then there was you

Also by Mona Shroff

Then, Now, Always

MONA SHROFF

then there was you

HQN

ISBN-13: 978-1-335-41855-5

Then There Was You

Recycling programs
for this product may
not exist in your area.

HQN
22 Adelaide St. West, 40th Floor
Toronto, Ontario M5H 4E3, Canada
www.Harlequin.com

Printed in Spain

To Anand,
You are the embodiment of your name,
bringing happiness and joy everywhere you go,
especially to my heart.

then there was you

CHAPTER ONE

ANNIKA

FIRSTS WERE ALWAYS ripe with possibilities. First steps. First friend. First love. But nothing was ever quite like the first day of school. Especially not this year. This year, Annika Mehta was in charge of her first classroom. The familiar aromas of chalk and paper, crayons and paint took on new meaning as Annika surveyed her summer handiwork. She was proud of the setup. Science area, art area, reading nook (complete with small cushy pillows), math section with beads and plenty of paper. It had taken her a while to get here, and she inhaled, satisfied.

That was when the butterflies hit. Annika hadn't been this nervous since her student-teaching days, and that was mostly because the parents all thought she looked too young to be a teacher, which always amused her, as she was actually a few years older than most student teachers. Now, however, Annika was the head teacher. She put her hand to her stomach, as if doing so would calm the fluttering. She inhaled the familiar scents of cut grass and city exhaust as she opened a few windows. The air was cool right now, but the stickiness proved that summer still prevailed despite the fact that it was after Labor Day.

She was ready. Or at least as ready as she'd ever be.

A knock and shuffling at the door gave her butterflies

new wings, but they settled as she greeted the first of her students.

"Good morning, Allison!" Annika walked over and made eye contact with the little girl, then turned to the mother. "Good morning, Mrs. Peterson."

"Good morning. Good to see you again," Mrs. Peterson replied, her smile warm and welcoming.

Annika gave her full attention to the child. "Do you remember where things go?" Orientation had been a few days ago, but Allison nodded.

"I do, Ms. Mehta." She beamed and looked at her mother, as if asking permission to go.

Mrs. Peterson smiled, tilting her head at her daughter. "You'll have to ask Ms. Mehta when you're in her classroom."

"Oh. Ms. Mehta, can I go put my things away?"

Annika grinned, relaxing. "Of course."

Allison walked over to the coatrack and placed her backpack and lunch in the appropriate cubby.

Mrs. Peterson sighed. "She's talked about nothing else but this classroom since meeting you. We're very excited about her kindergarten year."

"Me, too." Annika smiled.

Mrs. Peterson waved at her daughter and placed her hand on her heart. "They grow so fast." She smiled at Annika, her eyes moist, before gripping Annika's hand in both of hers. "Thank you."

"It's going to be a wonderful year, Mrs. Peterson," Annika assured her.

Other students and parents followed soon after, leaving Annika so busy and energized there just wasn't room for butterflies.

The buzz of animated children filled her classroom,

with only two of them so far having shed any tears. With a few minutes left in drop-off, Annika turned for a moment to observe the members of her class who were there. A small group had gathered around the books, another couple had pulled out blocks to play with and others were simply coloring quietly.

"Ah. Excuse me?" a male voice called from the door.

Annika walked over and addressed the child who stood with the man. "Good morning, Mitch. Do you remember me?"

Large brown eyes looked up at her, a small, shy smile breaking through on Mitch's face. Annika turned her attention to the man with him. "Hi, I'm Ms. Mehta." She extended her hand. "I don't believe we met at orientation."

The man stiffened, merely glancing at her hand. "Are you the teacher?"

Annika smiled, keeping her hand extended. "Yes, I am."

He looked around and behind her, his brow furrowed and a small frown forming at his mouth. "There's no one else here?"

Annika pressed her lips together and forced the smile to stay put. Here it was. The typical *No way you're old enough to teach*. Good skin and genetics were a blessing and a curse. Hopefully, she'd still look young when she was fifty.

"No need. I'm the teacher. Annika Mehta. I'm new, but completely qualified." She laughed. "I can assure you, they won't let just anyone teach here."

The man stared at her extended hand, then looked at her, his eyes hardening. "Clearly, that's not true. Seems they'll let anyone teach."

Confused, Annika dropped her hand. "I'm sorry?" She paused. "I only look young. This is my first classroom on my own, but I have done extensive training—"

The man scoffed. "It's not your age." He nudged his son forward, narrowing his eyes, a scowl settling in on his face. "Go on, now, Mitch. Your mother will get you later."

Mitch ran to the cubbies, and his father turned on his heel and headed out the door. Annika stood frozen to her spot. Not her age? He couldn't possibly have meant… No, that didn't happen. Not in this day and age. Not to her.

She was shaking, her body understanding fully what her mind was trying to wrap itself around. That it wasn't her age, it was her skin color. She hadn't thought it possible, but for the first time she could feel the brown of her skin, as if brown was something less than and something dirty. Rage at this man boiled inside her, intense and sharp. She raged even more at the fact that someone could even for a second make her feel less than she was. Being brown, *being Indian*, was a part of her. She squared her shoulders and fought the hot tears that came to her eyes, clogging her throat with a hundred things she wanted to scream at that man. Not the very least of which was *What are you teaching your son?*

She pulled the plastic strip from her pocket. Her name and birthdate were typed on it, along with other numbers she still did not understand. She inhaled, as if she was infusing courage from the air. She squeezed the hospital band and placed it back in her pocket, where it had been for the past five months.

Mitch. Her first day. She had a class to teach. She fought back fiery tears and swallowed hard at the lump of anger. She plastered a smile on her face and readied herself for class.

She turned and clapped a short rhythm. She did it again, this time clearing her throat. Her gaze landed on Mitch, and he clapped back at her, copying her rhythm. Her heart swelled and she grinned, focusing on the smiles of the children, as she repeated the clapping pattern again. This time, a few children joined Mitch in answering her. She walked to the edge of the circle, continuing the game, until all the children had joined her.

"Good morning, class. Do you remember my name?" She paused, then allowed her heart to be light at the chorus of "Ms. Mehta" that came to her from her students.

"That's right." She floated her gaze around the circle at each child. "We're going to have a wonderful year."

That's a promise.

CHAPTER TWO

DANIEL

DANIEL LAY DOWN in his room at base, shoes still on his feet. The helicopter was clean, equipment ready to go, all paperwork up-to-date. He'd earned himself a bit of a lie-down. He closed his eyes, and the image of Annika Mehta, twenty-seven, popped immediately into his brain. It had been five months since he'd cared for her in the ER, but every time he closed his eyes, there she was, in all her beauty and pain.

He had unwittingly memorized the emergency address she left. He should just go down there and see how she was. Irrational. Stalker, much? Definitely losing it. He relaxed all his muscles and attempted to clear his mind so sleep would come. Just as he hit that place between sleeping and waking, an intense and insistent buzzer jerked him awake. Immediately alert, he grabbed his belt and helmet as he quickly but calmly entered the hallway.

"Base" was where the flight medics and pilot waited for cases to come their way. Daniel's room was one of three in the house, with a bed, small desk and a chest of draw-ers. They had a fully stocked kitchen and three bathrooms. Shifts were twenty-four hours, so base was Daniel's home a couple of days a week. His own apartment in Baltimore was simply a place for him to sleep between shifts on the helicopter and shifts in the ER.

"Gunshot wounds at a bar. EMTs are already there, but the patient needs to get to Hopkins." Crista rolled her eyes as she donned her helmet. "When will they learn that alcohol and guns don't mix?"

Daniel followed Crista outside to the helipad. The downwash had churned up fallen leaves, and Daniel squinted to avoid flying debris as he bent over at the waist and followed his partner onto the helicopter. Crista shivered in the unexpected fall chill despite the fact that they each had on an extra layer. When they'd gone up in the afternoon, it had been decidedly warm and muggy. More August than early September.

The pilot was already gearing up. Daniel sat with his back to the pilot and fastened his five-point harness. Crista took the seat that would be next to their patient. He plugged in his helmet so he could communicate with the pilot and donned his night-vision goggles just as the roar of the blades and engine reached a peak and the chopper lifted off.

Daniel cleared his mind, the intense vibrations of the chopper just part of his background. This wasn't that different from being a nurse practitioner in the ER, in that you never knew what you were facing until you were facing it. Both jobs were intense in different ways, keeping his mind from wandering to painful things.

A few minutes into the flight, the pilot spoke to Daniel through his helmet. "Daniel?"

"Yes, sir?"

"I need an open field to land near 131 North Charles."

Daniel knew these parts like the back of his hand. And

he knew that address. His heart leaped. "Repeat that address?"

"It's 131 North Charles."

How the hell was Annika Mehta's emergency address a bar? That made no sense. Why would she give a bar address as her emergency contact?

"Daniel!" The pilot was waiting on him. "Any ideas?"

"Yeah, sorry." Daniel mentally shook himself and told the pilot about a high school football field about half a mile from that location. He closed his eyes and pushed thoughts of Annika Mehta out of his mind. If the EMTs had called for the chopper, he was going to need to focus.

A few minutes later, the pilot landed them smoothly in the field. Daniel and Crista grabbed their gear bags and ran for the red flashing lights of the fire truck that would serve as their ride to the site. Daniel barely even registered the siren as they approached the bar. Blue-and-red flashing lights became visible—at least two cop cars as well as an ambulance were parked as if thrown in a semicircle in front of the bar.

"Phil's Place," Crista chuckled.

"What?"

She shrugged. "It's the bar. Kind of place I'd go to."

"Yeah, sure." Daniel scanned the area. Not looking for beautiful women with dark curly hair. No. Not at all.

Sirens blipped, red and blue lights flashed, a flurry of activity around the ambulance and the police cars. Daniel automatically tuned out every distraction and focused on the bleeding man thrashing about on the gurney. The EMTs had him strapped down while treating his wounds, but it didn't deter his attempts to be free of his restraints.

"Let me out!" His voice was strangled with sobs, taking the fight out of him, but he continued to twist against the straps around his wrists. "I don't want to live! I can't—" His wail of pain distracted Daniel for a quick moment before he registered it clinically. An EMT was cleaning one of the man's wounds.

Daniel met Crista's eyes and stepped up, taking the lead. He motioned for light. The scent of gunpowder confirmed shots fired, and a quick scan revealed one gunshot wound in the man's shoulder and another in his upper thigh.

"What happened, Andy?" Daniel asked the EMT. The patient was crying out in a nonstop stream that quickly became background noise as Daniel's focus narrowed to his patient and how he was going to best care for him in a quick and efficient manner.

"Looks like he tried suicide by cop."

Daniel flicked his gaze to the EMT. "Seriously?" This was not entirely uncommon, but still not your run-of-the-mill gunshot wound.

"Yeah. Apparently, he buried his wife today." The heft in Andy's voice was metered by the clinical tone that was a side effect of their job, where life-changing events became information.

Daniel approached his patient with new eyes. Young, male, late twenties, maybe a few years younger than Daniel. A nod of silent communication to Crista, who started her clinical assessment while Daniel addressed the patient. "So, hey. What's your name?"

"Mark."

"Okay, listen up, Mark. I'm Daniel. This is Crista. She's the best. We're going to fix you up, get you to a hospital."

"Don't bother." Mark started crying. "My wife..."

"Yeah, I know." Daniel motioned to Crista as he continued to address Mark. "I need you to focus."

"Daniel, he's…uh…got a child." Andy didn't meet Daniel's eyes.

Daniel froze. The words came to him as if from a tunnel, shattering his fine-tuned focus, and transporting him instead to the scene of a hectic ER filled with doctors and nurses frantically trying to take care of a little girl. Daniel suddenly felt as though Andy were speaking a different language, and he couldn't decipher the words and numbers the EMT was rattling off.

"Daniel. Hey, Daniel, are you listening?"

"Give me the vitals, Andy." Crista stepped in front of Daniel, and he let himself be shoved aside as she took over.

Daniel registered Andy saying something to him—maybe an apology—just as Crista barked, "Forget him. Just give me the rest of the information."

Daniel caught her eye as Andy finished speaking. Her gaze was fierce, but her words weren't without concern. "You working tonight, Daniel?"

"Yeah." He snapped out of it. "Yeah, I'm working."

"Well, let's get to it. It's going to take us both." She turned to her patient. "I hear you got a kid?"

"Yeah. A little boy." Mark turned his focus to Daniel. "You have kids?"

"No." Daniel needed to say something to Mark, something comforting, but he couldn't do it. Silence hung in the air for a moment before Mark started wailing his grief once more.

Yet again, Daniel froze.

He felt, rather than heard, Crista's curse before she addressed Mark herself. "Listen, Mark. What's your little boy's name? Huh? Look at me, Mark. What's his name?"

"Nick." Mark stopped thrashing about. "His name is Nick."

Crista grinned as she stabilized Mark for the chopper ride. "Nick. That's a great name. How old is he?" She leaned closer to Daniel for a split second, elbowing him painfully in the ribs. "Snap out of it, huh?" she hissed.

Daniel grunted, glaring at Crista for the jab, though it was well deserved. To say she looked unapologetic was an understatement. He took over caring for Mark's wounds as Crista continued to talk.

"He's seven."

"Well, Mark. Seems that little Nick needs a father, don't you think? I mean, who's going to teach him to throw a ball?"

Mark looked away as he considered her words. Daniel continued with the business of medicine. He could not participate in a conversation where a father needed to be goaded back to caring for his child.

Mark looked at Daniel. "You married?" Why did this guy feel the need to keep talking to him?

"Not anymore." Daniel's words were clipped. They had an IV going, and the bleeding was temporarily under control, but they needed to get Mark onto the chopper. He caught Crista's eye and nodded, indicating that they were ready to move.

"Too bad. I loved my Lisa. She—she was everything," Mark sobbed again as they moved him into the ambulance.

Daniel couldn't hold his peace any longer. "Maybe she was—I don't know," he growled. "But what I do know is that you have a little boy. You're a father. Nothing trumps that. Nothing." His voice was gruff and filled with anger—not at all the comforting tone of a paramedic or a nurse practitioner. "You want your little boy in foster care?"

Crista glared at him, burning holes right through him. "Daniel!" Personal stuff had no place on the job. Besides, if there was no other family, little Nick was headed into the system for the foreseeable future, just based on Mark's activities tonight.

But Mark was staring at him. "No—of course not!" He looked wildly around and tried to sit up. "I need to get to him."

Daniel pushed him down. "You're not going anywhere except into this ambulance and onto the helicopter. Your family will watch Nick until we get you patched up."

"My brother. Call my brother."

Crista took the brother's information as Daniel did a sweep of the area to make sure they had gathered all of their equipment, and that was when he saw her. Annika Mehta. He would have missed her in the dark, except that she stood under a streetlight. For the third time that night, Daniel froze midjob. Her wild curls were pushed into a ponytail, but the curve of her jaw and cheekbones were already familiar to him. She was unmistakable. Was it possible that she was even more striking now?

She wore a dark apron with *Phil's Place* emblazoned across it. In the dim light of the street, her brown skin looked almost golden, and she didn't smile at anyone. As he watched her, she folded her arms across the name and shivered in the cool air. An older man with salt and pepper in his beard started herding people back into the bar. Her gaze passed over Daniel, and he had the sensation of being scanned. She was too far away for him to know if she recognized him, but then how could she? She had never even opened her eyes that night. His stomach did a flip at the possibility.

The older man spoke. "All right, now. Nothing left to see. Come on back in. Next round's on the house."

Daniel was lost in her movements as she slowly turned

and followed the customers back into the bar. She hung her head slightly, and as she passed the older man, he rested a hand on her shoulder. She lifted her face to him and smiled. Daniel just barely caught that smile in the faded light, but it put his heart in a viselike grip. He couldn't remember ever having seen something so beautiful, yet so sad.

"Daniel!" Crista called out to him. "If I have to corral you in one more time tonight…!" Crista always looked out for Daniel, but she couldn't be expected to save lives alone.

"Yeah, okay. I'm with you." Daniel took an extra second and caught a quick glimpse of Annika Mehta through the large window of the bar. She was behind the bar, pouring beers, warmth exuding from her very being. A few pieces of hair escaped the ponytail, and she tucked them behind her ear. The movement was so casual, yet so intimate, that Daniel suddenly longed to be the one tucking back those rogue pieces of hair himself.

"Goddamn it, Daniel!"

The trance broken, Daniel forced himself to break his gaze. He followed Crista to the ambulance that took them and their patient to the chopper.

Once back in flight, Daniel focused on a now-compliant and regretful Mark and getting him safely to the surgeons who could help him.

Thoughts of Annika standing in the streetlight floated in and out of his mind, unbidden. Her smile warmed him. He could think of nothing else except what it might feel like to hold her again. A tiny amount of lightness crept into him. This was all new to him. He hadn't felt anything like this in almost five years.

It felt like hope.

CHAPTER THREE

ANNIKA

ANNIKA SHIVERED IN the night chill while the EMTs tended to the gunshot victim. Well, the victim had fired first, clearly distraught by the death of his wife. He'd gone on and on about it inside the bar. Annika hadn't really paid him much attention. Her mind was still reeling from the realization that one of her student's parents had quite bluntly insulted her on the basis of her skin color. On her very first day teaching.

When the distraught man had pulled the gun on himself, Phil had pushed the button that he'd always had in his bar—the one that summoned the police. Phil managed to talk the man outside before the cops showed. One thing led to another, and before Annika knew what was happening, the man had fired his gun at the police, who were forced to return fire.

She glanced up in the night sky as she heard the helicopter, and shortly thereafter a fire engine arrived. Two flight medics disembarked the chopper. They approached the EMTs with the calm sense of urgency that was second nature to emergency personnel.

The one in the lead was tall and well built—that was apparent even in his flight suit. His stride was long and purposeful, and Annika could tell from where she stood that he was completely unaware of his own presence and was singularly focused on his patient. He called for light and began to prepare his patient for helicopter travel. He spoke to the EMT, then he froze.

Annika watched him with curiosity. Working in a bar, she had seen more than one paramedic administer care. But she'd rarely seen one falter at the scene. He had been listening to the EMT as he worked, and suddenly, in the middle of a life-saving situation, he'd stopped. It was only for a second or two, before he gathered himself. But by then it looked like his partner had taken over.

Once they stabilized their patient, the medics packed their stuff and made to leave. The one in charge looked in her direction and stopped. As if he knew her. Annika did not meet his gaze. Men often looked at her, and she found the easiest thing was to not make eye contact. Who had given him permission to look at her like that? Was he looking at her because she was brown? Was that something people noticed all the time? She'd never had these thoughts before today.

No, this man was looking at her like he knew her. Ridiculous. He didn't know her.

No one really did.

CHAPTER FOUR

DANIEL

DANIEL LEANED ON his bike and closed his eyes against the intermittent flashing of the Phil's Place sign. He could still see red light pulsing from behind his eyelids. She was in there. He should go in. He wanted to go in. Last night, he'd stood in this spot for an hour, then gone home. There was alcohol in there. And while he and alcohol were not enemies, they certainly were not friends.

He caught his reflection in one of the windows to Phil's Place and quickly looked away. Large windows gave him a view of the older man with salt-and-pepper hair standing behind the bar. The red neon Phil's Place sign obstructed his view of anything more.

He didn't even want a drink. But Annika Mehta was in there.

Jesus Christ. He didn't know what disgusted him more: his fear of a drink or his fear of facing a woman.

What the fuck was wrong with him? Before he could think too much more about it, he grabbed the wrought-iron door handle and pulled. A couple of scantily clad young girls followed by a couple of very drunk young men nearly fell on him as he opened the door. Much giggling ensued as Daniel pushed past them.

Daniel braced himself for the stale aroma of old alcohol and the dank darkness typical of such establishments. He paused at the welcoming aroma of hearty food in the well-lit, simply appointed establishment. A piano in the corner caught his eye. He firmly ignored it.

Phil's Place bustled, even at nine thirty on a Thursday night. The door jingled, announcing his entrance, but no one seemed to care. He found himself a spot at the bar and dipped his chin in the older man's direction. Must be Phil. He was expertly filling beers and nodded his acknowledgment. Daniel waited.

He scanned the place, looking for that ponytail. Wouldn't it just be his luck that he came in on the day that she was off? But what if she was here? What would he say to her anyway? He should leave. If he told her how he knew her, it would only bring to the surface something she may want to forget.

This was a bad idea. He turned on his stool and made to leave when a woman's voice called to him.

"Weren't you here the other night?"

Daniel turned to face mahogany-brown eyes that were narrowed at him. The woman's lips were pursed, and her brow furrowed with the question. She wore her hair back in a ponytail, which Daniel knew hid beautiful dark tight curls. Even though he'd walked in here looking for her, he was caught off guard, and a few extra seconds ticked by before he gathered himself to speak. A slight flush built in her cheeks as he stared at her.

"Um, no. I think I would remember that."

"Sure, you were here—with the fire engine." She pointed to his jeans and T-shirt. "You were wearing a uniform, but I'm pretty sure it was you."

"Ah, yes. The gunshot victim." Daniel nodded. He couldn't take his eyes off her.

"Yeah. You were the one who faltered." There was no challenge in her voice, just fact.

"Excuse me?"

"You just stopped in the middle of treating that man."

"How could you possibly know that?"

"I saw. Most people watch the victim. I watch the medics." She shrugged. "Excuse me if I stepped on your manhood."

Daniel grinned. *She'd noticed him.* "I hesitated a moment, and my partner took over." He studied her face. "In any case, it happens almost never. And my partner is great."

"So, I wasn't wrong. You faltered." She waved her hand at the bar. "Can I get you something?"

Her flowery scent wafted toward him as he sat down again. "Bourbon. Rocks."

She left to retrieve his drink without so much as another word. He tried not to stare as she chose the bottle and the glass, plunking a large ice cube into it before pouring him two fingers of what looked like relatively cheap bourbon. Her movement was fluid and graceful. She was just a couple of inches shorter than Phil, whom Daniel put as a couple of inches shorter than his own six foot one.

Phil muttered something to her that made her smile and shake her head as she walked back to Daniel with his drink. The smile transformed her. It was light and pure and filled with humor. He didn't think he would ever be able to get enough of that smile.

So lost was he in her smile and movements that he startled when she set his drink down. He swirled it around. *Say something.* Conversation was not coming easy. Forget conversation—speaking was a challenge. Annika walked away.

Daniel stared at the drink. It wasn't that he couldn't control how much he drank. It was what happened to him when he did. He let everyone believe that he had stopped drinking because he couldn't afford to lose his job, but the truth was something darker.

"Aren't you going to drink it?" Annika was back, a look of bewilderment on her face.

"I don't drink."

"You know this is a *bar*?" She raised her eyebrows and spoke slowly, as if he were daft. "And that is a *drink*."

He could watch her talk forever.

"Yes." Wow, he was a stirring conversationalist. Why was he here? He should just drop some cash and leave and never return. No good was going to come of this. There was a reason he didn't get involved with women. Just like there was a reason he didn't drink bourbon.

She shrugged and started to leave again.

"I'm not an alcoholic." The words spilled out of him.

"Okay. If you say so." She started walking away.

"In case you were thinking I was some sort of alcoholic, testing myself or something."

"Whatever." The smile was gone, replaced by impatience.

"It's just that the effects of alcohol remind me…of things." Things he needed to forget. Why was he explaining himself? "Anyway, I haven't had a drink in a while."

"Listen, I'm not your AA counselor or whatever. Drink it, don't drink it, I do not care. Either way, you owe me eight bucks."

Daniel stared at her. She wore her brashness like a shield. Like something she could put on as needed. Or take off. He had a feeling it did not come off very often or for just anybody.

"Hey, Annika." A young man with a very trim beard and glasses nodded as he walked past Annika and donned an apron similar to hers.

Annika's face brightened. "Hey, Bobby."

"Harassing the customers again, or just the hot ones?" He swept his approving glance over Daniel as he tied his apron.

Daniel bit back a grin as Annika flushed before him yet again. Even through her silky brown skin, the deep color broke through. Annika folded her arms across her chest and pointedly turned her back on Bobby.

Even so, a wave of jealousy passed over Daniel as he observed the easy familiarity between Annika and Bobby. No. Nothing weird about that. Nothing messed up about sitting in this bar with a drink he wasn't going to touch, either. *This was a mistake.* He opened his wallet to pull out some cash. He shouldn't have come to begin with.

"You want food, since you're just observing your alcohol?" Her voice had softened a bit.

His stomach growled. He had forgotten to eat. "What's good?"

"It's Baltimore."

"So, something with crab?"

She shrugged, her arms still crossed. "Mrs. P. makes the best cream of crab soup. All those fancy seafood places are no competition."

"Okay, I'll have that."

"Should I bring you a spoon so you can eat it or you going to just stare at it?" Her lips turned into a snarky half smile, which felt like it was just for him. "I mean, you might be a vegetarian who just likes to order crab soup."

Daniel raised an eyebrow. "Bring the damn spoon."

She was trying hard to be tough. Not let anyone in. Daniel recognized that for sure.

He couldn't help watching Annika while he waited for his soup. Her regular customers were fond of her, and the new ones were clearly taken by her warmth. Underneath all that sass, Annika was quick to put on a genuine smile for her customers. It just wasn't the same one she saved for people close to her. Like Phil, who seemed more like an uncle to her than a boss, the way he held her shoulder and spoke quietly, concern and amusement taking turns on his face.

The bourbon sat steadfast in his periphery. The ice melted, changing the color from a deep golden to a weak yellow. Condensation collected on the glass and dripped down the side.

Not that Daniel noticed.

He imagined the warm liquid sliding down his throat, relaxing his muscles and making him forget. It was dangerous to forget. Mostly because once the alcohol wore off, he was forced to remember. It was remembering that ruined him every time.

He pointedly ignored the weakening amber liquid and focused instead on Annika. He easily recalled how her body had fit perfectly with his when he'd held her. How he was able to give her a modicum of comfort when she had clung to him as if he were a lifesaver and she was drowning. How, in her sorrow, she had needed him, and how he, too, had ended up finding comfort with her in his arms.

His phone buzzed and displayed a picture of a pretty brunette with green eyes. Emma. At least once a day, every day.

Though Emma's call never irritated him, today he wanted to watch Annika. "Hey, Em."

"Did you eat?" The beauty of siblings was that you could forgo the niceties, like *Hello. How are you?* Or so Emma believed.

"I'm eating now." He glanced toward the kitchen. He would be eating soon.

"Great." Pause. "So, Daniel, how about coming up this weekend, taking Charlie fishing? Michael's away and I don't know anything about fishing."

"Sorry. I can't. Working." He cringed inwardly at his lie. Whatever, he'd pick up another shift and then it would be true.

"Yeah, okay." She sighed deeply. She knew he was lying, but Daniel knew she wouldn't press it. "Make sure you eat."

"Yeah, thanks."

"Call Mom sometime."

"I just talked to her." Big sisters were so bossy.

Annika was laughing at something Bobby said. That green monster reared its head in Daniel's belly. He barely registered Emma's voice.

"Last week."

"Mmm. Okay. I'll call them."

"Love you." She hung up.

It wasn't unusual or even unexpected that Emma was concerned about his eating, since he had gone a period where he routinely forgot to do even that. She also believed that Daniel would heal if he spent some time with his nephew. But even seeing Charlie once or twice a year at a family function that he forced himself to go to was too hard. Come to think of it, he couldn't remember the last time he'd seen Charlie. Was it last year or maybe the year before? Jeez. He was a crappy uncle.

Charlie had been born a week before his Sara. The little

boy was like a little clock, marking the passage of time. Right now, Charlie's clock had wound through ten years. Sara's clock had stopped five years ago.

CHAPTER FIVE

ANNIKA

ANNIKA PUT IN the soup order, then tended to her regulars. They didn't study her; they were so involved in escaping their own sad lives they couldn't be bothered to pay any more attention to her than was required.

She refilled drinks and wiped off tables, her head filled with so many thoughts that she didn't hear Mrs. P. banging the bell to indicate the soup was ready. It wasn't until Phil was standing in front of her that she looked up.

"What's going on, Anni? Still letting that bigoted parent get to you?"

No one called her Anni. Her name was Annika, and she always insisted people take the extra millisecond to say the last syllable. But when Phil said it, he filled those two syllables with so much affection that Annika couldn't yell at him. Though right now it made her want to cry.

"No." She forced a smile. It had been a few weeks since all that, but it still got to her from time to time. "Maybe a little. Just everything."

"You need some extra time off?" Phil shook his head.

"No, Phil. Really, I need to come in. Besides, it's been five months since..." She trailed off. She still couldn't say it. What kind of wimp wallowed for five months? She hadn't been pregnant that long, just under three months, though she had been with Steven for close to a year. Her pregnancy had been thoroughly unexpected, and to say that it had caused uproar in her family was an understatement.

Despite her family's lack of enthusiasm, Annika had allowed herself to become excited at the prospect of being a mother. She had been in love, she was getting married and she was having a baby. Her path may not have been straight, but she was happy. Her family had been in the midst of quickly throwing together a wedding until blinding cramps had her in the ER in the middle of the night, changing her life again.

"I need to work."

Phil grinned at her. "Well, then, let's get out of your head and back to work, eh? That new guy's waiting to stare into his soup."

Annika let out a small chuckle. Even though she had tried not to, she'd been watching Chopper Guy while she worked. He hadn't so much as sipped his bourbon as he had stared at it. And from time to time, he scanned the room and rested his gaze on her. Though she pretended not to notice, every time those green eyes found her, a little thrill went through her body.

"Got it, boss."

Phil placed a hand on her shoulder. "Clara has your favorite waiting in the back."

Mrs. P. was forever feeding her, but Annika was still grateful every time she remembered to save a generous bowl of the crab soup for her.

"Nothing gets between Clara and feeding the ones she loves." Phil grinned and squeezed Annika's shoulder. "She's got plenty."

Content with love, Annika smiled and headed for the window that opened to the kitchen. Clara, or Mrs. P., as everyone else called her, was quiet and introverted, the yin to Phil's yang. Her cooking was amazing, and more than once she hit Annika up for Indian recipes, always looking for new dishes to learn. On cue, Mrs. P. hit the bell again for Annika to pick up the soup.

Annika grabbed the soup, inhaling the comforting aroma of cream and spices. This soup rivaled her mother's *khichdi* for best comfort food ever.

She brought it to chiseled-jawed, double-dimpled, green-eyed, superhot Chopper Guy. Oh, God! Was she a teenager again? She showed him the spoon before pointedly placing it next to the bowl. "So you don't have to stare at it."

Chopper Guy rewarded her mockery with a laugh. And what a reward it was. His eyes crinkled and his mouth opened wide, revealing almost perfect teeth. One of the very side ones was slightly crooked, and it caught her eye and her curiosity. It was the sound of his laugh that drew her attention. It started as a low rumble, almost as if he hadn't laughed in a while and needed to warm up. Then it progressed to a more abandoned sound, not loud, but rumbling and free. The laugh gave her a reason to look at his mouth. She was drawn to that mouth, more than seemed normal. If looking at a guy's mouth even qualified as normal.

The truth was, she had recognized him as soon as he'd entered the bar. It was the walk. Sure, he was tall and muscular and had that chiseled jaw and great hair, but she remembered the quiet confidence of his gait from the other night. The way he had moved efficiently and gracefully, completely unaware of his own presence.

The laugh ended in a smile, perfect lips parted just slightly over those almost perfect teeth, with a dimple on each side, and her knees actually weakened a bit as she stood there.

Annika had no trouble believing that all he had to do was turn on that smile and women would swoon.

His eyes met hers, and something jumped in her belly. How could you not notice those eyes? With dark chestnut hair—just long enough to tempt one to run her fingers through it, yet short enough to be professional—and skin the color of desert sand, one expected rich brown eyes. So, when Chopper Guy flashed fiery green eyes at her—and he did flash them, intentionally or not—one had to look twice. She just didn't have to melt like she did.

Right now, those eyes studied her, and her belly fluttering was getting out of control. It was bad enough that Bobby had to announce that Chopper Guy was superhot (Bobby always noticed the hot ones, and always tried to set Annika up with the ones he wasn't interested in), but she had gone all hot and sweaty with embarrassment. Bobby had grinned when he noticed, so she knew Chopper Guy had noticed, too.

He granted her a playful version of that smile and picked up the spoon. "I don't have a questionable history with cream of crab soup."

How many versions of that smile were there? She wouldn't mind finding out. But the smile disappeared as he brought the spoon to his mouth. "Mmm."

It was almost a groan, and Annika swallowed hard. She was salivating. And it wasn't because of the soup.

"You were not kidding." Chopper Guy landed his gaze on her again.

Who reacted to a groan like that? "I don't kid about soup." Fantastic. She was talking to this hot guy about *soup.* Clearly, she was not ready to be in the company of attractive men.

Thankfully, Chopper Guy directed his appreciation toward the kitchen, where Mrs. P. stood in the window, watching them. Mrs. P. nodded and returned to the back, accepting his broad grin and thumbs-up.

Chopper Guy took another spoonful and turned those green eyes on her. "Thank you."

"Just doing my job." She needed to walk away from him, but her knees had once more turned to jelly. So she stood frozen for a moment longer than necessary.

Amusement filled his eyes as he leaned toward her and whispered, "You going to watch me eat?"

Annika flushed. He was very close, and *damn* if he didn't smell amazing. A combination of some musky cologne, soap and something deliciously unidentifiable. With great effort, she gathered herself and leaned away. "Well, it would certainly be more entertaining than watching you drink." She smiled at him and nodded at his bourbon before finally making her legs walk away from him.

This guy was trouble.

CHAPTER SIX

ANNIKA

MILD NAUSEA CLAWED at Annika's stomach as she drove the thirty-five minutes from her apartment in Baltimore to her childhood home in Columbia, Maryland. She'd been making this trip more often these past few months since... everything.

When she had been with Steven, she'd ignored the obvious strain her relationship with him had put on her relationship with her family. She had told herself they simply didn't understand, and they would come to love him, just as she did.

But they had seen what she had not, and while she'd chalked up their resistance to Steven to his not being Indian, or that she was pregnant outside of wedlock, the reality was that they hadn't liked Steven because he was selfish and didn't really have her best interests at heart. They loved her, and so had ultimately gone along with her decision, but a distance had crept between them. She missed that closeness and was working to get it back.

Problem was, her parents were pushing for her to get married. Like, soon, before she could make another mistake.

Her teenage brother, Nilay, was out on the driveway playing basketball with his friends. They were dressed in shorts and muscle shirts, seemingly oblivious to the October chill. They stopped playing as she drove up, and Nilay ran to her car.

She parked in the street, and before she was fully out the door, her brother had grabbed her in a sweaty bear hug.

"My sister's home!"

"Ugh, Nilay, you stink!" Annika squirmed to get out of his grasp, but it was really nice to be hugged by him.

"You missed me, Didi. Admit it."

Annika always melted a little when he called her Didi. He managed to roll up all his affection into that one little endearment, so it meant much more than "big sister."

"If I admit it, will you let me breathe fresh air?"

He let her go. "It's not that bad." He sniffed his armpit. "Well, maybe it is."

"Gross." She waved to his buddies. "Your muscles are coming along, I see."

His eyes widened. "You think?" He looked at them. "I've been lifting…"

Annika giggled, causing him to roll his eyes and return to his game.

She turned to the house. The front door currently had a paper jack-o'-lantern taped to it, something she must have made in grade school. She studied it for a moment. Sure, her kindergarten students could make something like this. Maybe her mother would let her take this home so she could use it as an example for her class.

Small pumpkins decorated the three steps leading to the door. Along with the pumpkins, tea lights flickered in decorative *diya*, and a colorful *rangoli* design done in colored chalk brightened up the small landing. Jack-o'-lanterns and rangoli. Halloween and Diwali settling in on the same stoop—pretty much summed up how she was raised.

"Hello?" She inhaled the scent of her childhood, cinnamon and cloves sautéing with onion and garlic. Pair that aroma with the sound of the exhaust fan attempting to remove the strongest of the scents, and she was twelve years old again, trying and failing to avoid the cooking lesson with her mother. Cooking was a life skill, and one should know the basics, her mother would insist. Sadly, even now, cooking was not something Annika enjoyed. Hence the pity food from Mrs. P.

She took off her shoes just inside the front door and dropped her purse.

"What? Is that Annika?" Her mother's *W*s still sounded like *V*s, something her brother always teased their mother about.

"Yes, Mom. It's me." Annika slipped on indoor clogs and found her way to the kitchen.

Usha Mehta still kept her hair in a single long braid down her back and was only an inch shorter than her daughter. She wore a simple red tunic with gold bordering over jeans. Annika let her mother pull her into a deep hug, enjoying the cinnamon-and-clove scent that always seemed to surround her even when she wasn't cooking. It didn't matter how old she got—there was nothing like being hugged by her mom.

"No work today?" Annika glanced at her mother's attire. Her mother worked part-time as a pharmacist, and she wouldn't be caught dead wearing jeans to work.

The older woman shook her head. "Tomorrow." She wrinkled her nose. "You smell like you saw your brother."

"He gave me a sweaty hug." Annika shook her head and smiled. "You put the diya out early."

Her mother shrugged. "Just easier. Diwali is coming soon, anyway. You are in time to help me make *rotli*."

Despite Annika's distaste for cooking, Annika and her mother had built their relationship making the fresh hot flatbread together for the family. They had many a heart-to-heart while her mother rolled out the flatbread and Annika baked it on a flat pan, then topped each one with ghee. They'd also had many an argument while Annika was a teenager and groused about whatever it was that irritated her that day. Nilay always said the rotli didn't taste as good on the days they argued. Maybe he was right. In any case, rotli making was their thing.

Her mom picked up the thin rolling pin reserved solely for making rotli and dusted the countertop with flour. Annika kneaded the dough and started making small balls, which her mother would roll flat.

Her mother smiled at her, pride in her eyes. "You still make excellent *lua*."

Annika got about halfway through the dough, then switched to baking. Her mother's skills were good enough that she would be able to make the lua and roll the rotli while Annika baked each piece.

"How are you?" Her mother side-eyed her, a tentative pause in her voice.

"I'm good." Similar caution in Annika's voice. She thought of the hospital band in her pocket and blinked away the burn behind her eyes.

Silence.

"Beta." Her mother stopped her work and forced Annika to look at her. "It is okay to be sad."

Her nose prickled as tears built again. Annika nodded her head, afraid to speak, and swallowed hard. She squeezed her mother's hand. Long, thin fingers, small calluses, soft skin—all familiar comfort for Annika. She inhaled deeply and found her voice. "Yeah, okay."

Her mother squeezed back and smiled before turning again to her work.

Small silence as grief weighed on them for a moment.

"How is Naya?" A forced lightness in her mother's voice told Annika they were moving to other, less demanding topics.

"She's good." Annika relaxed. "Law school is kicking her butt." *Especially since she doesn't want to be a lawyer.*

"Veena-kaki wants Naya to meet Urmila-auntie's son. Do you remember Ravi? He's a lawyer now."

Annika smirked. Naya's mom was persistent. Annika's dad and his brother were so alike; it was interesting that their wives were so different. Veena-kaki kept trying to set her daughter up, and Naya had agreed to the match-making, just as she had agreed to go to law school. But Annika suspected her cousin didn't want to get married any more than she wanted to be a lawyer. She simply did what was expected of her. It kept everyone happy. Except for maybe Naya.

As much as her own mother wanted her to be married, Annika was relieved she hadn't tried to set her up yet.

"Mom, I don't really think Naya wants to get married. She wants to see the world after law school. Maybe join the Peace Corps." She planted the idea in her mother, hoping it would get back to Veena-kaki.

Her mother shrugged. "Well, you never know."

"Where's Papa?" Annika used her fingers to flip the rotli over to bake the other side.

"He should be home any minute. How is work?" Her mother's bangles jiggled and clanked on the counter as she quickly and efficiently rolled out the flatbread.

Here was another point of contention, although with the boyfriend and pregnancy it had sort of fallen to the wayside. Annika had been pre-med in college and had the grades and MCAT scores to go to medical school. As the time loomed closer to apply to those schools, however, Annika had been filled with dread. What she wanted was to be a kindergarten teacher. Not a doctor or a lawyer or an engineer.

"Work is great, Mom. I love it," she said automatically, almost in defiance of what she thought her mother was thinking. She placed the rotli directly on the gas, allowing it to puff up. The kitchen took on the comforting aroma of fresh bread, and Annika allowed herself to sink into it.

"Glad to hear it" came the automatic reply.

"Glad to hear what?" Her father was home. She turned to him. If there was any doubt what her brother would look like in thirty years, all one had to do was look at their father. Anil Mehta stood a few inches taller than his daughter, and a few shades darker. He had a full head of hair, though there was a good deal of salt in the pepper, and he still parted it on the side as he had all his life. He was handsome in that mild-mannered, Clark Kent kind of way, and his eyes still lit up when he saw his wife. Her mother offered her cheek and her father kissed it, smiling.

His smile faded slightly, taking on a shadow of firmness as he turned to Annika. She did her best to ignore it.

"Hi, Papa. Just telling Mom how much I love teaching." She continued to cook the rotli as she spoke.

"That is good to know that your education is at least making you happy, even if it won't buy you a future."

Who said Indian men didn't understand sarcasm?

"Have you thought about what we suggested?" He pierced her with his gaze. Nothing like getting right to it.

"I did. But I'm not ready to get married."

They may not have *actually* set her up, but they certainly didn't stop talking to her about it.

"No one is ever 'ready' to get married, beta." Her father's voice was calm, but already starting to show agitation.

"Papa, I want to meet someone on my own." An image of Chopper Guy flashed before her. She shook it from her head. Not going there.

Her father waved a dismissive hand. "You want to find someone and fall in love—a very American concept. Your mother and I were arranged by our parents. Love grew over time. Do you doubt that your mother and I love each other?"

The affection in his eyes as he pecked her mother on the cheek was definite proof of their bond. "Of course not, Papa. It's just that…marrying a stranger is not for me."

"He won't be a stranger. You can date him, get to know him—just let us set you up with some nice boys." This was her mother, pleading with her.

"Why can't I meet someone on my own, in my own time?"

"We allowed that, Annika. And look how it turned out." And there it was. Another failure for Annika. She did not have the energy for this argument right now.

Her mother placed her hand on her father's arm and gave him a look that told him to let it go in no uncertain terms. "Go. Get changed. We will have dinner together."

Anil Mehta grunted and left to change his clothes.

Annika continued to make rotli without making eye contact with her mother.

Nilay came down from showering and started to set the table, taking the *shak* to the table. He returned to the kitchen, his mouth full of spicy green bean and potato. Annika shook her head as their mother scolded him.

"Can't you wait five minutes until we sit down? Take the raita and the rice, but do not pick at them, too."

Nilay swallowed and treated his mother to a smile as he picked up the yogurt-and-cucumber salad as well as the rice. "Is it my fault you're a great cook?"

Annika rolled her eyes and made the gagging motion at him.

Her mother tried not to smile as she raised her rolling pin at him while she called him a wiseass in Gujarati. Nilay laughed and scooted out of her reach, taking the food to the table. They would leave the dal to simmer on the stove until it was time for that course. Annika spread ghee on the last rotli and brought the warm stack to the table.

By the time the table was set, her father had returned to the kitchen after changing. Annika was about to sit down across from her mother when the doorbell rang.

Her father looked blankly at Annika. "Can you see to that, beta?"

"Um, sure." Puzzled, Annika went to the door. She opened it to find a very handsome man standing there. Did Amazon deliver handsome men now?

Tall, with a lean muscular build and brown skin, the man seemed as surprised to see her as she was him. He hesitated a moment before speaking. "Um, hi. I was looking for Usha-auntie or Anil-uncle."

"Oh, yeah, sure. They're my parents." She stepped aside to let him in.

He seemed to study her as he stepped into the house. Then his face lit up. "Annika? Wow! It's been forever."

Crap. She probably knew him, but she couldn't place him. She definitely did not grow up with anyone this attractive. Her puzzlement must have shown loud and clear, because he chuckled.

"It's Sajan. Sajan Shah. We were in that dance together, senior year of high school."

Nope. She would've remembered someone who looked like him.

"Well, my senior year. You might have been a freshman?"

"Oh!" She covered her mouth with her hand. He had been awkward and skinny, and not nearly this tall, not nearly this muscular, but now that he mentioned it, she did remember those hazel eyes. "Hey, Sajan! It has been a lifetime. Whatever happened to you? I feel like we never saw you after that performance."

"We moved to Virginia, but I work in Baltimore now, so my parents recently moved back to the area. I was on my way to see them, and they asked me to stop here and pick something up for them."

"Ah, Sajan!" Annika's father's voice boomed from behind her. "So good to see you again. Come. Come in. We were just sitting down to dinner. Come join us."

"Oh, no, Uncle. I couldn't. My parents asked me to pick up some diya. They seem to have misplaced theirs in the move."

"Of course, we have the diya set aside for you. But come and eat a little. I insist. And I assure you, your parents won't mind a bit, huh?" Her father could barely meet her eyes, and Annika knew in that moment she was being set up. The question was, was Sajan in on it? She stole a glance at him, but it was obvious that he, too, had figured out what was going on, and he was just as surprised as she was.

"I'm sure Sajan has better things to do." She glared at her father.

"Yeah, I'll just get those diya and be on my way."

"No, I insist." Her father's tone was such that there was no arguing with him.

"But Uncle, I'm on call, and I really—"

"Well, then, you should eat when you have a moment." Annika's mother had shown up to chime in. "And it seems you have a moment."

Annika closed her eyes. Her dad you could argue with, but not her mom. When Mom insisted you eat, you sat your butt down and ate. She knew Sajan had no choice now but to have dinner with her and her family.

She glanced at him. He was well aware of his predicament. He bent down to take off his shoes. "Well, Auntie, who could say no to your cooking?"

"Fantastic!" Her father boomed and rubbed his hands together in victory. "Come." He led the way to the dining table.

Clearly, Sajan's parents and her parents thought they would make a great couple. They also knew neither of them would agree to an official "meeting," so they had cooked up this ruse. She glanced at him again out of the corner of her eye. He definitely had a slight deer-in-headlights look about him.

Annika's mother filled everyone's plates, heaping extra food on Sajan's plate, despite his protests. After the customary prayer, there was no sound, not even the clinking of silverware, as most of the food was eaten by hand. Annika was fuming that her parents would stoop to tricking her into meeting men. Even handsome men. So, she did not feel obliged to make conversation. If her parents were so keen on Sajan, they could talk to him.

"So, Sajan, your father tells me you are a physician at Hopkins." Her father attempted conversation in the void.

Annika's insides tightened. Seriously, he was a doctor? Could they *be* more cliché?

"Yes, Uncle. I'm on staff there."

"And your specialty?" He appeared to be waiting to hear this with bated breath. As if he didn't already know.

"Pulmonology, sir."

"Well, that sounds exciting. Doesn't it, Annika?"

Was he kidding? She looked up at poor Sajan and tried a genuine smile for his sake, but she knew it fell short. "Sure, Dad. Exciting."

"I think it's cool," Nilay said in between bites. Of course he did. Nilay had known since he was born that he wanted to be a doctor. He relished everything about medicine.

Sajan smiled at him. "Thanks. I really enjoy it."

"Tell me about some cool cases." How Nilay could speak and continuously eat was nothing short of miraculous.

Sajan obliged and began describing a case. Nilay listened, rapt, and asked questions. Annika was relieved and immensely grateful to her little brother for moving the conversation along. Her parents could make her eat dinner with Sajan, but that was it. She was not going to be forced into conversation. She glanced at Sajan again and caught him looking at her, hazel eyes slightly amused. How much did he even know about her and her past?

"So, Annika. What do you do?" Sajan asked, as if it were the most normal thing in the world.

Wait. It kind of was.

Okay, fine. She could go along for one dinner. After all, he was quite easy on the eyes, and her parents' faces held genuine smiles for the first time in a while.

"I'm a kindergarten teacher."

She waited for the surprised eyebrow raise, but it never came.

"That is something I could never do. A room full of kindergarten kids would eat me alive." He smiled, clearly impressed.

"You just have to know how to deal with them."

"Well, that is an enviable skill."

"It's because she's childlike herself," Nilay quipped.

Annika rolled her eyes at her brother, but he wasn't wrong. Children made sense to her. They were honest and open, and eager to learn. She couldn't help the real smile that appeared on her face. It was nice to be complimented on her choice of career for a change. "Well, thank you."

Her father grunted, but said nothing. Her mother glanced around the table, assessing each person.

"You don't approve, Uncle?"

Annika snapped her gaze to Sajan and her father. What business was it of his?

"Well, Annika was a strong candidate for medical school. She could have gained admission to Johns Hopkins. But she tossed it all away to teach small children."

"Uncle, bright energetic teachers for young children are badly needed. What Annika is doing is very much in demand."

That was nice of him to say, but it wasn't anything she hadn't already said to her father. She certainly didn't need anyone to defend her. She tensed at Sajan's presumption. She opened her mouth to say just that when her father answered him.

"Well, I'm glad that you see it that way, Sajan." Annika just about fell over at the conciliatory tone her father took. He turned to her, his eyebrows raised, as if to say, *See, Sajan thinks it's great you're a teacher.* He must really want her to like this guy.

"These days, it can be dangerous." Her mother spoke softly, but her concern was clear.

"Mom, I've told you. We have security precautions." On this, Annika was patient. The world was becoming a different place, and school shootings were not unheard of. It seemed anyone who wanted to could get a gun. There had been an incident in her school a few years ago, and strict protocols were now in place.

Nilay spoke up. "Yeah, but what about that dad from the first day." His eyes blazed as he clenched his jaw.

Annika had shared that story with her brother, and he'd wasted no time telling their parents.

"Exactly!" her mother compounded. "I worry about these things. Her safety—"

Annika was about to make an attempt to allay her mother's fears, when her father surprised her.

"Usha. That is not a reason. We cannot be afraid of such ignorance. People like that exist in every facet of society." He sighed and looked at his wife. "Don't you remember when we tried to buy this house thirty years ago?"

Usha nodded. "Yes." She glanced at Sajan. "Our own real estate agent told us we could never afford this house. He assumed we had very little income."

Sajan's eye bugged out. "What?"

Nilay chimed in. "Yep. But Papa bought the house and made it work." He beamed with pride at his father.

Sajan stared at her. "What happened to you?"

She relayed her story. Sajan's eyes darkened in anger, and he stopped eating for a minute.

"What are you doing about it?"

"Well, I told my principal, and I'm going to be me. I'm going to teach. *All* the children."

"That's right," her father quipped. "Don't let that fool scare you from what you want."

"What kind of security is there?" Sajan's brow was still furrowed.

"Anyone entering the building has to sign in and out. If a teacher wants to come in early, he or she has to be escorted by the officer on duty. There's always an officer on duty."

Sajan nodded his approval. "We have similar things at the hospital. Though it's harder to monitor, given that it's a hospital."

Annika nodded her understanding. She stared at him. Then it struck her, like lightning. Her parents looked happy and relaxed. Her mother looked at her with an extra little twinkle in her eye. They had never looked this way when she had brought Steven over.

They had been right about Steven. There had been a reason they were uncomfortable around him, and it had had nothing to do with the fact that he wasn't Indian. Annika had hidden behind that reason and had been unable or unwilling to see that Steven simply was not the man for her. It took a miscarriage and Steven leaving for her to figure that out. Unbidden, her heart ached at the thought of what she lost.

"So how long have you been teaching?" Sajan asked as Usha refilled his plate, despite his insistence that he could not eat another bite.

"Well, this is my first year with my own classroom."

"That must be very exciting." He beamed at her.

"It really is." Happy to have a receptive audience and to change to a more positive topic, Annika told him all about her class and basic lesson plans.

"So, parents' night comes up soon?" he asked.

"Oh, not until early January, and it's during the school day, so they can see how their children spend their time in school."

"Good luck."

The conversation turned to Diwali celebrations and who was still in the area that Sajan might remember. The evening passed amiably and quickly, everyone seeming to have had a nice time. Even her.

After Sajan left, laden with leftovers and the diya he had come for, they cleaned up together. Everyone in the house had a job: her dad did dishes, her mom put away the food, Nilay did floors and Annika wiped the countertops.

"I told you I wasn't ready to meet people." She scrubbed the countertop with her back to her father and mother.

"But it wasn't so bad, eh?" her mother replied.

"It was fine, I suppose."

"So, you like him?" her father asked.

Annika stopped scrubbing and turned to face her parents. They stopped what they were doing and looked at her expectantly. "He's a nice guy. But that doesn't mean that I 'like' him." She made sure to use air quotes around the word *like*. "There's no…spark." An image of Chopper Guy suddenly flashed in her mind.

"That spark will come. You'll see." Her mother was beaming.

"Mom. Seriously, nothing has changed." She made eye contact with them both. "Don't do this again."

They weren't listening to her. They were already envisioning how great it would be to have Sajan in their family. She saw it in their eyes. They were happy. Their happiness soothed her troubled heart.

Maybe she should give Sajan a chance.

Chopper Guy's laugh echoed in her ear, putting a small smile on her face.

Maybe.

CHAPTER SEVEN

DANIEL

AT THE BUZZ, Daniel reached over and grabbed his phone from his nightstand. It was one of only a few pieces of furniture in his apartment.

The phone screen displayed a text from his sister. Are you up? Don't forget to eat.

Daniel closed his eyes and lay back in bed. He'd been having a great dream starring the one and only Annika. His sister's text had interrupted right at the good part, and he wanted to get back to it.

No dice. The phone buzzed again, demanding his attention. He threw a text back. Overnight shift. I'll eat.

He got out of bed and hit the shower. By the time he got home from his overnight, it had been close to 8:00 a.m., and he had crashed.

Annika had seemed fine at the bar the other night. No need to go back again. It wasn't as though he was looking for a girlfriend. He'd tried that already and it hadn't worked out. Since then, he simply dealt in the occasional one-night stand. But Annika Mehta was not a one-night stand.

Though he *had* just promised his sister he would eat. And there wasn't any food in his apartment. Mrs. P. seemed like a great cook. Maybe he'd head over to the bar for more of that soup. A man had to eat, right? If Annika happened to be there, well, then, she was there.

Daniel hopped on his motorcycle and took a route through the city that landed him in front of Phil's Place. Huh. Might as well go in now. He *was* hungry. And Emma would be calling to check up on him anyway.

His stomach lurched in anticipation of seeing Annika again. He walked in to find the place as busy as it had been the last time he'd been in. It was almost five, afternoon was giving way to evening, and the bar bustled with happy-hour energy. In no time, Daniel scanned the room and found the ponytail he'd been looking for. She caught his eye, and at her smile, nerves that had been on edge since his last visit settled. He walked up to the bar and sat down.

"You'll have to move over two seats." Bobby was looking at him, eyebrows raised.

"What?"

"Move over two seats—" he indicated the desired stool "—and you'll be in Annika's section."

Daniel flushed. "Oh, I didn't come here for… I mean… the soup the other night was so good. I thought I'd—"

Bobby stared him down and waited patiently for him to finish rambling. Sensing defeat, Daniel stood and moved down two seats into Annika's section. Bobby's expression did not change, but he bellowed out, "Annika, someone in your section."

As Bobby walked back to the register, he looked Daniel in the eye. "You're welcome."

Before Daniel could answer, Annika was in front of him. "Didn't have enough stare time with your bourbon?"

He chuckled. "Actually, I will have another. And whatever your next recommendation is on the menu."

"Today, Mrs. P. is making Cubans. Hence the crowd. You may have to wait."

"I'll take the bourbon while I wait."

She made a face like he was crazy and rolled her eyes, but she went to get the drink.

She placed his glass down in front of him, making eye contact. "Don't go all wild on me and take a sip."

Her lips pursed and those brown eyes taunted, and it was all Daniel could do to not reach out and touch her. When was the last time he'd felt like touching a woman? Not that he hadn't *touched* a woman in five years, but those women were forgotten before morning. Right now, he wanted to simply touch her face, see if her skin was as soft as it appeared.

Not that he would want to stop at that.

"Don't you work? Or is it just the helicopter thing?"

He swiveled his glass around, a smile pulling at the corners of his mouth at her tone. "I do. Just not right now." Two could play this game.

Bobby sidled up behind Annika and leaned toward Daniel. "She's only asking because she works two jobs."

Annika shook her head at Bobby. "That's not why. Just making conversation."

Something inside Daniel flipped, excited that Annika wanted to make conversation with him. "Yeah? What's the other job?"

"I'm a kindergarten teacher." A gorgeous flush filled her cheeks. She was clearly proud of her vocation, but Daniel barely noticed. His head was spinning, and lead had filled his stomach. A small voice inside his head was screaming for him to leave this bar and never return to Annika Mehta. Painful images started their all-too-familiar slideshow in his head. He gripped his glass.

A crash from the kitchen jolted Daniel back to the present, and he released his hold on the glass. In an instant, Annika's expression went from playful to worried, and she dashed to the back, Bobby at her heels. Daniel followed.

"Mrs. P., you okay?" Annika stopped midstep, and Daniel was forced to grab her arms to keep from falling into her.

"Sorry," he mumbled as he quickly let go. Her skin was soft and warm—and as much as he might have thought he wanted to know how soft her skin was, he really did not need to know that.

Pots, pans and utensils were all over the floor. A few bowls still rolled and spun before finally clattering to a stop. Behind Mrs. P., a couple of old wooden shelves were still swinging as they held on to the wall by only a nail or two.

"Yeah, I'm fine." Mrs. P. stepped away from the chaos, lifting a shaky hand to her mouth. One of the shelves gave up the fight and fell to the floor with a thud. "But these shelves have seen better days."

Annika went to the older woman and wrapped her arms around her. Daniel tapped Annika's shoulder. "Mind if I take a look?"

Annika nodded and stepped back.

"I'm fine!" Mrs. P. insisted.

"Can you just let—" Annika looked at him.

"Daniel."

"*Daniel* take a look? We don't need our best cook injured."

It was a grudging Mrs. P. that Daniel took a quick look at. "Did anything hit your head?" he asked as he checked her eye movements and reflexes. She shook her head. "No pain?"

"I'm fine, young man."

Daniel nodded at her. "Let me know if that changes."

He glanced behind Mrs. P. to find Phil checking out the damage. "Well, this is the last thing we need."

Daniel walked past Annika to inspect the shelves.

Phil scratched his head. "Gonna have to call someone to fix up these shelves. Too much for me."

"I can do it." What was he saying? He shouldn't be anywhere near Annika. Not two minutes ago, he had been on his way to bolting out the door. Daniel pulled the old shelves out of the wall with ease. "Well, my brother-in-law can. I'll help him make up some simple shelves, and I can install them. We could probably do cabinets, there and there." He nodded toward some cabinets that had seen better days, as well. It was like he was programmed to hurt himself and couldn't stop talking.

"Seriously? You can do that?" Phil raised his eyebrows.

Say no. Say no. He caught Annika gaping at him, and it sent a thrill through him. "Sure." Daniel shrugged.

"I didn't catch your name, young man." Phil turned his gruff voice toward Daniel with new interest.

"Oh." Daniel extended his hand to Phil. "It's Daniel, sir. Daniel Bliant."

"All right, then, son, you're hired." Phil clapped him on the back.

"I can give you an estimate, so you'll know what to expect."

"Why? You planning on cheating me?"

"Uh, no, sir."

"Then we're fine." Phil was firm. Daniel opened his mouth to protest, but Phil cut him off. He held out his hand to Daniel. "We'll shake on it like men, and that'll be it."

Daniel grinned and shook it. Clearly, there was no arguing with Phil. "Deal. I'll give you a fair price." How much was his peace of mind worth? Because he would have none working here, side by side with Annika.

"Damn straight you will." Phil winked at him. He looked over at Annika and Bobby. "Who's taking care of the customers?"

Annika and Bobby looked at each other and scrambled out to the front, but not before Annika turned and caught Daniel's eye. Her small smile lit up her face and zinged through his body. He caught himself staring, and smiled back. She nodded and took off before Phil could say any more.

Daniel assessed the damage and started picking up the debris.

"So what's your other job? I mean besides the helicopter?" Annika had returned.

"Uh…" He hesitated. If she found out he was a nurse practitioner in the ER, she might wonder what he knew. "I work at Hopkins."

Her eyebrows shot up. "You're a doctor? How do you have time for—"

"I'm a nurse practitioner." He gave in. "Working. That's my vice. Not the alcohol."

Satisfied, she started to leave. She came back again. "Why are you doing all this? I mean, you don't know any of us."

Because he'd thought of nothing else but her for the past five months. Not to mention that he apparently enjoyed torturing himself.

Daniel shrugged. "I just happened to be at the right place at the right time. Besides, I'm pretty good with my hands." He cringed. Did he just flirt with her?

She flushed, but did not break eye contact. "Well, I

guess we'll have to see about that." She smirked and returned to her customers.

Oh, damn.

CHAPTER EIGHT

ANNIKA

AFTER SCHOOL, ANNIKA approached the bar for her shift, trying not to speed up her pace. Every day for the past three weeks, she'd found herself walking a bit faster to the bar in anticipation of seeing Daniel. At this rate, she'd be running there within the week.

Daniel had not been in last night since he'd been on the chopper, so he was probably there tonight. *Why did she even know his schedule?* The door jingled to announce her arrival in the quiet bar, and sure enough, a familiar and quite muscular back was sitting in her section at the end of the bar. Daniel turned on his bar stool.

Annika swallowed hard. He really was magnificent. His green-gray T-shirt fit tight across his broad shoulders and muscular chest. Biceps bulged from the shirtsleeves, leading to strong forearms and hands. He held his bourbon and raised it to her, a smile playing at his ever-so-full and kissable lips. Even from where she stood frozen and taking in his beauty, she saw the amusement in those knee-melting green eyes. *Kissable?* Where did that come from?

She forced her feet to move at a normal, casual pace, convinced that if she walked as fast as she really wanted to, he'd see her attraction to him. Because of course the silly grin on her face revealed nothing. If Naya were here, she'd roll her eyes.

Danger. Danger. A voice that sounded like her mother—complete with Indian accent—came from the back of her head. Though, truth be told, it was hard to hear that voice over the hammering of her heart. Honestly, it was like she was in high school. It had been getting worse over the past few weeks since Daniel was at the bar most days, helping Phil get the kitchen back in order.

"How was class today?" Daniel called out to her as she passed him on her way to the back. She grinned, strangely comforted by the fact that he asked that question every day without fail. His lips would tighten almost imperceptibly, and he didn't quite make eye contact, betraying to her that it cost him something to ask it. While she was sure it made him sad, she had no idea why. Today, his eyelid twitched as he asked, "Has Mitch found his voice yet?"

Annika shook her head. Mitch was a young five, having just made the age cutoff date for the class. But he didn't speak. He managed to interact with the other children without needing to be verbal, but his mother was concerned he wasn't socializing well. While Mitch's father chose not to speak to Annika at all in the rare instance he did pickup or drop-off, his mother did speak to her, possibly only for Mitch's sake.

From those interactions, Annika learned that Mitch spoke at home and for his speech therapist, but Annika had yet to hear his voice. Even with the special education department and the school counselor in communication with the parents, they were having a hard time figuring out what was happening. In a moment of frustration, she had spoken to Daniel about it. Mitch was her student, and she was moved to find a way to help him.

"Not yet, and the other kids are picking up on it. They interact with him less and less." She informed him over her shoulder as she continued back to the kitchen and removed her coat.

"What about the parents?"

Annika hadn't shared with Daniel what Mitch's father had said to her, and she didn't feel the need to do so now.

"The mom tells me what goes on at home. We're working together on trying to figure out what's going on." She dropped her backpack and surveyed the kitchen. New cabinets, a fine stainless-steel countertop below them and gorgeous shelves made up the new and improved kitchen. It looked done. Her heart sank a bit. "Wow!" She forced some excitement into her voice as she called out to the front. "You finished."

"Well, just about." His voice was almost in her ear.

She started. She hadn't heard him come up behind her. Despite the heat coming off his body, she was suddenly frozen and at a loss for words.

"I just need to get a few knobs, and we're all set back here." Daniel walked past her, a grin playing at his mouth.

His subtle earthy scent did nothing to slow her heartbeat. This was not good. She couldn't possibly have feelings for him. It was a physical reaction. He was undoubtedly hot, that was all it was. Because there was no way her parents would go for a guy who was a nurse practitioner. Not when Sajan was a surgeon. Not when the last guy she chose on her own had been such an asshole.

"Then I guess you won't be coming back." She tried to keep the sadness from her voice as she looked up at him. She failed.

He stepped close enough that his body—that very fine body—blocked out her view of everything else, and his scent surrounded her. She could get lost here. He smiled down at her, his eyes never leaving hers. "Well, I'm addicted to Mrs. P.'s cooking. And I do need somewhere to stare at my bourbon."

In an instant she had visions of Daniel continuing to come to the bar, of talking to him daily, as she'd quickly gotten used to. Of doing more than talking… She quickly squashed the thrill of excitement that flashed through her body at the idea that Daniel didn't want to go elsewhere to stare at a drink. That he wanted to come here. To see her. Really, she should not be entertaining fantasies of Daniel— of any kind. It was better if he didn't return to the bar. He had *complicated* written all over him and his mysterious bourbon. She did not need that.

Being close enough to be enveloped in his body heat wasn't helping. "Sure. Whatever." As if to compensate for her wayward thoughts, her attempt at nonchalance came out as complete indifference.

His eyes darkened below a briefly furrowed brow. He opened his mouth to speak, but Annika interrupted him. "I mean, it's your bourbon. Go wherever you like." Now she sounded downright mean.

He frowned as if hurt or disappointed. Time to get away before she did something she would regret further. Like take it all back and fall into his arms.

He shook his head at her. "Annika…" His phone rang out the tune of the Harry Potter theme. Even Annika knew that was his sister.

She stepped back from him. "You should take that." She grabbed her apron and headed out into the bar so he could talk.

She heard his footsteps as he followed her out.

It wasn't that Annika was eavesdropping. But Daniel

took his calls at the bar and didn't make any attempt at hiding his conversation. So, she was bound to hear some stuff. Though she hardly liked to admit it, she was curious about the rest of his life. Especially about that bourbon. Now she'd probably never find out.

It was just the beginning of happy hour. She was listening to his end of a conversation with his sister, Emma, when the door jingled, and her heart lightened.

Nilay entered the bar as if he entered bars all the time. He carried a brown paper bag that Annika knew had food from home.

She looked behind him, ready to tense at the sight of her father, but no one was there. "Did you drive here yourself?" She grinned. Her baby brother had a driver's license.

He leaned over and gave her a hug as he placed a shopping bag on top of the bar. "Yes, Didi, I did." He beamed. "And I passed Papa's test, too, which means I can drive anywhere!"

Her father strongly believed that the MVA test was not enough, so he'd given them both an extra "driving test" when they were learning how to drive. Once they passed his test, he let them have the freedom they wanted. As a result, Annika, and now her brother, were both excellent drivers.

"Nice!" Annika high-fived her brother. "Did he do the 'squirrel' thing?"

Nilay shook his head, rolling his eyes. "Every chance he got."

"Something smells amazing!" Daniel tapped his phone off and came and sat in her section, near Nilay.

Nilay just stared at him, before turning to Annika, with a *Who is this guy?* look on his face.

"Daniel Bliant." Daniel extended his hand to Nilay. Nilay just stared at it.

"Nilay, Daniel's a…friend of mine." She widened her eyes at him to prompt some manners.

Nilay smiled as he got the hint and shook Daniel's hand. "Nilay Mehta. I'm her brother."

Annika moved the bag to her side of the bar, and the aroma of garlic, onions and garam masala wafted by. "My mom sent food from home." Annika indicated the bag.

"Takes me back." Daniel raised his eyebrows at her. He turned to Nilay. "What's the squirrel thing?"

Nilay and Annika stared at him. Annika pursed her lips as Daniel flushed. "What?" He looked from one sibling to the other as if he'd been caught doing something wrong. "You weren't whispering."

"Uh-huh." Annika nodded at him, though she knew she was just as guilty of listening to his conversations.

He leaned toward her, and Annika's stomach did a flip at the intimate tease in his voice. "I know you listen when I talk to Emma."

She froze. *Busted.*

Daniel grinned and sat back from her, triumph all over his face.

Nilay narrowed his eyes at his sister. "What's going on here?"

"Nothing." Annika was quick to answer but did not look at Daniel. "Nothing at all. Why don't you explain the squirrel thing to Daniel, and I'll go get you both some food."

"Ooh! Did Mrs. P. make that soup?" Nilay called as she walked to the kitchen. She heard him start the explanation, just as she entered the kitchen.

The soup was hot and fresh, and Nilay dived into it as soon as she placed it in front of him.

Daniel thanked her, letting his gaze rest on her a moment longer than necessary, making her wonder if their earlier conversation was still on his mind. She turned away from him and watched her brother eat as if he hadn't eaten in days, throwing her a cursory "Thanks, Didi."

"Little brothers." Annika mumbled under her breath as she rolled her eyes at Nilay again.

"Guess I'll have to remember to be nicer to my older sister." Daniel smiled all the way out to both dimples, and Annika found her knees were suddenly made of jelly.

She filed away the knowledge that Daniel's sister was older. "See that you do," she somehow managed, before leaving to tend to other customers.

Nilay and Daniel continued to chat amiably about driving and food, while enjoying their snack. Watching them gave her a warm feeling in her chest that she had long since forgotten. She forgot that she was trying to not like Daniel and was lost in that stolen moment of happiness when the door jingled and a familiar blond head reared in.

The blood drained from her head. He looked the same. No less than five women of varying ages turned to watch him walk in, expensive suit fitting like a glove, lopsided grin plastered to his face. He was aware of every eye.

Steven.

When they were together, he had never come down to the bar to see her or even have a meal, but now here he was. Walking like he owned the room, soaking up every last bit of female attention.

He was with a few of his colleagues from work. Before she could move toward the door to make him leave, he and his friends entered and sat down at Bobby's end of the bar. She froze. Her sudden stop caught Nilay's eye, and it took him only a moment to follow her gaze and absorb what was happening. Before she could say anything, Nilay bolted up and out of his stool toward them. Annika recovered control over her body and followed him, trying to stop what she knew would not end well for anyone. In her periphery, she caught a surprised Daniel turning and walking toward Nilay.

"What the hell are you doing here?" Nilay demanded.

Nilay had seen through Steven the first time they'd met. Annika had blown off her brother's concerns as childish, but she wouldn't ever make that mistake again. She came around and stood in front of her brother to face Steven.

"Leave, Steven." Annika gritted her teeth in an attempt to not empty her stomach right there and then. How she was not screaming at the top of her lungs, she had no idea.

Steven was completely stunned, clearly having no idea what bar he had walked into. But in true Steven style, he quickly assessed the situation and recovered.

"Hey, kid." He swept his gaze past Annika to Nilay.

"Don't you *hey, kid* me."

Annika felt Nilay try to push past her. She held her ground. "Just leave, Steven."

Steven nodded, blue eyes finally resting on Annika. "How have you been?"

Annika paused, seeing something there she hadn't expected to see.

"How has she been?" Nilay was almost shouting. "How has she been? Are you crazy? You, of all people, *do not* get to ask that. *Now leave!* Before I make you." With that, Nilay was able to push past his sister, so he was toe-to-toe with Steven.

Steven chuckled. "You're going to make me?"

At sixteen, Nilay was taller than Annika, but he was skin and bones. He was forever lifting weights and drinking protein smoothies to "bulk up," but it hadn't taken yet. Next to Steven's tall, muscular build, Nilay looked even more like a kid. Nilay did not seem perturbed by the fact that Steven towered a good six inches over him. Not to mention that Steven probably also had a good twenty pounds of pure muscle that Nilay did not. He glared at Steven as if warning him that his death was impending.

Steven inhaled and exhaled with exaggeration. "Listen, kid. I didn't even know she worked here."

Nilay stepped up closer, almost in Steven's face. "Fine. You're forgiven for entering. Now leave."

"Nilay, it's fine." Customers were starting to notice. The last thing Annika wanted was trouble for Phil. "I can handle this." She noted some movement from Daniel in her periphery.

Nilay addressed Annika, his eyes never leaving Steven. "I know you can. But if I had done my job as a brother before, this asshole never would have had a chance to hurt you."

Steven's blue eyes turned to ice. "Who the hell are you calling an asshole?" He put his hand on Nilay's chest and shoved him.

Nilay lost his balance and fell back into Annika. Annika also lost her balance and fell back into the closest table. While the table had been vacated, she hadn't had a chance to clean it off. She tried to use the table to regain her balance, but instead she and Nilay went down with the table. Wineglasses shattered, beer mugs clunked and a searing pain went up her left arm.

"Nilay, get off me!"

"I'm trying." Nilay stood and offered his hand to Annika to help her stand. She reached for him. "Aw, jeez, Didi, you're bleeding."

Sure enough, there was a large gash on the palm of her left hand. Blood oozed from the gaping wound. Nilay led her to a chair away from all the debris. Daniel was kneeling by her side in an instant, no sign of Steven or his friends.

"What the hell...?" Mrs. P. materialized at Daniel's side. "How can I help?"

"Where's Steven?" Annika searched the bar, even as a wave of nausea gripped her at the sight of her wound. She turned her focus to Daniel. His brow furrowed as he gently examined her hand with a professional eye. Pain throbbed from her hand, up her arm, and the sight of the blood was not helping her stomach. She tried not to notice the gentleness of his touch, or how it sent an electrical current through her.

"Well, our Daniel pulled him off your brother. Now Phil's got him, don't you worry, hon." Mrs. P. comforted her, pride in her husband all over her face. "He's not too old to take care of a troublemaker like that."

Daniel glanced up at Mrs. P. "Let's get some fresh towels to clean this off." He looked at Annika. "Can you stand?"

She paused before nodding. Her stomach was settling, and there was no light-headedness. He held her injured hand gingerly and wrapped his other arm around her waist. With no apparent effort on his part, he lifted her to standing. If her hand hadn't been throbbing with pain, she might have actually enjoyed his proximity. *Who was she kidding?* She was totally enjoying his proximity, pain or not.

His face was inches from hers as he scanned her face. "Steady?"

He was so close she was unable to speak, so she nodded again and allowed him to lead her to the sink as Mrs. P. went to the back to grab towels.

"How's she doing?" Phil asked as he returned to the bar.

Daniel wrapped her hand with a clean towel, before finally settling his gaze on Annika.

"Well, she needs stitches." He turned to her. "Let's go."

"Go? Go where?"

"The ER." He hesitated, then looked her in the eye. "I can do them for you."

Annika shot a look at Nilay. He set his lips in a straight line. "You have to go," her brother said.

"Can't you just do them here?" She knew she sounded like a little girl, but she couldn't face the ER. Especially not right after seeing Steven.

"No." Daniel grinned at her. "They frown on us taking lidocaine home."

"Young lady." Mrs. P. came close and spoke. "Anni, you do what this young man says. I know it's hard going back there…" Mrs. P.'s blue eyes met hers with understanding.

Annika's hand throbbed. Her heart began to race, and she started to sweat, her breaths shallow. "I don't like the ER."

Bobby had already started righting tables and Phil was sweeping. The few customers slowly went back to their conversations now that the excitement was over.

"No one does." Daniel leaned in and spoke quietly, gently, and Annika tried not to concentrate on how sexy he sounded when all he was doing was trying to take care of her. "I'll do them myself. You won't feel a thing."

"Don't you have a bag with all that stuff in it?" Annika bit her bottom lip. "Actually, I'll be fine." She looked at Nilay. "Maybe Sajan could do it."

Nilay shook his head like she was an idiot. "You'd still have to go to the hospital."

"Who's Sajan?" Was it her imagination, or did Daniel tense up and seem irritated?

"No one. A friend." She instantly regretted bringing up Sajan's name. What was wrong with her? Why did it matter?

Daniel studied her for a moment and seemed to relax some. "Okay. We'll go elsewhere."

"Not the ER?"

"Not the ER. But we'll have to take your car. All I have is my bike." He put his hand out for her car keys.

"I'll drive," Nilay spoke up.

She looked from one grim man to the other. "But no ER?"

Nilay looked to Daniel. Daniel raised his hands. "I promise." He side-eyed Nilay. "How long have you had your license?"

"A week."

"He passed the squirrel test," Annika assured Daniel. "And I'm not going without him."

Daniel sighed, resigned. "Let's go."

IT WAS DECIDED that Nilay would drive and Daniel would direct from the passenger's side, leaving Annika in the back seat. Nilay kept up a stream of conversation while he drove.

Daniel was suddenly interested in the traffic. "Watch out for that guy."

Nilay easily maneuvered out of the way. "So I saw you help Phil get rid of Steven."

Daniel shrugged.

"Could you show me that move sometime?"

Daniel side-eyed Nilay. "We just met. You don't know anything about me."

Nilay grinned. "I know people. Trust me."

Daniel turned his head to Annika in the back, his eyebrows raised. Annika nodded. "It's true. He's got some kind of radar or something."

Daniel shrugged. "Sure, kid." He nodded at Annika's hand. "How's it feel?"

Her hand was pounding, but it was nothing to how the rest of her was shaking from the encounter with Steven. How had she ever thought she loved him? Honestly, if there really was a radar that detected the character of a person, hers was permanently broken. She met Daniel's concerned gaze, unsure of what her own face revealed.

"It'll be fine."

He narrowed his eyes at her as if he wanted to ask her something, but instead he nodded and faced front again. "Almost there."

Annika studied his profile, enjoying the lines of his face as he spoke to Nilay and laughed at something her brother said. That warm feeling of contentment passed over her again as she watched them. She shook her head of it. No point in going there. *Your radar is broken, remember?*

But Nilay definitely liked him, and he had great radar. Maybe...

As they approached a small building with a large field, she sat up straight. "You're taking me to your chopper base, Chopper Guy?" Oh, shit, did she say that out loud?

"What did you call me?" Amusement dripped from his voice, and he turned to face her, his face lit up, green eyes dancing.

"Nothing." Annika focused her gaze out the window. Her face heated in response to his smile, even though she couldn't see it. Thank goodness for brown skin.

Nilay's face lit up. "This is a chopper base? You're a flight medic?"

Daniel nodded. "Yes, on the side."

"Wow."

Annika grinned to herself. Her little brother was completely starstruck. Just when Daniel couldn't get any cooler, he turned out to be a helicopter flight medic. She sighed, slightly disappointed. Nilay's radar was most likely tainted by the fact that he thought Daniel's jobs were amazing.

"So…do you carry a gun?" Nilay started his questions.

Annika rolled her eyes in the back seat.

"No," Daniel answered. "There's no need. We're not cops."

"Right. So what do you get to do?"

"Well, we start IVs, stop bleeding, do minor procedures if necessary. Basically, we stabilize the patient so we can airlift them to the surgeons as quickly as possible."

"What's some of the worst you've seen?"

"Well, there was the gunshot wound a month ago at Phil's Place."

Too late, Annika began shaking her head from the back seat in an effort to get Daniel to not mention that.

"There was a gunshot at Didi's bar?" Nilay's voice filled with alarm.

"Uh—" Daniel side-eyed Annika.

"It was nothing. No need to mention this at home." She glared at Daniel. *Thanks a lot.*

"What do you mean *nothing*?"

"Hey, there's a spot. Think you can get it in there?" Daniel interrupted.

Nilay concentrated on his parking, and Daniel offered information about the base before Nilay could continue with his interrogation.

Daniel held Annika's arm for support as he guided them through the door and into the building. Normally, Annika would have insisted she could walk on her own—her feet were not injured!—but she wasn't inclined to say no to being this close to him. She might never get another chance.

"The base is set up much like a house. We have three bedrooms, one for each of us and one for the pilot. That way we can rest in between calls," Daniel told them as he led them to a small room with a single bed and a desk.

By this time, Nilay was bouncing with excitement and asking about everything he saw. Daniel sat Annika on the bed and turned to Nilay. "You're free to look around while I do this, just don't touch anything."

"Seriously? Awesome! I promise—I won't touch anything. Where's the chopper?" He started to bounce away, then turned back. "You're okay, right, Didi? I mean, I can stay if you need me."

Annika shook her head. "I'm fine. Go ahead."

She had barely finished before Nilay was off.

Daniel had opened a black bag, rummaged through it and pulled out a small pouch, which turned out to be a suture kit. "Sorry about telling him about the incident at the bar. I guess I wasn't thinking."

Annika shrugged. "It's fine. It's only a problem if he tells my parents, which he won't because he thinks all this—" she waved with her good hand "—is supercool."

He placed a small nightstand in front of Annika before he turned to open an overhead cabinet and get things set up. The muscles of his back and arms flexed as he reached inside the cabinet and pulled out a clean sheet, which he draped over the small nightstand, placing Annika's injured hand on top of it. He left the room for a minute and returned, drying his hands on a clean paper towel. He pulled up a chair and sat down across from her, donned gloves and proceeded to set up his instruments.

His breath came steady and sure, his movements graceful and practiced. He filled the small space, and she was mesmerized. More than aware of the fact that she sat on a bed he slept in and that they were very much alone.

When all seemed set, he gently removed the makeshift bandage he had put on. He cleaned the wound and readied a needle. "This will pinch. It's just lidocaine."

It did pinch, and Annika squeezed her eyes shut, trying not to flinch.

"So, who was the asshole?" Daniel did not look up from his work.

"No one." Tears welled in her eyes. Everything came back. She concentrated on her hand, but when he looked at her, she had to bite her lip to keep the tears from falling. She failed.

"Well, 'no one' really had your brother riled up." He spoke softly, but Annika caught an edge in his voice.

Annika wiped away her tears and swallowed hard. "Why do you care?"

"Because I do." His lips pressed together, but kindness filled his eyes when he stole a glance at her.

More silence.

"Steven. He's the asshole." She found herself speaking into the silence. Must be a technique they taught in nursing school. *How to get people to spill their guts without saying anything.* "I'm not sure what that says about my taste in men, but we were engaged—and then we weren't."

"Seems like you dodged a bullet there."

Annika stared at him.

He looked up as if he could feel her gaze. "You know, him being an asshole and all that." Daniel's touch was gentle as he started the stitches, sending a small thrill through her.

Annika snuck a glance at him as he focused on his work. Long dark lashes framed those green eyes perfectly. His hair was thick, the color of brown autumn leaves that had fallen, with just a touch of wave. Her fingers wiggled at the thought of running them through it. *Wait, what?*

"Whoa, easy there." Daniel glanced at her. "No wiggly fingers."

"Sorry." She kept still and changed the subject to cover her flush. "Where is everybody?"

"Out on a call. Which is good." He didn't look up. Probably a good thing, as Annika could still feel the heat in her face from her wayward thoughts.

"Why?"

"Technically, I shouldn't be treating you here." If he hadn't already been looking at her hand, Annika had the distinct feeling he would have avoided her gaze.

"Why are you treating me, then?" She tried to keep still.

"You need stitches."

"You could have forced me to go to the ER."

"Yes. I could have. But you looked terrified of the ER, so I came up with plan B." He glanced up at her and flushed, almost embarrassed, then quickly bent back to his work. "You seem to really like teaching."

Annika smiled. "I love it. Chase Creek Elementary all the way!"

Daniel froze for a split second as she pumped her good hand.

"Oh. I'm sorry, no sudden movements. I do get a bit overexcited about my job." She slowly put her hand down and concentrated on being still. This must be how her students felt all the time. "I really love being with the children and watching them discover how the world works." She switched gears. "My parents wanted me to go to medical school—but I couldn't do it. I took a year or so off after college—after I had decided against med school—to save up some money for grad school. Teaching is part of me. It's like I need to do it." She hadn't talked about this in forever, but it felt easy to share with him.

"Well, that's something we have in common."

"You teach?" She grinned.

He chuckled, a low rumble that Annika could have listened to forever. "No. Med school. I applied after nursing school. Pressure from everyone—" he lifted his gaze to her and rolled his eyes "—about not living up to my full potential, and I got in. But it wasn't for me. I decided to do my graduate work toward my DNP instead."

"So why do you do this?" She indicated the base with her good hand.

"Um...well." He hesitated, suddenly unable to meet her eyes. "This is just a side gig—like you working Phil's. I like to keep busy."

"I work at Phil's because I need the money." She shrugged, then grinned at him as an idea struck her. "You should come to my class and talk about this. The kids will find it exciting. The helicopter, the whole thing."

For the second time in a few minutes, his entire body seemed to stiffen, almost imperceptibly. She couldn't stop watching him as he clenched his jaw and then almost forcibly relaxed it.

"Oh, I doubt that. They're a little young for trauma." He maintained concentration on her hand, though he was holding the needle and not stitching. "Maybe I can arrange a visit from the local fire department instead. That fire engine is very popular with the kindergarten-age set.

A firefighter friend of mine, Lance, loves showing it off." He looked up at her, the tension still in his face, even as he smiled at her. "The kids love it."

Annika paused a moment, trying to figure out what put that tiny bit of fear in his eyes. "Sure." She finally managed. "The children would love that fire engine! Let's make it happen."

He grinned wide, the tension finally leaving his face and body. "Consider it done."

Annika inhaled the scent of him, clean and fresh, mixed with the sharp scent of rubbing alcohol.

The combination was strangely comforting, maybe even familiar. Her eyes met his, and she was powerless to look away, her guard slipping just a bit more.

"So…I was pregnant."

Daniel paused in his work, his mouth set in a line, but his eyes were warm, and he said nothing, waiting for her to continue. Her guard melted away, and tears prickled at her nose. Daniel was mid-stitch, and even in her state she could appreciate that he was conflicted between wanting to touch her and breaking sterile. Silence stretched between them while Annika gathered herself.

"With his baby."

Daniel nodded, finished the last stitch, applied antibiotic ointment, and wrapped up her wound with gauze and a small splint.

"Initially, he was great. He proposed, and said he loved me and wanted a family with me." She paused, forcing herself to speak with clinical detachment. "Five months ago, I had cramps and bleeding in the middle of the night. He drove me to the ER. By the time he parked the car and found me, I had…lost…" She shook her head and swallowed her unspent tears. So much for detachment. "I had

been waiting for him, but when he got there, he—he—"
She searched the room for the words she still couldn't believe. "He broke up with me right in the ER. Said the only
reason he proposed was to do 'the right thing.' And today,
he acted like it was nothing!"

She thought about the hospital band that she always
carried. It reminded her of the worst day of her life. Of
that night. It reminded her that if she could survive that,
she was stronger than she thought. But those damn tears
burned behind her eyes again. They filled her eyes, though
she was determined they not fall. "I was so stupid!" Well,
so much for no tears falling.

His work finally done, Daniel pushed aside the suture
tray, tossed his gloves and scooted his stool up to the edge
of the bed where she sat. He was level with her, and he
cupped her face with his hands, wiping away her tears with
his thumbs. Rough calluses rubbed against her skin, and
it was all she could do to not melt into his tender touch
right there.

"No, you were not stupid. He was." Daniel moved closer.
She could see the small brown flecks in the green of his
eyes. She was so moved by the determination in them that
she believed him.

"I felt like such a failure." Tears were free-flowing.
"I lost my baby, not to mention the man I thought I—"
It was ridiculous to say the word *love* here, because she
could see clearly that what she and Steven had had was nowhere near love. She swallowed hard, and her next words
came out of the sadness she'd been feeling for these past
months. "You know, I didn't even know I wanted to be a
mother. I was always all about my career. Family would
come in time, I kept telling my parents. But when I found
out I was pregnant, I wanted that baby so bad. I wanted to

be a mother. Then, when it was…all over, it was like the world continued and I was standing still. Stuck in that moment." She could still feel that pit of despair in her belly from time to time.

Something flashed in Daniel's eyes: recognition, sympathy, understanding? It was as if he knew how hollow she'd felt.

"It sounds ridiculous, I know," she sniffled. Out of nowhere, Daniel handed her a tissue with his free hand. She half smiled her gratitude as she dabbed at her eyes.

"No." His voice was low and gruff, as if he fought off emotion. "No, it's not ridiculous. A loss…is a loss."

Something in his voice—a hitch, or a momentary heaviness—made her catch his eye. "Did you lose somebody?"

He met her gaze with such sorrow Annika caught her breath. The slightest flick of his eyes and the moment was gone. "Just something I learned in my line of work."

"I'm sorry. I don't know why I'm dumping all this on you now. We hardly know each other, and I know I should be past this by now."

"That's not true." Daniel tipped her face up from where he still held her. "We know each other. We're…friends, right?"

She nodded, but her heart sank just a bit. Sure. That was what they were. Friends.

"I mean, at least I know you well enough to know that any man who let you go is not in his right mind. And certainly breaking up with someone in the ER is probably one of the lowest things I've ever—" He paused, pressing his lips together before speaking. "Anyway, it's horrible."

He rolled his stool even closer to her. Close enough that she could feel his breath on her. "Listen, you lost a baby, someone you loved—you need to grieve. You shouldn't feel ashamed or like less of anything. There's no time line for these things. You did nothing wrong. It wasn't your fault." Anger flashed in his eyes. "And it was shitty of that asshole or anyone to make you feel like you were somehow at fault."

She just stared at him, allowing his words to fill her and enter her heart and mind. Tears continued to fall, but she had no desire to stop them. She had been scared but excited to become a mother. No matter what the circumstances. She might have been pregnant only eight to ten weeks, but it was enough for her to start to make plans, see the future. It was enough for her to fall in love.

Daniel continued to wipe aside her tears with his thumb. He stayed firm and strong, his eyes never leaving hers as her tears fell.

"I…I feel so empty."

He nodded.

"I…I…" She never finished her sentence, because she was flat-out crying. Daniel pulled her close, wrapped his arms around her and held her while she sobbed. She was enveloped in comfort and strength and couldn't remember the last time she'd felt so safe.

Or could she? Such a feeling of comfort and stability—and familiarity—flashed through her, but, like an elusive dream, it was gone before she could grab it.

When the wave of sobbing passed her, she kept her face burrowed into his shoulder for a minute, enjoying the scent of him, and the comfort of his body, before pushing back to look at him.

"And Steven is a goddamn fucking asshole." Not a new thought, but the pronouncement felt good. She wiped away her tears and tried to get herself back together.

Her proclamation earned her a small smile and a chuckle. "Yes. That he is."

She was keenly aware of the intensity of his gaze and the rapid hammering of her own heart. His face was only a few inches from hers, and she shifted her gaze to his mouth. Without really meaning to, she found herself studying his lips and wondering how they would feel against hers.

The thundering of helicopter blades startled her, and she jumped away from him. He closed his eyes as he shook his head at the sound. When he opened his eyes, his lips were set in a grim line, shyly invoking both dimples, almost as if he'd been caught red-handed.

"Better find your brother."

CHAPTER NINE

DANIEL

DANIEL STOOD AT the sound of the chopper. Maybe a bit too fast. He usually heard it before it got this close, but clearly his focus was diverted.

"Um, here. Take this for pain." He handed her some ibuprofen and a glass of water.

Annika looked almost relieved. He started putting the suture kit back together and cleaned up.

"You can take more in eight hours if it still hurts." He tossed the words over his shoulder as if he were talking to any patient as he quickly went to drop off instruments for sterilization. He needed the distance to clear his head.

What was he thinking? She was sobbing into his arms about losing her baby—finally allowing herself to feel the pain—and all he could think about was kissing her? Honestly, he had a problem. He did not need to be kissing Annika Mehta. Especially since she told him how badly she wanted to be a mother.

Except that she hadn't pulled away from him.

And he hadn't wanted her to.

He had almost told her the truth. He hadn't told anyone about Sara since she'd died. The people who knew were people he knew when she was alive. And outside of work colleagues, he didn't really hang out with anyone from back then.

He was keenly familiar with how it felt when your world stopped but everything else continued. How people went to work, loved each other, laughed together and basically continued to live their lives. He had had trouble believing any of that was still possible when a beautiful little girl had been so violently ripped from the earth.

He returned to find Annika standing and waiting for him. Her eyes were swollen. Her nose was still red, and her left hand was bandaged, but her smile threw him off balance and he had to stop in his tracks to gather himself. So much for clearing his head.

He finished straightening up, putting away any sign of the fact that he had just treated somebody, aware that she watched his every movement. "Exactly how much trouble can you get into?"

Daniel shrugged one shoulder. "Let's just say you had a tour." He took her good hand and guided her out the door. Her hand was warm and fit perfectly into his, and when she squeezed it, a thrill shifted through his body that he probably should not have enjoyed so much.

"Come on." Daniel led the way out. But—just his luck—Crista was on her way in.

"Hey, Daniel! What are you doing—" Crista stopped as she saw Annika. Her gaze shifted back to Daniel, grazing over their clasped hands.

"Hey, Crista. Just a quick tour." He turned toward Annika. "Crista, this is Annika. Annika, my colleague, Crista."

Crista held out her hand for Annika to shake. Disappointment flooded him as she released his hand to shake Crista's. He grimaced to himself. *Ridiculous. He hardly knew her; she shouldn't affect him like this.* His reprimand was quickly forgotten as she took his hand and righted his world again.

"Oh, my. That doesn't look too good." A wide-eyed Crista nodded at Annika's bandaged hand. She didn't even bother hiding her smirk to Daniel. "You should have some-one look at that for you."

Annika flushed, darting a glance at Daniel, but rallied. "Oh, this? This is old…" Daniel gently squeezed her hand as if they shared a joke.

Crista raised an eyebrow at them. "Uh-huh. Yeah, prob-ably all healed up by now." Crista's smirk was quickly headed to an outright laugh. Of course, Nilay chose that moment to barge in.

"Hey, did you see the chopper?" He was breathing heavy and his face carried that excited flush all boys seemed to get from seeing anything that flies. "That was seriously cool!"

Daniel made introductions without actually making eye contact with Crista. "This is Annika's brother. He drove."

"Uh-huh." Crista leaned into Daniel and whispered, "Might want to get the hell out of here before Andrea sees."

Daniel threw her a grateful grin. "You're the best." He glanced at Annika and nodded toward the door, then ad-dressed Crista again. "I'm on shift in two days. See you then." Daniel gently guided Annika with a small tug of her hand and dismissed Crista with a wave as they walked past her. "Let's go, kid."

Once in the car, Annika turned to Daniel. "Are you in trouble?"

"Nah. Crista won't say anything. Trust me."

"Who's Andrea?"

"Oh, she's the pilot. Kind of a stickler for the rules."

Alarm flashed across her face. "You sure you're not in trouble?"

Daniel nodded. "Yes. We got out before Andrea got in. No problem." He'd be doing Crista's share of the cleaning for a month, but it was worth it.

Nilay chatted almost the whole car ride, asking question after question. Annika teased her brother, laughing at his antics and excitement, the way only an older sister can. It reminded Daniel of better days with Emma. He didn't see her as much these days. It was too hard to see her son.

Something inside Annika seemed to have been released, and the professional in Daniel knew it was because she had shared some of her most personal fears with him. It was basic—a medical degree was not necessary to know that talking about the difficult things was a step toward healing.

He just couldn't do it himself.

But seeing Annika this happy—it was delightful. She had almost completely shed her armor for the moment. A large grin formed almost automatically at the realization that her happiness made *him* happy. And he wasn't used to any kind of happy. Daniel tried to force his expression into something neutral, so as not to appear ridiculous to her, but he couldn't stop. Being with Annika made him want to smile.

Huh.

"Hey, Daniel, I know we just met, but could I come as a ride along on the chopper one time? I won't get in the way—but I'm thinking about med school, and it would be awesome to see what happens," Nilay said.

"Nilay," Annika started in her big-sister voice, "I'm sure Daniel has better things—"

"No, actually, it's fine. We do it from time to time."

Daniel looked at Nilay. "I'll do you one better. You can come and shadow me at the ER, too."

"The ER? Seriously?"

"Yes."

This was the second chance today that he'd had to tell Annika the truth about how he met her—how he'd really met her—and he couldn't bring himself to do it. It was cowardly and he knew it. But the smile on her face and the unspoken closeness when he caught her eye stirred something within him that he had forgotten was even there. What difference did it make *how* they actually met, when the connection was clearly there now?

"What? Are you serious? That would be beyond— I mean that would be so— I promise I won't get in the way."

"Great." Daniel chuckled at Nilay's wide-eyed gratitude. "I'll have some forms for you, and a parent will have to sign off on it."

"No problem!" Nilay was about busting out of his seat.

"Eyes on the road!" Annika and Daniel spoke together.

AT ANNIKA'S REQUEST, Nilay dropped her off at the bar, and Daniel got out, as well. He loitered outside the bar while Annika and her brother said goodbye.

It was properly dark now, a crispness lingering in the air. Not quite winter, but not summer, either. They stood alone in the streetlight, suddenly awkward with each other, and spoke at the same time.

"Listen, about what I told you."

"You should rest that."

Daniel smiled. "Sorry, you go."

Annika met his eyes, bit her bottom lip. *Damn.* "Just about what I told you… Thank you for listening and for…

everything." She broke his gaze as a flush colored her cheeks. "I'm sorry I fell apart…"

Daniel held up a hand. "Don't apologize for having feelings."

Gratitude washed over her face as she nodded at him. "I do feel much better now, thanks. I just don't want you to feel sorry for me."

"I don't feel sorry for you. You've had to deal with some hard situations." He paused. "I wish I had your strength."

"You wish you had my strength? You must have missed the earlier show." Annika shook her head.

Daniel fixed her in his gaze. "That was no show—it was real—sometimes you have to cry and swear. That takes strength." Again, he was great at giving advice. Just don't ask him to actually apply it himself. "You're…well, you're stronger than you think."

She did not break eye contact, but did flash him a smile, and it was the most pleasant of electrical currents that flared through him again. It was like a drug. And possibly just as addictive.

"What were you saying?"

"Oh, just to rest your hand. Grab your bag." He jutted his chin toward the door. "I can drive your car home."

"It's just a cut. I'll be fine." She examined her bandaged hand as if seeing it for the first time.

"Just a *cut*?" Daniel ran a hand through his hair. "You have seven stitches in there."

"It's my left hand." Annika shrugged, but her eyes seemed glued to him. She cleared her throat. "And besides, I can't leave Phil by himself. They have to clean up and serve customers. Bobby's been covering for me, so I need to send him home."

Daniel sighed. "Okay. Let's go." He started for the bar.

"Go where?"

"Into the bar." He opened the door and waited for her.

"Aren't you going home?" Brown eyes widened and she didn't move.

"No, I'm going to be your other hand." *Or any other part she needed him to be.*

Annika jerked her head back, her mouth dropping open for a moment, before she curved it into a smile. "You're what?"

Daniel flushed. "I'll carry your tray, so you can rest that hand."

"I can carry it. I do it every day." But she was still smiling.

"I know you can." Daniel couldn't meet her eyes. She obviously didn't know he'd been watching her all this time. "But today, you'll bust open my handiwork. I worked hard on those stitches, and I'll be damned if you wreck them."

She pursed her lips together as if she didn't believe carrying the tray would harm her in any way. But her voice was surprisingly soft. "You should go home."

"So should you," he answered, as something quiet but real passed between them. He wondered once again what her lips would taste like when he kissed her. The way she looked at him, he was sure her thoughts were the same.

Annika broke the silence that built between them. "Well, I suppose that's how friends help each other."

"Um, yeah, sure." Daniel nodded. "We did decide we were friends." *Damn it.* He didn't want to be *friends* with Annika. Though he didn't really think he could be anything more. He simply needed to stop thinking about kissing her.

"Fine." She rolled her eyes. "Just don't spill anything."

Daniel chuckled as she passed. "As if."

LUCKILY, ANNIKA'S SHIFT had only three hours left in it. Unfortunately, they were the busiest three hours of the night. Annika donned her apron and started taking table orders. Daniel waited by the bar. The first of Annika's orders was filled, and Daniel grabbed the tray before Annika could protest.

True to his word, Daniel carried all of Annika's drink and food orders and did not so much as spill a drop anywhere. While Annika did not seem any less irritated with her shadow, she did at least seem grateful.

By 1:00 a.m. the stragglers had left, and Annika went into the kitchen to help Mrs. P. with the next day's menu.

Daniel found himself standing in front of the bar piano. It was an older upright with a dark wood finish, covered in a thin layer of dust. As far as he knew, no one played it anymore. Bobby had mentioned that it used to be played every night, but none of the current employees knew how to play.

His muscles tensed at the familiar keys. He used to play for Sara when she couldn't—or wouldn't—sleep. The last time he played was the night before...well, the last time he played for her was the last time he'd played.

"PLAY THE GOOD-NIGHT song for me, Daddy, pleeeaase?" He agreed, but before he started, she held up two fingers. "Two times, Daddy, okay?"

"I just got home from work, honey. I only have time for one song." She pouted, but took the song only one time.

It would've taken him five minutes to play it a second time. His shift had been long and grueling, and he was covering the early shift for a sick colleague the next day. He had wanted to get her to bed so he could eat and get some sleep. The agony of regret was a hole in his gut. Not to mention the irony of the fact that he never slept well anymore and routinely forgot to eat.

An image of Annika laughing in the car, followed by the pain on her face as she opened up to him, flashed through his mind. Without thought, he sat down on the bench, his fingers automatically finding the cool keys. He ran his fingers up and down the keyboard a few times, the keys all at once familiar and foreign. He had expected to find fear and anguish here, but instead he found that warm feeling of greeting a long-lost friend, a level of peace he hadn't known for years. Without thought, he played out a soft lullaby.

Images of Annika were replaced by blue eyes, soft brown curls and sticky kisses. His heart ached, and a familiar burning built up behind his eyes and prickled at his nose. He inhaled deeply and willed the sensation away as he continued to play. He transitioned from the soft lullaby to a rowdier children's song, to some of the first classical pieces he'd ever learned. The music seemed to flow from his fingers, and he became lost in the melodies and harmonies of the sounds he produced. He could almost hear her voice, but tonight he did not run from it as he usually did. That was new.

So involved was he that he didn't notice Annika until her floral scent reached him and the warmth from her body radiated to him. She sat with her legs facing out and held a glass of watered-down bourbon in her good hand.

"Sorry, I didn't mean to startle you. It's a beautiful piece." She looked at him, then at the keyboard. "You've been coming here for weeks, and you've never played before."

Daniel shrugged. "You've never had a bourbon before."

"Says you." She grinned. "This was yours." She sipped

it, then met his eyes. "I drink yours every day." She turned in the seat so she was now facing the keyboard.

"Do you, now?" The smile on his face showed exactly what he was feeling, but he was powerless to stop it. That was just what seemed to happen around Annika. He kept playing.

She nodded and finished the drink, reaching up to place the glass on the case of the piano. "I do. Haven't you noticed that I started pouring you the good stuff?"

She had turned away from him to put down the glass, inadvertently tossing her loosened ponytail. Her soft locks threw off a light fruity scent he recalled from his time with her in the hospital. He had indeed noticed that she was pouring more expensive bourbon, but he hadn't given it much thought.

He chuckled. "How's the hand? Any pain?"

She placed her good hand on the keyboard and played a small melody by popular artist Ron Pope that spoke of longing and hope. "Feels fine." Her voice became soft; she raised her injured hand. "Thank you, again, for not making me go to the ER."

He shrugged. Stray curls escaped the loosened ponytail, making her even more beautiful. "I didn't know you could play."

"I'm better with both hands." She darted her eyes away from him and cleared her throat. "What's the tune you were playing? Seems familiar."

"It's a lullaby. I used to play it…" He opened his mouth to say *for my daughter*, but the words stuck to his tongue. "For my nephew. But he's big now, and I don't see him much."

She furrowed her brow. "You talk to your sister every day—it seems like you're close."

He smirked at her. "I knew you were eavesdropping."

A slight pink flush poked through her beautiful brown skin, and he momentarily forgot how to draw breath.

"Well, uh—yeah. Everyone knows that—you talk at the bar, and you don't exactly whisper." She fidgeted with the hem of her shirt but released it in one quick motion as she locked her gaze on his. "Her name is Emma, and it seems she worries about whether you eat or not." She rolled her eyes. "Common knowledge."

He laughed, but his heart thumped at the knowledge that she had paid such close attention to him, and he planted his gaze in hers. "We are close. I just—don't see my nephew often." He shrugged it off, better to close the topic. "It's fine." The scant space between them was charged with their not touching.

"I suspect it has something to do with this bourbon." She tilted her head in the direction of the glass she had emptied. "We don't have to talk about it, but it's okay to not be fine."

He couldn't have looked away from her if his life depended on it. "We, um…well, we all have issues." He happily drowned in her attention.

She grinned. "You do come here almost every day and pay for bourbon that you stare at." Her voice dropped. "That is most certainly not normal."

"Very true. I'm trouble, and you're probably better off keeping your distance." He said the words in a rough whisper with little to no conviction as he leaned ever so slightly closer to her.

"Is that so?" Her voice was a hoarse whisper.

Daniel decreased the distance between them, shifting his gaze to her mouth. Everything around them fell away, his only thought how her lips would feel on his. "I'm really sorry that chopper came when it did."

"Me, too." Her words were barely a whisper, almost as if she didn't want to break this spell.

Daniel gently touched his lips to hers. When she didn't pull back, he pressed his mouth to hers, his heart racing even faster when she pressed back. She opened her mouth to him, allowing him to deepen their kiss. He placed his hand on her jaw, his fingers on her neck, and pulled her closer to him. She tasted sweet and smoky like his bourbon, and she kissed him back, leaning her body into him.

His other hand found her waist, and she moaned softly as his thumb grazed the small gap between her shirt and her jeans. He couldn't get enough of her; he didn't think he ever would. She pressed into him, as if she couldn't get enough of him, either. They needed to come up for air, but right now breathing was overrated.

"Annika!" A door slammed, and a woman's voice shouted out. "There you are."

Annika flew out of Daniel's arms, leaving him stunned and disoriented.

"Naya, what are you doing here?" She croaked out the words, breathy and distracted.

Something inside Daniel lifted, learning he could affect her that way. Then that something plummeted into his belly as he noticed who had interrupted them. Gray eyes met his with a flicker of recognition. It was the cousin he had met in the ER that night. Annika's night.

She shifted her gaze to her cousin. "Do you know what time it is? Nilay told me you got stitches today, and then you were late coming home and you're not answering your cell, and I just had the most amazing date ever…and…well, it seems so did you." She looked from Annika to Daniel and back to her cousin, a question forming on her face.

"No, we're not on a date." Annika spoke fast.

Daniel cut his eyes to her. She bit her bottom lip. The same lip he'd just had in his mouth.

"Oh." The girl widened her eyes at her cousin, now completely ignoring Daniel. "Is that wise?"

Without even looking at Annika, he felt her stiffen at the judgment.

Gray Eyes bit her bottom lip. "Sorry, I didn't mean—"

"Whatever," Annika sighed. "What's going on?"

The girl hesitated, then broke into a large grin. "I wanted to tell you about my date." She glanced at Daniel again but paused this time. "Wait, don't I know you?"

Damn. "Well…" Daniel glanced at Annika.

"How could you possibly know him?" Annika seemed puzzled.

Naya snapped her fingers. "In the ER. The night that—" She looked at Annika and back at Daniel, her eyes wide. "You were her ER nurse. You were just making out with your ER nurse?" She stopped short of doling out that judgment. But not short enough.

Annika threw her cousin a withering glance. "He wasn't my ER nurse. I had a woman. Amy, Anna or something. I met Daniel here, at the bar. And anyway, he's an NP."

"Not 'Chopper Guy'? Who stares at bourbon?"

Annika tightened her lips and nodded almost imperceptibly.

She'd talked about him to her family? A pleasant sensation floated through him. It had been so long since he'd felt it that he almost didn't recognize it for what it was. Happiness.

"Well, whatever. This is the guy who was in your room when I got there that night." The cousin was almost curt.

That lightness he felt a few moments ago dropped away in an instant, becoming something akin to cement in his stomach.

"That's not even possible. Daniel's an NP at the Hopkins ER…" Annika trailed off, as some realization kicked in. She turned to him. "Or maybe it is? It's such a big place—it didn't even occur to me that you might've been working the night I came in." Her voice was small, disbelieving. Like she didn't want to believe what she already knew was true. "Were you? Were you working that night?" Horror colored her whisper.

He opened his mouth, nothing came out.

"Daniel!" she said, her voice gaining strength as his silence put things together for her. "Were you in my room that night?" Her eyes darted all over his face, searching for the truth but begging him to deny it.

He managed a nod.

She shook her head as if it couldn't be true. "No, that can't be." She glanced at her cousin, who watched her with a grim expression. She took a few steps away from him, then walked back to him. "No, there's a mistake. You would've told me."

Daniel brought himself up to his full height, as if doing so would protect him from her wrath, however deserved it may be. He was stiff and unmoving, his insides roiling with dread, the taste of her still on his tongue. "It's true."

She shook her head, and the confusion in her eyes turned to anger, those beautiful brown eyes that he imagined diving into turned to coal.

"You knew—this whole time—about Steven's and my—" She whispered the next word, *baby*. Her good hand fell to her belly, as if her baby were still with her, and Daniel's heart broke for her. "You knew." Her voice got stronger as anger settled in. "You *knew*, and you let me go on and on—I haven't opened up to anyone about—" Her voice hitched. "And what the hell was that kiss? What do you do? Stalk the most vulnerable patients and see if you can get them into bed?" She was almost screaming now.

What had he been thinking? That he could find her, and she would have feelings for him? *That he had any right to have feelings for her?* What had he done, really, anyway? Holding her that night was as much for him as it had been for her. He had no business being in any kind of relationship anyway. Guilt and fear paralyzed him.

"You couldn't just say, *Hey, I was there that night. I'm sorry for what happened*?"

"What difference would that have made?" He found his voice, but he barely recognized it, he sounded so weak. Though she seemed to have a point.

"None! You're right. It's creepy either way." She advanced on him, eyes narrowed, her mouth twisted in a sick smirk. "What the fuck were you doing in my room if you weren't assigned to me?"

How could he explain that?

Angry tears swam in her eyes. "Leave. Now." This time, her voice cracked, and she gasped for control. She was trying not to cry in front of him. Well, he could at least do that for her.

He forced his legs to move just as he did that day in the ER. He stopped at the door, turning his head slightly so she could hear him. "Two weeks. Your stitches should be healed in two weeks."

Without waiting for her to say more, he opened the door and stalked out into the biting chill. Somehow, he reached his bike, his vision blurred by his own angry tears. Interestingly, he and Annika were angry at the same person.

Screw the helmet. He needed to ride.

CHAPTER TEN

ANNIKA

ANNIKA WATCHED HIM walk out of the bar and flinched when she heard the rev of his bike. What the hell had just happened? Never mind, she knew the answer. She'd started having feelings for a guy who turned out to be a liar, and possibly a stalker. How was that any different from having feelings for a guy who was self-centered? Honestly, her judgment was *way* off. If Naya hadn't walked in on them, she'd never have known he was in her room that night.

His kiss still had her head spinning, and she shivered in the coolness left behind from where his warm body had touched hers. *Forget him. Move on.*

She blinked back her tears and turned to see Naya staring at her with one eyebrow raised.

"What?"

"That looked like some kiss."

"Well, looks can be deceiving. Obviously." She recovered the shakiness from her voice and shrugged her shoulders as if that kind of kiss happened all the time.

"He never told you he was your nurse?" Naya looked behind her at the door Daniel had just left from.

"He wasn't my nurse. He's a practitioner."

"But he was in your room." She shook her head and turned back to Annika.

"He never told me, Naya." She sighed, exasperated, her patience running thin.

"What did he tell you?" Her cousin wasn't letting this go.

"Nothing." He had just listened. He had just held her and told her that she'd done nothing wrong. That it was okay to grieve even though she'd never even seen her baby. That it was okay to cry. Not to mention he knew right off that Steven was an asshole. Though he probably knew that from that night in the ER.

"Well, I guess it's good you know now, before things got too serious." Naya's tone settled it. Let it go. Move on.

"Good thing I have you to save me."

Her cousin's eyes softened, as did her tone. "That's not what I meant. I just meant..."

Annika raised her hand in surrender. "It's okay. I know what you meant. It's okay to say it. My judgment sucks. Plain and simple."

"Maybe you're still getting over Steven." Naya was backtracking, trying to spare her feelings.

Annika examined her injured hand. "I doubt that. This is what happens when Steven's around." She shook her head at her hand, trying not to recall Daniel's gentle touch or how it had made her feel. Or how he had made her feel. Light. Happy. Naya was right. Let it go. He'd lied to her, and she had been fool enough to believe him.

Annika inhaled and focused on her cousin. "Did you say something about a date?"

Naya flushed. "I did."

"With who?" Annika suspected she already knew.

"Ravi Shah." Naya tried and failed to suppress her giddy smile.

"Another guy your mom set you up with?" Annika

grinned. Naya was the "good" one. She was the one who was in law school and loved cooking and met the boys her parents suggested for her. Naya was well on her way to marriage, career, children—all the things that shouted "My parents did a fabulous job raising me!" Forget the fact that she hated law school (and the law, for that matter). What she really wanted to do was join the Peace Corps. She was attending law school to attain her law degree, fulfilling her parents' requirements, and then she intended to join the Peace Corps. She had said as much to her parents.

They were ignoring her.

To say the setups were less than successful was an understatement. But Naya dutifully met them all.

Annika walked to the door, with Naya following her. This was perfect. She could concentrate on Naya's latest disaster to take her mind off Daniel.

"Let me guess. He's a doctor who still lets his mother dress him?"

Naya shook her head. "No, that was two months ago."

Annika locked up and handed her car keys to Naya. "A lawyer who expects you to work and do all the housework."

"Anish, three months ago." Naya smiled. "But he is a lawyer."

Annika mock groaned as Naya opened the car door and sat in the driver's seat. Annika got into the car and studied her cousin. There was something different about her. The smile. It was...real. Plus, she was biting her bottom lip. Annika narrowed her eyes. It was hard to say in the darkness, but she could have sworn that Naya was *blushing*.

"You like him!" It came out as more of an accusation than anything else, really.

"He's...nice." Even if Naya hadn't giggled in that moment, her huge smile and definite flush would have given her away.

"You like him," Annika repeated, smiling at her cousin. "He's more than nice. You know he's Urmila-auntie's son?"

"Yes, I know."

They didn't know much about Urmila-auntie; she wasn't in their parents' closest circle of friends, but both of their mothers always talked about how kind she was, and they totally coveted her wardrobe.

"Are you seeing him again?"

Naya nodded, that grin still on her face. "He's cooking for me."

"He cooks, too?" Annika widened her eyes. "Does he know that you like to bake?"

"Well, he'll find out tomorrow when I show up with my famous rose truffles."

"You mean *our* famous rose truffles." Annika poked Naya with her bandaged hand as they pulled up to their apartment. Both girls loved baking. Annika couldn't really cook to save her life, but baking cookies, and her specialty, chocolate truffles, was how she relaxed, an outlet for her creativity. She and Naya particularly liked mixing Indian flavors into the items they baked, and the rose-flavored chocolate truffles were by far their favorite.

"Not like you're making them with that hand," Naya teased.

"Well, I'll supervise." Annika grinned.

They walked into their apartment, each lost in their own thoughts. Naya headed for her room and turned back to Annika. "What's the deal with you and the hot NP?"

Annika shrugged. Daniel clearly had no business being in her room that night, so why was he, if he wasn't a crazy person? In any case, Daniel had lied to her, so the slight ache in her heart when she thought of him walking out of the bar had no bearing on anything.

"He might make a good rebound guy or something? You know, until you're ready to settle down?"

Annika flinched. Which was unreasonable, because Daniel wasn't going to be *any* kind of guy. But the implication was clear: he should not be the guy she settled down with.

"Although," Naya continued, "he could be psycho."

"Even if he's not, he lied to me." She didn't get that creepy-psycho feeling from him, but lying was a deal breaker. If nothing else, she had considered him a friend— though the truth was, she hadn't really wanted to simply be his friend. So she'd let her guard down and had maybe the most amazing kiss she'd ever had. She licked her lips, still longing to have a taste of him, but then berated herself for being so weak. No, there would not be a rebound guy for her, but it would be a while before she forgot that kiss. "Deal breaker."

Maybe her parents were right. Maybe she just needed to settle down with someone dependable. Someone from a good family who was friendly and easygoing and didn't have a weird relationship with beverages and children. Someone like Sajan. Love would grow, just like it had for her parents. And they were perfectly happy.

Naya shrugged. "Glad to hear it." She walked into her room, then walked right back out. "You know what was really great?" Annika swore there were stars in her cousin's eyes.

"Do tell," Annika sighed as she walked to her room.

"He just sort of *got* me. Without really trying. The other guys were kind of weird. But Ravi grew up here, like we did. And he just—understood."

A pit grew in Annika's stomach as she nodded. "I know what you mean." It was what she had felt when Sajan had stopped by. The ease with which her family got to know him. The ease her parents felt around him. The fact that he automatically understood her reasons for becoming a teacher. It was refreshing. All the more reason to stop whatever she was feeling for Daniel. Even if she had continued to see Daniel, her family would never approve. Her dad would never understand Daniel's reasons for becoming an NP as opposed to a doctor. It was too hard going against your family all the time.

So why the pit in her stomach?

"Annika. Did you hear me?"

"What?"

"My parents are hosting a party of some sort this weekend, and they're making me attend. Come with and make it bearable."

Still distracted by thoughts of Daniel, she nodded. "Sure. Whatever you need."

CHAPTER ELEVEN

DANIEL

From: amteaches@balt.school.edu
To: lworthfire@balt.fire.gov
Cc: dblianter@hop.hosp.edu

Dear Lance,
Thank you so much for doing this! The children will be thrilled. There will be twenty children, me and four parent chaperones. The school administration has arranged for our bus to arrive by 9:30 a.m. Does that work for you?
   Please let me know if you need any more information.

Thanks again!
Best,
Annika Mehta

From: lworthfire@balt.fire.gov
To: amteaches@balt.school.edu
Cc: dblianter@hop.hosp.edu

Annika,
Looking forward to it!
Thanks to Daniel for setting this up!

Lance

Daniel read and reread the email thread. He had arranged for Annika's class to visit the fire station as he had promised. It was easy enough, since he and Lance had saved more than one life together.

He continued to analyze her email for the slightest sign that she may have thawed some, but he swore that even her emails were terse and carried her anger and sense of betrayal. It was what he deserved, so when she refused to even glance his way when he went to the bar to put the finishing touches on the cabinets, he tried to shrug it off. Easier said than done, as he couldn't ignore the way his heart skipped a beat when she entered the bar, or the fact that he smiled when he heard her laugh. In fact, he wouldn't have thought it possible to be *more* aware of her now that she was ignoring him, but he was.

Whatever, he'd finish up these cabinets, and then he would no longer have a reason to show up at the bar. It was for the best, he told himself. He didn't need to be involved with someone he would end up hurting in the end. He just couldn't shake the feeling that there had been something more in that kiss. Never mind. She was probably convinced he was some sort of creepy stalker, anyway. She was better off without him. Definitely. She'd told him how badly she'd wanted her baby; she clearly wanted to be a mother someday. That was the deal breaker. He should have backed off right then. He was better off, just trudging along alone.

Sure he was.

A child's wailing caught his attention, and he went to open the door between the kitchen and the bar. A mother was desperately trying to calm her distraught son. Annika walked around to the front of the bar, holding a bubbly pink drink in a plastic to-go cup. She knelt down to the child, offering the drink and speaking quietly to him.

The little boy sniffled and his chest heaved, but he eyed the drink. Daniel found himself smiling as Annika handed the Shirley Temple to the little boy. She had a way with kids, that was for sure. He was frozen to his spot as Annika leaned against the bar and waved goodbye to mother and son.

Bobby was drying glasses behind the bar. "You'll make a great mom one day."

She turned to face him, and Daniel's heart skipped a beat at the look of joy on her face. "I certainly hope so." She grinned at Bobby, then caught Daniel watching her.

Heat blazed through him, powerful and unnerving as he caught her gaze. Her eyes hardened as her smile faltered, and she busied herself with collecting used glasses. Daniel noticed that she still had a small bandage on her left hand, but the splint was gone. The dressing looked fresh, so he was confident it was clean and without infection. Had the infamous *Sajan* re-dressed it? Jealousy, green and ugly, boiled in him for a moment. He shook his head. He had no right to be jealous. Annika was not his.

Daniel took his cue and turned back to his work in the kitchen. She would make a great mother one day. A pit formed in his stomach as he shut down the whisperings of what could have been.

He would never have her.

Because he would never be a father again.

CHAPTER TWELVE

ANNIKA

ANNIKA PUSHED ASIDE thoughts of Daniel, yet again, as she walked into her aunt's house without knocking. She just hadn't expected her reaction to him when she caught him watching her at the bar. She was angry at him. There was no reason for her heart to leap like that when she saw him. And there was certainly no reason for her to be able to feel his eyes watching her, making her sweat like a teenager.

To his credit, he did not try to talk to her, which was probably smart, so the disappointment she felt was quite unreasonable. If Daniel had already lied to her—and he had—then the future could bring only more of the same. She shook her head as if she could physically knock out thoughts of him.

Sounds of laughter and music and the scent of freshly fried samosas greeted her like a childhood friend, cocooning her as she entered and took off her shoes. There were matching shoes to every kind of Indian outfit there was, but as soon as Indian people got anywhere, they took off said shoes. Yet she and Naya always had to have the perfect shoes to match the outfit.

Annika made her way to the kitchen, which was no easy feat, as she was greeted along the way by various aunties and uncles she hadn't seen in some time. Everyone wanted to hear how the teaching was going, how she managed living in Baltimore. Most everyone was genuinely interested in what was going on with her; after all, she had grown up with these people. If it seemed like a few of the aunties were giving her the side-eye, well, it must have been her imagination.

"Oh, here's the stranger!" A jovial voice, paired with twinkling eyes and a broad smile, stopped her pilgrimage just as she approached the kitchen.

"Mehul-kaka!" Annika grinned from ear to ear. Her father's younger brother always had a special place in her heart. His accent was light but ever present, same as her father's. He had shaved his mustache, and both brothers had long since given up oiling their hair.

And when things had gone bad—he was the one who spoke sense to her father. She threw her arms around him in a tight hug. "I'm not a stranger. I just saw you at Diwali."

"That party was two weeks ago, beta." He returned the hug with gusto. "And you were preoccupied with a certain young man." He raised his eyebrows with a wink.

She did an internal eye roll. You couldn't talk to a guy around here without starting the rumor mill. "Mehul-kaka, Sajan is just a friend."

The eyebrows came down, and he shrugged. "Hmm. Can't blame a kaka for trying to get information. My daughter tells me nothing."

"When there's something to tell, Naya will tell it."

Mehul-kaka sighed, resting his arm around her shoulders as he escorted her to the kitchen. "In the meantime, make sure Kaki gives you hot-hot samosa."

Annika rolled her eyes at the literal translation of *garam-garam*. The words actually meant hot-hot, but the connotation was fresh and hot. Her family loved the word-play. Her kaka laughed and made eye contact with his wife. Veena-kaki's eyes lit up at the sight of Annika. "Maybe she can bribe information from you with good food." He chuckled and left her in the kitchen.

The kitchen was, as always, a hotbed of activity. Aunties sat or stood in small clusters around the room, depending on what part of the samosa they were working on. At one end, far from the stove, a couple of aunties rolled out the dough for flatbread that would be the outer covering. Next was the filling station, as Annika's head interpreted it, which comprised another few aunties. The last station was the closing station, where the filled samosas were squeezed shut before frying. This task was usually given to ten-year-old girls who wanted to help. And sure enough, two young girls were sealing samosas and looking very pleased with themselves. A third girl did the work, a slight scowl on her face. She eyed the boys running around with a ball with more than a little longing. It was as if Annika was watching herself at that age.

Amid all this, small children ran around playing, marginally supervised by the socializing adults. Bollywood music played in the background, and somewhere, young teen girls giggled as they practiced Bollywood moves.

In all the time she'd dated Steven, she had not once brought him to one of these parties. It was difficult to explain the chaos and the camaraderie that was mixed in with the gossip and judgment. Though arrival and departure times were loose, children roamed freely, and people ate constantly, standing or sitting anywhere there was a spot, there were definite rules of etiquette that needed to be followed. He never would have understood, he never would have fit in, and he hadn't really wanted to. And she had known it.

To be honest, sometimes these parties seemed more work and annoyance than they were worth, and when Annika was in her early twenties, the rebel in her took charge and she stopped going. The gossip and the judgment of her career choice was irritating, so she saw no point in it. She started coming back after the breakup with Steven and found she didn't quite hate them anymore. There was a sense of comfort in being surrounded by people who have known you your whole life that Annika found healing.

She navigated her way around the clusters of people before finally making it over to her aunt. She hugged her tight and took in her calming scent, a combination of baby powder, Avon hand cream and frying oil. It was a scent as calming to her as her own mother's. She deftly avoided the hot skimmer that kaki was using for frying samosas. Veena-kaki was rounder and shorter than her mother, but she and Naya shared those gray eyes that stunned anyone who saw them. She positioned her gray gaze on Annika now.

"Annika, beta. So good to see you."

Honestly, she just saw them, but it was becoming clear that her family was worried about her.

"You, too, Kaki. Here—" she reached for the skimmer "—let me help you."

Veena-kaki carefully moved the utensil away from her. "Nonsense. You enjoy. I have my friends here to help." She jutted her chin toward the aunties rolling out the dough. "And your parents are coming soon." She shoved a plate of samosas at Annika. "Here, eat a few while they are still garam-garam, before everyone else eats them all."

"Thanks, Kaki." She smiled to herself as the words *hot-hot* flashed through her mind. She couldn't help it. Annika took the plate and moved out of her way.

Annika greeted a few more uncles and aunties while she hunted for her favorite cilantro chutney. She finally located both the savory cilantro chutney and the tangy-sweet tamarind chutney while catching up with some friends she hadn't seen in a long time. Naya still hadn't arrived.

Her garam-garam samosas were lukewarm by the time she finally got a small break and was able to take that first bite. She was just enjoying the tang of the tamarind chutney mixed with the spices inside the samosa when a familiar voice called to her.

"Hey, Annika."

Sajan. She should have known her kaka and kaki would invite his family. The rest of town was here, after all.

Annika looked up at hazel eyes grinning at her, her mouth filled with samosa, and managed a nod while she chewed.

"I was a waiter for a while, and they trained us to talk to people just as they were putting food into their mouths." He grinned at her.

Annika managed to chew and swallow without incident before she greeted him. "I'd say you learned very well."

He chuckled and looked around. "It's good to see you again. If I didn't know better, I'd think some of these aunties were having parties just to put us together."

"They're bored. They need excitement." Annika tried to laugh off Sajan's comment, but she knew it really could be the truth. She put nothing past these women.

"Well, in any case, it's nice to see a familiar face. I feel like I must've known some of these people growing up here, but it's been a while, so I might as well be in a room of strangers."

"Some of them you must remember from Diwali? But I can introduce you around."

"Yeah?" He looked a bit too excited at that prospect.

"Sure. Let's eat first. These samosas won't last long." She handed him one and grinned. "They were hot-hot." She giggled, but Sajan just looked at her for a moment, confused.

"Ah—I get it." His face lit up with understanding, but not necessarily amusement. "Garam-garam."

Annika waved it off. The moment had passed. They both ate a few samosas while Annika pointed out people that Sajan may have known when he lived here.

"What happened to your hand?" Sajan nodded at her injury.

Annika shrugged and willed herself not to flush. Like that ever worked. "A few stitches. Broken glass. Happened right after Diwali." She had hoped it was less noticeable without the full dressing, but clearly even a small bandage didn't escape a surgeon's eye. True to Daniel's word, her hand was almost healed.

"So the stitches should be almost out."

Annika bit into a samosa and nodded.

A few of Sajan's friends came over and joined them in their snack. Among them was Reena, a girl who had been a year ahead of Annika at school. Reena had been one of the dancers in the group she was in with Sajan back in high school, and Annika remembered her as being quite shy. She must have come out of her shell in college, because there was nothing shy about her now—or about her interest in Sajan, to which Sajan seemed oblivious.

Annika held a beer in her right hand and popped the last bit of samosa into her mouth with her left.

"Ooh! What happened?" Reena nodded at Annika's injury.

Annika waved her hand. "Oh, nothing. Just cut myself on some glass."

Reena's eye's widened. "Enough for stitches? That must have been painful."

Annika shrugged. "Yes, it was." But she had been well taken care of by a certain nurse practitioner.

Reena giggled. "Was it painful or not? From the way you're smiling, it almost seems like you enjoyed it."

Annika curbed the smile that had crept across her face. "No. I mean yes, it did hurt." She held up her beer. "I should probably cut myself off."

Reena shook her head but seemed to accept that Annika's grin was due to too much alcohol and, thankfully, dropped the subject.

Annika glanced once more at her hand, and her thoughts quickly drifted back to Daniel and his confession that he had in fact been in her room at the ER. Try as she might, Annika could not remember his face. She did recall having a sense of peace and finally crying herself to sleep, but no recollection of Daniel. Honestly, she needed to move on. No way should she be involved with someone of such questionable character.

The conversation around her shifted to medicine, and she attempted to appear engaged, even as her thoughts drifted back to that kiss. Sadly, she had absolutely no problem remembering how his lips had felt on hers. Or the fact that she'd never been kissed the way he had kissed her.

She was jostled out of her daydream by a playful bump to her shoulder. Naya stood next to her, gorgeous in skinny jeans topped with a deep purple *kurta* top. But it was the sparkle in her eye that made her look. A very handsome man with a trim beard and nearly black eyes stood a few inches taller than Naya, his shoulder grazing hers as if he couldn't bear not touching her.

Annika raised an eyebrow at her cousin. Naya widened her eyes. "Ravi—" she tilted her head toward him "—this is Annika."

Ravi immediately turned his gaze to Annika and smiled broadly as he extended his hand. "So nice to finally meet the big-sister-cousin-best-friend I've heard so much about."

Annika shook his hand. "Very nice to meet you, too. I've heard quite a bit about you, as well."

Ravi's whole face lit up with adoration as he turned to look at Naya. Annika's heart melted for her cousin.

"Only the best things, though," Annika added with a laugh.

Ravi chuckled. "I'm just thrilled she's talking about me at all."

Naya rolled her eyes, but it did nothing to hide her flush. Naya was completely smitten with Ravi, and clearly Ravi was just as taken with Naya.

Annika turned to Naya and hugged her close. "Where have you been?" she whispered.

Naya responded with a small, mischief-filled grin as she pulled back from the hug. She flicked her gaze to Sajan and whispered, "Doesn't look like you were too bored. Introduce us."

Annika treated her cousin to a small eye roll as she spoke. "Sajan, this is my cousin Naya and her boyfriend, Ravi. Naya, Sajan."

Naya shook Sajan's hand with a knowing look in her eye that irritated Annika. Ravi remembered Sajan from their high school days, so they immediately started playing the do-you-remember-so-and-so game.

Annika teased her cousin with that same knowing

look that had irritated her, the way only sisters can. Naya flushed and shot her a mild glare. There was a small lull in the conversation as Ravi and some of the guys went in search of more beer, and Annika could hear the aunties next to them talking.

"You wouldn't believe—she was nearly three months along, and she missed."

"Oh, *hai*. How terrible!"

Annika tensed. The accents were thick, and Annika could envision the hand movements and judgment-filled scowls that accompanied the words.

"Well, maybe for the best. She was engaged to a *dhoriyo*, and they broke up after she missed."

They had to be talking about her. She was the only one who had been engaged to a white guy and had a miscarriage. How could they possibly know this? She felt the heat rise to her face, even as fresh tears pricked her eyes. Naya leaned imperceptibly toward her in support.

"Ah, so it was for the best that she missed."

"That is why Usha-ben is so keen to get her married quickly, before all of this gets known, eh? They have even approached Poorvi Shah about her son. As if." The auntie sniffed. "Who would give their son to such a girl? Pregnant before marriage? It is disgraceful."

She felt Sajan tense beside her and heard Reena's intake of breath. Poorvi Shah was his mother. There was only one Usha-ben in the group, and everyone knew she was Annika's mother. Annika could not bring herself to look up at any of them. Twenty-seven years old, living on her own, working two jobs, but the shame of having a miscarriage and being dumped had her unable to make eye contact.

Before Annika realized what was happening, Naya had spun around to face the aunties. They exchanged glances and pursed lips, even as their faces flushed from being caught gossiping by the daughter of their host.

"You should be ashamed of yourselves, gossiping in such a manner in my parents' home, about their niece!" Naya's eyes were ablaze. "My cousin has done nothing disgraceful, nor should she be 'grateful' for her loss. It's you who are disgraceful."

The aunties had the decency to appear abashed as Naya reprimanded them, but as their gazes drifted over to Annika, she clearly saw their disdain. Daniel's words came to her, clear as if he had been standing next to her: she had nothing to be ashamed of, and no one should make her feel so. Annika turned and looked them in the eye, forcing her chin up in defiance she hardly felt, daring them to continue judging her. Maybe they were right. She *had* dodged a bullet in Steven—he wasn't right for her—and maybe it had been careless to get pregnant before she was ready. But she'd be damned if she was going to let them know that.

She felt Sajan's hand on her shoulder, but she couldn't face him. Facing Sajan was different from facing a bunch of gossiping aunties. She stepped aside from him and made for the door. She couldn't imagine how the aunties had found out—her family would never discuss this as gossip. That she had been engaged to Steven was common knowledge, but her pregnancy and miscarriage were supposed to have been a well-kept secret.

She heard Naya behind her as she grabbed her shoes and headed out the door. It was November, but she hadn't brought a coat, so she shivered in the moonlight. All of her bravado was gone, and the reality that she had lost her baby hollowed out her body so her baby's absence was a physical thing. She thought she was over it, but here she was, crying about it for the second time in a few weeks.

She felt for the hospital band in her purse. Would it ever stop hurting? And now humiliation was added to the fire. She turned to Naya.

"How? How did they find out?" A sob escaped Annika as Naya wrapped her arms around her. She didn't give a rat's ass about the gossip, but she knew her parents cared. She knew one thing the aunties had said was true: if her parents wanted her to marry inside the community, it would be hard if the truth was out. They would be mortified, knowing that everyone knew their daughter had been pregnant before she got married.

"I don't know, honey. But the community is small, and it just takes one candy striper to have seen you in the hospital to figure it all out."

"They're right, you know," Annika cried into Naya's shoulder. "I made a colossal mess of my life, trying to follow my dreams and be this independent woman. I'm better off without Steven, but I never would have seen that if it weren't for..."

"Stop that talk right now." Naya grabbed her by the shoulders and pulled her back so she could look into her eyes. "You would have seen through Steven sooner or later—and miscarriages are losses that you have to grieve, not punishments for bad judgment. You did nothing wrong—you deserve to be happy just like everybody else. Those aunties could use a punishment of sorts, though."

"Now everybody knows." Annika's shoulders sagged in defeat.

"So what? The people who care about you don't care."

"My mom and dad care." More tears threatened at the thought of her parents finding out people were gossiping about her.

"You can't be worrying about all that." Naya was steadfast.

"I can't be worrying about failing my parents on every front?"

Naya rolled her eyes. "You aren't failing your parents. You made your choices. Some of them didn't work out. But some did. You're a fabulous teacher."

Annika smiled in spite of herself. "I am."

"See? Come on. Let's go home and order pizza, eat ice cream out of the carton and drink wine out of the bottle."

"Can I pick the ice cream?"

"Fine, but then I pick the wine."

"What about Ravi?" Annika glanced at the house.

"I'll text him. He'll understand." Naya pulled out her phone as she spoke.

The door behind them opened and Sajan stepped out. "Hey." He looked right at Annika, a softness in his face. "Are you okay? Those aunties—" he pursed his lips, a darkness coming across his eyes "—are totally out of line. I just gave them a piece of my mind. Of course they had no idea that Poorvi Shah's son was standing there the whole time."

"I'm okay." Annika was grateful, but she didn't want to talk to him about all this. "Thanks for checking."

"We're having ice cream and wine. Want to join?" Naya turned toward Sajan and ignored the glare Annika shot her.

Sajan smiled. "Sounds great, but I have to get back to the hospital." He looked at Annika. "Maybe another time?"

"Sure. She'd love that," Naya answered for her.

"Awesome." Sajan's eyes never left Annika. "Well, I better get going." He brushed past her and turned after a couple of steps. "You should just ignore them. They simply have nothing better to do."

"Will do." Annika waved him off. He really was very kind. And not bad to look at. Maybe she really needed to give him a chance. She shivered in the cold and started walking toward her car. "It's freezing out here, come on." Naya followed.

They settled into the car and started the drive to Baltimore. "You should've seen Sajan's face when those aunties were talking." Naya side-eyed Annika as she drove. "He looked about ready to punch them."

Humph. Interesting. But instead of Sajan, it was an image of Daniel that entered her mind. Daniel comforting her at the base. She pushed it aside, too drained to think about either Sajan or Daniel. Her father's words came to her. *Love will grow over time.* She closed her eyes, leaned her head back, and released a sigh.

CHAPTER THIRTEEN

DANIEL

"DANIEL! YOUR GRANDMOTHER is asking you to do this." Emma didn't usually get bossy, and she generally accepted Daniel's excuses to not see Charlie, but their grandmother was aging, and she asked very little. Not to mention that she had helped raise Daniel and Emma while their parents worked. "If she wasn't eighty-four years old and nursing a broken foot, she would go herself."

His stomach fell into knots. He really did not want to go to a wedding. "There's no one else to go and represent the family?"

"If there was, do you think I would bother asking you?"

He deserved her withering tone. It was true. His family gave him all the leeway he wanted or needed. It was as if, since he lost Sara, they just didn't want to push him, for fear that he would break apart. Only Emma dared. "Just get dressed, go to the wedding for a couple of hours, show your face, say hello and leave."

Daniel closed his eyes. "Yeah, okay. I'll do it. Text me the details."

"Oh, Daniel! That's great. Thanks. She'll be so happy." Emma softened almost immediately. "And who knows, you may even enjoy yourself. Take a date or meet someone new, you know. A woman."

Daniel nearly growled. Images of Annika filled his brain, and he did his best to shake them out. "You know that's not good for anybody."

It did not deter Emma's enthusiasm. "You never know…"

"Just send me the details." He was not entertaining the possibility of *entertaining*.

"Fine. Make sure you wear the appropriate clothing."

"Oh my God, Em. I'm a grown man. I can figure out what to wear to a wedding."

"You know what I mean. Not American clothes—"

"Yeah, yeah, I got it." He looked up and saw Nilay pulling in. "I gotta go, Em." He tapped the phone off.

NILAY HAD A definite presence. Daniel chuckled to himself. The teenager was bright and energetic, but he was not quiet. Forget that it was 5:30 a.m. and the sun wasn't even up yet—Nilay was hyper in the seat next to Daniel.

This time Daniel drove Nilay's car as they headed out to the chopper base. Annika or no Annika, Daniel had promised Nilay a ride along on the chopper, and the kid got all his paperwork together. So today was the day. Luckily, Nilay chatted nonstop the whole ride, which kept Daniel from giving in to the temptation of asking about Annika.

Nilay held a box of doughnuts and a box of bagels on his lap and started to reach for a doughnut. "Hey, hey. Not for you," Daniel reprimanded.

"What do you mean?"

"The night shift was up and out all night. They're probably starving. We'll eat what your mom sent." The car smelled of spicy Indian food that Nilay's mother had made for them. Daniel's stomach growled despite the early hour.

Nilay's eyes widened and he flushed. "Oh, right. Sorry." He closed the lid. "Of course."

"You can have one after they eat."

"Sure."

Daniel drove in silence for a minute or so. "So, did the kids like the fire station the other day?" Weak. He was very weak. He knew they had; Lance had texted him right after.

"What kids?"

Daniel sighed. "Never mind." His need to talk about Annika—or maybe even get info about her from Nilay— was ridiculous. She was better off without him.

Nilay glanced up at him. "Oh, you mean Annika's kids. At the school. Yeah—she said they had a great time. It was awesome you could set that up. She didn't tell you herself?"

"She did. I mean, she sent me an email." She'd cc'd him in her email to Lance.

"Email? Not even a text? That's harsh. What'd you do to piss her off?"

"She didn't tell you?"

"My sister's love life is not something we discuss. Well, not usually. And whatever it is—it can't be too bad."

"I'm not part of her love life—what do you know about it anyway?"

"I know plenty. I listen and pay attention even when people think I'm not listening." For the first time, Nilay's voice went quiet. "Especially after the last guy." He set his jaw and stared straight ahead for a moment. He turned to Daniel. "Not that you're anything like he was, but I... Well, I have to look out for her."

"Is that why you're here?"

"No." He grinned. "I'm here because this is going to be awesome. Checking you out is part of the bonus."

"Well, no worries. Your sister and I are not a thing."

Nilay shook his head in disbelief. "She may be mad right now, but she'll get over it."

Daniel shrugged.

"She told me to behave myself when I came out here with you and not be a pain," Nilay continued, "and not bother you. She wouldn't have made a point to call me about all that if she wasn't thinking about forgiving you."

Daniel's traitorous heart did a flip. He didn't really deserve that forgiveness, though clearly he was ready to accept it.

"You've got a stupid look on your face."

Daniel knew he did. But try as he might, he couldn't remove the grin. He might still have a chance. He parked the car and they both got out, heading for the front entrance this time, so Daniel could sign Nilay in.

"Make no mistake about it." Nilay stopped and looked Daniel square in the eye, that seriousness back in his eyes for a moment. "You saw what happened in the bar. I'm not afraid of much. If you hurt her, I'll have to hurt you. I don't care that your muscles are twice the size of mine." He glanced at Daniel's biceps and swallowed hard, the intensity of his gaze unwavering. "Well, maybe I do—but it won't stop me. Understood?"

Daniel stood frozen for a moment. And in that moment, he was not standing in front of a young boy who was half his age, and easily half his size. He was facing a brother who cared enough for his sister that nothing else mattered. Daniel knew this was another reason he should run from Annika: Nilay would just be another person he hurt when he hurt her. "That won't be necessary. I'd never do anything to hurt her."

But that meant he couldn't see her again—ever.

Nilay nodded and broke into a smile, a regular teenager again. "I knew you were a good guy."

They entered the building, and Nilay presented his ID

while Daniel chatted with the administrator and signed him in.

Nilay was a hit with the night shift as he placed doughnuts and bagels on the food table. He was enjoying a doughnut and getting his questions answered when Crista and the pilot, Andrea, came on duty. Daniel made introductions and waited for Andrea to start briefing.

Crista's smirk said more than Daniel wanted to deal with at the moment, so he did everything he could to avoid eye contact with her.

"So, you want to be a flight medic?" she asked Nilay.

"Well, actually, I don't know. I kind of want to go to med school, but this seems really interesting, and Daniel said I could tag along. And I brought food my mom cooked." He smiled. "Indian food."

Crista's eyes lit up at that. "You brought Indian food? Kid, you can observe here anytime."

Andrea cleared her throat. "You guys okay if we start working here?"

Crista high-fived Nilay and turned to Andrea. "Let's hear the brief, already."

Andrea sighed and went through the pilot's brief, going over the weather, maintenance and what the role of the observer should be. She finished up and fixed a hard stare on Nilay. "Stick with Daniel, don't get in the way."

Wide-eyed and stiff, Nilay nodded. Daniel clapped a hand on his shoulder. "Don't mind her. She's just giving you a hard time. Come on, I'll show you where to put your stuff." He led Nilay back to the room he'd had Annika in for her stitches. A small closet had a couple of shelves in it, one of which belonged to Daniel. He squeezed Nilay's backpack onto it and put on his flight suit.

"Now what?" Nilay bounced, unable to sit still.

"Now we wait."

Crista came over and stood in the doorway. "Hey, Nilay, how's your sister's hand doing?"

"Oh, she's doing great. Daniel's awesome at stitches."

Daniel closed his eyes and shook his head. Nilay needed to understand what a secret was.

"That he is." Crista grinned wide, her eyes dancing with knowledge. "Well, kid. Andrea informed me that the chopper needs cleaning, and she can be convinced to tell you all about flying while you do it."

Nilay's face lit up like a kid at Christmas. "I get to hang out on the chopper? Sure! I'll do whatever!" He glanced at Daniel before leaving. "Okay?"

"Yeah, sure. Make yourself useful."

Nilay bounded out of the small room, leaving Daniel alone with Crista and her grin.

"What?" Better to get this over with. Crista wasn't going to let it be.

"What's going on with you? You've got the little brother here, you're making him very happy—clearly you did her stitches here."

Daniel shrugged. "Yeah, so?"

"So, why do you look so miserable? Usually a girlfriend is a good thing. God knows you haven't had one in years."

"She's not my girlfriend."

"Well, usually people don't entertain the siblings of one-night stands…"

"She's not a one-night stand." He growled. But now he was envisioning her in his bed. Not that it wasn't a regular recurring dream of his.

Crista widened her eyes and tilted her head. "So what is she?"

Daniel sighed and dropped onto his bed before looking up at Crista. "Nothing. She's nothing."

Crista shook her head. "Lie to me all you want. But don't lie to yourself. She's something. I saw you two the other day. That girl has a thing for you, and you definitely have something for her." She jabbed her thumb in the direction Nilay had gone in.

Daniel shrugged. "I fucked it up."

Crista rolled her eyes. "That just makes you a normal male. Fix it. You actually looked happy with her." She moved closer to him and forced him to look her in the eye. "You deserve some happy."

Did he, though? If it came at someone else's expense? Before he could respond, an alarm sounded, and both he and Crista sprang into action, quickly gathering their bags.

"Nilay!" Daniel called. "We gotta go."

The teenager was at his side in an instant. Daniel handed him an extra helmet. "Put this on. Let's go." He hesitated a moment. "You sure you're okay with seeing trauma?"

"I'm sure."

If Nilay was in any way nervous, he hid it well. Daniel nodded and headed for the chopper, donning his own helmet and securing it while he communicated with the pilot. The chopper's blades were already spinning when he arrived. He and Crista made sure Nilay was securely fastened in the chopper before securing themselves and going down the checklist with Andrea.

Andrea's voice was clear in his ear. "Walk around."

"Complete."

Andrea again. "Steps and skids."

"Are clear."

"Seat belts and doors."

"All secure."

"Drugs, blood, medical equipment."

"All on board."

"Cell phones, pagers, radios."

"All on board."

"Stretcher."

"Secured."

"Oxygen bottles."

"Secured."

Daniel secured himself and made his "off call" to dispatch. "Medevac Ten responding, four souls, two hours' fuel." He listened to the dispatcher on the headset give him the details as they took off.

He sighed and made eye contact with Crista. "Bar brawl."

At Nilay's wide-eyed expression, he answered, "Nope, not too early—these are the ones that were out all night getting drunk, and now they fight." He shrugged and shook his head.

The vibrations and noise of the chopper were familiar to Daniel, but he was impressed by how Nilay took it all in stride. The chopper landed in a field and the ambulance was already waiting for them.

"We'll do it hot," came the order from Andrea.

Daniel nodded as he got off the chopper behind Nilay, pushing the boy's head down so he was bent at the waist as they exited behind Crista. "She wants us to move fast, so she's not turning off the blades."

They approached the ambulance to find the patient strapped to the stretcher with a large piece of glass protruding from his arm. Crista spoke to the EMTs while Daniel explained to Nilay, "He has a penetrating injury to his arm. With the amount of blood we see in the gauze, there may be a major blood vessel involved, which is why they called us." He dropped his bag and crouched down to open it, pulling out multiple packets of gauze. "This is QuikClot. It's a special gauze that has clotting agents in it to promote quick blood clotting, so our patient doesn't bleed out." He glanced at Nilay. There was a lot of blood, but damn, the kid was listening and observing the patient with no sign of even going pale. "Here, put on these gloves and let's open a few of these packets and apply them."

Nilay did exactly as he was told. He moved naturally, as if he'd done this his whole life. Daniel smiled as he applied the QuikClot Nilay handed him. "You're a natural."

"Thanks."

"We're attaching a monitor to the patient so we can continuously monitor blood pressure. We'll also monitor his oxygen levels and heart rate for any rhythm changes."

"All right, boys. Let's move." Crista was ready.

As Crista and Daniel loaded their patient into the waiting chopper, Nilay was already seated, buckled, helmeted and ready for liftoff.

Daniel smiled at him.

Nilay grinned and mouthed, "This is awesome!"

CHAPTER FOURTEEN

ANNIKA

NAYA PATTED DOWN her sari for the billionth time, and Annika couldn't help her grin.

"Oh my God, Naya, it's going to be fine. You look amazing. That burgundy looks like you were born to wear it, so stop fussing. I'm never wrong."

They were in the parking lot outside of the hotel where the wedding would take place, waiting to be part of the *jaan*, the groom's procession, which should start in the next fifteen minutes. She raised her face to absorb the warmth from the midmorning sun in the November chill as the *dol* player tested out his beat. The dol player held the single drum with a strap around his neck, so the drum lay horizontal at his waist. He played one side with a stick and the other side with his hand.

The loud drumbeat was as synonymous with weddings as a bride and groom and the scent of burning incense. The crowd responded to the *taka-taka-tum* with cries of enthusiasm as they began to move their bodies to the beat of the dol. The jaan would dance the groom to the entrance of the hall, where the bride's family would greet him.

Naya spared her a glance. "I'm not fussing. I'm just not used to wearing a sari. Not everyone has your grace." She scowled.

Annika laughed. "You're all worked up because Ravi is going to be here with his family. It's cute—I've never seen you so nervous over a guy before." She grabbed Naya's hand. "I said, stop fussing. You are an amazing and accomplished woman. There's nothing to be nervous about." She squeezed her hand. "And didn't both sets of parents agree to the initial meeting anyway? It's like you have preapproval."

Naya held up her hands. "Of course. I'm being ridiculous. I just want them to like *me*, not the résumé." Her gaze dropped to Annika. "You're looking pretty damn amazing in that sari yourself. Sometimes I'm right. That purple is working for you. Wait until Sajan sees." She wiggled her eyebrows.

"Thanks." She glanced down, seeming to notice the color for the first time. Truth was, she was no more comfortable in a sari than Naya was. They only wore them on special occasions, so while she could manage it, they both relied heavily on safety pins. She tried to be excited to see Sajan, but it was all she could do to smile back at Naya at the mention of his name.

"You do know what color sari you put on today, don't you?" Nothing got past this girl.

Annika gave her cousin her best "duh" look, but the truth was that she was distracted—she couldn't stop thinking about Daniel. He had kept his distance since their little fallout, presumably respecting her wishes. But thoughts of him kept finding their way into her mind. At least once a day, one of her students mentioned that fire truck. Even the bar seemed a bit empty without him to flirt with. And then there was her brother, FaceTiming her with his "Daniel is so awesome" commentary. She had rolled her eyes at him, but her heart had clung to every word Nilay said about Daniel.

Then there was that kiss, of course. She only continued to replay that moment fifty times a day.

"Oh, shit, Annika." Naya squeezed Annika's arm, even as a small smile crept onto her face. "You didn't tell me *he* was coming."

"Who?" Was it some guy Naya had been set up with? How was Annika supposed to keep track of a list that long? There were five hundred people coming to this wedding, so it was more than possible to be surprised by someone's attendance. She narrowed her gaze at her cousin.

Naya let out a long breath. "Damn, but that man is fine."

Annika started to spin around, but Naya tugged at her arm. "Turn slowly. Don't make a scene."

Annika turned slowly. Time seemed to slow down and her breath caught as she watched Daniel catch stares from every woman he walked past, regardless of their age. And who could blame them?

Daniel was wearing a simple emerald-green sherwani with fitted cream-colored bottoms and matching scarf, which he simply hung around his neck. The tunic fit him perfectly, moving and stretching with his muscles as he walked toward her. He was clearly oblivious of the attention he was getting, his gaze set only on her. What was he doing here? And where did he get that outfit?

As he got closer, she noted that the green of his eyes matched the green of the tunic, and when he smiled deeply enough to show both dimples, she had to inhale deeply to get oxygen to her brain, lest her knees go out from under her. Just as he was close enough for her speak to him, Nilay appeared by his side.

"Hey, Daniel! What are you doing here?"

Daniel spared Nilay a glance but answered while look-ing at Annika. "I'm on the bride's side. Friends of my grandmother."

Try as she might, Annika could not break the hold his gaze had on her. She was supposed to be pissed off at him, but right in this minute, she could not remember why. Ev-erything around her fell away, her complete focus on those green eyes and the man they belonged to.

"Annika, beta, there you are." Her father's voice snapped her to attention, and she quickly turned toward him, as if gazing at Daniel had been wrong. "And look who I found."

"Papa." She hugged her father, then was met with the hazel-brown eyes that belonged to one Dr. Sajan Shah. He was very handsome in a silver and navy sherwani that flat-tered his brown skin. The tunic was well fitting, though she thought he had a little more room to move around than Daniel seemed to. Her heart sank a bit, and she pointedly fixed her gaze on Sajan. She shouldn't care that Sajan's presence might hurt Daniel. "Hey, Sajan! What a surprise."

He laughed. "Is it, though? We keep finding ourselves at all these functions. Seems almost inevitable at this point." He leaned in for a friendly hug, and Annika stiffened. "How's the hand?"

She held out her hand, which was now free of its ban-dage, aware that Daniel followed her movement. "Pretty good. No more stitches."

Sajan took her hand in his and brought it closer to ex-amine. Maybe it was because he was looking at it as a doc-tor, but his touch didn't affect her the way Daniel's did. "Someone did a nice job with those stitches. Who did it?"

"What?" Maybe if she pretended not to hear, she wouldn't have to answer.

"The stitches. Who did them?" Sajan appeared amused.

"Oh, uh...well." She lifted her hand as though the answer was somewhere on it.

"I did them," Daniel answered for her. "Dr. Shah." Daniel was beaming as he held out his hand to Sajan.

"Daniel?" Sajan also broke out into a huge grin as he reached for Daniel's hand. "Sorry—it took me a minute—didn't quite get there without the scrubs."

Clearly, both men not only knew each other but were quite happy to see each other.

"Same here," Daniel chuckled as they shook hands, smiling.

"So that's your work?" Sajan raised an impressed eyebrow.

"Well." Daniel flushed. "I happened to be in the right place at the right time."

Annika just gaped from one man to the other.

"This is so cool." Of course Nilay would love this. He turned to his father. "Papa, this is Daniel Bliant, my mentor." Nilay took over, and Annika was once more grateful for her brother's gregarious nature. "And apparently, he knows Sajan—sounds like from work."

"Exactly." Sajan grinned in Annika's father's direction. "Daniel is one of the best."

Her father shook Daniel's hand. "Well, first, my son can't say enough about you, and now Sajan—you must indeed be one of the best. I am impressed that you have time to work on the helicopter with a doctor's schedule. Quite impressive."

"Nice to meet you, sir. But I'm actually an NP in the ER."

Annika's father's smile faltered just enough to be noticeable, but not enough to be considered rude. Annika tensed. Her father was far from a chauvinist, but he was big on fulfilling your potential. And anything less than med school or law school was not fulfilling that potential. He'd had that conversation with Annika many times.

"You didn't want to just become a doctor…or maybe you couldn't get in?"

And there it was.

"Well, no, sir. I did get in—but it wasn't for me."

"Ah, just like my daughter—medical school 'just wasn't for her'—now she teaches little children." If there was such a thing as having negative pride in your children, Anil Mehta had it for his daughter. And it showed in his voice and in his demeanor. "Well, at least you are still in the medical field—and Nilay speaks very highly of you." He smiled with some semblance of warmth.

She snuck a glance at Daniel. If he was offended or hurt by her father's comments, it didn't show. He nodded politely at the older man, his gaze flicking toward Annika for only the smallest fraction of a second as he clenched his jaw. That was all it took for him to portray his sympathy to her for lack of parental support. She answered with the most minute eye roll.

"Daniel and I work together quite often, Uncle, and he has saved quite a few lives," Sajan said into the silence.

Her father nodded, slapping Sajan fondly on the back. "But not quite as many as you, eh, Doctor?"

"Papa!" Annika chided her father before she could help herself. "Don't judge so quickly." *Wait, what?* What did she care if he was rude to Daniel? She was angry with him. He had *lied* to her—and could be a stalker for all she knew. But she hadn't kept Nilay from him, and she never got any stalker-like vibes from him. Daniel wasn't really anyone to her anyway. Was he? Her father opened his mouth to say something, but before he could, Nilay was tugging at her elbow.

"Annika? Annika? Are you coming? Hello?"

"What?" Her residual irritation with her father landed on Nilay, who was thankfully oblivious.

"*Garba*, Didi! The jaan is starting!" Nilay was already bouncing to the beat in his eagerness to join the dancing.

She had somehow blocked out the call of the dol. But now she heard it beckoning to them, loud and clear. She grabbed her brother's hand. "Well, let's go!"

"Come on, Daniel," Nilay called over his shoulder.

"Well, I'm on the bride's side…"

Nilay grabbed Daniel by a biceps to make him move. "So what? Just come. Sajan and I will show you how."

"That won't be necessary."

Annika heard the confidence in Daniel's voice, but when she turned to him, he simply raised his eyebrows at her and motioned for her to move.

Annika loved being part of the jaan. Dancing in the street (or parking lot) was one of the many highlights of the wedding. This groom had opted out of the traditional horse in favor of a fancy sports car with the top down. He sat on top of the back seat, dressed in his fancy turban and white-and-red wedding outfit, holding a coconut with leaves.

Annika and Nilay joined the dancers in front of the car. Sajan stood to the side and joined in the clapping. These were the groom's friends and family, and they would dance the procession to the hotel entrance to celebrate the joy of the day. The dol was in full swing, its beat revving up the dancers. Annika joined a group of her friends in a small circle and danced garba, which was a line dance done in a circle. Skirts twirled, hands clapped, and hips swayed, faster and faster in time with the beat of the dol. A few men joined in the garba, and Annika actually stopped, causing the girl behind her to trip, when she recognized Daniel in his emerald-green sherwani, easily moving to the complicated steps and beat of the drum.

Her flub did not go unnoticed by Daniel, who winked at her but kept pace and didn't miss a beat. Annika was forced to step out of the circle so as not to cause a backup. She inhaled deeply to gather herself. Daniel was dancing garba like he'd done it all his life. There was a natural, masculine grace about the way his body moved, the way his feet kept the beat, the way his arms moved in sync with everyone else's.

As his part of the circle came her way, Annika picked up the step and joined the circle in front of Daniel. Just for fun, she motioned to Naya and a couple of friends to change up the step to a yet more complicated one. Having done this together all their lives, the girls quickly and gracefully switched up the step. After missing only one or two beats, Daniel easily made the switch, as well. Annika couldn't help the impressed grin on her face. Daniel was holding out on more than being in her room that night, and suddenly she was curious about all of it.

They finished the garba in a synchronized fury of clapped beats, quick feet and excited calls, many people dropping out, while Annika and Daniel remained the last two with the stamina to continue. At the final call, she caught his eye, slightly out of breath, and they took a small bow to the cheers of the other members of the jaan.

The dol slowed its beat, starting a bhangra. This was a dance from northern India, done with the shoulders to start, but then also progressing to hip swaying, twirling and complicated footwork. Though both men and women danced bhangra, the men's and women's steps differed slightly. As the dol beat sped up, the men jumped and squatted, using their scarves to accent the beat. Annika usually had no problem keeping up, but she had never really done it in a sari. Not to mention her left hand was still a bit sensitive.

Her sari and hand ignored, Annika and Naya—and she noticed Ravi as well, and, from the sidelines, Sajan—joined the guys as the beat got faster, and they quickly approached the hotel entrance. Some sari goddess must have been looking out for her, because as Annika kept up, her sari gracefully flowed, not once getting in her way. Daniel danced next to her, and she was aware of his every movement, as well as his gaze upon her. From the corner of her eye, she saw gray and blue, which meant Sajan was dancing on her other side. She dared a glance at Daniel and was captured by the amusement in his eyes. That was all it took, and she missed a beat, caught her sari underfoot and was falling, her newly stitched hand ready to brace her fall, when she was caught midfall. Strong hands encircled her waist and held her as she fought for balance, her injured hand flailing in the air.

"Whoa, there." Daniel dodged the errant hand, avoiding a smack in the face. "Careful with my handiwork."

Annika grabbed what she could with her good hand and found herself clinging to a whole lot of biceps. Or steady rock, because that was what it felt like. Daniel pulled her up to standing, where she avoided the green gaze by checking her sari and all the surrounding area as if her very life depended on it.

"Are you okay?" Sajan was at her other side.

"Yes. I'm fine—just tripped over my own sari." She flushed. "Not used to bhangra in a sari."

Sajan's brow furrowed. "Maybe skip the dancing for a while? Until you're healed."

"I'm fine." She tried not to sound irritated, but really, she was a grown woman.

"Sajan!" A hushed male voice called out to him, grabbing him and dragging him toward the groom. "We need you to guard the shoes." Sajan nodded and left, leaving her alone with Daniel.

The jaan had moved past them; the music changed to a more subdued yet still festive tune as the bride's mother approached the groom to greet him.

A tuxedoed server approached with deep-fried fritters as a snack, and Annika gratefully reached for one. Naya was standing next to her and reached for one, too. The girls looked at each other and automatically moved their heads from side to side. "Hot-hot." They proclaimed and burst into giggles.

Daniel took a fritter and raised it to them. "Garam-garam," he said, and both girls promptly stopped their giggles to stare at him, astonished. He took a bite, then pointed to the door where Auntie approached and circled the groom's smiling face with an herb packet.

Annika finished her fritter and leaned toward Daniel. "She's warning him. Giving him the option to leave now, with no further ramifications." She started to explain, still looking at the groom. "It's equivalent to 'speak now or forever hold your peace.' Because—"

"Because if he crosses the threshold, he's committed to marrying her daughter. There's no turning back." Daniel turned toward her.

"That's right." Annika finally looked up at him, forcing her jaw closed. Who was this man? He was staring down at her the way he had right before he kissed her that night. She should look away, but he held her with his gaze as sure as if he'd been holding her in his arms.

Cheering from the crowd snapped Daniel's head around. "We're going in."

They followed the procession of the groom with the bride's parents leading him to the four-poster *mandap*, where the wedding ceremony would take place. The bride would enter once the groom was seated and blessed.

They approached the mandap and the groom paused.

"He's going to have to take off his shoes," Daniel whispered.

"Yeah. I know." Duh. How did *he* know?

The groom would have to remove his shoes before entering the mandap, and someone from the bride's side— usually a cousin or a sibling—would try to steal them in an effort to get the groom to pay up to get them back later. Members of the groom's side were tasked with not letting that happen. It was one of many games played at weddings. Annika loved how the fun always balanced the solemnness of the occasion. It was like saying that, yes, marriage was a serious business, but don't forget to enjoy life, too.

"How do you know—"

But before she could finish, he had grabbed her hand and taken a few steps toward the groom's back. Sure enough, the groom stopped and slipped off his fancy slippers, and as he did so, two little girls no more than seven years old popped in from nowhere and made a grab for them. A teenage boy wearing the groom's colors beat them to it and snagged the coveted shoes. But before he could tuck them away, another teen boy made a grab for them. He got ahold, but the groom's boy did not let go. Both boys from opposing camps held strong to the shoes, their faces filled with determination, and pulling and shoving ensued.

Annika's heart jumped. The boys were starting to create a scene, which was not the purpose of the game. She started toward the boys to break them up before it escalated any further. Daniel got to them before she did.

He laid a firm hand on each boy, towering over them. They froze.

"Boys." He spoke in a low whisper. "You know it's way more fun if they get the shoes." Daniel smiled at them, and the boys handed over the shoes, which Daniel promptly handed to the two little girls. They grabbed the shoes from Daniel and quickly flittered away just in case he changed his mind.

"Thanks, Uncle!" The girls squealed in delight as they took off with the shoes. When they were far enough away, they turned around and stuck their tongues out at the boys who had been fighting.

Daniel returned to her side. People who had been watching the spectacle returned their attention to the groom. Annika knew her mouth was open, but she couldn't shut it. This man just kept getting more and more fascinating. "How do you know that?"

"What?"

"How do you know that it's more fun when they get the shoes?"

Daniel crooked a half smile at her. "Come on. You'll miss the wedding." He turned and waited for her.

The priest had started his blessings for the groom. It would be a few minutes before they called for the bride. The man she'd come to know and just observed was not a creepy stalker. If he'd been in her room, there was a reason. Maybe it was time she found out. She caught Daniel's eye and moved to the back of the room and out into the lobby as more guests entered the wedding hall. She found a small alcove with relative privacy and stepped into it. Daniel followed.

She tilted her head up to him, her gaze sweeping over his mouth and landing on his eyes. She wasted no time getting to the point. "What happened that night, Daniel?"

Daniel stared at her a moment, a war waging in his eyes. He shook his head and started to leave. "It doesn't matter."

She reached out and grabbed his arm. "Yes. It does." This time she gripped his eyes in hers. "It matters to me."

Once more she found turbulence in the flick of his eyes, the set of his mouth. He fidgeted, clearly having a disagreement within himself. He shook his head at her, and fear flickered in her belly. Had she lost him forever without an explanation? His gaze landed on her hand on his arm, and he stilled and softened. She withdrew her hand, worried she'd overstepped her bounds, but his gaze lingered for a moment where her hand had been, and she considered for a moment replacing it. But the moment was gone.

"Do you remember being carried to the wheelchair?" His voice was low and gravelly. She was forced to step closer so she could hear him, and she was instantly within some warm protective force of his. It was not unpleasant. "When you tried to check in?"

She remembered being lifted and feeling secure, but the pain and her fear had been her main focus. She nodded, unable to stop looking at him.

"That was me." He sighed and looked away at something she could not see, as if asking permission to continue talking to her. "You told me your fiancé was parking the car." He met her eyes again and continued.

"My colleague Amy was assigned to you, but...I couldn't stop checking on you. I heard the asshole break up with you right there in the ER as I was coming to check on you. I heard you scream, and I started to come in and see what had happened, when I saw you throw your engagement ring at him. When he emerged from your room clutching his eye, I was proud of you—which was very odd, because I didn't even know you. But you were so strong, even in this horrible moment. It was incredible."

His eyes widened and he studied her face, and she knew the hardest part was yet to come. "I peeked in and saw you kneeling on the floor, your phone in your hand. You must've texted Naya. And then you crumpled into a ball. On the floor." He stopped and fixed his eyes on hers, begging her to understand. "I couldn't leave you there. I wasn't even really thinking. I just knew I couldn't leave you alone." He took a deep breath and continued. "I picked you up to lay you in the bed, but you clutched my scrubs in your hand and cried, as if letting go of me would undo you. I know how it sounds, but I just stood there, holding you, until you fell asleep in my arms. I couldn't leave you. I didn't *want* to leave you. Once you fell asleep, I laid you down on the bed. I was covering you with a blanket when Naya came in. She assumed I was your nurse, and I didn't correct her." He stopped and swallowed, his eyes never leaving hers. "I lost someone—"

"Didi!" Annika started as Nilay stopped in front of them. He glanced at Daniel, then back at her. "Sorry, but, uh, the bride's on her way." He looked from one to the other. "Okay. Well, thought you'd want to know." He made a hasty retreat.

She gave Daniel a small smile. "You were saying?"

He shook his head. "Never mind."

Silence floated thick between them.

"How did you find me?" It was a whisper. He had taken care of her that night. He—his arms—that was the moment of peace and comfort she remembered. It was real.

And it was him. She moved closer to him, her heart racing in her chest.

"I did have the address to the bar—you put it on your intake form—but I didn't come looking for you until we had that call that night. The truth is, I would have eventually, because I couldn't get you out of my mind." He sighed. "I'm sorry. I should have told you from the start. There's no good reason for not having told you that."

She searched his face for the lie, but it wasn't there. He opened his mouth as if he had something more to say, but he snapped it shut, as if a decision had been made.

She had gone home with a vague feeling of having been safe for a time. It was because of him. He hadn't told her, because it was outside of what his duties were. He had been there for her in her most dire time of need, in that moment of absolute despair, when she had been completely alone. But what had he suffered that he could recognize her anguish so clearly? He was so close, and he smelled of the outdoors mixed with traces of cologne.

With her heels on, the top of her head was just above his chin. She tilted her chin up at him, searching his features for his secret, but all she saw there was the same struggle she'd watched him have earlier. The same struggle she'd had, as well. Time to put an end to it. Sajan might be the more practical choice, but her heart was choosing Daniel.

A small voice told her this was not the place, but she ignored it. She shifted her gaze from his eyes to his lips, and she could have sworn she heard a small groan. Whether it came from her or from him she couldn't even be sure. Their breath mingled in the scant space between their mouths. Before she could change her mind, she gave in to what she wanted, and placed her lips on his.

That was all it took. Daniel seemed to lose his battle,

and he pressed against her, his body already familiar to hers, as if they belonged together. He opened his mouth to her and kissed her with abandon. She melted into him, and thankfully he wrapped an arm around her, because she was certain she could not stand on jelly knees. She might have kissed him forever in that little alcove had not the sound of the dol startled them both back to reality. She jumped away from him again, as if she had been doing something wrong. But there had been nothing wrong with that kiss.

She bit her bottom lip, still tasting him, and gave him a small smile. "Where'd you learn to dance like that?"

His lips were swollen from her kiss, and maybe he wore a hint of her lipstick, but his smile was relaxed, if far from satisfied. Amusement colored those green eyes; mystery framed his smile.

"What are you doing next weekend? I'll show you."

CHAPTER FIFTEEN

DANIEL

BALLOONS FLEW FROM the mailbox, a clear indication that a party was happening. Annika refused to ride on Daniel's bike, so they had taken her car. As she parked in the street in front of the house, a huge bouncy castle in the backyard came into view, and loud music blared from somewhere. Daniel's stomach clenched and sweat formed on his upper lip. He inhaled deeply and reached over to squeeze Annika's hand. Her smile sent instant ripples of calm through his body, settling his stomach, his heartbeat returning to normal.

They exited the car to an unseasonably warm afternoon for late November. It was as if the weather gods had decided to gift Daniel's nephew, Charlie, a warm day for his birthday party.

Daniel took Annika's hand again as if it were the most natural thing in the world. He was light with feelings he had suppressed for the better part of five years. Annika was about to meet his family, and he couldn't think of anything he'd rather be doing. Except for maybe being alone with her. Hopefully there'd be plenty of time for that in the future. He almost laughed out loud at himself. He hadn't thought about the future in the last few years, either.

A small voice in the back of his head nagged him,

threatening to ruin his light feelings: he hadn't yet told Annika about Sara. Among other things. It wasn't time yet, he told that voice. He didn't want her to be with him because she felt sorry for him. Her feelings had to be real.

She seemed to have forgiven him for the ER, but at the sight of the balloons and the bouncy house, her face became panicked.

"Daniel, I know you said we were meeting your family." She swallowed. "But I was thinking a casual coffee, maybe lunch." Her eyes were wide as she turned to face him. "But this looks like a family function—a party."

"It is." He nodded. "I thought it would be easier—you know, the focus would be spread out."

She inhaled deeply, weighing this. "Yes. Okay. Makes sense." She nodded vigorously. "Let's do it."

"It'll be fine." He pulled her closer to his side. "You'll see."

This didn't seem the right time to tell her that he hadn't brought a girl home since Sheila. The truth was, even though he didn't have any idea what he was doing with Annika, the only way to explain himself was for her to meet his family. Not to mention if he was going to see his nephew, it would help to have Annika at his side. He was already calmer just having her here.

Hmm.

"About time we saw you, live and in person." Emma walked out of the house before he reached the door and trapped him in a hug.

"Yeah, sis. I missed you all, too," Daniel whispered. Guilt, sharp and intense, shot through him when Emma finally let him go, her eyes shiny with tears. "Aw, Em. Don't."

She waved him off and turned to Annika. "Emma," he said, "this is Annika. Annika, my big sister, Emma."

Annika smiled at Emma and held out her hand, but Emma pulled her in for a hug. Shock sprang to her face, but she seemed to recover quickly and returned the hug. His sister's eyes were still wet when she released Annika. "I'm sorry," she sniffled. "But Danny hasn't been to a birthday in—well, a long time."

Daniel rolled his eyes and shoved his hands into his pockets. "Jeez, Em. Can we not do the 'Danny' thing?" He looked around. They still stood on Emma's front porch. Clearly, she had wanted a minute with him before everyone else got to him. "Where is he, anyway?"

As if in answer, a dark-haired blue-jeaned blur whooshed up and stopped in front of Emma. "Hey, Mom. When are we cutting the cake?"

Daniel's heart was beating too fast; he felt the blood drain away from his head. This—this grown-up little boy could *not* be his nephew. Had that much time passed? Annika leaned toward him, probably because he looked like he was going to pass out. But when he looked at her, her concern was laced with confusion.

"Emma's right. I haven't been to a birthday party in a while." That was all the explanation he could muster right now.

There had been an incident. It was the first birthday after Sara. Emma had made him come to the party because it had meant a lot to young Charlie to have his uncle there. A little girl who looked just like Sara—at least the brown curls and blue eyes part—had asked Daniel to cut her a piece of cake and Daniel had frozen. Emma had had to convince him that the little girl was not his Sara. Ever since then, he avoided groups of children. Until this birthday party. Until Annika.

Emma was talking to her son. "Soon, don't worry. Charlie, I have a surprise for you."

Charlie's eyes lit up, and he did a little jig. "What?"

"Look who came to your party." She turned him to face Daniel. "Uncle Danny is here."

Charlie narrowed his eyes as if trying to place Daniel, but, as Daniel had anticipated, recognition never lit up his face.

The young boy held out his hand and plastered a polite smile to his face. "Nice to meet you, Uncle Danny."

Daniel's heart broke a little more. He had changed this boy's diapers, stayed up nights with him. He had played with him, given him his first soccer ball, and here he was, ten years old, offering to shake his hand as if he were a stranger. What had he done, staying away for so long? Not that he hadn't seen his sister and his parents. It was Charlie he avoided.

Daniel's hand shook even as he offered it to Charlie. Considering the furtive glances from his sister, and the continued quizzical look on Annika's face, he wasn't doing a good job of hiding his anxiety. "We've met before."

"I'm sorry, I don't remember."

"Well, it's been a while, and I've been away." Daniel forced out the words as he studied his nephew. "The last time I saw you, you were five. And only about this big." He held his hand low to the ground. "Not nearly the grown-up boy I see here." Tears pricked at his eyes, but he forced them back. "I hear you're a pretty good soccer player. Maybe we could catch a game?"

Charlie's eyes lit up. "That would be awesome!"

Daniel grinned, finally feeling the warmth of the sun.

"It's a date. I'll get us tickets." Annika placed a hand on his shoulder, offering support, though she couldn't even know why. He relaxed under her touch.

"Can I go, Mom? Huh? Can I?" Charlie nearly bounced with excitement.

"Of course. Now go see to your friends. Cake in ten minutes."

Charlie started to run off, but he turned back after a few steps. "You're not leaving soon, are you?"

"Not a chance."

CHAPTER SIXTEEN

ANNIKA

DANIEL'S MOTHER WAS an older version of Emma, her skin slightly browner, with eyes to match. She embraced her son a bit too long, making Annika wonder if Daniel had been avoiding more than just Charlie.

Daniel's father, a tall man with a full head of graying hair and the same green eyes as his children, stayed back a bit, his eyes narrowed at his son.

Daniel stepped back from his mother, finally fixing his gaze on his father. When Daniel had looked at his mother, his eyes were the green of a meadow, promising everything light and wonderful. The green he rested on his father, however, was reminiscent of a murky body of water. The older man pressed his lips together.

Daniel extended his hand. "Dad."

A small storm brewed in the older man's eyes, and he waited a beat before shaking Daniel's hand. "Son. About time you came to see your mother."

His mother placed a hand on her husband's arm. "Ned—"

"Mom, I'm fine." Daniel turned to his father, his lips mashed together as if keeping in words that were better off not being said. "I'm here now."

"Yeah, well. It shouldn't be that hard for a man to come

see his family every so often. Your sister here talks of nothing but you. And her kid, does he even know who you are? I mean, I know you've had it rough, but you aren't the only one who—"

"Dad!" Daniel's voice was hard and firm as he cut off his father. "Let it go." He made a small motion toward Annika.

Daniel wasn't the only one who *what?* What didn't she know? Annika studied his family, but both his sister and mother were looking between Daniel and his father as if waiting for the inevitable storm to rage.

His father stopped and glanced at Annika, as if seeing her for the first time, and nodded. "Yeah, okay. I don't suppose we should be airing dirty laundry when Daniel has finally seen fit to bring a girl home."

Daniel clenched his fists, staring at his father. It was Emma who brought life back to the room.

"Everyone, this is Annika."

"Annika? What a lovely name."

Annika spun around at the sound of a voice with an Indian accent. The tension in the room all but melted away as the newcomer drew them all in. An elderly woman with paper-thin brown skin, white hair and pure love in her black eyes rolled into the kitchen in an electric chair.

"Ba!" Daniel caught Annika's eye and raised one eyebrow as he brushed past her to greet his grandmother. Annika gaped when he bent down to touch the older woman's feet in greeting. But Ba stopped him halfway, and Daniel leaned over to embrace her. "What's with the wheels, Ba? Getting lazy?" he chuckled, and Annika almost fell over.

Ba? Touching of feet? What the hell was happening here?

"Bahu waqt ti na dekayoo, beta." Which Annika un-

derstood perfectly as she, too, was fluent in Gujarati. She should be—it was all they spoke in her home when she was growing up. "And my foot is broken. I'm sure you heard." If Annika wasn't mistaken, the old woman rolled her eyes and shot a look at Daniel's mother. "Which means that I can't go to weddings!"

"I'm sorry. But I went. And you didn't miss much. Just an amazing dol, great food, fun people." Daniel laughed and ducked his head, but not before his grandmother managed a playful smack on his head.

"Ba, there's someone I want you to meet." He stood and held out his hand toward Annika. "This is Annika. Annika, this is Ba."

Annika tried to keep the astonishment from her face as she automatically pressed her hands together and bowed slightly in namaste. *"Kem cho?"*

Daniel's grandmother beamed. "Ha! You got one that speaks the language."

Annika's heart was racing, and her mind buzzed with incomprehension. She was still trying to wrap her head around what was happening when Daniel spoke.

"Hoon tho bolu chun, neh?"

He did speak it. He had an accent, but still.

His grandmother harrumphed as grandmothers do and continued in Gujarati. "Yes, but how often do you come to see your grandmother?"

In contrast to his father asking this question, Daniel grinned and answered her back in Gujarati. "I'll try to come more."

"So has your father met Daniel yet?" Ba addressed Annika with a slightly crooked smile.

"Ba—" Daniel sounded a bit like a teenager "—can we not do this?"

"You hush, I'm talking to Annika. Besides, you brought her here."

"Ba…"

She turned to face her grandson. "Isn't she your girl-friend?"

Daniel flushed bright red. "Umm…we're…"

"Friends. Ba, we're just friends." Annika helped. Is that what they were? Kissing-type friends?

Ba narrowed her eyes at her grandson. "You did not bring a booty call here to meet your family, did you?" She said *booty call* in English, and Annika could barely contain her gasp.

"Oh my God, Ba! Stop!" Daniel was all kinds of crim-son, much to the amusement of his sister and mother. "How do you even know that word?" Even his father had cracked a small smile.

Annika wasn't sure what surprised her more: Daniel speaking Gujarati or Ba knowing the phrase *booty call*. She was blushing, but she managed to keep smiling and looking at Ba, all the while wishing there was a hole she could disappear into. She did not, however, miss the twin-kle in Ba's eye.

"What?" Ba asked innocently. "It's a question."

"Well, I think he brought me here to meet you because I caught him doing garba and bhangra like a boss at that wedding last weekend," Annika said. "But now that I've met you all, I see that he's been holding out on me."

Ba chuckled. "He always liked fooling people. Look at him—dark brown hair, green eyes. No one would suspect he had an old Gujarati grandmother."

"Aw, Ba. You're not old." Daniel gazed upon his grand-mother with such love and affection that Annika almost didn't recognize him. She'd watched a lot of things play upon his face, but this kind of love hadn't been one of them.

She laughed again. "I am, but don't think I'm too old to knock sense into you. About time you came to see Charlie."

The affection he had for his grandmother never left his eyes, but his face went blank, as surely as if he had put on a mask to cover whatever emotion his nephew elicited.

"Why haven't you seen Charlie for a while?" Annika was puzzled, but the atmosphere in the room had again gone from jovial to something hard yet delicate. No eyes met hers, and certainly no one looked at Daniel. No one except his father, who scowled and shook his head. What didn't she know?

A car door slammed, and it seemed to break the trance. "That's Michael with the replacement cake." Emma nodded at the smashed cake next to the sink. She smiled widely, as if to remind everyone that they were at a birthday party.

The family jumped on her suggestion with more than a little bit of gusto. Everyone, it seemed, needed to be involved with getting the cake ready for cutting. Even Ba rolled farther into the kitchen and started looking for candles. Everyone except for Daniel. He kept his distance. Still with his family, but just at the edge.

Annika sidled over. She'd find out about the nephew later. She had a more pressing question. "So, one-quarter Indian, huh?" She raised an eyebrow. "And Gujarati at that? Daniel Bliant, you've been holding out." She nudged him with her shoulder.

Thankfully, his tension seemed to slip away, and he pursed his lips at her, amusement replacing the pain in his eyes. "No one ever believed I was part Indian. Especially other Indians. But Ba lived next door my whole life, and I was raised by her as much as my own parents." He shrugged. "I would tell people, but they wouldn't believe me. It used to piss me off, until my grandparents told me that maybe I should show people who I was instead of telling them. So I did." He caught her eye. "I still do."

"So you decided to show me who you are?"

"Well, I don't hide who I am. It's just…people know you're Indian when they look at you. For me, they have to investigate further." He met her eyes. "The opportunity presented itself, so…"

She held his gaze, while something definitely more than friendship passed between them. Daniel Bliant was trouble.

"There's more, Annika. I want… I *need* to be honest with you." His words and the look on his face set something churning in her belly. "What my family keeps dancing around…" Before she could think too much about it, the moment was broken by the sound of Daniel's phone chirping.

Daniel sighed and reluctantly reached into his pocket for the phone. Whatever he saw there caused him to furrow his brow.

"Everything okay?" What *more*? What did he need to be honest about?

He shook his head. "Probably not. It's my ex-wife. She wants to see me. Says it's important."

Ex-wife? Daniel had been *married*? What else didn't she know? Was that what the bourbon was about? She looked around and watched as Emma cut a piece of cake. She might as well have been cutting another piece of the puzzle that was Daniel's life. Was this the *more*? She forced her face into a neutral expression. She did not, after all, have any real claim over him. "You were married?" She couldn't keep the surprise from her voice.

"Yes." He nodded and looked back at her, apprehension in his eyes. "I wasn't trying to keep that from you, I swear—and we've been divorced for three years."

"Does she ask to see you often?"

He frowned. "Last time she got in touch, she wanted to tell me she was getting married. So, no." He glanced at his watch. "We have time for cake. No big hurry."

Annika's heart sank. She was getting more questions than answers here. And she *wanted* answers. All of them.

SHE AND DANIEL talked nonstop on the way back to her apartment. She learned about his experiences growing up, and how they were similar yet different from her own experiences. He was proud of his Indian roots and felt a great deal of frustration having to prove his heritage to Indians and non-Indians alike. He could have just let everyone believe he was white. It would have been easier.

"But I couldn't have done that. It was like hiding a part of myself—as if I was ashamed of that part of me. I wasn't. I'm not." He sighed. "I just got tired of the arguments. And I found that seeing was believing. So now I show." He grinned, clearly proud of himself.

"Yeah, you do," Annika chuckled. "Meanwhile, I was always just trying to fit in. I wasn't trying to ignore being Indian, but keeping my Indian side separate so I could be like the other kids."

"Did you? Fit in?"

Annika shrugged. It was the classic immigrant story of straddling two cultures. Speaking Gujarati at home, learning how to make Indian food, going to temple, studying. But at school she spoke English, played soccer, and ate peanut-butter-and-jelly sandwiches.

"I tried. But I *was* different, and I loved being Indian. I loved garba and being able to speak two languages. It took me a while, but I found a balance." But now that she had some distance, she saw how she'd hidden the Indian side of her from Steven. More reason she was better off without him. "Although sometimes, I have the issue of people looking at me and seeing only the Indian part of me." She rolled her eyes. "Shocked that I'm not a doctor or a lawyer. Kind of the opposite of you."

Daniel glanced at her and smiled that smile that she swore was just for her. "You have to get to know us."

Annika's heart swelled as she realized that she and Daniel understood each other on a level that she could not even verbalize. They weren't the same. But the bond still formed.

"Your family is great. And I loved meeting Ba." Annika bit her lip and turned to face him. "Thanks for introducing me."

Daniel glanced at her, a smile on his lips. "I wanted them to meet you." He turned back to the road. He had insisted on driving home. "Sorry we had to leave early. It's just that Sheila, my ex, really doesn't ever ask to see me unless it's important."

"So you're still friends?" Annika did her best to keep her voice light and breezy, like this was a casual question whose answer had no bearing on her whatsoever. Wait. It was a casual question.

"It's complicated." Daniel sighed. "We've been divorced for three years, but we parted on civil terms. She remarried a year ago." He shrugged. "We wanted different things."

"What different things?" Maybe not so light and breezy anymore, but she wanted to know.

The air between them turned electric with tension. He remained silent for so long that Annika was sure he wouldn't answer her, and her heart sank. She stared at the road ahead and was about to tell him to never mind, forget the whole thing, when he said her name. He glanced at her quickly and then back at the road.

"She wanted children."

"And you didn't?"

"No." He sighed heavily.

The next obvious question was, did he not want children, period? Or did he just not want children with his ex? But Annika wasn't ready to ask that of him. They weren't even dating. They were…what? They just got done telling *his* family they were friends, and *her* family, aside from Nilay, didn't really know he was part of her life. No: two kisses, no matter how amazing, did not warrant the "Do you want to have kids one day?" question. She held her tongue.

A voice that sounded like her father harrumphed in the back of her mind. She ignored it.

They drove for a bit in silence.

"I guess we both have kind of tough fathers, huh?" Annika was curious.

Daniel shook his head. "To say the least."

"My dad just thinks I keep making the wrong decisions in my life. Teacher versus med school. Steven versus… I don't know." She had almost said Sajan. "Not Steven, I guess. What's your dad all bent out of shape about?"

Daniel's knuckles went white and his eyes went blank.

"Nothing. Just father-son bullshit." Daniel's voice was thick with emotion. "I'll just never be the man he wants me to be."

"Well, what does—"

"Don't worry about it, Annika." He cut her off as he pulled up in front of her building. "It's a lost cause." He closed his eyes and inhaled deeply. "I'm sorry. It's just…

me and my dad...basically, he doesn't agree with how I live my life."

His face was closed to her, and she knew when a conversation was over. "I get it." She smiled. "Parents are... complicated."

Daniel offered more questions than answers. Her parents' imminent disapproval rang in her ears. Her attraction to Daniel aside, it didn't really make any sense for her to get more involved with him with all these unanswered mysteries surrounding him. It was as if she was being given fair warning about trouble ahead.

They got out of the car, and he tossed back her keys and got his helmet from the back seat.

"Thanks for driving back," she said as she started toward her building. He followed. "I thought you were going to see your ex." She nodded toward his bike.

"Well, yeah. But I'm walking you to your door."

Annika almost laughed, but he was totally serious. "Not necessary. I'll be fine."

He shrugged. "Whatever. Let's go."

Resigned, but in no hurry for her time with Daniel to end, she continued toward the building. She unlocked the door, and Daniel held it as he followed her in. When she turned to say goodbye, he grinned. "Your *actual* door."

She shrugged and led the way up the steps to her third-floor apartment. Suddenly, Daniel was very chatty, sharing a humorous story about moving Emma into her first apartment, and his ba being firm about putting a small Ganesha in it.

Annika tapped the necklace she always wore, the one with a pendant of the elephant-headed deity. "Remover of obstacles. Can't ever hurt."

In front of her door, Daniel stood behind her while she

fumbled with her keys. The fact that she could feel the heat from his body did not improve her ability to fit the key into the lock. She finally succeeded and opened the door, motioning for Daniel to follow.

"Might as well have chai before you go," she said, turning into the kitchen to clear her head.

Daniel stood just inside the doorway, his hands in his pockets, an almost shy smile on his face. He fixed his eyes on hers, and she was forced to rest her hand on the counter to steady herself. "Tempting," he said, pursing his mouth, suggesting the temptation was more than just the chai.

Annika held his gaze a beat too long before responding. "Of course, you have to go. Sheila." The thought of him going to see his ex irritated her. She held her hands out. "Well, I'm safe and sound." A jealous growl escaped her throat. "Thank you."

Daniel did not break eye contact. "Yeah. I should go." But instead, he moved a few steps into her apartment. Closer to her. Suddenly, the electric tension that had followed them from the car crackled and sparked. Against her better judgment, Annika walked to him. Close enough to see the struggle on his face, the war that seemed to always be waging in his eyes. Close enough to feel the heat from his body. Her irritation melted away.

She nodded. "Mmm-hmm."

He stood for a moment longer, watching her, the thick, electric silence stretching between them.

"Yeah, okay." Then, in one quick motion, he turned and walked out.

Well, okay.

Annika let out a breath and shut the door behind him. She didn't get the feeling he was still in love with Sheila, but there was something there she couldn't place. A few kisses and meeting each other's families didn't make them a couple—she'd been pissed at him until last week, for God's sake. So she needed to give up the irritation that he was going to see Sheila.

His family had been lovely to her, and Annika couldn't remember the last time she'd felt so comfortable around people she'd only just met—it certainly hadn't been this way with Steven's family.

A giggle from Naya's room grabbed her attention. When was the last time she heard Naya giggle? Annika crept toward her door, which was slightly ajar. Another giggle. Annika knocked.

"I'm on the phone. Come in," Naya called. Annika slowly pushed open the door to find Naya FaceTiming. As soon as Naya caught her eye, she motioned for Annika to come in.

"Ravi, I'll be there in an hour. Promise." After another giggle and what Annika could have sworn was a kissy-face (or two), Naya tapped her phone off and glanced shyly at Annika.

"Don't tell your parents or mine."

Annika rolled her eyes. "That you're spending the night at your boyfriend's? Naya, most women our age do."

"You know they'll flip out. It's not 'what we do.'" Naya did a perfect accent and head bob. "Especially after—never mind." She waved her hand and looked away from Annika.

"Especially after what happened with me, you were going to say."

Naya lowered her head, sheepish. "Yes, but I didn't mean it that way. I just meant…"

"Uh-huh."

"I just mean your parents might be pressuring you to

get married, but the whole situation has my parents freaking out a bit, too."

"But you're the 'good one.'" Annika made the air quotes. "They should know that by now."

Naya set her lips in a stern line and placed her hands firmly on Annika's shoulders. "You're not bad. I'm not good. We just are who we are."

"You know what I mean. I seem to consistently do things that cause my parents anxiety." Ignoring warning signs.

"You have to live your life, Annika. You're a great teacher—"

"You know that doesn't really matter to them." Annika waved it off; she was done with this conversation.

"So, where were you all day?" Naya didn't wait for an answer. "Let me guess, out with a certain tall, dark and handsome?"

Annika froze. How had Naya known she was out with Daniel?

"How is dear Sajan?" Naya dragged out Sajan's name in that singsong-y way they used to when they were kids. Oh.

"You weren't out with Sajan?"

"Um, no." She didn't feel like explaining who it was, so she turned and headed for her room.

"Then who was it?" Naya had followed her.

"No one."

"'No one' left awfully quickly."

"We're just friends, and he had somewhere to be." Annika shrugged and entered her room. Again, Naya followed. This woman had no boundaries.

"So why won't you tell me who it—" She pointed a finger at Annika. "This is someone you *like*." She narrowed her eyes and gasped, shaking her finger at her. "You were out with that *nurse*, from the bar, and you were dancing with him last weekend. What was his name? Daniel! You were out with that Daniel, weren't you?"

It sounded scarily like an accusation, but hadn't Naya been the one to tell her to go for it?

"He's a nurse *practitioner*," Annika defended him. "And everyone was dancing." She defended herself.

"Yeah, but who knew that he could garba like that? And he couldn't take his eyes off you." Naya's eyes widened. "But what about Sajan?"

"What about him? He's nice, but—"

"Weren't you at the wedding? Everyone was talking about what a great couple you two would make."

"Who is everyone?"

"Your parents. And mine."

Annika raised her eyebrows.

"And maybe his," Naya added.

"What? I never said— I didn't do— I really hate the gossip thing." Annika flopped down onto her bed.

"I knew it—you were out with Daniel!"

"What if I was?"

"I thought he was a stalker or something?"

"He's not. In fact, he's very, very…" *Sweet. Kind. Sexy. Distracted by his ex-wife. Weird aversion to his nephew.* What *was* she doing? Sajan was sweet and kind and handsome by anyone's standards. He didn't come with secrets, or ex-wives, or weird bourbon issues. He'd grown up like she did—he would *get* her—like Naya and Ravi.

But Daniel *did* understand her.

Her parents already liked Sajan.

"Annika? Hellooo? Annika?" Naya was waving her hand in front of Annika's face. "Where'd you go?"

"Nowhere. How's Ravi?" Just as she'd hoped, Naya's eyes got all dreamy, and she forgot about lecturing Annika.

"He's awesome." But then she snapped her gaze to Annika. "Nice try. But we're talking about you."

"There's nothing to talk about. I'm not seeing either of them right now." It was true, nothing had really happened with Sajan, and Daniel was…complicated.

"Your dad will pitch a fit if you try to date Daniel." Naya had her arms folded across her body.

"Why do you say that? He was perfectly civil at the wedding."

"Well, yeah. You weren't dating him then. Trust me, Sajan will be easier. And better in the long run. No big cultural divide. Remember, Steven's one redeeming quality was that he was a lawyer. Daniel is an NP, not going to help." She raised her eyebrows at Annika. "Where did dear Daniel run off to anyway?"

"He went to see his ex-wife." The words fell out of her mouth before she could filter them. She could have told Naya that Daniel was part Indian, but that really shouldn't make a difference.

"He's *divorced*?" Naya said it like it was a bad word.

Annika shrugged. "So?"

"So get out before you get in too deep. You'll never sell him to your parents. Especially not after Steven."

That could be true. Naya had a compelling argument. After all the drama with Steven, Sajan would be…comfortable, easy. He was a good man. Her feelings for him would grow. Just like her father said.

Daniel offered more questions than answers. Her parents' imminent disapproval rang in her ears. Her attraction to Daniel aside, it didn't really make any sense for her to get more involved with him with all these mysteries surrounding him. It was as if she was being given fair warning about trouble ahead.

Too bad her heart did a rapid fire every time she thought of Daniel.

CHAPTER SEVENTEEN

DANIEL

DANIEL MOUNTED HIS bike and drove away from Annika, his body heavy with regret. Every part of him had longed to kiss her, but if he had, he'd still be up there with her. And he couldn't bail on Sheila. She asked for very little.

Annika had been completely comfortable around his family. By the time they'd left, she had even succeeded in getting a smile from his dad, when she told the story about how a child had cut a chunk of her hair when she was an intern. She had simply offered the left-handed boy a pair of left-handed scissors.

"What happened when you told the parents?" his father had asked.

Annika had shaken her head, tossing those gorgeous curls. "Well, it turns out that the parents were trying to get him to do everything right-handed. They were trying to get him to be something he wasn't. So, when I asked him to use the left-handed scissors, he was confused."

His mother had smiled at her. "And he cut your hair."

Annika had shrugged. She had hit a nerve and was completely unaware. His father had gone quiet. It didn't matter. Ned Bliant could not understand why his son was unable to let go of the past and move forward. *That's what men do, son. You take care of your wife. Pay the bills, work over-*

time, cook if you need to. Men don't wallow in themselves.
Just take care of business. You'll be fine soon enough."

His father would never forgive him for divorcing Sheila,
even though it had been Sheila's idea. Somehow, Ned saw
the divorce as Daniel shirking his responsibilities. And
that was just as unforgivable as being in pain.

Daniel shook thoughts of his father from his mind. He
had to focus on the task at hand. Sheila's text was perplex-
ing. They had parted amiably, if not quite friends, and Daniel had even attended her wedding. Jim was a good guy,
and he treated Sheila well. In fact, under different circumstances, he and Jim might have been friends. There was no
ill will between him and his ex-wife, just the shared bond
of belonging to a club no one really wanted to be a part of.
Stranger things had bonded people together.

They certainly did not hang out together. He knew it was
hard for Sheila to look at him. Sara had had his smile, with
both dimples. Hell, there were days he couldn't look in the
mirror. Basically, Daniel tried not to force her to see him.

He pulled into the older neighborhood, the acrid, sweet
scent of burning leaves taking him back to a time of what
should have been domestic bliss. Anger swelled in his chest
as he thought about how all that was ripped away from
him because someone with a vendetta had access to a gun.

He parked in front of his old house and sat on his bike,
listening to trash cans being dragged to the curb, whistles
calling dogs back in and the low chatter of neighbors con-
versing as they passed one another. The mundane sounds
of a life he would never have again. He breathed deeply
of the cool autumn air and calmed his anger before trying to face Sheila.

They'd argued about gun control, as well. At the time,

Sheila was too wounded to feel the outrage, but outrage was all Daniel allowed himself to feel.

He took in the small home he had shared with his little family. A small front porch, carport at the side, small front yard with the same azaleas he'd planted. Someone was doing the upkeep: everything looked neat and in its place.

For some reason, Sheila had kept the house, even though Sara had lived in it. Or maybe she kept it *because* Sara had lived in it. Maybe the house was how she hung on to Sara.

Daniel stared straight ahead and focused on the door even as dread grew steadily in his stomach. He approached the door purposefully, putting one foot in front of the other, taking in the chipped white paint, the grain of the wood, the weight of the door knocker. The house seemed to close in around him, reminding him that a beautiful little girl used to live here, and that she didn't anymore. The less he saw, the better. He picked up the door knocker, letting it fall with a squeak and thud. He could almost hear her little feet rush to open the door.

"It's open." Daniel heard Sheila call from inside. He turned the knob and forced himself to step into a house that was no longer his.

The familiar smell hit him first. It was a mixture of whatever had been made for dinner last night and whatever candle Sheila had burned after. But Daniel swore that Sara's scent still clung to the air. Maybe he imagined it, but what did that matter? "Hey, Sheila. It's me."

"In the kitchen, Daniel."

Daniel stood in his old foyer. The house was small. A starter house, their agent had called it. Something they would grow out of one day. He hadn't thought they'd grow out of it in quite the way they had.

Everything was all at once familiar and strange. The

little bench they used to keep for Sara to put on her shoes was no longer there. In its place was a mat. A set of men's running shoes was neatly placed in the middle. They would be Jim's.

Out of habit, he slipped off his shoes and placed them next to Jim's, taking small, hesitant steps toward the kitchen. "How's Jim? He's not home?"

Sheila sat at a small dining table, surrounded by papers. "He's fine. He's at a conference this weekend. Come on in, Daniel. I have coffee." She moved aside a few stacks. "Sorry, I have to get these charts done before surgery tomorrow."

"What do you have?" He sat down across from her.

"Back-to-back-to-back cataracts." She smiled. She and Daniel had always loved talking about medicine. Jim was an ophthalmologist, as well. Daniel could only assume their conversations were interesting. "Want some coffee?"

"Sure."

Sheila locked eyes with him as she stood. Daniel understood in that instant why she had called him. He clenched his jaw as blood rushed to his head and his ears pounded.

"You're pregnant." He spit the accusation out from in between his teeth, unable to even open his mouth. He grazed over her swollen belly with an experienced eye. "Like, five, six months."

Sheila swallowed hard and went to fetch the coffee. Her hand shook as she placed the mug in front him. "Yes. I'm due end of March. I wanted to tell you in person." She looked down at him, blue eyes hesitant.

Daniel's grip around his coffee mug became dangerous for the ceramic. The heat from the liquid pressed into his hands. This was what she had wanted. A couple of years after Sara died, Sheila started talking about having another baby. Daniel had been beside himself. There was no way to replace Sara. She was one of a kind. You couldn't have another child like you got another puppy.

Sheila had insisted that she wasn't replacing Sara, just moving forward, but Daniel had remained adamant. No more children.

"I guess you got what you wanted." Daniel's voice was harsh.

"I was hoping you would be happy. A child is…"

"You can't replace Sara," Daniel growled.

Tears shimmered in her eyes. "I'm not trying to replace her. No one could ever replace our angel…"

"Damn right." Daniel slammed down the mug, sloshing coffee onto the table, splashing her charts. He stood so abruptly he nearly knocked over his chair. He turned and headed for the door.

"Daniel." Sheila grabbed his arm to stop him. "Daniel, we were going to ask you to be the baby's godfather."

"You—what?" He shook his head, threw his hands up in the air and then down again, violently. "I'm no one's *father* anymore!" His voice was harsher than he'd intended, but the thought of being anyone's any kind of father—no. He couldn't do it. "And I never will be."

"Fine. But you need to find a way to deal with this." She swallowed hard.

"I deal with it," he snapped.

"By what? Working twenty hours a day? Drinking?"

"I haven't had a drink since before we divorced. You know that."

Her gaze faltered a bit. "That doesn't mean you've dealt with this."

"Listen, just because you married Mr. Stable and forgot about Sara, doesn't mean that I have to."

"Forgot? How dare you?" Sheila was almost growling. "She was my daughter, too. I lost her the same as you. You think I don't think about her every day? That I don't miss her? Every. Damn. Day?" Her voice cracked and her eyes refilled with tears.

"I don't know, Sheila, you tell me. You're the one having a replacement baby." He regretted the words the instant he said them, but the wound on her face told him he could never take it back.

"Get out." Her calm was more threatening than any scream could be. "Get out, you bastard, and don't come back."

Daniel stormed toward the door, stepped into his shoes and left, slamming the door behind him, not looking back.

He tore out of the neighborhood on his bike and stopped at the first liquor store he found.

Daniel parked his bike, grabbed the brown bag and took off his helmet. Someone was exiting the building, so he didn't have to buzz up and risk rejection. His brain whirred with images of Sara and Sheila, and his ears echoed with Sheila's guttural "Get out!" Maybe he was out of line, but he couldn't accept her replacing their daughter. And he certainly wouldn't be anyone's godfather. He just couldn't.

He found his way back up to the apartment. If he could get in this easily, he was going to have a word with Annika about her personal security. He found the door he wanted and knocked before he lost his nerve. "Annika. It's Daniel."

She cracked open the door and peeked out, and just the sight of those brown eyes calmed his breathing some. She closed the door and unlatched the chain, and it seemed a year before Daniel could see her eyes again.

"Hey… Daniel." She eyed him with trepidation as he walked past her as if he lived there.

"Can I have two glasses, please?" He was brusque and he knew it, but his breath was short and his mind would not settle.

She opened a cabinet, pulled out two short tumblers and set them in front of him. He set down his helmet as the weight of her gaze bore through him. Undaunted, he opened the bourbon and poured them each two fingers.

"What's going on, Daniel?" There was no anger in her voice, but her tone demanded an answer.

He raised his glass to her and waited until she did the same. He took a gulp of his bourbon and enjoyed the burn as it flowed through his body and warmed him. Annika's mouth gaped open.

"Sheila's having another baby." He said it as if that explained everything, then turned to examine his surroundings. They were standing between her small kitchen and the dining area, the bourbon bottle resting on the high granite countertop that was large enough to serve as a breakfast bar. The small dining room was open to the adjoining family room. In the back of the family room, an open door led to a bedroom. A small statue of Ganesha stood on the counter. *Remover of obstacles, ha.* Obstacles were never removed—only added.

Annika sipped her drink. "Your ex-wife is having a baby, so you're drinking?" She narrowed her eyes, her gaze penetrating. "Are you still in love with her?"

"No." He had the presence of mind to catch the worry in her voice. "That's not the problem."

"Okay, Daniel. What's the problem?"

He gulped down his drink, poured another. Some might call it liquid courage, but it was never that for him. It was more like liquid memories. His muscles relaxed. Even his mind calmed a bit. He focused on those brown eyes as if they were his lifeline. Where to begin? "She's having a replacement baby."

Her eyes narrowed and she tilted her head, confused. "Replacement?"

Finally, he was ready to tell her everything. "Sheila's new baby is going to replace the child we had." He wasn't making any sense to Annika, he knew it, but how did you tell someone that you had a beautiful girl at one time, but now you didn't?

"You had a child…" Her voice drifted off, and then her eyes met his, and she gasped. Her next words were barely a whisper. "Daniel, what happened to *your*—"

"Sara." However softly he spoke her name, it was still too loud for him. "She was five."

"Was?" She walked toward him and stopped just two steps from him. Tears shone in her eyes. "Sara." Her breath hitched.

At the sound of his daughter's name on her breath, the sound of her surprise and sorrow, tears prickled at his nose. Tears he had never allowed before blurred his vision and clogged his throat.

"Beautiful name."

Daniel nodded slowly. If he moved too fast, he would lose his mind. A tear escaped, falling directly to the floor as if even his own tears needed to escape his sorrow. He took another gulp of his bourbon and spoke. His first words had to fight the backlog of emotion in his throat. "She had curly brown hair and blue eyes, and she loved school."

Annika smiled through her tears. "She looked like Sheila?"

He nodded, his mouth automatically forming a frown. "Except when she smiled."

Annika nodded, knowledge in her eyes. "The dimples."

"Yeah." He could barely even whisper. Her smile had been a miniature version of his from the start. Everyone had commented on it. He had thrilled in seeing that little piece of him in another human being. In the end, it was the thing that he had come to avoid.

"She, uh…she had made a card for her teacher and wanted to go to school early to give it to her. Sheila said no, but I felt bad because the night before I had played only one song for her on the piano, instead of two, because I was tired." Self-loathing overwhelmed him as it did when he thought of that second song. "I was such an ass. It would've taken three minutes to play that damn song, then I wouldn't have felt guilty, and then…" He polished off his bourbon.

A sound like a laugh escaped him, but it was mean. "So, I took her." Nausea flooded him at the memory. Sara had hopped out of the car and grabbed his hand. Her tiny five-year-old-little-girl voice clear as if she were standing in front of him.

Thanks to the bourbon.

"Thank you, Daddy. Ms. Groller is going to love this card. She's the best teacher I ever had. I love her almost as much as I love you and Mommy."

The air had been warm that day. It was close to the end of the school year, so Sara had on her favorite blue dress with small white dots and flowers. Daniel had left the house in his blue scrubs. There must have been lavender growing nearby, because Sara had commented on the pretty smell, but Daniel had found it cloying.

She had taken his hand in hers and smiled up at him as they walked up to the doors to be buzzed in. He remembered thinking that her hands were sticky again, and that no matter how many times a day he washed her hands, they always seemed to be sticky.

The school wouldn't be open to students for another thirty minutes. They waited outside, the sun growing warmer as they stood, the thick lavender scent turning Daniel's stomach. Daniel was ready to take Sara and wait in the car until the building opened, when Ms. Groller herself opened the door.

Sara's eyes lit up upon seeing her teacher, her smile wide, those all too familiar dimples melting his heart.

"I took her hand—you know she could only hold three of my fingers in her whole hand." He held up his hand and gazed at it as if Sara's tiny hand might miraculously show up. "We followed her teacher to her classroom."

The thick scent of lavender filled his nostrils, making him almost gag. He closed his eyes to shake it. It wasn't real. There was no lavender in this room. He opened his eyes, his gaze resting on those beautiful brown eyes. Annika watched him, no sign of the discomfort most people wore when he inadvertently mentioned Sara. Their faces closed, as if, by being too close to him, they might inadvertently lose their own child and become a member of that club no one wanted to belong to.

Annika rested her hand on his, squeezing tight. He allowed it.

His heart began to pound as if it were all happening again. He couldn't ignore it.

It had been cooler in the building, and the hairs on his arms had stood on end. Sara had chattered away with her teacher as Daniel followed behind them.

He shivered from the memory of the chill.

"Come on, Daddy!"

His sneakers made soft squishing noises on the tile floor as he followed behind his daughter, allowing her to lead the way. "I'm right behind you, babe."

End-of-the-year displays lined the walls. Bright yellow construction-paper suns with children's names on them floated along walls outside Sara's classroom.

He entered the classroom behind Sara and Ms. Groller. Sunlight streamed in from the window, making yellow bands across the room. Sara walked right up to her desk, opened her backpack and took out her homemade card.

"This is for you, Ms. Groller. I made it." No inhibitions. No concern that her love would not be well received. The innocence of youth. Pride swelled in his little girl as she watched her teacher ooh and aah over the craftsmanship.

After Ms. Groller admired the card, Sara went to hang her backpack where it belonged.

"I could never get Sara to hang up her backpack at home, but at school, she was Miss This-Is-Where-It-Goes." His mouth went dry. "There she was, hanging it up like she owned the place." He'd had another moment of parental pride.

"Sorry she's so early, but—" Daniel threw up his hands in surrender "—she had to get that to you." He looked around. "Is there anything I can help you with before I head out?"

"No, not at all. Sara is a wonderful helper." The teacher smiled broadly at her little charge. "We'll manage, won't we?"

Sara nodded proudly.

"Okay, then. Off to work I go." He knelt down to kiss Sara goodbye. She smelled like baby powder and lotion

and that mysterious essence that made children smell so precious.

Try as he would, Daniel could never quite exactly remember Sara's scent. He closed his eyes and inhaled deeply, as if he could extract that scent from the air around him. It didn't seem fair that he could easily remember the offensive odor of the lavender, even feel the chill of the school building, but the little baby smell of his daughter was lost to him.

"Bye, Daddy." She waved him off. She felt safe.

"Bye, sweetheart." Daniel stood and nodded at the teacher as he left.

"I left. I left my sweet little girl at school and I went to work."

"Daniel." Annika's eyes were wide; her breath was coming fast. "Daniel, where did Sara go to school?"

He met her gaze with nausea in his belly, unable to say the name of the school.

It was enough for Annika. She gasped. "Chase Creek. Sara went to my school, didn't she?" Tears filled her eyes. "There was a shooting…"

"I *left*." He spat out the word and pounded the granite, relishing the zing of pain that flew up his arm. "I was at work and he came…and he…" He hung his head as he leaned against the granite counter with one hand. Sweat beaded on him, his skin went cold. He couldn't say the words.

A gunman had entered the building twenty minutes after he left and shot the teacher and Sara. He had shot five other people, too, because they were in his way. Four teachers and another student. Seven people. Seven people dead because an unstable man that Ms. Groller had dated one time found access to a gun. Because even though the gunman had a history of violent behavior, even though Ms. Groller had obtained a restraining order, he still had a gun. Because it was easier to get a gun than to get help. He had a gun and he took seven innocent lives before taking his own. Daniel didn't even get the satisfaction of facing the man while he rotted in jail. Rage built again, and he fisted his hands. Annika took one of his fists in her hands, forcing him to look at her.

The rage melted away, and he dropped his head and shook away the tears that threatened his eyes again. "What if I had stayed? Just an extra twenty minutes?" His breath caught. "I could have saved them."

"Or you could have been killed with them."

The thought had occurred to him more than once. It didn't seem like the worst option.

He recalled being in the ER. His own voice seemed to be coming to him from far away as he tried to explain to Annika. "The next thing I knew, the ambulance was in the bay. Everyone was scurrying about—normal for the ER. I heard snippets—gunshot wound, child, school shooting—I didn't think anything of it, past what my job entailed, until they brought her in." He glanced up, trying to catch a glimpse of Annika's eyes, but tears pooled, blurring his vision. "I saw her—" his voice cracked and his knees buckled and nausea swept over him as if he was actually seeing her "—on the gurney." He could barely stand.

"The staff—they tried to keep me from her. But she was my little girl—I had to save her." He could still feel the strength in the hands and arms that had tried to restrain him—tried to keep me from his Sara. He had easily fought them off, colleagues or no. *That was his daughter.* "She looked like she was sleeping, but blood—was everywhere. The docs took her right back—I tried to follow, but I heard Sheila screaming for me. Somehow she had heard and came in after the ambulance." He could still hear her calling out his name. It was one of his recurring nightmares.

"Daniel—where is she? Where is she? Daniel, go fix her. Go fix her! Daniel!"

"I went to Sheila, because I couldn't let her see—and I knew. I knew—" His voice failed and his body was too heavy and his knees finally gave way as he fell onto them to the cold tile floor. He pressed his palms to his eyes as if he could press away the memory of that vision. "I couldn't let Sheila see what had happened to our little girl."

Soft fingers threaded into his hair. Annika skimmed his face with her fingers. Then she was kneeling in front of him. He kept his eyes shut to keep the tears away. He couldn't look at her.

She spoke so softly, her voice smooth, comforting. "Daniel, I'm so very sorry."

She took his face in her hands, and at her gentle touch, he broke. He couldn't fight the tears that he had kept at bay for five years. He kept his hands over his eyes as if he could stop them. But there was no stopping them now.

Annika pulled him closer to her. He rested his head on her shoulder as sobs racked his body. Visions of Sara's life came at him. Her birth, Sara crawling, toddling, falling, scraping a knee, going to school. All that and now she was gone. He cried for all the things Sara would never do: play soccer, dance, graduate high school, fall in love, get married. His heart broke again for everything that Sara lost, and with her, everything that he had lost, too.

Annika's fingers were soft and strong, offering soothing comfort. At some point, the waves calmed. Cool hands wiped his cheeks. Daniel hazarded a glance at her. Brown eyes swept across him like a comforting blanket, no accusation, no pity. It looked like love, but he couldn't be sure.

No one had looked at him like that in a very long time.

CHAPTER EIGHTEEN

ANNIKA

ANNIKA HELD DANIEL'S face in her hands. She used her thumbs to wipe away residual wetness as she held his gaze. The green she loved so much in his eyes was flecked with brown and even black.

He had been holding this inside him for five years. Trying to will it away, forcing normalcy into his life where there simply could be none.

This was why he had held her in the ER. She knew it, as if she'd always known it. He understood her pain. She had felt so empty, so lost after losing her baby. People had expected she would get over it and move on—after all, her baby hadn't even been born. But she had still felt the loss. Her heart ached for Daniel—he had actually held his child and watched her grow. He had seen himself in her.

"Who took care of you, Daniel? Who was there for you?" A day's worth of scruff was rough against her hands.

He shook his head, looked away from her and shrugged as if he didn't understand the question.

"You took care of Sheila." She couldn't move her hands from the curve of his jaw. They belonged there.

He nodded.

"Made all the…arrangements, handled the well-wishers. Made sure she ate?"

"That's what…men…do."

Realization hit her like a brick. "That's what your father says." Anger toward the older man flashed through her, followed quickly by pity, then sadness.

All this time, Daniel had kept his loss to himself. Provided and cared for someone else, never succumbing to his grief.

Until now.

His lips parted. "I'm sor—"

She stopped his apology with her fingers. "Don't." His gaze shifted to her mouth. Without thought, she straightened so she could reach him and gently placed her lips on his.

He moved slowly at first. Small tentative kisses, as if unsure what she wanted. She leaned closer to him, opening her mouth to him. His response to her invitation was immediate and frantic. His hands on either side of her head were strong yet gentle, and he pulled her close, moving his mouth on hers as if he were parched and she was water. He tasted smoky like the bourbon and smelled of leather and the outdoors. When he moved his body closer to her, she met him halfway, so not even air could get between them.

He released their kiss and placed hot full lips on the cool skin of her neck and she shivered, a small moan escaping her. She was losing herself in his touch. He pulled back, and Annika had to suppress a whimper. She opened her eyes and found him looking at her, his eyes hooded with desire. He touched his lips to hers again, gently to start, but Annika wanted more, and within seconds her need took over and she took his mouth with hers.

Daniel responded in kind. Every kiss, every touch was fueled by his passion and his grief. She recognized his need to *feel* something again as it mirrored her own need. She did not resist. She did not want to.

He stopped, resting his forehead against hers, his fingers in her hair, his breath coming hard and fast. "Tell me to stop."

Without breaking her gaze, she reached down, grabbed the hem of her T-shirt and yanked it over her head. "I don't want to stop." All of her fears and sorrows were at the surface. She wanted this. She needed *this man*.

This man, who not only had his sorrows but understood hers, and looked at her like she could fix everything. Maybe she could.

Her breath came heavy as she leaned toward him and slipped her thumb just under his shirt, rubbing his skin. She captured his groan in her mouth as she kissed him again. He reached over his head and pulled off his shirt, kissing her deeper and drawing her closer.

They were skin to skin, and she reveled in the closeness and the feel of hard muscle against her body. She drew her hand down his chest muscles, across his abs, stopping only to undo the button to his jeans. She looked him in the eye. "I'm not stopping."

His eyes darkened as he ran his hands down her sides, grazing the sides of her breasts, enticing her yet closer. He bent slightly and lifted her, turning, so when he laid her down, her bare back found plush carpet and not cold tile. She could feel his restraint as he gently kissed her face and neck.

"Daniel." She cupped his face in her hands and forced him to look at her. "Don't hold back." Breath escaped him as he closed his eyes and inhaled deeply. When he opened them again, they were loving, but hurt and angry all at the same time. She felt his grief, and she saw his healing. She brought his face to hers and kissed him fiercely with all the love she had. As if she could infuse love and strength into him with her kiss, and his pain would go away.

He responded with his mouth and hands roaming her body. He kissed her face, her neck, and when he approached her ear, he whispered, "You make me feel like I can breathe."

Annika gripped his bare shoulders, pulling him closer as she met his eyes once more. She'd never forget the way he looked at her right now. "So, breathe."

CHAPTER NINETEEN

DANIEL

WHEN DANIEL WOKE, it was to find himself pleasantly entangled in Annika's arms and legs. At some point they had made it to her bed, and he was surrounded by her scent, fruity and bold, uniquely Annika. She held him with a fierceness he had never known, and when he turned to her, he was met with big brown eyes and that sassy mouth curved into a smile. "Hey."

He turned and pulled her on top of him, where she leaned her forearms on his bare chest to look at him. "Hey, yourself."

"You're still here."

"Do you want me to leave?"

"Do you want to leave?"

"Not really."

"So, stay." She smiled. And he melted. "Daniel?"

"Hmm?"

"What happened after all that?" She looked him in the eye. "Did you ever talk to someone?"

"No, I—" He looked past her, up at the ceiling. "Sheila couldn't get out of bed for months. She stopped going to work, stopped seeing her friends, everything she loved." Annika shifted so she was lying next to him. He turned to face her. "I was the husband, the fath—" He shrugged.

"I took the job on the chopper. I cooked. Forced Sheila to eat. Paid the bills. That was my job." *That was what men did. They handled business. Right?*

"Yes, but didn't you go to therapy?"

"Who had time for that? Sheila's friends and sister all came by regularly to help her cope. She eventually saw a therapist."

"What about you?"

"I had my sister. She would bring food when I worked double shifts, but she would bring Charlie with her. Seeing him just reminded me of what Sara wasn't doing. What she would never do. So, she came less and less." He sighed and looked away. "She made me see a therapist. I went for a few months, but all they talked about was how I was supporting my wife."

"You drank."

"Yes." Most people had not been surprised to find him drunk more than a few times. "I drank. Just a little at first, but as time passed, two drinks became four, four became five or six or the whole bottle—and at some point, I realized that when I drank, I thought that Sara was still—" Tears burned again; he blinked them back. "But then when I sobered up, it was like losing her all over again."

He would wake up screaming Sara's name; Sheila would regress and fall apart into tears, inconsolable. For his part, he would be reliving the day she died every time he came to. "It had to stop." He met her eyes. Annika watched him, steady and sure, small flecks of gold in those healing brown eyes. He relaxed yet further under her loving gaze.

"That's why you stare at it."

He nodded. "After a while, I knew I had to either stay sober or stay drunk." He met her gaze. "It would have been easier to stay drunk, but Sheila wasn't functioning, so I couldn't lose my job. One of us had to keep it together. So, I stopped drinking." He sighed. "Honestly, if I hadn't felt like she needed me to be sober, I might still be drunk."

"So, what happened between you two?"

"A couple years later, Sheila wanted to have another baby." Anger welled up inside him as he remembered what had brought him here tonight. "But I didn't want to re-place Sara."

Annika placed her hand on his chest. He felt his heart hammer against the palm of her hand.

"She wanted another baby and I didn't, so she asked for a divorce. I just don't think it helped that Sara looked a bit like me." He gave a one-shouldered shrug. "I have days I can't look in the mirror, either."

"So now she's married to someone else and having a baby?"

Daniel nodded. He couldn't trust his voice.

"So?" Annika raised an eyebrow and appeared genu-inely confused.

"So...she can't replace Sara." Wasn't this obvious?

Annika raised herself onto one elbow, her voice soft and soothing. "She's not replacing her. She's giving her a sibling. She's moving on."

"How can she move on?" Daniel snapped.

"How can she not?" Annika challenged him, her tone even and without accusation.

Daniel was silent. He couldn't even consider moving on; he'd lose Sara all over again. But if Sheila was able to find happiness... His throat was tight, and his vision blurred again. "I just don't know what I'm supposed to do with the knowledge that Sara has a sibling in the world."

"What else did Sheila say?"

"She asked me to be the baby's godfather." He mumbled the words as if they were scandalous.

"That's not a bad thing."

He snapped his head to her in disbelief. "What do you mean?"

"I mean it gives you a chance to be involved, to be a part of Sara."

There was no way he could do that. Even the thought of that threatened to drag his heart down. He shook off the thought. He didn't want to think about that now. Not while he was here in the bed of the most beautiful woman he knew.

"You don't have to decide now." Annika forced him to look at her. "But you should talk to somebody. I know some people who can help you process—"

Daniel cut her off with a kiss. The last thing he needed or wanted was to have a standing appointment that required him to talk about Sara. "It's okay. I really don't want to talk about my ex-wife right now, do you? Because if you do, that's really weird." He ran his hands down her spine and thrilled at her moan as she pressed closer to him. This was what he needed. Just her. He hadn't had this lightness in his heart in a long time. That feeling that everything would be okay, that hint of a feeling that he could actually be happy. That he *was* happy.

She melted into his arms and wiggled closer to him. She grinned into his mouth. "Again?"

He kissed her neck, turned her onto her back and slowly, gently worked his way down, his mouth never leaving her skin. "And again. And again." He stole a sideways glance at her. "We have all night."

CHAPTER TWENTY

ANNIKA

"YOU'D REALLY UPSET Mrs. P. if she knew you could cook like this." Annika groaned in pleasure as she enjoyed another mouthful of the best omelet she'd ever had.

"Keep making sounds like that, and you may never get to finish it." Daniel kissed the back of her neck, sending warm shivers throughout her body.

They had spent the night alternately sleeping and making love, until, exhausted, Annika finally decided they needed to eat. It was early Saturday morning, and Naya was still at Ravi's.

Annika leaned back into his kiss and was rewarded with his hands on her body and hard muscle supporting her. She moaned again. "You'll get no argument from me." She was wearing his shirt, so Daniel was currently shirtless, his hair pleasantly rumpled and jeans slung low. As he came around to sit across from her, she couldn't complain about the view.

"Ha! You're the one who wanted to eat in the first place."

"You have a shift!" Annika said.

"That I do." He glanced at his phone. "But I still have time." He grinned wickedly at her. "Eat fast, you're wasting precious time."

"Why is your sister so worried about you eating when you can cook for yourself?"

Annika regretted the question immediately as his eyes darkened, and the sexy grin disappeared into sadness. "Because I don't usually have food in my fridge to cook. It's easier to grab something on the go. And besides—" his eyes lit up again "—I needed an excuse to show up at the bar to see you."

Annika relished the last bit of that omelet and gulped her coffee before going to him. He turned toward her in his chair; she brought her legs around him, straddling him. "I'm done."

"I thought you'd eat forever." His voice was oh so husky with desire for her, and she was heady with the effect she had on him. He wrapped strong calloused hands under her shirt and around her waist, kissing her like he hadn't spent the whole evening doing just that. And more. Annika was just surrendering to him when the door opened. Annika flew out of Daniel's lap and onto the floor, looking up to find Naya standing in the doorway.

Naya's eyes widened and then quickly scrunched shut. "Oh, God. Oh, God. I'm sorry. I swear I didn't see anything."

Annika scrambled to standing. Naya opened one eye slowly.

"It's fine, Naya." Annika smiled. "We're dressed." She glanced at Daniel, who widened his eyes at her. She shifted so she stood in front of him, partially blocking him from view. "Well, sort of."

Naya opened her other eye and tilted her head to peek behind Annika. Her eyes widened again before she quickly shifted her gaze to Annika. "Daniel?" she stage-whispered, as if Daniel couldn't hear them.

Annika flushed and glared at Naya. Daniel chuckled softly behind her as he stood up and waved, grinning. "Hey, Naya. Your timing is impeccable—every time."

It was Naya's turn to flush as she waved back. "Yeah, sorry about that."

Awkward silence floated around for a beat until Naya spoke. "Yeah. So, I'll just pop into my room and grab a few things. I'll be gone before you know it."

"No. It's fine. Daniel has a shift soon anyway. No need to run off."

"Yeah, don't run off on my account." But he didn't move.

Naya looked at both of them and raised her eyebrows. "Uh-huh. Okay." She bolted for her room.

"I should go." He looked down at her as he placed a hand on either side of her face.

"You'll need your shirt."

"That I will." He smirked at her as he kissed her and started to unbutton the shirt.

"She'll be out any minute."

"I doubt that," Daniel managed between kisses. "We've scared her off."

"True." She led him back to her room. "But I need clothes, and you really do have to go."

AFTER DANIEL LEFT, she showered and changed and grabbed a fresh cup of coffee before peeking into her cousin's room. Naya was putting away clean laundry.

"Hey." Annika brought the warm mug of coffee to her lips and sipped.

Naya looked up at her, tight-lipped. "Hey, yourself."

Okay. Annika flushed. "So… Ravi, huh?"

Naya couldn't meet her eyes, and Annika swore she saw her cousin swoon. She'd never seen Naya quite so smitten.

Naya looked at her and tried to shrug casually but failed as giggles escaped her mouth. "Are you giggling?"

Naya shook her head as she continued to giggle. "I know it seems weird, we haven't known each other that long, but we...fit. He's easy. And I've never been so comfortable to just be myself with someone, you know?"

She did know.

"And the thing is...he feels the same way." She giggled again.

Naya's laughter was contagious, and Annika found herself giggling along with her cousin. "So...maybe he's the one?"

Naya shrugged. "What about you? Pretty hot rebound guy you've got yourself."

All the lightness in Annika's heart fell into her belly with a thud. Rebound guy? Is that what Daniel was?

Naya stared at her. "He *is* the rebound guy. You know that, right?"

When she didn't answer, Naya pressed on. "He's the guy who helps you get the asshole out of your system. He's not the settle-down guy."

"I know what a rebound guy is," she snapped back, not bothering to hide her irritation.

Naya held up her hands in surrender and actually looked at her with *pity*. "We've discussed this. Your parents will never go for it."

Annika opened her mouth to protest, but Naya cut her off. "Why put them through that? Why put yourself through that? They think you should be with Sajan, and after the Steven fiasco, you're not going to convince them otherwise."

"They'll never trust my judgment."

Naya nodded, shrugging. "Maybe trying it their way will work. Plus, it's not like you needed this guy for more than that anyway, right? And it's not like you can trust him."

"Sure, right." Annika forced a smile onto her face, but a deep pit formed in her stomach. Daniel didn't feel like the rebound guy. Not at all.

CHAPTER TWENTY-ONE

DANIEL

WHAT EXACTLY WAS the protocol after you bared your soul to someone? As Daniel finished his shift, he found himself automatically heading toward Annika's apartment instead of his own. He had hated having to leave her to go to work, and he couldn't wait to see her again, so it seemed only logical to go back to her apartment. But she wouldn't have stayed in her apartment waiting for him—that was ridiculous. She had two jobs and a life.

Truth was, Daniel couldn't remember the last time he had looked forward to going anywhere. He had been alone in his grief, and when he wasn't working, his mind would wander to painful corners. Work kept him away from those corners. So, he worked. And worked more, with the goal of coming home so completely exhausted that he simply fell directly into sleep.

But now, there was *her*. She kept those painful corners far from him, and he couldn't wait to get back to her. It was more than just not being alone. For the first time in years he felt the desire to be in someone's company. He didn't just *want* to know everything about her—he *needed* to know. He wanted to take his time learning about her, savoring her. While he couldn't wait to get back to her, he wished time would stand still when they were together.

Emma's voice came unbidden into his head. *You want a relationship.*

He did. No one was more surprised than he was.

He had left her Saturday morning for his shift. It was currently Saturday evening. Date night.

When he pulled up in front of her apartment building and saw that her car was still parked there, his stomach did a little flip. Before he could think too much about it, he found himself knocking on her door. He heard footsteps and a slight pause as she looked through the peephole— he hoped. He really had to talk to her about the lack of security in this building. After what felt like an eternity, the door opened, but instead of the warm brown eyes he craved, he was met with cold gray ones.

"Hey." Naya pursed her lips as she examined him. "You're back."

"Yeah." He looked past Naya into the apartment to catch of glimpse of Annika, but nothing. "Is she here?"

Naya stepped aside to let him in. "Yep. She has a shift soon, though. She's in the shower."

The friendly Naya of his last few encounters seemed to be missing, replaced by this distant version. "Is everything okay?" Daniel ventured as he walked past her into the apartment.

Naya looked him up and down, and Daniel had the distinct impression of being assessed. She frowned. "Listen, she's been through a lot."

He turned to face Naya. "I know." He thought he knew where this was going. "I made a mistake, not telling her how I knew her, and I don't intend on doing anything else to hurt her."

This earned him a small smile. "I understand that, but that's not what I mean." She paused and took a deep breath.

"I mean, she's been through a lot, and what she needs is stability. Someone she can rely on." She focused her gaze on him.

Daniel felt his stomach drop. "Yeah?" Not going where he thought it would.

"Well, you're divorced. You have a questionable relationship with alcohol. It's not like you're a successful surgeon who—" Naya stopped abruptly as if she'd revealed too much.

"Wow. Say what you mean, don't hold back. I may not be *Dr. Sajan Shah*—" he raised an eyebrow and pointedly paused at the name, causing Naya to flush "—but I care about Annika, and I would never hurt her. And besides, she hasn't really shown any interest in Sajan, has she?" The last bit came out a bit cockier than he'd intended, but there was a significant part of him that worried that maybe she would be better off with the good surgeon.

"Hasn't she?" Naya raised an eyebrow at him.

A vise gripped his heart, and before he could respond, Annika stepped out of the bathroom in nothing but a thigh-length bathrobe, and Daniel lost the ability to speak. Her hair was damp and wavy, her skin glowed and what he could see of her long legs was enough to bring him back to his knees.

Annika's face and eyes lit up as they landed on him, and he knew he had made the right choice coming here. "Hey, you."

It was all the invitation he needed. In two steps, he was in front of her, his lips pressed against hers. He put everything he felt into that kiss. How much he needed her. How she was saving him. He kissed her as if he hadn't seen her in ten years, instead of ten hours. In return, he found no doubt in her kiss. She wanted *him*.

Any doubt Naya had placed in front of him was gone. There was no way Annika could kiss him like this and still want another man. Handsome surgeon or not.

"Ahem."

Annika pulled back slowly but stayed in his arms. They turned to face Naya. "Yes?"

"You're going to make out while I'm standing right here?" Her previous chill had warmed some, though Daniel was sure it wasn't all gone.

"Well, it saves you having to walk in on us." Daniel grinned at her.

Though she tried to fight it, Naya smiled at him. "I suppose I should be grateful for that." Her phone buzzed and she glanced at it. "That would be Ravi." She grabbed her coat and bag and headed toward the door. Just as she opened it, she turned back to them. "Hey, Chopper Guy. Remember what I said."

Daniel nodded, and Naya left.

"What is she talking about? What did she say to you?"

"Nothing, really."

Annika narrowed her eyes at him. "She called you the rebound guy, didn't she?"

Daniel widened his eyes and shook his head. "No."

Annika's mouth formed an O, like she realized she shouldn't have spoken.

"Am I?" His mouth went dry as he realized right then that there was no way he could stand it if he was just the guy who prepped her for the next guy. For Sajan. He wanted more than that. It scared the crap out of him, but he couldn't imagine not being with her. "The rebound guy?"

She was silent a moment as she studied his face, then stepped back to look at all of him. "You're wearing the same clothes as this morning."

So what? Why wouldn't she answer the question? "Yeah, well. I haven't been home yet."

She smirked at him, and he was reminded of when he met her at the bar that first time, and something inside him loosened. She led him to the sofa. "So you left here, went to work, then came straight here from the hospital?"

He sat down next to her. "Yes."

She kneeled on the sofa, facing him, a smile spreading across her face. "That's what I was hoping you'd say." She leaned into him and pressed her lips to his, opening her mouth to him. "You are so *not* the rebound guy."

Daniel lifted her to his lap. "Thank God," he managed between kissing her. He groaned and pulled her closer. "Damn, I missed you."

Annika pulled back, mischief in her eyes. She loosened the belt around her bathrobe, letting it fall open. "I have a couple of hours before my shift. Prove it."

"I HAVE TO SAY, I'm loving this." Emma beamed as Daniel and Annika entered her home. Christmas lights were up outside, and inside, the tree held a place of honor in the corner of the main room. Stockings decorated the mantelpiece, one for each family member, including him. Small ceramic houses with little lights made a small village on an end table, and every other surface was adorned with either a Santa statue or a reindeer or a snowman. In short, Christmas had thrown up all over his sister's house, as it did every year right after Thanksgiving. In fact, Emma pretty much overdecorated for every holiday. Good thing Annika had missed the Diwali explosion. He smiled to himself. God, he missed hanging out with his sister.

"I just saw you at the kid's party." Daniel hugged his sister.

"That was before Thanksgiving! But two times in three weeks is a goddamn record for you, Danny." She pulled Annika in for a hug. "Great to see you again, too."

"Em, can we kill the 'Danny' shit?"

She simply shrugged and waved him off. Apparently not.

"Something smells amazing." Annika inhaled deeply.

"Come on into the kitchen. Michael's pouring wine." Emma hesitated a beat as she took coats and flicked her gaze Daniel's way.

"It's fine, Em. I can have a glass of wine." Wine didn't affect him like bourbon did.

She looked doubtful but said nothing more about it.

Daniel took Annika's hand as they walked into the kitchen. From the slightly amused look that passed between Emma and Michael as he handed them wine, Daniel knew they had been talking about him and Annika before they arrived.

"You did a wonderful job with those cabinets for Phil's Place, Michael. They're beautiful." Annika sipped her wine as she and Michael discussed carpentry while Emma fussed over the food.

Daniel inhaled deeply, taking in the savory aromas of roasted garlic and tomatoes. It took him back in time. "Remember when we tried to teach the kids how to cook?" He blurted out the words without thought.

Emma froze mid-stir, her eyes wide and confused. Michael had also turned to him, frozen midsentence. Annika also stopped, her wineglass halfway to her mouth.

"What did you say?" Emma found her voice first.

"I said—"

"No, I heard you. You've just never— I mean…you said…*kids*." She let out a breath on the last word, almost as if she were afraid to say it herself. Tears swam in her eyes, a small smile breaking through.

Daniel let out a breath, as well. He had referred to *kids*. He wasn't even thinking about it—the words had just come from a very happy memory. "I guess I did." He let out a breath and smiled at his sister. The memory was of teaching three-year-olds Charlie and Sara how to stir sauce. Nothing major, just him and his sister and their children enjoying a quiet evening at home. The memory warmed him.

"You haven't… I mean…it's a memory…from…" Emma dropped what she was doing and came over to Daniel, tears in her eyes, and hugged him.

Daniel chuckled and hugged her back. "From before." That's how life was divided for him. Before Sara and after Sara. "I know. It's weird…"

Emma pulled back and looked up at him, tears shamelessly running down her face. "Well, I certainly remember it. They made a huge mess!" She laughed and glanced at Annika over Daniel's shoulder before gazing back at her brother and wiping her eyes. "Seems like things might be looking up for you."

Daniel turned to look at Annika, who also had tears shining in her eyes, and she'd never looked more beautiful. This woman was incredible. Just being near her made him feel more whole than he had in five years.

Emma squeezed his arm and let go, a smile still on her face, though Daniel thought he may have caught a glimpse of concern in her eyes.

"Come, let's sit by the fire. Dinner will be a bit." Emma grabbed her glass of wine and took Michael's hand. Daniel took Annika's hand and led the way.

He sat next to Annika on the sofa and sipped his wine, letting the alcohol warm him, before placing the glass down and resting his arm around Annika's shoulder. She continued her conversation with Michael but leaned back slightly into Daniel, pressing her body into his chest. It was tantalizing and reassuring and loving all at once, and it confirmed for Daniel in that moment that he was home. She was the reason he could remember Sara without breaking down. She was his home.

Daniel relaxed for what felt like the first time in years. Annika was beside him, smiling and laughing, her hand occasionally grazing his thigh or arm, and the jolt he felt from that went beyond simple desire into pure happiness. It was clear that his sister and brother-in-law were both quite taken with Annika. And with good reason.

While Annika and Michael discussed the latest movie they'd each seen, Emma rose and asked Daniel to help her in the kitchen. Daniel nearly refused as he suspected what was on her mind, but Emma's face made it clear he was coming to the kitchen.

Once in the kitchen, Emma shut the door and checked on the homemade lasagna. Stalling.

"I know what you're going to say, Emma."

"Hmm. Do you? Then why do I have to say it?"

Daniel shrugged. "You don't."

"Don't be a wiseass. You know you have to tell her."

"I told her about…Sara." He had to pause before saying her name, and the sound of it weighed on his heart.

"Did you tell her all of it? The fallout?"

"No." He looked away from her piercing gaze.

"Don't you look away from me, Daniel Bliant. You're lying to that poor girl, leading her on. She clearly cares about you. I haven't seen you look at a woman like that— ever. Not even Sheila."

"It's fine, Em."

"How can you say that? Have you changed your mind? Are you willing to become a father again someday?"

"Sure."

"*Sure?* That's your answer?" Emma's eyes grew wide and slightly dangerous. "What the hell kind of answer is that, Danny?"

"Didn't you see how I was able to remember Sa—her—just a bit ago?" Damn it, why was it so hard to say her name?

"Yes, I did." Emma softened, her tone revealing that she noticed her brother's struggle. "Don't get me wrong, that's wonderful. And if she's helping to bring that out in you, I'm all for it. But Danny, there's a big difference between remembering Sara for a moment and becoming a father again. I'm all for you having more children one day—I just don't know if you're ready for it. You need to talk to—"

"Don't say I need to talk to somebody. I tried that. It doesn't work for me. *Working*, staying busy, that works for me."

"Says our father."

Daniel clenched his jaw. "Says me."

Emma stared him down the way only big sisters could. Daniel didn't want to argue with her. He softened. "Em, when I'm with her, I'm better. When I'm with her, I can actually be around children again. We've just barely started dating. Who knows where this goes?"

"I'm just saying it's not fair to her."

He stepped closer to his sister and took her hands. "I won't hurt her." A little voice in the back of his head chided him. He ignored it.

"Hey, you two! Are we eating tonight or what?" Michael and Annika entered the kitchen carrying the empty cheese board and wineglasses.

Emma put on her biggest smile and directed it toward Annika. "We're ready. Annika, grab the salad while these two refill our glasses." Annika brushed past Daniel to get to the salad, and as he inhaled her familiar, comforting scent, he knew what he had told his sister was true. He could do anything with this woman by his side. Anything.

CHAPTER TWENTY-TWO

ANNIKA

"WHAT'S THE SECURITY like when you go in early?" Daniel's face was grim, and it was the first time he had even referenced her school in any way. They talked plenty about her teaching and the class, but never about exactly where she went.

He was getting ready to leave her apartment for the ER night shift, so he wouldn't see her before she left in the morning to get to school early for Parents' Visitation. She looked up from where she was putting final touches on the week's lesson plan.

"A security officer will walk me to the classroom and clear it before returning to his post in the front of the school." She was very matter-of-fact. Daniel simply needed to know she was safe. He'd offered to take her to school, but he had a shift, not to mention he'd have to enter the building. And if his face was any indication, he was not up for that task.

"A rent-a-cop or a real live police officer?"

Her phone chirped. She ignored it.

"A police officer." She knew where this was coming from, and to be honest, as a teacher these days, one would have to be irresponsible to not consider the reality of what was happening in the world around them. But Annika did not live her life in fear. She was cautious and careful, but not fearful.

He nodded, his mouth downturned, eyes grim, clearly not convinced. "Can you text me when you get there? And when you get home?"

"You sound like my parents. They made me do that my whole first month."

Daniel did not comment. Clearly, he thought that was a completely reasonable response.

"I'll be fine." She put aside her papers and walked over to him. "Daniel." She wrapped her arms around him. His body was a rock. Not that she ever found his body soft, but he was completely rigid. "Daniel. Look at me."

"You're going *early*." Fear and apprehension widened his eyes as he implored her to understand what he wasn't saying.

She softened, squeezed him tight. "Okay. I'll text you. I promise."

Her phone chirped again.

Daniel smiled. It was forced, she knew, but he was trying. "Better check that."

She picked up her phone. Text from Sajan. No problem! I'd be happy to come for Career Day at your school.

She smiled. Career Day was months away, but he'd already said yes to her request.

"Good news?" Daniel was gathering his things.

"Yes. Sajan can do Career Day. So I can check 'doctor' off the list." She grinned.

"That's great." His smile may have faltered a bit, but he was supremely worried about her day tomorrow.

She stepped closer to kiss him. "Now, go. Save lives."

DANIEL STILL REFUSED to talk to a therapist, insisting he was fine now that he had Annika. And while that warmed her heart, it also scared her. Not dealing with such a loss could do things to a person. Destructive things.

Though, to his credit, no matter how often Annika broached the subject of therapy, Daniel never asked if she had told her parents about him. "All in good time" was Annika's approach. All this with Daniel was so new; she didn't really know where it was going. And really, why tell them if she didn't have a plan?

Annika was up early that next morning to get to school and set up for her first ever Parents' Visitation. A glance outside confirmed the light January snowfall that had been predicted, but nothing was sticking, so it would be school as usual. Parents' Visitation was the day all the parents came to the classroom to observe their children. She had discussed this with the children, how they were supposed to do their work like normal, so their parents could see how well they worked in school. Annika couldn't help but feel that the success of this day was a reflection of her abilities as a teacher, so she wanted to be there early enough to get things together and gather herself.

She was particularly concerned about Mitch, the little boy who would not speak or interact with the other children. He'd been evaluated and had exhausted the school's considerable resources but still was not showing improvement at school. She'd had a meeting with Mitch's mother and learned that he spoke nonstop at home. Annika had done some research and had requested an IEP meeting, which would involve the parents and school officials. The meeting was for tomorrow.

Her heels clacked loudly in the empty hallway, and had she been alone, she might have found it eerie. But she was accompanied by the soft-shoed officer who patrolled the school. Police presence had become commonplace at the school, and she generally did not spend too much time concerned about it. But with Daniel's concerns fresh on her mind, she looked at the school through different eyes as she followed procedure and walked behind Officer Keely.

"Big day today?" Officer Keely grinned at her.

"Does it show? I'm more nervous than I've ever been."

Officer Keely chuckled and shook his head as they reached her classroom. "You'll be great, Ms. Mehta. The kids love you. I've heard talk around the school that every one of your kids loves you the best."

Annika inhaled deeply and smiled at the man. He was probably about her age and wore a wedding band. Putting himself in harm's way for the school. For the children. For her. The thought made her shudder. "Thanks for saying that. I appreciate it."

Officer Keely walked into her classroom while she waited at the door. This was protocol now. Her heart grew heavy as she glanced down the familiar hallway and into her classroom. She had still been a student in teachers college watching the news in horror as grim journalists covered the shooting that had ripped terror through this place. The walls had been repainted, repairs had been done and Officer Keely had been employed.

Teachers should not have to be concerned with gunmen while trying to develop the minds of the future. Children should not have to learn drills in case of an active shooter. Parents should not have to consider purchasing bulletproof backpacks for their children's protection. Annika shuddered at the thought that there even existed such a thing as a bulletproof backpack. Children shouldn't die because they had wanted to give their teacher a homemade birthday card.

Officer Keely flicked on the lights, looked around and must have found everything in order, because he beckoned her in.

The name of the school had been fresh enough in her parents' minds that when she was offered the job here, they were solidly against it. She'd taken the job anyway. Hence the texting. She really did not do things that made her parents' lives easier, did she? She pulled out her phone and texted Daniel.

I'm at school. Safe and sound.

The response was almost immediate.

OK. Great. I'll see you at Phil's. Good luck!

She could almost hear his sigh of relief.

It was no wonder Daniel had suggested the fire station instead of coming to the school. How could he ever enter this building again? Tears burned at her eyes, and her heart ached for him.

"I only hope you're still teaching here when my little one enters kindergarten."

Annika's eyes flew open. "Meg is pregnant?"

He nodded, his happy grin filling his face.

"That is fantastic news! Congratulations!"

"Thank you. Well, you have a great day, Ms. Mehta. I'm sure all will go well."

She watched Officer Keely leave and then turned to her classroom. The chairs were arranged in a circle for circle time, then the children would put them with the desks that were in groups of four around the room at different stations. There was the reading-writing area, the math area, the science area and the history area. Each area had materials for the children to use and work on. Annika would go over the lesson for each area, and the children would rotate throughout the morning. The feeling was almost Montessori, but it wasn't true Montessori, as she—and not the students—determined when the children moved on to the next area.

Today they would work on the letter *F*, learn addition using beads, color frogs in science and build log cabins like Abraham Lincoln's. She made sure each station had all the supplies it needed and all was ready to go when her first students started trickling in. The parents were asked to stay in the office until all the children had arrived and were ready for the circle.

There was a spark in the air as the children hung up their coats and found their way to the circle. Having your parents watch you was very exciting, and the children seemed to have extra energy and were more than a little bit chatty. The buzz of chatter, and the scraping of chairs and extra loud squeals of delight were no match for Annika. Her heart broke for the children whose parents would be unable to attend today. She hugged away frowns and tears and assured them they could take work home to show their parents tonight. She handled all of that with calm and ease. They were children, after all, and excitement was part of the job description.

Eventually, even the most rambunctious of the group found their way to the circle, and to Annika's delight, they were right on schedule. Everyone sat quietly for the morning announcements and the special welcome for the parents. She began her address to the students just as the parents filed in and took their seats in the back of the room. Annika relished the fact that not one of the students turned their heads to look. They went over the date, the weather and the lessons for the day. She gave each student a schedule of their day, so they would know which station to go to and so they wouldn't be with the same children all day.

She dismissed them to their first lesson, and each child took his or her chair with him to the desks that were at the stations. At the reading-writing station, two students accidentally banged chairs. It happened at least once a day and was never really a problem. Both children giggled and apologized and went about their business. Annika sighed. Perfect.

She assessed the room and found one child struggling with his chair. It happened every day, and Annika let him be, because he always made it and consequently felt good about himself. Today, the child's mother stood and helped him bring the chair over.

"I can do it, Mom," Jeff insisted, throwing the other children a furtive glance, as none of the other parents were helping their children.

Annika stepped in. "Mrs. Delancey, Jeff moves his chair every day and is quite successful. I'm sure if you watched, you'd be proud."

"Ms. Mehta." Mrs. Delancey's eyes were hard. "If you're telling me that Jeff struggles like this every day, and no one helps him, I am appalled. It's too big for him."

"Mrs. Delancey, please, give him a chance. If we find he's still struggling, I'll move the chair myself."

Mrs. Delancey pressed her lips together and raised an eyebrow, but she took a step back and waited. Sure enough, Jeff managed to move his chair where it needed to be. He turned and beamed at his mother, who softened instantly and gave her son a double thumbs-up, and a small concil-iatory nod to Annika.

Crisis averted. Things were going smoothly. Annika smiled to herself, proud that her children were doing so well. She relaxed.

That was her first mistake.

Annika had barely sighed relief when loud voices erupted from across the room.

She turned to find two girls screaming at each other. Ashley, her dark locks shaking with indignation, was screaming at Miranda, who was wailing with her little fists balled at her sides.

"You took my spot, Ashley!"

"You grabbed the green pencil from me!"

"Did not. I don't even like your stupid pencil."

"My pencil is not stupid!" Ashley stamped her foot and shoved Miranda before Annika could get over to them.

Before Annika could do anything, both Ashley's and Miranda's mothers were at their daughters' sides.

Miranda's mother clutched her daughter, soothing her while Ashley's mother tried to explain that we do not shove, even if the other person uses bad words. Jeff, of the successful chair move, was currently drawing on the little boy next to him, who had started to cry.

Both girls' mothers were glaring darts at each other, and now the other children started crying from all the com-motion in the room.

Annika tried to pacify each child in turn but to no avail, and the parents were turning on her faster than anything. Out of the corner of her eye, she caught Mitch edging his way toward the back wall, away from the commotion, his eyes wide with fear. Mitch's father was glaring at her, a level of superior satisfaction emitting from his smile.

Now all of the parents of the crying children were trying simultaneously to calm their children and chastise Annika for losing control in the first place. Miranda's and Ashley's mothers had now started yelling at each other, and more than one parent was asking Annika what the hell was going on. In the midst of all this, her classroom phone rang. She glanced in its direction and then promptly ignored it. Another child had decided to simply lie on the floor and scream.

Annika stood in the middle of the room and clapped out a pattern. Mayhem continued. She clapped it out again. A couple of children copied her. She did it again, and some of the crying stopped and a few more children answered. She did it again and again, until all of the children answered her and the crying had stopped. She continued the pattern as she went to the closet and pulled out a colorful parachute. She handed each child a part of it, until they all stood in a circle, and then she engaged them in play.

"Ms. Mehta."

Annika snapped to attention as the principal entered the room.

"Mrs. Colter," she addressed the principal, "if you would be so kind as to escort our parents to the cafeteria for a coffee break, the children and I have some regrouping to do." Many of the parents were reluctant to allow Annika to do anything with their children, but the principal seemed to have decided to give Annika a chance to regain her classroom, and she encouraged the parents to come with her. Annika saw the disappointment in their eyes and in the set of their mouths. She did her best to ignore it all.

As the principal left, she whispered to Annika, "We called to tell you your father is here."

Annika snapped her head to the principal. "He was here?"

"He's still here."

Annika nodded. "I can't come now."

The principal nodded. "Of course."

"Bring the parents back in ten minutes."

The principal nodded.

It was in that moment that Annika made eye contact with Mitch's mother. She wished she hadn't. The look of disappointment and disgust on the woman's face was enough to have Annika curling up into a ball on the floor herself. Instead, she felt the old hospital band in her pocket, plastered a smile on her face, found her happiest singsong voice and turned to her class.

"Okay, who's ready to run under the parachute?"

In a clattering of shoes and grumbled mutterings, the parents left with the principal as she regained control over her classroom.

By the time the principal returned with the parents, the children were so engaged in their work they hardly noticed the reentry of their parents. Annika immersed herself in teaching the children and was barely aware of the parental presence herself.

Thankfully, today was a half day, and when the morning finally ended, the children went home with their parents. It took Annika close to an hour to straighten up her classroom, after which she worked on mid-year assessments.

It was late afternoon before she remembered that her father had been at the school. She called him.

He answered on the first ring.

"Papa? I heard you were at the school today. Is everything okay?"

"Yes, I came to see what you did." His voice was clipped.

"Uh-huh." She wasn't going to ask. She didn't need to.

"I heard the parents complaining about you. About how you lost control of the classroom."

"Mmm-hmm."

He sighed, his frustration and irritation with her clear. "Maybe if you listened to us, did what we said, you wouldn't keep finding yourself in situations you can't handle."

Her heart sank, but her anger raged. She was tired of trying to make people happy. "I did handle it, Papa," she snapped. "You just didn't hang around long enough to see that."

Her hands shook as she disconnected the call.

What was the point of trying to please people who would never see it? It didn't matter how good she was—they would *always* think teaching was beneath her. She thought of Daniel. Wait until they found out she was with Daniel, and not Sajan. She didn't care if they approved. There was no point in trying to make them happy. Even if they were her parents.

CHAPTER TWENTY-THREE

DANIEL

HE KNEW AS soon as she walked into the bar that something was wrong. The quiet, calm feeling he would get when he saw her floated away as he noted the stiffness in her body, the set of her lips. Her face lit up for a brief moment before it slowly clouded over, and damn if he wouldn't do whatever it took to fix whatever had put that sadness in her eyes. The fatigue he felt after an overtime, overnight shift melted away in an instant, as his focus became only her.

She walked to the back to put away her stuff as she always did. Daniel followed.

"Hey. How did it go?" Her back was to him, and when she turned to look at him, her face crumpled. He pulled her into his arms, and she buried her face into his chest.

"It was awful. The kids fought, the parents fought. The principal came. It was awful."

"At Parents' Visitation? The parents fought?" Comical images filled his head, but Daniel suppressed his chuckle as Annika was clearly distressed, and comical though it may be, parents fighting was never good. Daniel kissed the top of her head and stroked her hair. "I'm sure you regained control, and all ended well."

She shook her head without looking up. "Nope. The

principal had to come take the parents while I took care of the kids."

"Well, you handled the kids."

She pulled back and looked up at him. "My dad was there." Tears fell from her eyes. This was the real problem. Daniel's heart dropped into his stomach.

"What do you mean he was there? How could he get to the classroom?" Daniel may not have gone back to the school, but he had attended every board meeting until certain policies were put in place. The main one being that no one, *no one*, went near the classrooms without an escort.

"No, he didn't get to come back. He was waiting in the office. He heard the parents complaining while they waited for me to regain control." Annika sighed. "They pretty much blamed me for everything."

Daniel knew that Annika wanted nothing more than to impress her parents. Which was part of the reason she was afraid to tell them about him. He pushed that thought aside for now.

A sob escaped her, and Daniel found himself angry at her father for not believing in her. "So now he's confident that I'm a failure." She sniffled.

"You're not a failure. You're a great teacher."

"You don't know that." She burrowed deeper into his chest. He wrapped his arms around her, trying to protect her. But her pain came from within.

"Well, not firsthand, but you're good at everything."

She pulled back to give him a withering look.

"Fine." He pulled her close again. "I don't *actually* know, but…" He paused, holding her tight. Why shouldn't he actually know? He could go to the school, as an observer, or for Career Day. He knew she was great, but maybe she would believe him if he actually saw her teach.

"Fine, I'll come for Career Day. Talk about how awesome it is to be an NP." He spoke quickly, before he changed his mind. How was he going to walk into that building?

Annika tensed and pulled back. "No. You don't want to do that."

"Why not?"

"You do remember where I work?" She stared at him. "I never should have told you Sajan was coming—"

"This has nothing to do with Sajan." Well, mostly nothing. His stomach was in knots, but at the moment he didn't care. He placed his hand on the side of her head. "I would do anything for you." It was completely true. It didn't matter about the building. He would do anything to make her happy. "I love you."

"But Daniel, you don't have to—wait, what did you say?" Her nose and eyes were swollen and red rimmed, her cheeks were flushed, but she smiled and looked at him with such pure love that he wanted to freeze that moment in time.

Heat rose to his face. "I said I would come to Career—"

"No, not that."

A silly, dopey grin took over his face. "I said that I love you."

She gave him her crooked smile. "This was the most romantic way you could think of to tell me you loved me?" She looked around. "Standing in the back of a bar while I cry?"

"It's perfect." Daniel leaned down and kissed her. "Don't complain. I said I would come to your class."

She pulled back. "You don't have to…just the offer is enough…"

"I'll be fine." Of course he would. The building haunted

his nightmares, but for her, for the woman he loved, he'd figure out a way to walk into it. "Besides, little boys should know that nurse practitioner is an option, don't you think?" *Not just surgeon.* Jealousy did not look good on him, and he needed to let that go.

"Well, sure, of course. But I don't want you to do anything you aren't ready for."

"I'm ready." He ignored the panic that streaked through his body at just the *thought* of entering that school.

She pulled back from him and studied his face, no doubt looking for anything that would tell her he wasn't ready to go back into the building where he had last seen his daughter alive. He simply focused on how much he loved her. On how it broke his heart to see her unhappy. On how he didn't even really care that she didn't tell her parents about him, because he was willing to take any part of her she was willing to give.

"Daniel…"

"I got customers here, Anni," Phil bellowed from out front.

Daniel pursed his mouth in amusement and tilted his head toward the front. "You better go. You may need this job after that fiasco today."

She lightly smacked his arm as she narrowed her eyes at him, her grin poking through despite her efforts to hide it. "Ha ha. And you say you love me."

"But I do." He stroked her cheek with his thumb, getting lost once again in those brown eyes. He slowly drew his thumb over her bottom lip, before leaning down to gently suck it into his mouth. Her hiss of breath was all the encouragement he needed to open her mouth and deepen their kiss. She moved closer to him, whispering his name, and for a moment he forgot where they were.

"Anni, let's go!" Even Phil's bellow did not have the power to shake them from each other, though Annika did pull back.

They were both a bit dizzy from lack of oxygen when he let her go. Her lips were swollen and her eyes were glassy when they met his.

She straightened out her apron and cleared her throat. "Okay, then."

Daniel swore she wobbled a bit as she headed out front. He was an idiot to even entertain jealousy.

Maybe he'd drop a hint to Nilay to have their father stop by the classroom on Career Day. He could finally see what a fabulous teacher his daughter was.

DANIEL MOVED AROUND his small kitchen with comfort and ease, as if he'd been cooking here all his life, when the truth was, he couldn't remember the last time he'd actually done anything more than nuke something. Tonight was different. A new beginning all around. He'd bought food to fill and stock his refrigerator as well as his pantry. He even had wineglasses and wine to fill them.

As he cooked, he paused to hit the FaceTime button on his phone. "Hey, Em," he said as she picked up.

"Danny! What's up?" She was half-off the screen, as she was clearly cooking, as well. "You know all I can see is the fridge, right?"

Daniel paused in front of his phone. "Hey. I'm putting away groceries. Remember that chicken Mom used to make with the sauce and—"

"You bought groceries?" She had stopped whatever she was doing, and now her face filled the screen.

"Yes, I bought groceries." He held up his hands like he couldn't imagine why that should surprise her.

"Wow, Danny, that's awesome."

"Focus, Em. The saucy-chicken recipe?"

"You're going to make it?"

"Again with the surprised face. Yes, Emma. I. Am. Cooking. Dinner."

She grinned, a knowing—and annoying—twinkle in her eye. "For Annika."

Nothing got past her. Though this wasn't that hard. "Maybe."

"Danny—" she squealed, like only a big sister could.

"Daniel."

"Whatever. This is for real, isn't it?" Emma's voice got serious.

"I'm making dinner."

"Did you tell her?"

"Tell her what?" He turned away from the phone to put vegetables in the fridge.

"Daniel. You know exactly what I'm talking about." Her voice took on that big-sister tone he was so familiar with.

"Now you call me Daniel."

"Did you tell her you won't be a father again?" Emma's stern face filled his phone screen.

"No need."

"Daniel Bliant. Do not lead that girl on. You're clearly involved with her if you are actually buying groceries and cooking for her. She has a right to know that parenting is not something you can handle. I mean, you can barely handle pediatric patients."

"Em. It's a nonissue. I can do it."

"What do you mean you can do it? Do what? Be a father?" She paused for breath, her disbelief oozing through the screen.

He thought about Annika and how she had brought

lightness to his life these past few weeks. He thought about how he missed her when he went to work. How he couldn't wait to come back to her after every shift. How she made him feel invincible.

He had avoided doing a double shift in the past few weeks just so he'd have time to see her. He tried to work when she was working so they could be together when they were off. He was even going to cut his chopper shift down to one a week. His colleagues were giving him crap about being lazy these days.

He needed her. And she needed him. If that meant he would have to be a father again, then so be it.

"Yes, Em. That's what I am saying."

"Danny, are you sure?" All the disbelief was gone from her face, and she was in full concerned big-sister mode.

"Yes, I'm sure." There was a slight pit in his stomach, but he ignored it. "I'd do anything for her." Even walk into that school building again. He had meant it when he told Annika he would come to school for Career Day.

Silence. He sighed. "You going to give me that recipe, or do I have to call Mom?"

"Just be careful, Daniel." Emma's voice was small and resigned.

"I'll be fine."

Emma sighed. "Did you buy fresh basil? Because the dried stuff won't taste the same."

HE HAD JUST opened a bottle of red and was letting it breathe when there was an insistent knock at his door. He wiped his hands and nearly leaped to answer it. He opened the door, and Annika flew into his arms in a rush of jasmine-scented hair.

She kissed him like she hadn't seen him in a week, though they had just seen each other yesterday evening.

He managed to bring her into the apartment and shut the door, all while still kissing her. When they came up for air, she smirked at him. "Hi."

"With a hello like that, we may never make it to dinner."

She grinned. "At least let me take off my coat." As she unwrapped her coat and scarf and gloves, Daniel tossed all of it onto the sofa and gathered her in his arms again. He would never be able to have enough of her.

"Aren't you going to show me your place?"

He pulled back from her. "Of course." He pressed his mouth against hers, walking backward as he kissed her. "Let's start with the bedroom."

"Something smells amazing." Annika stretched the length of the bed and entwined one of her legs with his.

"Well, I cooked for you."

"Perfect, because I've built up quite the appetite." She tried to get out of bed, but Daniel was too quick and had her wrapped in his arms before she even sat up.

"In a minute." Daniel's voice was husky as he kissed her neck.

Annika moaned in pleasure. "We may need more than a minute."

He was still trailing kisses over her when the phone rang. It was his landline, so they both ignored it. It went to voice mail. Daniel froze at the sound of the voice.

"Hi, Daniel. This is Gus from…well, you know where from. Uh, listen, I'm kind of hoping you've changed your mind about things since the last time we talked… Anyway, I'm calling because there's a gun-control rally coming up, and we could really use your voice. I know you had said you weren't interested, but it's been a year since the last one. I spoke last time, and it made an impact. We need to hear from parents and survivors of gunshot victims… We need to make sure no other parent goes through this again. Anyway. You know how to reach me."

Daniel pulled back and sat up. What the fuck was Gus doing, calling him after all this time?

Annika sat up and looked at him. "Is Gus…?"

"Yes. He lost his son the same day as…" Daniel swung his legs to the floor, away from Annika. "He's become an activist. Gun control." He let his voice turn bitter, as it did every time he thought of Gus. "As if gun control *now* will bring our children back to us. Or make our grief go away."

"People grieve differently."

"Well, Gus should keep his grieving to himself. What difference does it make to legislators or anyone else if I get up and pour my heart out over losing… What difference?" He stood, pulling on his pants. Annika watched him from the bed, a sheet covering her.

"Well, you never know…"

"One thing I do know is what happens when you do stand up." Memories he had quite successfully suppressed—until now—flooded his mind. His heart beat rapidly and he started to sweat.

Annika moved closer to the edge of the bed where he stood. "What happened, Daniel?" Her voice was calm, but her eyes shone with concern.

"About a year after the incident, Gus and I, we spoke out. Did a few interviews, called for gun control. We called for waiting periods, background checks. We also called for better mental health care." He swallowed at the memory. "I was still drinking, but telling the story, speaking out and trying to change things, made me feel like I was *doing* something." There had been a light, showing him a path out of grief. It was only a pinprick of light, but it was something.

"Then Sheila got a call." He fisted his hands. "Some asshole had the balls to call our home and accuse us—" A lump of anger in his throat stopped him.

"Accused you? What could someone possibly accuse you of?"

Daniel found his voice, though it burned with anger. "They accused us of making the whole thing up just so we could come out against guns."

When Sheila, shaking from head to toe, had told him, he'd punched a hole in the kitchen wall. Sheila had taken to her bed again, and whatever small pinprick of light Daniel had seen was snuffed away, his world even darker, if possible, than before.

"They *what*?" Annika nearly shrieked. "Daniel, that's unforgivable. What did you do?"

He shrugged and flexed his fingers as if he could still feel the bruising from punching that wall. "What could I do? I stopped. I stopped everything. I went to work, tried to take care of Sheila."

Annika laid her hand on his chest. "I'm so sorry."

His heart calmed at her touch, and he sat down on the edge of the bed. "I just couldn't risk it again."

Annika wrapped her arms around him from behind and held him, and gratefully, he sank into her embrace, taking whatever she had to give. And what she had to give was everything. He couldn't remember the last time he'd felt so loved.

When they finally got out of bed, Daniel poured them each a glass of wine and set about making final prep for dinner. "So."

"So what?" Annika wandered around his small living room area, looking at photos and such. Daniel suddenly wished he had more than textbooks and a few family photos out to show for his life.

She was dressed simply, and she looked tantalizing. She'd had on her own blouse, but when she dressed, she'd grabbed his shirt before he had and put it on. It was sexier than hell, but his focus was shot.

"How was the meeting?"

She walked back to the kitchen, which was tiny, but it had a small breakfast bar open to the living area. She sat on a stool and sipped her wine.

"I mentioned to Mitch's mother that I thought he was suffering from what is known as selective mutism. It's a form of anxiety. Children are fine talking at home with their families where they feel safe, but once they get outside of their comfort zone, they freeze."

"Only the mother? The dad didn't come?"

Annika shook her head.

Daniel sighed, disgusted. "Un-fucking-believable. What kind of father can't even come to listen to you help his son?"

"Daniel. Not the point. The mom came, and at first she was reluctant to believe me, but I think I offered enough information for her to at least get him evaluated."

"Hmm." Daniel put aside his disdain for the father and clinked his glass with hers, his grin proud. "Nicely done."

Annika beamed. "You okay with that wine?"

Daniel nodded. "Just the one glass."

Annika hopped off the stool and went back to exploring Daniel's bookshelves. Daniel put the finishing touches on the salad while the chicken cooked.

"Oh! What's this?"

"What's wh—" Daniel froze as he looked at what Annika was holding up. She was holding one of his textbooks—and a small red paper heart. He felt the blood drain from his head and leaned against the counter. Annika was by his side in an instant.

"Daniel?"

Daniel hung his head for a moment to gather himself. Tears burned in his eyes when he finally looked up at her. "Well… Sara. Sara would cut out and leave those hearts everywhere." He shook his head.

"Why?"

"She said it was so that whenever anyone found them…" He paused and swallowed, unable to unglue his eyes from the small piece of paper that his daughter had actually touched. "They would know that they were loved." He cleared his throat and forced himself to look away from that little heart.

Annika broke out into a grin even as a tear rolled down her cheek. "What a lovely thought. She was amazing, your Sara."

"That she was." Daniel squeezed his eyes shut to stem the tears before turning his gaze to Annika again. "Where did you find that?"

"In one of your textbooks." She handed him the heart. "Guess she knew you'd need love someday."

Daniel took the small heart from Annika, his hand shaking. "Put it back in the book." He handed it back to her.

"You sure?"

"Yeah, I mean, I know it's there, whenever I want it."

Annika did as he asked, then sipped her wine. "Want to tell me about her?"

It had been so long since he'd talked about Sara to any-

one. He relived the memories on his own, afraid of forget-
ting even the smallest detail. Lest he forget her altogether.

Annika looked on, her eyes wide-open, her face patient and loving. "Maybe start slow, like what her favorite toy was?"

Daniel grinned. "She loved puzzles. She could knock
them out like that." He snapped his fingers. "I was constantly trying to find new ones for her."

Annika grinned, clearly impressed. Though whether
with him or with Sara, he couldn't tell. It didn't matter.
"She loved doing crafts, too." He laughed. "I learned a lot
about stringing beads, painting and decoupage. More than
I ever thought I'd want to know."

The timer went off for the chicken, and he stood to fill
their plates.

"Ooh! You know what decoupage is?" She bit her bottom lip, a glint in her eye. "Just when I thought you couldn't
get any sexier."

He could have said the same about her.

"Okay. So what were her quirks?"

Daniel thought about that as he placed their plates on
the table and sat down next to her. "Nothing on her plate
was allowed to touch."

Annika laughed. "Oh boy, that makes Indian food
tough."

Daniel shook his head. "Tell me about it."

She took her first bite of the dinner he had made them.
"Ooh. Wow. This is really good."

"You sound surprised."

She bit her bottom lip again, and Daniel barely suppressed a groan as he ran his tongue over the area of *his*
lip she had bitten.

"I don't mean to. I'm simply impressed." As if she knew

what he was feeling, mischief filled her eyes, and she released her lip into a small pout. "Very impressed."

"Sara was learning to cook a bit. She was my helper."

Annika nodded as she finished chewing. "She sounds completely amazing. And clearly you make a great dad. Decoupage is messy and time-consuming."

Daniel nodded. Sure, he'd make a great dad. He ignored the pit forming in his stomach and started eating. Under Annika's gentle prodding, he continued to share tidbits of Sara's life, sometimes remembering a small detail he had forgotten, at which point Annika would prod him to remember more.

She laughed with him.

She cried with him.

Just when he didn't think he could love this woman any more, he did.

CHAPTER TWENTY-FOUR

ANNIKA

ANNIKA WOKE TO the buzzing of her phone. She lunged at it, thinking it might be Daniel stopping by after his overnight shift, and all different parts of her body came suddenly alive with the anticipation of seeing him. Not the least of which was the rapid firing of her heart.

A pit formed in her belly when she saw it was her father. Ugh. She hadn't really spoken to her parents since she'd hung up on her dad. But there was no point to putting it off.

"Hi, Papa." She put the phone to her ear and lay back in her bed.

"Annika." He spoke her name with the same clipped tone he had used when she was a child and had broken one of the strict rules he'd had for her. The pit in her stomach grew. "Your mother and I are on our way. We need to talk to you."

Annika bolted up in her bed. This was new. They had always invited her to come home when they wanted to "talk." She took a moment to be grateful that Daniel had not spent the night. She glanced at the clock. Five after eight. Her parents would be here in half an hour. She quickly freshened up in the bathroom, being careful to put away Daniel's toothbrush. *Oh, crap.* What else of his was still here? She glanced around her small bedroom. Blue T-shirt thrown on the chair. Definitely a man's. She shoved it into a drawer. She pulled on leggings and a sweatshirt and gathered her hair into a ponytail. She spent the next fifteen minutes tidying up and hiding any piece of Daniel evidence she could find.

Defiance or no, she just wasn't ready to tell them about him yet.

Coward.

At the last minute, she knocked on Naya's door. Better make sure Ravi hadn't slept over.

"Mmm?" came the groan from the depths of Naya's room.

"My parents will be here in ten minutes. You don't have any company, do you?" Annika heard the sound of rustling and footsteps and Naya opened the door, looking every bit the hungover party girl, with tousled hair, black smears under her puffy eyes.

"What happened to you? I thought you had a quiet night in with Ravi last night?"

"In, yes. Quiet, not so much. His parents don't like me." Tears welled in her already red-rimmed swollen eyes.

"That's ridiculous! His parents helped set you up."

"They found out I want to join the Peace Corps when I graduate."

"So?"

"That's not what they expected from their daughter-in-law." Her eyes became alert for a nanosecond. "Wait, did you say your parents were coming? Here?"

Annika had momentarily forgotten her immediate freak-out, but now the panic returned. "My dad knows I flubbed parent visitation a few days ago." She stared at Naya. "They're coming to try to get me to go back to med school. I know it. And they're probably going to insist I date Sajan."

Naya rolled her eyes. "It's like your parents never learn." She shook her head.

"Wait, what do you mean?"

Naya's eyes widened. "Nothing. I mean nothing."

Annika narrowed her eyes. "Spit it out, Naya."

Just then, the buzzer sounded. Both girls started at it. Annika pointed at her cousin. "Well?"

"Later! Take care of this first." Naya nearly pushed Annika toward the buzzer before retreating to her room.

With a final glare at Naya's door, Annika hit the intercom button. "Hello?"

"We are here." Her father's voice was terse and to the point.

"Okay." Annika clicked the door open for them and turned on her Keurig. She placed a pot of water on the stove for her parents' chai. She had no idea what Naya was talking about, and right now, she was sure her parents were going to use her failure as a teacher to get her to agree to get together with Sajan. He was a nice enough guy, handsome, funny, but the thought of not being with Daniel nauseated her. Annika was so lost in thought she didn't hear the knocking at her door until her father's voice boomed from the other side.

"Hello? Annika?"

She started again and went to open the door, butterflies taking up all the space in her empty belly.

"Papa, Mummy." She smiled and hugged them as they came in. "I just put *pani* on for your chai."

"What about you?" her mother asked.

"I'm making my coffee."

Her mother carried a brown grocery bag that Annika

knew was filled with homemade food. "I brought some *tepla*. Go ahead and take it out. We'll have some with chai."

Her father had not really said anything. He looked around, and Annika went to tend to the chai for something to do. She added the chai masala and the loose tea to the heating water. She peeked in the bag, and right on top was some fresh mint from her parents' plant. She took a few leaves and tossed them into the tea. While she waited for it to boil, she put a K-Cup into her Keurig, shut it with a satisfying snap and waited for her coffee to brew. A little voice in her head reminded her that there was bourbon somewhere here, and that she might want some in her coffee right about now.

"Where is Naya?" her father asked, looking around as if Naya might materialize from thin air.

"Sleeping." The chai mixture had come to a boil, filling the apartment with the comforting aroma of cardamom, cinnamon and mint. She inhaled the scents of her childhood, allowing herself a brief moment of calm. Her coffee slurped as the mug filled, and she gladly turned her attention back to adding milk to the chai, and creamer to her coffee. Her mother had busied herself with taking out the homemade spicy flatbread she had brought along to have with the tea. She set the small table while Annika finished making the chai and brought the three steaming mugs of hot liquid to the table. Whatever her parents had come over to say, they didn't seem to be in a great hurry.

The three of them sat down together, and Annika took a much-needed first sip of her coffee and relished the warmth and sweetness of the liquid. She smiled to herself. Daniel had found it rather amusing that she valued coffee even more than food.

"Why are you smiling?"

She flinched again, as if her father could read her thoughts. "Coffee, Papa. You know how I love coffee."

Her father sipped his chai and broke off a piece of tepla. He chewed and swallowed before turning to her. "Your mother and I have been thinking that you have been teaching for a couple of years, and that is great." He said *great* like it wasn't really. "But now we think you should consider a career in which you can make a proper living."

"Is this because of what you saw at school the other day?"

"Annika—"

"Because that is part of my job. Dealing with children and their parents. It's what I'm trained to do. Sometimes we have bad days."

"That is fine. But you need to make some solid decisions about your future. I'm sure Hopkins will readmit you and—" he paused "—we have spoken with Sajan's parents, and I think Sajan is still interested."

"You what?" Annika slammed down her precious elixir, nearly spilling it in her complete surprise. "You talked to Sajan's parents? What am I? Twenty-one years old, fifty years ago?"

"We didn't think you would mind. You seem to like him," her mother chimed in.

"Sure, he's a nice guy, but that doesn't mean I want to marry him."

"Why not? Love can grow, just as it did for me and your mother." Her father shifted so he faced her. "And besides, we let you try it your way—and it didn't work out."

Did everyone need to remind her what a poor choice Steven had been? Didn't people get to make mistakes?

"I'm not going to medical school." She sat up and pressed her lips together. "I'm not marrying Sajan." She was with Daniel. It was about time they knew. "Listen, I have to tell you something."

Their eyes widened as if in wonder at what more she could say.

Her belly was overrun with butterflies, and she was starting to sweat profusely, but there was no way she was letting the idea of marrying Sajan go further. She took a deep breath and thought of the comfort she felt in Daniel's arms. "I've been seeing someone."

They stared at her in complete silence, with almost no reaction.

"Like, dating someone," she clarified, in case they didn't understand. Before she could say any more, there was a knock at the door. Her parents still sat in complete silence. Another knock. She didn't move.

"Aren't you going to answer that?" Her mother seemed to find her voice.

Annika stood and went to the door. Maybe it was Ravi, here for Naya.

She opened the door and was met with the fragrance of roses, followed by lips on hers that momentarily made her melt. Daniel wrapped his arms around her in the doorway and thoroughly kissed her good morning, weakening her body so she momentarily forgot where she was.

He walked her into the apartment, still kissing her, when the aroma of mint masala chai brought her back to her senses. She pushed away from him. He looked slightly hurt and confused until she tilted her head toward her parents, who had just watched him kiss her like he'd just returned from war. His lips were slightly swollen and wet, but to his credit, he simply pressed them together rather than draw attention by wiping his mouth.

His eyes filled with alarm, and Annika broke away

from his gaze and turned to face her quite ashen parents. "Mummy, Papa. As I was saying—" she glanced at Daniel with a small smile "—I'm seeing someone. And that someone is Daniel. Nilay's mentor." She made a small movement with her hand to indicate the man standing next to her, as if there were anyone else in the room. Like he hadn't just kissed her. In front of them.

Her father had his jaw clenched, and a vein was popping at his temple, whereas her mother's mouth went from gaping to tight-lipped. Neither one of them could tear their gaze away from Daniel.

Daniel, to his credit, did not try to brush off the fact that he had just been making out with their daughter. Instead, he stepped away from her as he brought his hands together and bowed his head slightly in the namaste greeting.

Her parents returned the greeting like robots, out of habit. It was clear they had no idea that they were even doing that. Annika swore she could see steam coming out her dad's ears.

"*This* is why you won't consider Sajan? This?" Her father spoke not only as if Daniel weren't there but as if he were nothing better than something stuck to his shoe. "He's a nurse, Annika. And he's divorced!" He said these things as if they were contagious incurable diseases.

Annika hazarded a glance at Daniel and found that he was looking at her. But if he was at all insulted by her father, he didn't show it. Concern for her settled onto his face, and it was in that moment, in the middle of all that chaos, with her father yelling at them, *insulting him*, her mother's disapproval mounting, that she knew she loved him. She had been falling for him all this time. For this man who, in the midst of this storm around them, was calm and supporting and oblivious of everything but her. There was no other man for her. Emboldened, she turned to her parents and said the first thing she thought of.

"Papa, his grandmother is Indian. And he's a nurse practitioner."

Anil seemed to swell up with anger. "Is that what you think? That I care if he is *Indian*? There are *plenty* of Indian idiots out there." His hands were flailing about as he tried to emphasize his point. "No! What I care about is that he did not have the ambition to become a doctor and instead chose to be a nurse. As a result, he has to moonlight on the helicopter to make ends meet. What kind of life is that? And being divorced shows lack of commitment."

Annika felt Daniel tense, and she risked another glance at him. His lips were pressed tight, jaw clenched, but he met her gaze with warning. He gave the slightest shake of his head. *I'm not worth it.*

He was wrong. Annika stepped in front of Daniel and faced her father. "You don't even know him."

"I know enough. Sajan is in a position to support you while you go to medical school." He said it like it was a done deal.

"I'm *not* going to medical school!"

"Why not?"

"Because I'm good at teaching. No, I'm *great* at teaching—and I love those children."

"But Sajan…" her mother started.

"I already told you."

Daniel leaned toward her ever so slightly, his chest pressed against her back. "I love those kids. I love what I do, and I love—Daniel. I love Daniel." She stared straight ahead, meeting her father's eyes, even as she felt Daniel tense behind her.

Her father gaped at her for a moment before he brushed

past them. "Think about what you are doing, Annika. What do you know about love? We only want what is best for you."

Her mother hesitated before joining her father at the door. "Beta, think about what we said. Every once in a while, we have a good idea." She glanced at Daniel with what Annika could have sworn was a trace of sadness. And with that, her parents opened the door and left.

Annika sagged right into Daniel as if she had just run a marathon. His arms were around her in an instant, providing the strength and comfort she needed right now. He led her to the sofa, and she curled up in his lap.

"So, um…good morning to you, too," Daniel chuckled.

"It's not funny."

"No, I suppose making out in front of your parents is not really comedy, or the best way to tell them about us." He pulled back to look at her. "You were telling them about us?"

"Well, yeah, before you came in and kissed me like I was the last woman on earth."

"You *are* the last woman on earth, for me."

"They're really trying to get me to marry Sajan. Besides, they should know about you."

"Not really the best way for them to find out."

She giggled despite the hollowness in her stomach. She felt his chuckle vibrate through her and decided it was the most amazing thing she'd ever felt. Well, almost.

"They don't like me." He was matter-of-fact.

She squeezed his hand. "They don't know you."

"They don't want to know me."

Annika sat up so she could look at him. "That's their loss. Listen, it's not easy. If you can't handle it, bail now." Better to find out now that he wouldn't be sticking around.

He pressed a finger to her lips. "That's not it at all. I'm

not trying to bail on you. But I don't want to cause trouble for you, either."

"You're not causing trouble."

"Hmm. That is true." He grinned at her, amusement playing in those green eyes she loved so much. "You're the troublemaker here." He kissed her neck. "But was this really the most romantic way you could think of to tell me you loved me?"

"You think you're in love with him?" Naya stood, incredulous, in the doorway of her bedroom. She had clearly been listening, waiting for the right moment to come out—preferably after Annika's parents had left.

"No, I *am* in love with him." She glanced at Daniel, and a ridiculous lightness came over her. She'd never felt this way before.

Naya smirked and rolled her eyes. "Okay, whatever."

Annika glanced at Daniel, then stood and walked over to Naya. "What exactly is your problem?"

Naya shrugged and looked over Annika's shoulder at Daniel. "We can talk later."

"We can talk now." They'd grown up together like sisters; confronting each other was nothing new. It was what they each valued most about their relationship. Annika crossed her arms over her chest.

Daniel stood and faced them. "Actually, I did just get off the overnight and could use a shower. Why don't you two talk, and I'll go."

No sooner had Daniel left the room than Annika turned to Naya. "What?"

"I'm just saying, you have a pattern."

Annika narrowed her eyes at her cousin. "Daniel is nothing like Steven."

"Maybe not, but still—don't you see it?"

"I honestly have no idea what you're talking about."

Naya took a deep breath. "Well, if you recall, the first time you met Steven, you thought he was attractive, but you weren't really sure about him."

"Yeah, okay."

"But when your parents got upset with you for going to school for teaching, you decided that Steven was the one for you."

"I didn't even know Steven when I decided against med school."

"No, but you dated him while you were in grad school, while your mom and dad were trying to get you to quit and go to med school."

"So?" Annika was defensive, but her indignation lost its punch as she realized what Naya was saying had a grain of truth. She had dated Steven in grad school. And her parents had been constantly nagging her to leave the program and go to med school. They couldn't understand how she had turned down Hopkins. It was nearly constant stress, and her only relief had been Steven. He had supported her graduate endeavors. Or had he? Now that she thought about it, he had listened while she complained about her parental pressure, but he hadn't really offered to help her do anything about it. In fact, he had insinuated more than once that her parents' beliefs were backward. She had been so convinced of his love for her that she'd told herself he just didn't understand Indian culture. Besides, she wanted to be modern and progressive, and being with Steven and not going to medical school were both of those.

"Wait. Are you saying that I'm doing the same thing with Daniel?"

"Aren't you?" Naya pursed her lips.

"No." She paused. "I mean, I don't think so." She no longer cared about being modern or progressive. She had deep passion for her work and no desire to become a doctor. Being a teacher was completely about following her passions. Her feelings for Daniel were such that she had never experienced before. In the short time they'd known each other, he'd become comfortable, reliable, steady. Sure, he had his issues, but who didn't?

"All I'm saying," Naya softened, taking Annika's hands in hers, "is consider the possibility that when you rebel, you don't necessarily make choices that are the best for you. Maybe you're turning away from Sajan because your parents actually like him. You wouldn't be the first girl who did that."

That couldn't possibly be the truth, could it? She glanced at her bedroom door as if she could see Daniel. He loved her, no doubt. Did she really love him, or was she acting out like a teenager?

A banging at the door interrupted her thoughts. Her attention snapped back to Naya, whose eyes had gone wide.

"It's like Grand Central this morning," Annika murmured as she went to the door.

She opened it to find a clearly unkempt Ravi midknock. "Thank God you're home. Is Naya here? She won't answer her phone or anything."

Annika stepped aside and let Ravi see Naya standing there. They made eye contact and Naya froze.

"Naya." Ravi sagged in relief. He said her name with such desperation, such relief and love, Annika almost teared up.

Naya pressed her lips together. "Ravi."

Annika could tell her cousin was trying to be cold, but she saw Naya's lip quiver.

"I'm going. I worked too hard—did what my parents wanted. I'm going."

Ravi narrowed his eyes and stepped closer. "Duh. Of course you are."

Naya couldn't hide the flick of surprise that fled across her face. Annika said nothing, as Ravi and Naya were clearly continuing a conversation that had started earlier. She stepped back into her room, leaving the door open a crack. She peeked out. Naya tightened her expression. "So that's it?"

"That's what?"

"Us. That's it. Because I'm going to the Peace Corps. No matter what. I'm not changing my dreams for a man— it's hard enough I have to mold them around my parents."

Annika felt Daniel come up behind her, his body just grazing hers. She turned to face him. His hair was dry, his clothes unchanged.

"You didn't shower?"

He pressed his lips together. "I did. Before I came here."

Her heart banged in her chest. "So you heard?"

He nodded. He flicked his gaze to the door.

Ravi's voice was firm, amusement lacing his words. "Have I asked you not to go?"

"Well, not in so many words, but your parents—" Naya's voice quivered.

"Have their own opinions. But they don't run my life. Or yours, for that matter."

"But you agreed to this setup. You're a lawyer when you want to be a chef."

Ravi nodded, though a frown creased his face. "All true. I agreed to the setup because I wanted to meet girls."

Annika and Daniel smiled at each other.

"I'm a lawyer, so I make good money and I can pursue

my dream to be a chef on my own." He stood directly in front of Naya and tilted her chin up to him. "Or I can join the Peace Corps with the woman I love."

Daniel smiled at this, and Annika melted.

"You—what?"

"You heard me. I'm going with you."

"But—"

"But what?"

"That's crazy."

"Is it crazy for me to want to be with you while you fulfill your dreams? You told me about the Peace Corps on our first date. I'm not an idiot. Nothing is going to stand in your way. Not me. Certainly not my parents. And it's not a reason to break up. We're in this together."

Relief washed over Annika. Ravi was a good guy.

"I don't want to come between you and your parents." Naya's voice was small. Her resolve was weakening as her feelings for Ravi took over.

"You won't."

Daniel was watching Annika, his eyes wary. He had heard everything Naya had told her.

Annika reached out and laid her hands on either side of his face, standing on her toes to reach. "I'm not rebelling. Maybe I dated Steven as an act of rebellion. But I'm with you because I love you." She pulled his face down to her, gently sliding her lips over his. "I'm with you because you are incredible. Because now that I have you, I don't want to be without you. I can't even remember what my life was like without you. I love you." She breathed the words into his mouth, kissing him harder, closing the space between their bodies, willing him to find in her kiss whatever he needed to believe her.

It was completely true. She did love him, and he was

the one for her. Her judgment was not off. This felt right, the way teaching felt right—like it was a part of her. Daniel was a part of her.

Daniel pulled back. "But your family—"

"Is being unreasonable. They don't even know you." She smiled. "Nilay thinks you're the coolest."

"What about her?" He motioned at the door.

"You mean the girl who is considering leaving the man who adores her because she can't stand not being accepted immediately? She likes you. She doesn't like the idea of you."

Ravi's agitated voice and Naya's sob broke through. Daniel's gaze flicked toward the door, then back to Annika.

"For the past five years, I have cut myself off from getting close to anyone. I went to work and I slept. That was it. I even cut myself off from my own heart because it was too painful to feel anything." He caressed the side of her face, his rough calluses stroking her skin. "You heal me. To say that I love you doesn't even begin to describe it." He sighed and glanced at the door, Naya and Ravi still arguing on the other side of it. "But I can't take you away from your family."

"You won't. We'll work on them. You'll see. My parents are reasonable people."

Daniel widened his eyes at her.

"Deep down." She grinned into his hand. "Way deep down. But you'll see. I'm not rebelling—I've got no reason to. I love you, too. Or didn't you hear me tell my parents? That has to be enough for now."

"It's more than enough." Daniel grinned as he finally leaned down to kiss her.

CHAPTER TWENTY-FIVE

DANIEL

HE HAD PROMISED. There was no reason he couldn't do this. He pulled into the parking lot of Chase Creek Elementary. He was just unnerved by Annika finding that paper heart last week. He parked the bike and removed his helmet, involuntarily holding his breath against the odor of lavender that he remembered. He climbed off the bike, still not breathing, and leaned against it. He had purchased the motorcycle when he and Sheila divorced. Everyone thought he was going through some kind of self-destructive, risk-taking phase. The truth was much less exciting. Men with families needed cars. Men without families did not.

He finally drew breath, the cloying scent of lavender filling his nostrils and sending him back in time. His head spun and nausea claimed him as he spiraled into the past and watched as a man and his young daughter entered the building.

The little girl able to hold only three of his fingers in her little hand.

No. He shut his eyes against the memory. Annika. He loved her and she loved him, and that would give him the strength to go into the building and keep his promise to her. But his legs wouldn't move, and he couldn't open his eyes.

He wasn't exactly sure how long he'd stood there, but

the next thing he became aware of was a familiar hand on his. Annika. Already, he could recognize her touch.

"Daniel?"

He slowly opened his eyes, and his gaze landed on those warm brown eyes he'd fallen in love with, and he exhaled, relaxing in an instant. His calm was fleeting, as he realized what had happened. And who was with her. His heart ratcheted up as he recognized Annika's father and *Sajan.*

Great. Not only had he failed by not being able to go in, but he had actually helped Sajan score points. Not that this was a game.

"Daniel, are you okay?" Annika narrowed her eyes at him.

He flicked his gaze away from where Sajan was observing him with obvious concern, and Annika's father had his lips pursed in righteous disappointment. He focused on the woman he loved. Whom he had just let down.

"I missed it, didn't I?"

She nodded and shrugged, her focus never leaving him. Her brow was furrowed and her mouth pursed as she darted her eyes over him, trying to see what was broken.

"So, no. I'm not okay." He turned his full attention on her. Forget the observers. "I'm sorry—I had every intention of doing this for you. But I got here, and that damn lavender—"

She shook her head. "No, Daniel, I'm the one who should be sorry, pushing you to do this when you weren't ready. Coming back here—" she waved her hand "—would challenge anyone in your position. I'm really sorry."

He had been utterly convinced that he would be able to go into that building. That his love for Annika would give him what he needed to take those steps.

"Everything okay, Daniel?" Sajan was genuinely concerned. He stepped closer. "Need anything?"

"What is going on?" Annika's father called out. He had remained a respectful distance away, presumably allowing Daniel some privacy.

Sajan turned to Mr. Mehta. "Uncle, this is where—"

"Nothing!" Daniel interrupted Sajan, staring the other man in the eye. "Nothing is going on." He wouldn't have his story blurted out in front of Annika's father for the sake of an excuse, or—God forbid—sympathy.

For his part, Sajan stopped talking, but he appeared supremely confused. He nodded at Daniel; he wouldn't tell his secret. But his face went blank when he saw Annika's hand on Daniel's arm. It was an intimate gesture, no doubt about it.

Sajan looked up at Daniel, a look on his face that Daniel had never seen in the good doctor. Anger? Jealousy? No need for him to worry. Daniel's heart felt like lead as the realization hit him. He'd be gone soon enough. There was no way Annika would keep him now. He'd never measure up, and she would always wonder if she wouldn't have been better off with Sajan.

Today was proof.

Annika's father stepped closer to Daniel. "Are you ill?" He said it with such genuine concern that Daniel almost didn't recognize the older man's voice. "Is that why you didn't come in?"

Mr. Mehta turned to Sajan. "Does he look pale to you?"

Sajan nodded. "Yes, Uncle, he does." Sajan met Daniel's eyes again, but this time with sadness. "But I'm sure he'll be fine. I'm sure Annika will see to that." He turned his gaze to her.

She looked him in the eye. "Sajan, I meant to—"

"Don't." He smiled sadly again, raking his eyes over her hand on Daniel's arm, over the scant distance between them. "Not necessary. We were never even dating." He turned toward Mr. Mehta. "Come, Uncle, I'll walk you to your car."

Annika's father pressed his lips together and shook his head in disappointment at Annika before turning and following Sajan.

Daniel watched the two men retreat, his body tense. Annika had just chosen him over Sajan in front of her dad. She squeezed his arm.

"I picked you long before today. Don't be so surprised."

He looked down at her. Was she reading his mind?

She smiled. "And don't worry." She tilted her head toward the building. "I'm sure there will come a time when you will be able to go in there. It's just not today." She shrugged. "And that's okay."

He didn't know what to say. He couldn't imagine what he had done to deserve this incredible woman. "Can we get out of here?"

"Sure," she said as she got onto his bike and grabbed his helmet. "Anywhere you want to go."

DESPITE ALL THE DRAMA, Ravi and Naya were back together. Having dinner together was Annika's idea, and Ravi had instantly agreed, inviting the three of them to his place. She figured that once Naya got to know Daniel, she would understand that he was not the rebound guy. Daniel himself was not so sure. He also suspected Annika wanted Naya to like him so she'd have another ally in the family.

"Relax. It'll be fine," Annika reassured a fidgety Daniel as they rode the elevator up to Ravi's apartment. "It's Naya and Ravi, not my dad."

"Honestly, I like my chances with your dad better. Naya is scary."

Annika waved a hand. "She's all bark. No real bite."

The building was one of the nicest in the city. Apparently, Ravi worked for a successful firm and did quite well for himself. Daniel took a deep breath when Annika knocked on the door. She squeezed his hand and he relaxed a bit.

Naya answered the door, giving her cousin a huge hug. She nodded at Daniel, acknowledging his existence with a simple hello.

Okay, so it was going to be one of those kinds of evenings.

"Something smells amazing!" Daniel said by way of greeting. Ugh. Mental face palm. Clearly he wasn't going to win anyone over with his conversational ability.

"That would be the dinner that Ravi cooked for us." Naya smiled proudly as the man in question came to greet them at the door, wearing an apron over jeans and a black T-shirt.

"Hey, man. Good to see you again." Ravi extended his hand to Daniel, his smile warm and welcoming.

Daniel shook his hand. "You, too."

Annika and Daniel took off their shoes and followed Naya and Ravi into the massive gourmet kitchen. "I hope you like chicken—I made my grandmother's chicken curry. Want a beer, Daniel?"

"Yeah, sure. That'd be great. And I love chicken curry. The spicier the better."

"Seriously?"

"Yes."

"Because I went easy on the heat, because I wasn't sure…"

"Didn't think the white guy could handle the heat, huh?"

Ravi had the grace to appear abashed. "Truthfully, yes. Guess I should know better." He opened a beer and handed it to Daniel. "I guess I should've known that someone who can do garba like you can also eat the heat."

Daniel took the beer and waited a beat. "Actually, my mom's mom is Indian. We grew up next door to her."

"Humph." Naya shrugged. *"Emma shu?"* She looked at Annika and rolled her eyes. *"Sajan bhi garba gayay che. Annay eh bhi thiku-thiku kayay."*

Annika opened her mouth, fired up and ready to defend Daniel. He pressed his hand to her back and addressed Naya himself. In Gujarati.

"Thamari vat sachu. Sajan does speak Gujarati, and he can eat spicy food. But he is not here right now." Daniel rested his gaze on Naya, amusement on his lips. He also couldn't resist pressing closer to Annika, as if to solidify that he was hers.

Naya's jaw dropped, and she managed a small smile. "No, I suppose you're right. Sajan is not here. You are."

Daniel had used the formal, respectful form of *you* in addressing Naya, and it did not go unnoticed.

"How about some of my special *pakora*?" Ravi brought out a plate of mixed-veggie fritters, breaking the tension as everyone turned toward the amazing aroma. The pakora quite literally melted in Daniel's mouth, and he reached for another.

"How'd you get that extra crunch?"

"Just a little bit of rice flour in the batter." Ravi beamed. "But wait till you try the chicken."

The evening progressed amiably, and true to Ravi's word, the chicken was incredible.

"Okay, I can't possibly eat more. Your chicken rivals my grandmother's." Daniel moved his plate aside.

"How about another beer?" Ravi started to stand.

Daniel waved him back to his seat. "Nah. I'm good."

"I'm thinking about opening a restaurant." Ravi sat down and looked around at the group.

"Well, count me in as a regular." Daniel smiled.

"Me, too." Annika grinned and squeezed Daniel's hand under the table.

So far so good.

For a minute.

"Seriously? I don't know why I'm surprised at you two." Naya threw her napkin down.

Daniel became slightly nauseated at the glare Naya was throwing them.

"What? We're being supportive. Ravi is a fabulous cook, and you said he's been going to culinary school," Annika threw back at her cousin.

"I mean, of course you two would support him." She glared at Daniel, sliding her eyes to Annika. "You do whatever you want, no matter who gets hurt."

Annika snapped her gaze to her cousin, but before she could spout out the rage building in her, Daniel laid a hand on Annika's thigh under the table and squeezed gently. He couldn't have her always in a position of defending him.

"Clearly, you're upset about this. Let's focus on that." Daniel used his best patient-soothing voice. "Why does this upset you?"

"Because," Naya sighed, "he just told his parents he's joining the Peace Corps with me, and they flipped out! They even told my parents. So now my parents are pissed at me for 'putting these ideas' in his head, as well." She paused for breath. "If he opens this restaurant, everyone will blame me as the 'bad influence'—especially his parents—and I can't—"

She broke off as sudden tears choked her. Annika reached for her cousin, but Ravi got there first. "Naya. How many times do I have to tell you? We're in this together. Who cares what they think? I've seen this a million times. Stubborn Indian parents opposed to the person their child chooses to marry. They almost always come around."

"Almost?"

Annika shook her head at her cousin. "I love you, Naya, but you have got to stop living your life for everyone else. Go with your heart for once. See what happens. This is your life, not theirs."

"And anyway," interjected Ravi, "being a chef, opening a restaurant, has always been my dream. I should just let my dreams go because you're afraid of what my parents will think of you?"

"Well," Daniel spoke up without thinking, "I don't think that's what she's saying. I think she just wants your parents to love her the way she is prepared to love them."

Both Naya and Ravi turned to glare at him, and Naya spoke first. "You know what? There's no way you understand what's going on here—I don't care that your grandmother is Indian. It's not the same."

Daniel seemed unfazed. "It's not about that. I'm just offering a different perspective."

"Perspective?" Naya said shrilly. "Now, that is something you two could both use." She waggled her finger between Daniel and Annika. "Whatever you two have going on, it can't last." She calmed her voice and turned to Annika. "Sweetie, I can see that you think you love each other, but he's not who your parents would want for you." She paused and gave Annika a meaningful glance that Daniel did not miss. "How much can you expect your parents to take?"

Annika seemed frozen to her chair, and Daniel's heart plummeted, even as his anger rose. Naya turned to Ravi and continued. "That's why this can't work. Daniel is right about one thing—I do want your parents to love and respect me, and if they can't, if they see me as the one leading you down a wrong road, I can't live like that. I love you, Ravi, but I'm not going to make you choose." Naya stood.

"What're you doing?" Ravi's eyes widened, and he stood, as well.

"I'm sorry." Naya shook her head and headed for the door. "I can't do this." With that, she donned her coat, turned and left.

CHAPTER TWENTY-SIX

ANNIKA

"OH MY GOD, ANNIKA! Come outside!" called an excited Nilay, poking his head through the door of the bar.

"I'm working."

"Two minutes." He looked around the restaurant. "It's practically empty." He glanced at the bar. "Hey, Daniel!"

Daniel waved to Nilay over his sandwich. "Hey, kid."

It was pretty empty and no one needed her, so Annika took off her apron and grabbed her jacket. "Fine." Daniel grabbed her hand as she walked past him and pulled her in for a kiss. She allowed herself to melt into him for a moment. She was definitely getting used to this.

With a heavy sigh, she pulled back. "Let me go see what he wants."

"Mmm. If you insist." Daniel let her go. "No hat?" He teased.

"Ha ha." She opened the door to the deep winter cold and wished she had grabbed her hat, and maybe a scarf. It was dusk, and the sun still peeked around a few clouds, shedding some light. The streetlamps would be on momentarily.

Nilay, wearing only a sweatshirt over his jeans and T-shirt, stood admiring Daniel's motorcycle.

She rubbed her hands together. "Aren't you cold?"

"Didi, check out this bike!" His eyes danced with excitement.

"Please tell me you didn't call me out here to look at Daniel's bike." She stomped her feet against the cold.

His eyes widened. "This? This is Daniel's bike? Seriously?"

"You did call me out here for this." The fragrant aroma of home cooking emitted from the brown bag he handed her. She pulled out her phone and texted Daniel to come outside. "Let Daniel come out here and talk to you about—"

"What is that stench?" A tall, muscular man had walked a couple of steps past them, but returned, his nose in the air, sniffing. Annika, always aware of her surroundings, had noticed him passing. He stood a good head over Nilay, his shoulders spanned the width of both hers and Nilay's, and he wasn't wearing a jacket, simply a dark-colored long-sleeved shirt, so tight it looked painted onto his skin, accentuating his beefy musculature. He took slow steps toward them. "I smell something…foreign." He wrinkled his nose and turned to them with a snarl. "Like it don't belong here."

Annika felt Nilay tense beside her. She grabbed his arm, her belly in fits. "Just ignore him."

Before Nilay had a chance to do anything, the man stepped closer, his eyes narrowed at Annika as she held the bag in front of her. "Why don't you just take that stench and go back to where you came from?" And he spat at her, spittle hitting the precious brown bag of food and dripping down onto the ground. Before she could fully register what happened, Nilay jumped in front of her, his small fists flailing.

"Nilay!" Annika dropped the bag, trying to reach her brother and pull him back before this deviant hurt him. "Stop! *No!*"

She was too slow, and the man shoved her aside as if he were flicking away a bug. He landed a meaty fist to Nilay's chest. Annika saw something on his fist catch the light and Nilay fell back, a rag doll in slow motion. Annika tried to reach him before he hit the sidewalk, but she was too far away. She grabbed at his shirt just as another pair of hands also grabbed at Nilay.

Daniel.

CHAPTER TWENTY-SEVEN

DANIEL

DANIEL HADN'T BOTHERED with a jacket; he was used to the cold. He walked out just as a man easily three times the size of Nilay landed a solid punch to the boy's chest. Annika was screaming and reaching for her brother. In two large steps, Daniel was close enough to grab Nilay so he didn't hit his head on the concrete. But in the second it took him to turn to the assailant, the asshole kicked Nilay in the leg, leaving it at an odd angle.

It was almost in slow motion that Daniel assessed that Annika was out of the way as he made a fist and aimed for the man's face. A flicker of something shiny flashed in front of his face, followed by a searing pain in his arm, and Daniel's punch never landed.

The assailant kicked the bag of food, scattering its contents all over the sidewalk, and took a few steps back, wielding the knife that had just cut Daniel.

Daniel brought himself to his full height and readied himself to face off with this animal. It was a foregone conclusion: he was going to rip this asshole's goddamn fucking face off. He calculated in a few seconds the various ways in which he could make this idiot pay for hurting Nilay. Throat punches seemed appropriate. He hadn't felt primal rage like this since Sara.

Annika's screams cut through his red haze, and he flicked his gaze to her. Sensing his moment of escape, the man turned and bolted. Daniel took a few steps after him, ready to give chase, but Annika's voice was further panicked now.

"Daniel!" she shrieked. "He's having trouble breathing!" She looked up at him from the sidewalk, panic all over her face. "You're bleeding! I'm calling 911." She pulled her phone from her jacket pocket.

He glanced down the street as the man disappeared into the crowd that had accumulated. Fucking coward.

He grunted as he knelt by Nilay's side, his own animal rage still lingering.

Daniel crouched down close to Nilay. "Can you breathe?"

Nilay nodded, but gripped his shirt. "Just barely."

"Where did he hit you?"

Nilay motioned at his chest. Daniel opened Nilay's sweatshirt and ripped the T-shirt. Bruises were starting to form. The bastard had worn brass knuckles. Sirens sounded in the distance. Daniel willed them to come faster.

He gingerly felt the area. Nilay flinched in pain and was clearly having trouble breathing. Damn it. He needed a stethoscope. Nilay definitely had a punctured lung, and dangerous pressure could be building up inside him as they spoke. The cops had arrived and were talking to Annika. She was trying to help them, but her attention was on her brother, and she kept eyeing Daniel's bloody arm.

The sirens drew closer as he tried to calm Nilay, and he overheard what Annika was telling the officer.

Fury infiltrated every cell in his body as he listened to Annika's story. "That bastard *spit* on you?" He stood, barely even aware that he left his patient's side, his fists clenched. He knew he should've chased the bastard down.

Annika turned to him, an angry storm ready to erupt from her eyes, and nodded.

"You should've let me—"

"I needed you here!" She pointed her finger down at her brother, shutting Daniel down with the ferocity of her hardened eyes. "Not off somewhere playing hero." She was shaking, and her rapid breaths fogged the cold air around her.

"Officer, can you take her inside?" Daniel didn't take his eyes off her. "It's freezing out here."

"I'm not going anywhere!" she growled.

The ambulance finally pulled up with a squeak and burp, and Daniel ran to it, almost colliding head-on with the EMT.

"Andy. I need your steth."

It was a mark of respect for Daniel that Andy handed over his stethoscope and nodded to his new partner to keep the engine running. "What's going on? Why is your arm bleeding?" Andy grabbed some gauze and followed Daniel.

Daniel managed normal language and turned his focus to his patient as Andy pressed the gauze to his arm. "Annika's brother, the kid—some asshole hit him in the chest. Brass knuckles. Kid's having trouble breathing. Leg's at a weird angle." He pressed the gauze to his skin and ignored the sharp sting. "I need to listen."

Daniel put on the steth and listened to Nilay's lungs with a calm he hardly felt, while Andy and his partner took vitals and assessed Nilay's broken leg.

Daniel's heart sank. Low breath sounds. "Tension pneumo. He looks blue." Daniel closed his eyes and focused. "I need to relieve that pressure now." He looked at Andy. "Got an eighteen-gauge in there?"

Andy stared Daniel down. "You don't know it's a tension pneumo."

"Yes, I do. He's gasping, turning blue—you have one in there or not? There's no time."

Andy's radio squawked. "Let's just get him in the bus. And to the ER."

"There's no time. Give me the needle, and we'll go." His fury seethed just below the surface, his words sharper than they needed to be.

"This your girlfriend's little brother?"

"Yes!" Daniel was nearly screaming now. He needed that needle. Now. "Goddamn it, Andy. I'm right. You know I am."

Andy hesitated, looking from Daniel to the weakening Nilay. "You better be right." He shoved his bag at Daniel while he and his partner finished the splint on Nilay's leg.

Daniel prepped the area, then readied the needle. Nilay's breath came out in small puffs. "This may hurt a bit, but I have to relieve the pressure, okay?"

He inserted it between Nilay's first two ribs, and the boy grimaced, trying—and failing—to stifle a groan. Within seconds, Nilay's breath came easier. Daniel secured the needle and called out to Andy. "We're good here. Let's load him up."

Andy nodded, and Daniel climbed onto the ambulance with Annika at his side. Andy glanced from one to the other. Neither showed signs of moving. He shook his head and banged on the window to the front.

"Let's go."

The siren wailed as the ambulance took off, Daniel and Andy watching closely over Nilay on the short trip. Andy grabbed Daniel's arm and removed the gauze. Daniel met Annika's eyes. "You might want to call your parents."

Andy assessed Daniel's wound. "Relatively superficial laceration. Not too bad, but deep enough for stitches. Should be fine. What happened?" He wrapped it in fresh gauze.

Annika relayed the story as Daniel simmered with anger. He was intimately familiar with a complete stranger harming someone he loved. Andy, too, looked about ready to punch someone.

"Did I get him?" asked Nilay, his voice a weak garble.

"No, Nilay. You did not." Annika was in his face. "He got you instead. How many times have I told you—fists are not the way. But *no*, do you listen…?"

"Couldn't let him get away with…"

"Yeah? Well, he got away—and he hurt you in the process." Annika's voice broke. Daniel put his good arm around her and held her close. She was shaking with fury.

"You gave him hell, kid."

Annika glared at Daniel, but before she could speak, the ambulance had arrived at the ER. Nilay was taken directly up to pulmonary for surgery. Daniel and Annika followed.

They waited in silence for the elevator, Annika fuming. Once the elevator doors had closed and they were alone, she snapped at him. "Do not encourage this behavior!"

"He was trying to protect you, teach that asshole a lesson. I can't fault him for that," he snapped back.

"I was fine. And that asshole was taught nothing. You can't change people's minds with violence." She paused, her nostrils flaring. "If you hadn't been right there…" Her voice broke again.

"He's going to be fine. He has to be," Daniel said, reaching for her and folding her into his arms. The elevator doors opened.

She nodded and led the way to the waiting room, where Annika's parents were just arriving, as well. Annika filled her parents in on what had happened.

"Who is the surgeon?" asked her father.

"I am." They all turned to find Sajan standing in the door. "He'll need a thoracostomy, but there's a chance of pulmonary contusion, which may not show itself for twenty-four hours or more." He glanced at them, finally nodding to Daniel. "Excellent work in the field. I'll let you know when I have something."

DANIEL SAT ACROSS from Annika and her parents, inhaling deeply to calm his nerves. Annika was right, violence was not the way, but if he had been in Nilay's place, he would have reacted with his fists first, as well. It would have been satisfying to land a punch on at least one deserving asshole. He had no way to avenge Sara, but punching this guy would've felt good. He flexed his fingers, the ache from the knife wound filtering up his arm. Damn it.

He found himself fixated on the way Annika's parents clung to each other, alternately reassuring each other and worrying aloud. He read the concern and panic in their eyes, the feelings they couldn't mask even if they had tried. The "what if" hung heavy and unsaid in the air.

The professional in him knew that Sajan was the best. He also knew that he himself had done everything in his power to get Nilay to the hospital ASAP. The professional in him knew that Nilay would be fine. He also knew that pulmonary contusion was likely and dangerous.

His heart rate quickened as he mentally listed all the other things that could be going on. Worry and pain colored Anil-uncle's face; the same parental tug pulled at Daniel, as well.

He and Sheila had sat just like Annika's parents that day in the ER. They didn't go to a waiting room; they had just taken one of the bays. Someone had brought them coffee, and Daniel couldn't imagine anything more mundane than coffee when waiting to hear if his baby girl had been shot to death.

What if Nilay wasn't fine? Sajan might be the best, but things went wrong all the time. Daniel's stomach churned. His breathing became uneven as he continued to count the ways in which things could go wrong. The ways in which he could have improved his care of Nilay before he even got to the hospital.

He stood and paced. What was he thinking? He should calm down. Nilay wasn't even his son. If something happened to Nilay, his family would never be the same. He froze midstep as a realization hit him. If something happened to Nilay, *Daniel* would never be the same. He tried to focus on the facts. Wave after wave of nausea churned his stomach.

He couldn't lose Nilay. He couldn't lose another child.

His hands shook. They had been rock steady when he was inserting that needle, but now... Now he couldn't make them stop shaking. Even fisted, they trembled. How could he possibly love another child and go through *this* again and again? He couldn't. Plain and simple. The not knowing, the wondering, and then, when the answer came down, the pure agony of having your heart ripped out whole.

No.

Annika's father paced the room, his brown skin ashen, his lips moving but no sound coming out. This was his son, and he was powerless. This man, who'd had the courage to leave one country in search of a better life, was now at the mercy of the skill of surgeons and the ability of the body to heal. He would be forced to accept and move on with whatever happened here tonight.

Annika held her mother while the older woman sat, her hands clasped in her lap, something between worry and terror in her eyes. There were no tears, just frowns of doubt, glimmers of hope, and that belly-sinking feeling that the worst might actually occur.

Daniel was overcome with helplessness and his gut wrenched, just as it had that day he'd sat in the ER bay with Sheila. Waiting. Powerless. Waiting to hear what he had already known was true. He shook his head, told himself that this was Nilay, not Sara, but it made no difference to his heart.

He willed himself to go and comfort Annika, to talk to her father. To at least go get them some coffee, mundane though that may be. But he was frozen to his spot. Almost paralyzed by the fear of losing Nilay. Nothing he did would be enough. It was all futile. What would happen would happen.

Suddenly it was clear. Daniel knew what he had to do. He met Annika's eye.

"Daniel." Annika came to his side, wrapping her arm in his so their bodies touched. "If it hadn't been for your quick thinking, we wouldn't have the hope we have now."

He wanted nothing more than to sink into her touch, but all he could think about were all the ways that Nilay could die. All the ways that things could go wrong. All the ways his heart would shatter again.

He faced Annika. This woman whom he loved with every cell in his body. Of this there was no doubt. But he was not what was best for her. Not by a long shot.

"Daniel? Are you okay? What's wrong?" His decision must have shown on his face, because concern replaced the relief in her voice.

Mr. Mehta slowed his pace and went to sit by his wife once more. He held her hand and forced a smile onto his face. She leaned against his shoulder.

Daniel took Annika and walked a short distance away from them. "Look at me." Brown eyes flecked with worry. He should be helping her get through this. She was brave enough to be with him when her family didn't approve. He should be telling her that everything would be okay.

Annika shouldn't be worried about him; she should be thinking about her brother and parents.

He tried to take her hands in his, but they shook uncontrollably. Instead, Annika covered his hands with hers, holding them steady. "It's okay, Daniel. Everything will be fine."

His heart raced and his stomach twisted with dread. She deserved far better than what he could offer. She needed what her parents had. She needed someone strong enough to lean on. He broke free of her hands and ran a shaky hand through his hair.

"What's going on?"

He shook his head, returning his gaze to her parents. "I can't do this."

She furrowed her brow. "Do what?"

He turned his full attention to her, aware that he might have a crazed look in his eye. "This." He motioned between the two of them. "I haven't been honest with you." He paused and then blurted everything out. "After Sara, I had decided that I would never be a father again. I even tried to get a vasectomy, but I was so young that the surgeon advised against it. But I *knew* I could never be a father again. Ever. I can't even be godfather to Sheila's baby, for God's sake."

Annika opened her mouth to say something, but he took her face in his hand and rested a thumb on her lips. One last time. "When I met you—when I fell in love with you, I thought I could. I wanted to be able to. It was the first time I wanted my own family again—because I couldn't imagine my life without you."

Still can't.

"I told myself that I was different now, time had passed, surely I was stronger...and that I could be a father if I had you by my side. But I don't have it in me." He glanced at her parents. "Look at them. It's agony."

He felt her swallow hard; her nostrils flared. She gasped as if she'd been punched in the gut. "You're breaking up with me."

"I love you. You make my heart race, you make me laugh, you have given me a taste of happiness, which is something I never thought I would know again. I've never loved anyone like this. And I am certain I never will again."

She reached into her pocket and pulled out what looked like a broken hospital band and held it out to him. He took it. "That's my band, from the night I lost my baby. From the night Steven left me." She lifted her chin and captured him in her gaze.

Daniel looked at the band; the lettering was faded, but it was definitely an ER band from his ER. He remembered seeing the tiny one on Sara's wrist. Where was it? Had they saved it? Did people do that? Should he have saved it?

"But it's a reminder of the worst time in your life."

She nodded. "It's also a reminder of what I survived."

The lettering blurred before his eyes. "You'll make a fabulous mother one day. But I...won't survive another...

I've barely survived losing... I can't be anyone's father ever again, because I can't do this—" he looked at her parents "—ever again." His eyes were wet, and it was difficult getting air into his lungs, but this was the right thing. It had to be.

Annika's skin had gone ashen and tears filled her eyes. Tears that he put there. Better a few tears now than an ocean later.

He let go of her sharply, as if she had scorched him, and stepped back. He needed to stop touching her. "I'm not the man for you. You deserve much more than...me."

The door to the waiting area opened, and Sajan entered. Daniel's heart fell into his stomach as the surgeon approached.

"He's fine." Sajan addressed Annika's parents. "His lungs will take a few weeks to heal, but we'll be monitoring him closely."

Annika's parents slumped against each other in relief, both of them tearing up. "Thank you, Sajan!" her father croaked out. "I knew he would be okay under your care. We owe you a debt of gratitude."

"Actually, Uncle, if it hadn't been for the quick thinking of his medics—" Sajan nodded in Daniel's direction "—I wouldn't have had much to work with." He smiled at Annika's father. "I need to get back."

Daniel turned to find Annika watching him. "See," she said, relief playing on her face, "he's fine—and thanks to you." Her hands shook as she reached for him.

Daniel craved nothing more than to allow her to wrap him in her arms, to believe in the fantasy that he could have a family, that he could have *her*. But that was exactly what it was. A fantasy. He had to stop lying to her. And to himself. He stepped out of her reach, because if she touched him now, he would cave. He would give in to his stupid heart and try to live the fantasy.

"No, Annika, don't. I'm not the one for you."

Panic rippled through him at the finality of losing his best source of comfort, of not having Annika by his side. He steeled himself, fought the lump that poked at the back of his throat. "Naya's right. Sajan can make you happy. Give you the life you deserve. I can't." He stepped farther back from her, lest he be tempted to touch her again.

"Daniel, you can get help. You only need to ask." She was pleading with him now.

He couldn't allow her to do that. He wasn't worth it.

He shook his head at her. "There's no help for me."

"Are you serious?" She narrowed her eyes and threw her next words at him in a low growl. "You're going to break up with me. In the—" her breath hitched "—hospital?"

The implication was clear. He was no better than Steven. Let her be angry. Anger was easier to deal with.

He spun around and walked toward the elevators, resisting the temptation to look back at her. If he looked, he'd take it all back and ask her to marry him.

That was lost to him now. Forever.

CHAPTER TWENTY-EIGHT

ANNIKA

ANNIKA SHUFFLED PAPERS, finished her lesson plans and put them into her bag. She threw in her sneakers for her shift at the bar. She'd just eat something at the bar today. Mrs. P. was on a mission to get Annika to eat more, but she simply hadn't had much of an appetite since that day in the hospital. Since Daniel left her.

She glanced at her reflection in the mirror by the door and pulled out some lipstick. Dark circles under her eyes advertised her lack of sleep. She applied the lipstick, vowing to stop being such a cliché and eat to Mrs. P.'s satisfaction whether she felt like it or not. Not eating and not sleeping were not going to convince Daniel that he'd made a mistake. No one could do that except Daniel himself.

Why she couldn't fall for normal, stable people was beyond her. The emptiness in her heart and gut were proof of her misguided feelings and had, many times during the past week, threatened to overcome her. But she had a class to teach, lesson plans to write, not to mention her parents were staying with her so they could be closer to the hospital. Whenever she had a minute, she went to see her brother.

She didn't have time to grieve over the fact that she thought she'd found her one true love but he turned out to be just another man who'd left her at the moment she needed him most. That he was lost in his own grief. That he wasn't hers anymore. The familiar burn prickled her eyes and nose. She closed her eyes and fought it back.

Daniel was just another failed relationship. Just another boyfriend. Just another someone she'd fallen for who'd decided she wasn't enough. She made poor decisions when it came to love, and it was time she listened to the people who really did love her. Her parents. Naya. Maybe she'd call Sajan in a week or two. She just couldn't handle anything right now.

These were the lies she told herself to get herself out of bed and back into her life.

"You don't have to work at the bar." Her father was having his chai. Even the familiar aroma of the cardamom and cinnamon failed to comfort her shattered heart. Her parents had taken over Naya's room, and Naya had gone home to visit her parents. Her mother had insisted upon spending the night at the hospital, and her father was on his way to relieve her. Though Nilay was out of danger, they needed to be with him. This was what they did.

"Yes, I do, Papa." She needed the money but left that fact unsaid, hanging between them.

"It's dangerous."

"I'm fine, Papa." She forced the irritation out of her voice. Her parents had enough to deal with right now.

"What happened with Daniel?"

She opened kitchen drawers, looking for nothing, as she avoided his question. She swallowed the lump in her throat that formed at the mention of Daniel's name, but there was no way to mask the sorrow in her face.

"Annika—"

"Papa!" She looked at him, calling on her anger. "What

difference does it make? You never liked him. You got what you wanted."

"I didn't want you to be unhappy."

"I'll be fine." She had no choice. He wasn't ready to move on. Not yet. Maybe someday he would be, and some other woman would benefit from that. The thought of Daniel with another woman burned like acid in her heart and had her blinking back tears—again.

"I know why he didn't come into the school building on Career Day."

Annika froze. "You do?"

"I heard him in the waiting room that day."

"Then you know—" Her breath caught.

"Yes, I know." Her father's face took on a distant, pained look, one that Annika had seen more than once. His eyes went soft. "You know what he has to do."

She sagged. "Papa. He won't. I've tried—"

"He has to be ready." Her father inhaled deeply and stood to face her. "You know, when I came to the school that day with Sajan, I saw how beautifully you handled those disappointed children." He paused and put a hand on her shoulder. Her father was not afraid to admit when he was wrong; it was one of the things she most respected about him. He lifted his chin and looked her in the eye, chagrin coloring his smile. "It was then that I realized I have let you down. You are my daughter, and you are following your heart—as you should. I was impressed. With skills like that, you should not have to work in a bar to make ends meet. It's a sad state of affairs for teachers, I am sorry to say. But I am proud of you."

Tears filled her eyes. She didn't realize how much she had wanted to hear those words and see the pride in her father's face. It didn't matter how old you got: you always wanted your parents to be proud of you. She hugged him, relaxing into her father's arms as if she were still a little girl. "Thanks, Papa."

He hugged her back and kissed the top of her head. "In the meantime, you should get to work. Come, I'll drive you."

AFTER SCHOOL BUT before her shift at Phil's, Annika went to see her brother at the hospital. Naya was sitting beside a drugged and sleeping Nilay. She and Naya had not spoken much since that dinner. It had been only ten days, but it seemed longer. Annika had reached out to her cousin, knowing that Naya would be hurting from her breakup with Ravi, but Naya had remained distant until Nilay's accident. Annika couldn't imagine her life without Naya and knew the feeling was mutual.

Annika walked in. "Hey."

Naya turned and smiled at her, but the smile did not reach her eyes. She had dark circles and her cheeks seemed sunken. Naya got up and hugged her. "Can you ever forgive me for being such a terrible best friend and sister?"

Annika hugged her tight and felt tears prickle at her nose. "It's forgotten—and anyway, you were a little bit right." She pulled back and tried to stem her tears. "He broke up with me, right in the waiting room. What is it with me and hospitals?" She tried to joke.

"What? That little fucker." Naya shook her head.

"Jeez, Naya. I did love him." *Still do*...

"Sorry, reflex. What happened? I was just starting to like him."

Annika raised an eyebrow at her cousin.

"Well," Naya continued, "I was trying to like him, anyway."

Annika shrugged. "There's not much to say. He has to deal with losing Sara. Right now, he deals by shutting down." She thought about Daniel's family. "And shutting everyone out." *Including her.* She swallowed hard. "That's what makes it so difficult. I have no doubt that he loves me. I actually think he feels like he's doing right by me. What is wrong with men?"

"By deciding *for you* that having children was more important than him?"

Annika sighed. She *should* probably be angrier about that, but she really couldn't muster the energy to be angry at someone who was hurting so much. Especially someone she loved with such ferocity.

"Give it a rest, Naya. Either way, he has to come to terms with his loss before he can—" *Be with someone again.* And she knew it wouldn't be her. When—if—he healed, he'd be a different person with different needs. Who knew if he'd still love her? She certainly couldn't wait around to just be disappointed. Boy, she really could pick them, couldn't she?

"You're too good for him." Naya grinned.

Annika rolled her eyes. "Whatever." She chuckled as she squeezed her cousin's hand. "How are you?"

Naya shrugged, but Annika caught the tears in her sunken eyes.

"Hey." Annika turned Naya's face toward her own. "Is it possible you're being stubborn and not seeing the big picture?"

"What's that?"

"That you and Ravi love each other and should be able to live your own lives."

"That's not—"

"Yes, it is. I'm not saying defy all authority. I'm saying

you're both grown adults. If he's willing to be with you with all his heart, his parents will come around. And if they don't—well, you can't live your life trying to make everyone else happy."

"Have you been talking to Ravi?"

"No, she has not." A deep but familiar rumble came from behind Annika, and Naya went even paler.

Annika turned to find a disheveled and weary Ravi standing in the door. He nodded at Annika, but addressed his words to Naya. "I knew you'd come to see Nilay. Annika is right. Talk to me, Naya. Come on."

"How did you even…know about Nilay?" Naya turned accusatory eyes on her cousin.

Annika held up her hands in surrender. "Not me."

"Daniel," Ravi confessed, flicking his gaze to Annika. "He called me."

That sharp pang that Annika was getting familiar with stabbed at her heart.

Naya, for her part, was frozen in her seat, her eyes filled with longing for the man in front of her.

Annika stood. "I'll just go…get some coffee…or something."

"No." Naya stood. "We'll go." She squeezed Annika's hand. "You visit with Nilay." Naya walked over to Ravi and took his hand. "Let's talk."

Annika settled into her chair next to Nilay's bed, prepared to watch him sleep as she had the past few days.

"Is she gone?" Nilay croaked from the bed.

Annika sat up. "Yes. Are you all right?"

Nilay raised a hand. "Fine. Can you press the button so I can sit up?"

Annika did as her brother asked. He actually looked

better. There was some color in his face, and he was smiling. "Hey! You look good!"

"Duh." He grinned. "I'm ready to kick some ass."

Annika shook her head. "Isn't that what put you here to begin with?"

"Listen, nobody messes with my sister."

"Yeah, okay, big guy." Annika smiled at him and shook her head.

Nilay's eyes got serious. "I mean it. If I ever find that guy—or even the dad at the school that insulted you—"

"What dad at the school?" Daniel's voice thundered from behind Annika, startling her. She jumped up and turned around to find him standing in the doorway, his unkempt jaw clenched and green eyes fierce. She leaned on the chair for support.

"Daniel, what are you doing here?" She had no idea how she sounded; she only hoped she didn't sound as heartbroken as she felt.

Daniel's mouth was set in a line, and he was clearly trying to avoid looking at her. "I came to see the kid." He lost his fight and looked at her, his voice and face immediately softening. "I walked by and saw you sitting here. I was leaving when I heard what he said." He pressed his lips together. "What guy at the school?"

"The dad who told her he didn't think 'her kind' should be teaching there," Nilay spoke up. "You know, the one with the kid who doesn't talk."

Now her brother decided to feel better and get all chatty.

"Mitch? Mitch's father said that to you?" Daniel's eyes widened. "That's why he never came to your meetings?"

"It doesn't matter." Annika turned her head to glare at her brother.

"It does matter!" Both men spoke in unison.

"I know it matters, but neither one of you is punching him." She pointed a finger at each of them.

"You really look like a mean teacher right now, pointing your finger like that," Nilay quipped.

She bit the inside of her lip to keep from smiling at him. "Good. Because I mean it."

Daniel was not amused. "You have to teach that guy a lesson, call the cops or whatever."

She turned back to Daniel. "I'll teach him a lesson my way."

"And what way is that?"

"By being me." She raised her chin at Daniel, her heart banging in her chest, as if it were trying to get out and go to him, where it belonged.

"What the hell does that mean?"

"It means—" she grabbed her purse and jacket "—that I'll handle it. It also means it's not your problem. Not anymore." She did her best to glare at him but was struck with a pang of sadness when his shoulders drooped and she knew she'd hurt him. "Bye, Nilay." She leaned down and kissed his forehead. "I need to get to work."

She brushed past Daniel, the very air that passed between them charged with the intensity of their not touching. It took every last piece of willpower she had to not give in to the desire to reach out to him. Why did he smell so good?

He stood stoic in the door as she passed, his gaze never leaving Nilay.

CHAPTER TWENTY-NINE

DANIEL

DANIEL SECURED THE sling on his last patient of the day, a fifteen-year-old budding daredevil who had an affinity for not quite succeeding in his tricks on his skateboard.

"You remember the instructions from last time?" Daniel grinned and raised an eyebrow.

The teen gave a small eye roll and an embarrassed grin. "Yes, sir."

Daniel looked at the boy's father. "Ortho will put on the cast tomorrow."

The boy's father shook his head behind him and gave a snort of laughter. "We'll be putting Dr. Cross's kids through college yet."

Daniel laughed with the father and shook both of their hands before heading out to the nurses' station to finish up for the day. His heart fell into his stomach at the sight of Anil Mehta seated in the waiting room. What the hell was Annika's father doing in the ER waiting room?

Daniel passed the nurses' station, glancing at the board, panic rising in his chest as he approached Mr. Mehta at nearly a run. "Uncle, is everything okay? Why are you in the ER?"

Mr. Mehta looked up from his phone and stood. "Hmm? Yes, yes." He held his hand up and gave a small smile. "Everyone is fine. No one is hurt. Sorry to have alarmed you, but I came to see you."

Daniel's heart still hammered in his chest, and he inhaled deeply to slow it, but even in his relief he couldn't imagine why Mr. Mehta had come to see him. "Okay. I just finished my shift. I'll be right back."

Daniel clocked out, sifting through the possibilities of what the older man could want with him. He grabbed his jacket and backpack and took a breath before walking toward the waiting area.

Mr. Mehta was waiting by the doors. As Daniel approached, Mr. Mehta nodded. "Coffee?"

"Sure." Daniel opened the door to a slight evening chill, then led the way down the block to the closest coffee shop. His heart rate had returned to normal, but now his stomach was in knots. Was Annika okay? Was he about to be berated or thanked for leaving her?

Mr. Mehta addressed the barista. "Tall coffee, room for cream." He turned to Daniel. "How about you?"

"Same." He pulled out his wallet.

Mr. Mehta smiled at Daniel's choice of beverage and addressed the barista again. "If you don't mind, we'd like our coffee in mugs as opposed to the to-go cups." The barista nodded, and Mr. Mehta waved away Daniel's offer to pay. "Don't be ridiculous. Put that away."

For some reason, this made Daniel defensive. "It's coffee. I can afford—"

Mr. Mehta stepped closer to the counter and swiped his card. "You misunderstand. This has nothing to do with whether you can afford to pay for coffee." He finished his transaction. "On the contrary, this has everything to do with what I owe you."

Daniel was speechless.

They fixed up their coffees and found a place to sit.

"I'm relieved you did not order the 'chai' tea." Mr. Mehta gave a small smile.

Daniel scowled. "'Tea tea?' Seriously. And it's not real chai anyway, is it?"

Mr. Mehta chuckled. "No. That it is not."

Daniel sat straight in his chair, both hands on his mug. "Is everything okay with Nilay?" he asked as Mr. Mehta took his first sip. "How's his recovery?"

A few people entered the shop, and the slurps and burps of the coffee machine mixed with the low volume of chatter.

"It may be some time before he can come home, but Nilay is progressing nicely. I suspect you already knew that."

Daniel nodded. He'd been visiting every day, just trying to keep clear of Annika when he did. It didn't stop Nilay from lecturing him about breaking his sister's heart. Daniel tried to ignore Nilay's words. Better he broke Annika's heart now than later on down the line.

"Well, Daniel." Mr. Mehta took another sip and gently set his mug down.

Daniel took a sip, allowing the hot liquid to warm him while he waited for the older man to continue. For mid-March, it was still cold, even though the sun was high.

Mr. Mehta raised his chin and looked Daniel in the eye. "I wanted to see you for a couple of reasons. Not the least of which is that I owe you deep gratitude for what you did for Nilay. Sajan insists it was your quick thinking that saved his life."

Daniel forced a smile. "Part of my job, sir. Nilay is a wonderful kid, and I'm just thankful that he's doing well."

"You weren't working that day, and you were injured, as

well." He glanced at the healing gash on Daniel's forearm. "But you put my son's care before yours, and for that I am eternally grateful." Mr. Mehta smiled, but it was something melancholy and weak. "Not only that, but you are modest, too. I should have known." He paused.

Daniel waited, as it seemed Mr. Mehta had more to say.

"I'm also here to apologize for underestimating you— actually, I should apologize for my rudeness the few times we have met. I'm afraid I prejudged you based on your chosen profession and my own biases. It's no excuse, especially when my son and daughter think so highly of you. You have no reason to accept my apology, but I offer it, nonetheless." He stopped and sipped his coffee.

A few beats of silence passed as Daniel digested what he had said. What Annika's father had said. All he could manage at first was a nod. "Thank you, Uncle." Still in shock, his voice was not much more than a croak. "That means a lot to me." He looked the older man in the eye. "It's not easy, being a father. Seems natural to want only the best for your children."

"True, but we have to separate what's best for them from what *we* want for them." Mr. Mehta shrugged with a small smile. "Sometimes—many times, in my case—that is not the same thing."

Daniel smiled his acknowledgment and went back to drinking his coffee. Mr. Mehta sat in silence for a moment, as if deciding whether or not to say something.

"Is there something else, Uncle?"

Mr. Mehta inhaled deeply and looked Daniel in the eye. "Yes, in fact, there is. I have one more thing."

Daniel finished his coffee and fiddled with his mug. It was taking all his self-control to not ask about Annika. It had been less than two weeks since he'd left her standing there in that waiting room, but only two days since he'd last seen her in Nilay's room. She had brushed past him that day, leaving behind a tangible vacuum.

Turns out he was as much of a jerk as Steven. Left her when she needed him most. While he wouldn't be forgiving himself for that anytime soon, he knew with all his heart that it had to be done.

Seeing her in Nilay's room a few days ago had only served to remind him of how much he loved her. Even now, his cells were dancing a small jig because he was talking to her father. Because of the *potential* that he might get some information about her.

Daniel wanted nothing more than to be the man she deserved, the man who could make her happy, but he wasn't, and he never would be. She was better off without him, and the sooner she accepted that, the sooner she could go on with her life and be truly happy.

He would just have to deal.

As if he had read Daniel's mind, Mr. Mehta shifted in his seat. "I did not mean to eavesdrop on your conversation that day in the waiting room, but I overheard what you told my daughter after she so very gallantly defended you to me. And I wanted to give you this." He slid a card across the table to Daniel. It said simply, "We are fathers."

Confused, Daniel looked at Mr. Mehta. "I don't have children."

"But you did."

A pit formed in Daniel's stomach. He wasn't going to talk about Sara here. Or anywhere.

Mr. Mehta held up his hands at the look on Daniel's face. "I'm not asking you to talk about it. And my daughter did not betray your confidence. I simply heard you mention it to her. In a public place. Before you broke her heart." He raised an eyebrow.

Daniel squirmed under his gaze. He was never going to please this man. "I would've thought my leaving was what you wanted."

The older man nodded. "Yes, I can see why you would think that. But as I said, as a father, you know it's about your children's happiness. And my daughter is not happy." Anil Mehta sighed. "But I'm not here for Annika. I'm here for you."

"I'm not a father." *Anymore.*

Mr. Mehta rested his hands on the table. "This is a support group for men like you. I know people, and this has come across my desk. I am passing along the information. Do with it what you will."

Daniel started to hand the card back. "I don't need this. But thank you."

Mr. Mehta raised his hand in protest. "Most men feel the same. But your ex-wife isn't the only person who lost a child."

Daniel flicked his eyes to the older man's. He found only compassion.

"Think about it." Mr. Mehta stood and extended his hand. "Thank you again, for everything."

Daniel shook his hand and nodded.

DANIEL IDLED HIS bike for a moment in front of the house. The sun was hiding behind clouds; the air carried the scent of freshly cut lawn and new mulch. Maybe he should have called first. He just wasn't sure that Sheila would actually take his call. Not after their last conversation.

Maybe it was because Annika's father had apologized to him. Or maybe he was just feeling guilty. But the truth was, he had been unduly harsh to Sheila, and he owed her an apology. Though they weren't really in each other's lives anymore, they were irreparably joined by a common past. Daniel could not let his apology go unsaid.

There were two cars in the driveway, meaning that Jim was home, too. Whatever. He was here to apologize—it didn't matter who else heard it.

He turned off his bike and tucked his helmet under one arm. The familiar dread of approaching the house Sara had lived in filled his stomach, but he pushed through and rang the doorbell.

The door opened, and he found himself face-to-face with a grim-faced Jim.

"Daniel."

"Jim. Is she home?"

"She is, but I can't have you upsetting her right now."

"I'm not here to—" He looked down at his feet, then back at Jim. "I just want to apologize for being such an ass."

A small smile flashed across Jim's face. He opened the door. "Good luck."

"Thanks." Daniel stepped across the threshold into the house. He ignored the assault to his senses that always dragged him back in time.

"Who is it, Jim?" Sheila's voice carried from the kitchen.

Daniel raised his eyebrows at Jim. Jim shrugged. Daniel was on his own. "It's me, Sheila." Daniel kept his shoes on and walked toward the kitchen. This wouldn't take long. He was met halfway by a very pregnant Sheila. She was just about due.

She narrowed her eyes and folded her arms across her chest. "Humph."

"Yeah." Daniel fidgeted with his helmet. "Listen, Sheila.

I'm sorry. I was out of line when you asked me to be your baby's godfather. I said things...that were cruel, and I'm sorry. If I could take it back, I would. You don't deserve that from me. You didn't when we were married, and you most certainly don't now."

Sheila stared at him, but her face had softened. "Well, you're right about that. And somehow, Daniel, you leave me speechless, no matter what the situation." She allowed herself a small smile and leaned on a chair. "You want to be—?"

Daniel cut her off. "I can't. You know I can't."

Sheila tried again. "It would be good for you."

Daniel shook his head. "Don't, Sheila. Please."

She nodded her surrender. Silence filled the space for a moment.

"Well, I won't take up any more of your time. Take care, Sheila." Daniel turned to leave. "Jim."

The other man stepped aside and walked him to the door in silence. The great thing about Jim was that he didn't feel the need to fill empty space with nonsense words. He extended a hand to Daniel. "Thanks for coming by. It really does mean the world to her. And to me."

Daniel shook Jim's hand and left the cloud of the past as he quickly headed off toward his bike. The sun finally made a showing, and Daniel raised his face to its warmth, his heart oddly light. He donned his helmet and was just getting ready to start his bike when he caught sight of Jim running toward him, arms flailing wildly. Daniel took off his helmet and dismounted his bike. He already knew what was happening.

"Her water broke, didn't it?"

A rather pale Jim nodded, his head bobbing up and down faster than necessary. Daniel put a hand on his shoulder and let out a small chuckle. Nervous first-time dads came through the ER all the time. "It's okay, Jim. Breathe."

Jim stilled his head and inhaled deeply, finding his voice again. "Daniel, the baby—"

"Yes, the baby is coming. Shall we go get Sheila?" Daniel asked as he started walking back into the house.

Jim didn't move.

"Babies are born in the ER all the time," Daniel said. "Come on. We'll get Sheila, her bag and your car keys."

Jim swallowed hard. "I'm going to be a dad."

Daniel grinned. "Yes. You are." Somehow, his reply held none of the angst it usually did when he watched men become fathers in his ER.

They walked back in to find Sheila grabbing her belly and moaning in pain.

"Jim," Daniel said, "go get her bag."

Jim tried to kiss his wife's cheek, but the glare she threw at him could have made laser holes in his head, so he bolted upstairs to get the bag.

"Sheila, breathe." Daniel moved toward her.

She took a deep breath and turned to Daniel with fear in her eyes.

"You'll be fine," Daniel reassured her.

She shook her head and tried to speak but was overcome with a contraction, and moaned aloud.

"Those are coming pretty fast and hard. Where are the keys?"

"Daniel. The baby," she gasped. "Not ready."

Daniel grinned at her. "Oh, the baby's ready. He or she is coming."

She shook her head again. "Listen to me!" she demanded. She took a deep breath and pointedly focused on Daniel. "The baby wasn't ready as of yesterday. Dr.

Goldberg said the baby needed to be turned because its feet are pointing down." She closed her eyes and moaned. "Not ready."

Oh, shit.

Daniel kicked in to work mode. "Let me feel the baby." He waited for Sheila to stand and nod her head. "Remember?"

He gently probed her belly, identifying body parts. It was a game he and Sheila used to play when she was pregnant with Sara. They would laugh as they tried to figure out what each bump was and cry happy tears when she would kick.

There was so much more to having this baby than Daniel had ever thought about. And Sheila was doing it. He felt Sheila's steady gaze on him and looked up to meet it. A pang of grief hit him with such force he was almost drawn down to his knees. There was panic and worry in Sheila's eyes that only he could understand. Daniel swallowed his grief and kissed her forehead. "It's going to be fine, Sheila. I promise."

Tears filled her eyes. "Don't promise if—"

"I would never." He took her hand and placed it on her lower abdomen. "The head is down."

She half sobbed, half laughed her relief. "Thank you, Daniel." She squeezed his hand. "Thank you for being here."

"Of course." He looked behind her as Jim came down with her suitcase. "Give me that, Jim." He took the bag. "Help her to the car." Daniel spotted the car keys hanging in the kitchen and grabbed them.

Daniel got into the driver's seat as Jim settled a moaning Sheila into the middle seat of the minivan. Jim shut the door and came around to Daniel. "You better sit with her in the back. You know, in case something happens."

"Nothing is going to happen. Get back there."

"Daniel! You get your ass back here and take care of this baby or else!" Sheila commanded from the back.

Jim raised his eyebrows and opened the driver's door. "Good luck," he whispered.

"I heard that, Jim," Sheila growled.

Daniel settled in next to her just as Jim started the car and pulled out. Sheila was in the middle of a contraction.

"Breathe, honey," Jim called from the front seat.

"If you tell me to goddamn breathe one more time, Jim…"

Jim focused on the road.

Daniel turned to Sheila as she screamed out in pain as another contraction racked her body. She'd tied her hair in a ponytail, but a few wisps escaped, sticking to the sweat on her face.

"Whoa, those are coming fast," Daniel said.

"What do you mean?" She lay back, trying to catch her breath.

"I mean they're coming fast. Let me check you."

Sheila's eyes nearly popped out of her head as she bolted upright. "Let you *what*?"

"Isn't that why I'm here? Besides, I'm a professional. Not to mention we were married once."

"We'll make it to the hospital. Right, Jim?" Sheila sounded desperate.

Jim's answer was drowned out by another scream as another contraction hit.

"Sheila. Let me check." Daniel was insistent. The baby could be on the way.

"Damn it, Sheila, let him check—what if the baby is coming?" Jim called out.

Sheila sighed and lay back in the minivan. Daniel checked and grinned at her. "I can feel the head. This is happening. Now. Like, right now."

Alarm filled her eyes.

"It's going to be fine." He glanced out the window. "We're almost there, but we're getting started here."

"I need to push, Daniel. *Jim!* I need to push."

Daniel was in work mode. His voice was calm and his movements were swift and efficient. Everything was clear to him. He hadn't lied: he *had* delivered many babies before. Just none in a moving car.

"You're fine, Sheila. Let Jim drive. We'll be there soon."

Sheila inhaled and did her breathing, Jim counting from the front.

"Okay," Daniel said, "when I say, go ahead and push."

Sheila groaned out the next contraction and pushed. Daniel got the head. He swept the baby's mouth. "Okay, Sheila. One more good push."

The next contraction came before he finished. Daniel held on while Sheila pushed out her baby. He wrapped the baby in Sheila's sweater just as they approached the ER bay. Jim slammed on the brakes and turned back to Daniel.

"What do you want me to do?"

Daniel grinned. "Come back here and meet your son." He couldn't remember the last time he was this happy. A *baby* had done that. "I'll get help."

"Son? It's a boy?" Jim ran around the car to the back seat and got in next to Sheila. Daniel walked into his ER and called for a gurney, ignoring the fact that he was covered in blood.

In no time, Sheila was in a bed, her little son cleaned

up, with Jim beaming beside her. Daniel washed up and went to check on her.

"Want to hold your godson, Daniel?" Jim held the baby out to him.

Daniel wanted nothing more, and no one was more surprised than he was. "I haven't agreed—"

Jim smiled. "It's all over your face. It's okay to hold him."

Daniel reached out with trembling hands and took the bundle from Jim. His hands had been steady when he delivered the child, but now his nervousness took over. Daniel gingerly cradled the infant in his arms and looked down at his face.

He gasped. "Sheila, he has her eyes."

Tears of joy fell to her cheeks as she nodded, but Daniel caught a fleeting sadness, as well. It occurred to him again how hard this must be for Sheila. Wonderful, but not without difficult memories.

"I mean, they're your eyes."

She grabbed Jim's hand and interlocked their fingers. "They're *her* eyes." Her grief for Sara and her joy for her new son were intertwined all in the same moment.

He had been so very wrong. A new baby didn't take away from Sara—a new baby helped to keep her alive. He returned his attention to the now sleeping baby in his arms. Daniel inhaled that baby smell and allowed himself to be taken back in time to Sara's birth. He really hadn't known what he was going to do with a baby. His excitement had been interlaced with apprehension. *Overwhelmed* didn't even begin to describe it. Each day his heart had swelled with love he hadn't even known he was capable of, and he had followed it, hoping he would be a good father. He kissed Sheila's forehead. "You make beautiful babies."

She flushed and turned to her husband. Jim's eyes filled with new-dad tears as he took in his son. Daniel reluctantly put the baby into their arms and stepped back. Jim kissed Sheila, and they both spent the next few minutes gazing at the wonder that was this newborn child.

"You got a name?"

Jim beamed. "Aaron. It means strength."

Daniel nodded, a calm and peace coming over him that he hadn't experienced in some time. Without consciously doing so, he imagined a similar scene with a baby whose eyes were so brown and soft they were almost black. He imagined creamy brown skin, and perfect little red lips. He imagined a baby that was his. His and Annika's.

The pit in his stomach was gone. It was replaced by an intense longing, as if a dam had broken, and what came through was that *this* was what he wanted. His fear had blocked him from seeing it, but this was what his life should be, risks and all.

CHAPTER THIRTY

ANNIKA

ANNIKA SEARCHED THE busy restaurant until familiar hazel-brown eyes met hers. Sajan raised his hand in greeting and smiled. Annika smiled back and walked toward the booth where he was seated. He was quite handsome, and the restaurant he'd chosen was trendy but tasteful. She willed herself to feel something—anything—for this wonderful man who could be part of her future.

Sajan stood as she approached the booth and waited while she settled herself in. *Good manners.* She was really reaching.

Popular music played and laughter sprang out spontaneously over the general chatter of the customers. It was early on a Saturday night, and anticipation of what the evening would bring buzzed in the air, creating a tangible excitement. Annika tried to tap into that energy.

"I'm so glad you called." Sajan beamed as he seated himself once again. "I have to admit, I was a bit surprised."

Annika tilted her head in question.

"I thought you and Daniel…"

She froze her face into the mask she used to hide the pang of pain that always followed mention of his name and shook her head. "Oh. Yes. Well, that's over." She waved her hand as if her relationship with Daniel had been inconsequential. *Well, it should be by now.*

Sajan narrowed his eyes and studied her a moment. "Okay."

The waiter arrived asking for their drink order. Sajan nodded at Annika.

"I'll have the Bee's Knees. Easy on the honey." Annika fidgeted.

"Manhattan." He looked at the waiter. "Thanks."

Annika smiled at Sajan. "Thanks again for everything you did for my brother. My parents are so grateful to have him back home."

Sajan shrugged. "Just doing my job. Besides, I meant what I said—if Daniel hadn't relieved the pressure in the field, things could have ended differently."

Annika swallowed hard.

"Did they ever find the guy?" Sajan's eyes darkened a bit in anger. Of course Nilay would have told him the whole story.

"No. But we didn't really have that much to go on."

"Well, your brother kept talking about having another shot at him." Sajan shook his head. "To be young, huh? Punches solve everything."

"Not necessarily."

"I agree. Violence is not going to stop violence."

Annika smiled for real this time. "I know. That's what I keep saying, but every other male I speak to simply wants to throw punches. For what? You're not going to change his mind by breaking bones." Here was something she could connect with Sajan over. Maybe this date had been a good idea.

"Very true."

Annika studied her menu in the silence that fell between them.

"How's your cousin?" Sajan asked. "I heard she's getting married."

Annika perked up. "Yes. She is." She shook her head. "End of June. She's barely giving us three to four months to plan. Her mom is out of her mind." She laughed. But it was forced.

"Well, good for her. Ravi's a great guy."

Annika nodded. "He really is. I'm very happy for her."

Their drinks arrived. Sajan held his out to her, and they clinked glasses. Annika took a sip, enjoying the tartness of the lemon juice, closing her eyes as the alcohol made its way through her body. She opened them to find Sajan watching her.

He put his drink down, laying his hands on either side of it, and fixed his gaze on her. "Why are we here, Annika?"

She put on a smile. "We're on date. I called you, asked you out, and here we are."

He leaned back and shook his head. "I get that. But why?"

"Why are we on a date?" Annika narrowed her eyes at him, as if that were a ridiculous question, when in reality she knew exactly what he was asking.

"Yes, Annika." He exhaled heavily. "Why are we on a date that you clearly do not want to be on?"

"That's not true. I like you and—" Annika sagged in her seat at his withering look. "I'm sorry. It's not you, I swear. I'm trying, I really am."

He sat back and straightened his back. "Jeez, Annika. My ego is pretty healthy, but come *on*."

"Sorry. I didn't mean it like that." She was an idiot. And possibly a terrible person. She had no business being here

on a date with Sajan when she clearly had no romantic feelings for him, and never would. She had great affection for
him as a friend, but that was all.

"Oh, God, Sajan. I'm an idiot." She started to reach into
her purse for cash to pay for their drinks. "You're right. I
never should have called when I'm—"

"Clearly still in love with Daniel." Sadness fell over Sajan's face, and he sank into his seat.

Annika pressed her lips together and faced him. "Is it
that obvious?"

Sajan nodded. "Yep."

"Ugh. I'm really sorry. You must think I'm awful—and
you wouldn't necessarily be wrong. You're a lovely person,
and I enjoy your company, and our parents—"

Sajan held his hand up to stop her. "Are wrong plenty of
times." He sighed. "And you're not an awful person. You're
trying to make your parents happy. And if it's any consola-
tion, I knew this couldn't be a real date when I accepted it."

"How'd you know that?"

He grinned. "I work with Daniel from time to time. He
looks worse than you." Sajan studied her a moment. "Want
to know what I think, as a friend?"

Annika smiled. "Of course."

"I'm guessing he broke up with you?"

Annika nodded.

"Daniel has some serious demons that he has not dealt
with. This breakup is about fear."

Annika sat up and stared at him, a light slowly going
on in her head.

"Daniel's a healer," Sajan continued. "And I don't mean
just his job. I mean that's who he is."

"And he can't heal himself." Annika spoke slowly as
the realization hit her. "He's afraid to heal himself. Be-

cause he's afraid of losing her all over again." Of course. This wasn't about her judgment. Daniel *was* a good man. A really good man. And his love for her was true. But she could not fight his demons for him. He had to do that on his own. He had to want to.

She pressed her lips together in a small smile and finished her drink. "Thank you." She placed her empty glass down. "Listen, I don't have any other plans tonight. Want another round? My treat." She let her eyes rest on him, hoping he'd agree. "I'll even spring for food."

"Well, if you're treating, hell yeah." He laughed and motioned for their waiter.

ANNIKA FINISHED PLEATING Naya's sari and pulled the pleated section down over her cousin's shoulder. "Stay still," she commanded through a mouthful of safety pins. She sounded like her mother. When the hell had that happened?

"It doesn't have to be perfect. We're just trying it on." Naya squirmed.

"Just stay still," Annika demanded as she pinned and wrapped Naya in her wedding sari until Naya was perfection. The sari was the traditional white with a red border, with fine beading throughout. Naya would make a beautiful bride.

"I think you do just a nice, simple updo, the red and white flowers accenting it, and that's good. What do you think?"

"I love it." Naya was slightly giddy. "What about you guys?"

"I had your mom get us all the same sari in that blue you like so much, right?"

Naya nodded her approval. "Honestly, whatever makes my mom happy at this point."

Annika grinned. A diva her cousin was not. Which boded well, since they had barely a few months to plan this thing.

"Lucky that Ravi was so persistent, eh?" Annika teased.

"Can't fight true love." Naya flushed.

"Too bad you didn't believe that a few months ago. We would've had more time to plan this." Annika studied her cousin.

"It's part of the compromise with his parents. We go to the Peace Corps, but we get married first." Naya shrugged. "Ravi and I had already wanted to be married, so pushing it up a few months seemed reasonable."

"To everyone but those of us who are planning."

"Stop complaining! You love this."

"I was talking about your mom."

"Yeah," Naya conceded. "She's going crazy." She shrugged. "She'll be fine."

Annika fidgeted with Naya's sari for another moment. "You should wear it like this, mermaid-style. It's super flattering."

"Whatever you say." Naya caught her reflection in the mirror and made eye contact with Annika. "What about you?"

"What about me?" Annika asked, distracted, as she slowly started to remove the sari.

"Heard you went on a date with Sajan." Naya raised her eyebrows.

Honestly, how did everyone know everyone else's business? "It wasn't a date." Well, it hadn't ended up as one. Even though Sajan had footed the bill no matter how hard she'd insisted on at least splitting it. She smiled. He'd make some woman happy one day. It just wasn't going to be her.

"Well, what was it?"

"Friends. Having dinner. It happens."

"Have you talked to Daniel?"

Annika stopped for a moment at the mention of his name. "No." She continued her task.

"Aren't you even going to fight for him?"

"I can't fight for him if he won't fight for himself." Annika tried to ignore the burn of tears by focusing on folding Naya's sari. *Would the tears ever stop?* "When I miscarried, it was awful. And when we heard those aunties talking like I should be grateful—" She stopped before the tears broke through. She swallowed hard. "But still, I had you and my parents and Daniel to support me. I had a counselor come to see me in the ER whom I turned to a few times for help. Daniel didn't have that support, nor did he seek counseling to help heal. He's buried the pain and simply functions. He's not living. He needs to want to *live* and not simply exist. When and if he wants that, he'll get help."

"So, what, you're just going to let him go?"

"Looks that way. It's been over a month and I haven't heard from him, except for the updates I get from Nilay. And those have stopped now Nilay is home."

"Actually…" Naya looked at her with sad eyes. "Nilay told me they FaceTime almost every day."

Of course they did. A fist wrapped itself around her heart. Daniel would not let Nilay go until he was well. He felt responsible. And he cared for Nilay.

Which was part of why she loved him. Caring about Nilay, loving her—these were proof that Daniel was perfectly capable of living and not simply existing. He just didn't think he deserved it. And she didn't know how to convince him.

CHAPTER THIRTY-ONE

DANIEL

DANIEL CHECKED THE address on the card against the building number. It was the right place. It had taken him only thirty-five minutes to get to Columbia from his apartment. He dismounted his bike. No need to go in. At least he knew where the place was. He could always come back later.

What did that mean, *get help*? Did that mean that he would forget Sara? Because no way that could happen. He thought about the number of times he had counseled patients on getting help with any of their issues. Many would come back and thank him—though their problems never went away, they simply found a way to cope. He leaned against his bike. The little voice in his head that held all of his professional information finally spoke up. *Get in there. Give it a chance.* But it was the daydream of a life with Annika that he held in the front of his mind that gave him momentum.

He locked his bike, grabbed his helmet and went into the building before he could change his mind. His father's voice sprang into his head. *"Men take care of business. Talking about things never did anyone any good. Let it go. Put it behind you."* Daniel pushed forward. He'd tried that. It wasn't working for him.

The floors of the building were still wet from being

mopped, and the familiar antiseptic scent of the cleaner reminded him of the ER, and oddly calmed his heartbeat. The suite was the first one in the building, and a few men passed him as he peeked in the door. Seemed like a typical setup, with chairs in a circle and simple refreshments on the side.

Daniel stepped into the room, his stomach in knots. What was he afraid of? He surveyed the men in the room. All of these men were fathers who had lost a child. Any one of them could have been his patient. There did not seem to be any pattern to them. Some were in expensive suits, some were in uniforms. They seemed to come from all walks of life, every socioeconomic class and every race. All the men greeted one another with friendly smiles and handshakes.

Daniel walked farther into the room, suddenly afraid to make eye contact, when a familiar accent stopped him. Definitely Indian. He turned to find Annika's father in conversation with a small group of men.

Wait, what?

He caught Daniel's eye and nodded, a small smile at his lips.

Mr. Mehta glanced at the clock and clapped his hands together. "Shall we get started, then?"

A hum of murmuring, and the scraping of chairs on the tile, as each man found a seat in the circle. A redheaded man standing near Daniel pulled out an extra chair and pointed to it. "Have a seat." He extended his hand. "I'm Ron. You look new."

Daniel shook Ron's hand. "Daniel. And yes, I am."

Ron's eyes softened. "Sorry for your loss. But good for you for coming here. If there's a way out of the hole you're in, Anil has the map."

Confused, Daniel took the seat Ron offered. Once everyone was settled, Mr. Mehta called the meeting to order.

"I am Anil Mehta, and I welcome you all. We will go around and see how everyone is doing, and while we do have someone here with us for the first time, I will break protocol just this once and introduce myself before we meet him. He is someone I have not *really* met up until now." Anil turned his gaze on Daniel, eyes warm and friendly. "My name is Anil Mehta, and I lost my son, Vipul, twenty-five years ago."

Daniel stared at him, barely registering the group chorus of *Welcome, Anil. We are sorry for your loss.* Annika had never mentioned—wait. Annika would have been a baby when—maybe she didn't know.

Mr. Mehta raised an eyebrow, as if to say, *We have more in common than either of us thought.*

Daniel nodded back and cleared his throat. "My name is Daniel Bliant." He paused and looked around the room at all these complete strangers. Black, Hispanic, white, wealthy, middle-class, well dressed, poorly dressed, fit, out of shape. All these men were grieving, had lost a child, just like him.

Mr. Mehta spoke. "It's okay, Daniel. We're all friends here. And we've all been where you are now."

Daniel was struck in that moment how similar Mr. Mehta's eyes were to Annika's. Comforting and strong. He nodded. "I'm Daniel, and I lost my daughter, Sara, close to five years ago. She was five." Tears sprang to his eyes, unannounced. He tried to blink them back, but one escaped. He hastily wiped it away as he glanced around the room, but not one man flinched or seemed surprised. His father would have been appalled.

"Welcome, Daniel. We are sorry for your loss," the group chorused.

Anil smiled and looked to Ron, who cleared his throat. "I'm Ron, and I lost my son, George, seven years ago. He was eight." He glanced at Daniel. "It was like the world stopped for me, but not for anyone else. I couldn't understand how life continued when my little boy was gone."

Daniel couldn't believe it. That was exactly how he'd felt in the aftermath of Sara's funeral. He had been so lost, his world had ended, but for some reason they still needed to eat and pay bills. While Daniel took care of all that, he'd had the sense that it was ridiculous. How was it possible to continue when there was now a gaping hole where there had once been a beautiful little girl? How was it possible that the earth even continued to spin? Daniel relaxed into his surroundings as the meeting progressed and fathers shared their latest setbacks and accomplishments. Then came Daniel's turn again.

"Anything you'd care to share today?" A kindness that Daniel had never heard from Mr. Mehta coated his words. "No pressure. But you could tell us what brought you here."

Daniel didn't know what had brought him there. He took in the faces that looked at him, some raw with emotion, others stoic now that they had shared. But not one of them looked at him with shame or disdain. They may not be smiling, but he'd just spent the last hour or more listening to their struggles and setbacks and progress in learning to live life again. Every man in this room had lost a piece of themselves, and they weren't living in fear of talking about it.

He stood and did something he hadn't done in a very long time. Maybe not even with Annika. He spoke from his heart.

"I'm here because I've been afraid for a long time. I've been afraid to care for another person. Until I found myself falling in love with the most amazing woman, and somehow, she loved me, too." He looked around the room, finally resting his gaze on Anil-uncle. "I ended up pushing her away."

"Why did you push her away?" Ron asked.

Daniel fixed his gaze on Anil-uncle. "I can't be the man she needs me to be. The man she deserves."

"Why not?" Anil asked.

"Because...because every time I care about someone, I'm filled with the fear that they will be ripped away from me."

"And now?" Anil asked.

Daniel sighed and looked around, his gaze resting on Mr. Mehta's face. "Now I'm tired. I'm so tired of being afraid."

Saying it out loud actually made him a little less tired. A little less afraid.

Anil smiled at him. "Then you have come to the right place. Thank you, Daniel."

After the meeting, a few men introduced themselves to Daniel before leaving, all of them offering words of support and encouragement. Daniel loitered until the last man had left and it was just him and Mr. Mehta.

Mr. Mehta spoke before Daniel even asked the question. "Vipul died when he was one year old. Annika was just two. She doesn't remember him, but we keep his memory alive. No secrets."

"Why didn't she tell me?"

"Would it have mattered? She doesn't remember him. Her strongest sense of loss is her miscarriage—which you know about." They walked out to the parking lot together.

"Why didn't she suggest this group?"

"You didn't want help. She tried, I heard her. Besides, I doubt she knows that I still come here. Children don't always know what their parents are up to, thank God." He chuckled. "I came to this group when Auntie was pregnant with Nilay. I didn't want to have another baby. I was already consumed with protecting Annika from every speck of dust. But we had a baby coming, and a friend suggested I try out this group. I was highly skeptical—what kind of man can't handle his own head? The way I grew up, men showed their strength by simply moving on. Go to work, make a living. They didn't talk about their feelings, let alone deal with them. I was doing what I had to—providing for my family, protecting, all the things a 'man' should do." Anil dropped his gaze and his tone went flat. "I was trying to make up for not protecting my Vipul. For not being able to save him." He shrugged, looked back at Daniel. "Every day, my wife would tell me something wonderful about the new baby to come, and every day I ignored her. As if by not acknowledging her pregnancy, somehow the baby would not come." Anil looked past Daniel, his voice gruff with emotion. "One day, I saw the love in her eyes turn to fear, and I realized that the distance I was putting between us had put that fear in her eyes. I had to make a change. I had to be the man she deserved." He gave Daniel a small smile. "So, I made myself come here." Anil stopped at his car.

Daniel nodded.

"What I found here was that while I was taking care of business, I was losing out on everything else—including my wife and daughter." He shrugged. "I wanted to be a better father for my daughter and new baby, and a better husband for my wife. So I kept coming back. I took over the group eight years ago when our leader moved out of the state. Many of these men had turned to alcohol and drugs and other destructive behaviors before they came here. Many of them were also workaholics. We are an adjunct to whatever regular therapy they seek."

"Why did you come to me?"

"Because you're a father. And you need help. Because I'm a father who can offer that help. Not to mention my daughter is in love with you." He handed Daniel another card. "This group is great. But sometimes we need more than what the group can offer. This guy—" he nodded at the card "—is one of us."

Daniel took the card, wondering about this brotherhood he seemed to have become an unwilling member of. As if he'd read Daniel's mind, Anil spoke. "None of us ever planned to be here. But here we are, and we do the best we can."

Daniel nodded and asked the question that had been burning in his mind. "How is she?"

Anil studied him for a moment. "Well, she was in love with you, and you left her. In the hospital. What do you think?"

Daniel looked away and grunted. "She should move on."

Anil shrugged. "Probably."

"She hasn't? But I thought you and Auntie were keen on Sajan."

Anil chuckled. "We were. But Annika is not. And when was the last time Annika did anything she did not want to do?"

A spark of hope lit Daniel's heart. The way he'd left her, he'd thought for sure…and that day, in Nilay's room. The way she had looked at him, as if he'd better not dare ask for her back. He thought for sure she'd started seeing Sajan.

Daniel looked Anil in the eye. "She's not why I'm here."

Anil raised an eyebrow.

"I mean, I'm not getting help just to get her back." Daniel sighed. "Quite frankly, I believe she can do better." The daydream be damned. He should put it to rest. There would never be a baby for them.

"That's quite possible." Anil grinned. "Why are you here, then? What do you hope to gain?"

"Peace. I want to put my agony and fear to rest."

"And?"

Damn it. "And I want her back."

CHAPTER THIRTY-TWO

ANNIKA

ANNIKA SQUIRMED IN her childhood bed, avoided opening her eyes. The smell of masala chai floated up to her from the kitchen, mixed with the clean scent of her sheets, and took her back to her childhood, where everything was warm and soft and sunny. No one was disappointed, no hearts were broken, big evil men hadn't punched her brother, and no children had been shot.

Annika wanted to live in that moment for as long as she could, because when she opened her eyes, she would have to acknowledge all those things. And the pain from that was too much today. But today was the day she had to face. It had been a year ago today that she and Steven had gone to the emergency room. A year ago today that Daniel had held her for the first time. A year ago today that she lost her baby. Her heart ached, but she had no more tears. Just as well; she had shed too many this past year. Time to move on.

Was that coffee she smelled? She opened her eyes. Her parents always had chai in the morning. They hadn't wanted her to be alone today, so they had insisted she come home for a few days. As it was currently spring break in Baltimore County, she had agreed. The truth of it was that she was grateful to be near her family today. She sat up in bed. The day was going to come whether she faced it or not. Better to face it. She washed up, donned an old Towson University sweatshirt, and followed the scent of chai and coffee to the kitchen.

"Jay Shree Krishna." The automatic greeting of praise to God fell from her lips without thought.

"Jay Shree Krishna." Her parents responded in unison. Her father glanced at her and went back to his chai. Her mother studied her.

"Where's Nilay?"

"School. A friend drove him," her mother answered. "How are you, beta?" Annika cringed at the caution in her mother's voice.

"I'm okay, Mom. Don't worry, I'm not going to crumble."

Her mother smiled. "Well, I should hope not. I raised my daughter to be strong."

"So, then, why are you so afraid to say anything?"

"We don't want you to yell at us," her father stated simply.

"I do not yell at—" She stopped because she was yelling. "Oh. Sorry about that," she finished, sheepishly. "I smell coffee."

Her mother brightened. "We made you some." She pointed at a brand-new coffeepot in the corner, filled with the life-giving liquid that Annika craved. She poured herself a mug and found her favorite creamer stocked in the fridge. *Jay Shree Krishna, indeed.*

She sat down with her parents and took that first, life-changing sip of coffee. Amazing. She sensed them watching her, but she said nothing. Her father spoke first.

"I'm glad you came home." He rested his hand on hers. "It's been too long that we saw you wake up in this house."

Her heart swelled. She hadn't realized how much she missed it until he said it. She squeezed his hand and smiled. "It really has."

Her father stood, taking his empty mug to the sink. "I must get to work." He kissed the top of her forehead, then her mother's cheek, before exiting the kitchen. He turned back as he left. "Annika, my car is in the shop, so I'm taking Mom's car to work. Tonight we both have meetings. Mom will drop me off. Do you mind picking me up from mine?"

Annika shrugged. "Sure. Text me the address."

Her father beamed, a little too happy about getting a ride from her. Whatever. Maybe she had been a bit extra difficult lately. "Great. See you then."

He left her alone with her mother. Her mother smiled at her and stood. "Toast?"

"Yeah." Annika stood as well, heading for the fridge. "Got any avocado?"

"Of course. In fact, I'll join you."

Her mother grabbed an avocado and began cutting it in silence. Annika put two pieces of bread in the toaster oven, then grabbed a lime and the salt. She waited for her mother to say something about her meeting up with Sajan.

"I'm sorry things didn't work out between you and Daniel." Her mother looked up from the avocado.

"What?" Annika didn't have a moment to even hide her astonishment.

"Well, it was clear how you felt about each other—"

"But you and Papa—I thought you didn't approve."

Her mother shrugged. "We didn't. Not at first." She sighed as she scooped the avocado into the bowl. She put down the spoon. "We were wrong, beta. But we didn't realize how wrong we were until that day in the hospital."

Her heart was in her throat; she couldn't speak. She truly loved Daniel and was certain that kind of love would not come for her again. Tears sprang to her eyes. Ugh. She was done crying.

"I really miss him."

Her mother shook her head and drew Annika into her arms. "I know. I'm sorry."

"And those aunties. At that party. What they said—it was so horrible."

"They are ashamed—I know this for a fact, because I told them off myself."

Annika pulled back to look at her mother. "You did what?"

"I told them they should be ashamed to say such things. My daughter should not be ashamed of something she has no control over. They always were gossips, those two. Kaki and I have decided they are no longer welcome in our homes."

"Mom!" Annika was shocked that her mild-mannered mother had been so forceful.

"Don't be so shocked. I might be quiet, but no one messes with my children."

The tears were coming down for real now, and Annika could not stop them.

Her mother held her close. "You have cried so much this year, beta. Get it all out."

As if permission from her mother had been all that she needed, Annika collapsed into her mother's arms. The scent of cinnamon and cloves enveloped her, and she found herself getting comfort from where she'd always gotten her comfort. Her mother held her close and whispered soothing motherly things as Annika sobbed out every last tear she had for the baby she'd lost and the man she loved.

IT WASN'T UNTIL she pulled into the parking lot that Annika realized which meeting her father was attending. Or running, rather. She had the windows down, the fresh scents of spring tickling her nose. It was past 7:00 p.m., but the spring sun was just starting to set. *Thank you, daylight saving time.* She pulled out her laptop to tweak next week's lesson plan.

Voices carried to her on a warm breeze, and she looked up to search for her father. That was when she saw him.

Daniel.

Walking out of the community center in a fitted black T-shirt and jeans. She told herself she didn't care, but her heart thumped in her chest, ready to betray her in a second. He continued talking to the man beside him. Her father. Her heart raced faster. What was happening here?

She froze, her gaze fixed on him. They were deep in conversation. Clearly Daniel had attended the meeting. Was this his first? How long had he been attending? So many questions she wanted answered. She was out of the car before she knew it.

Daniel turned his attention toward the parking lot and stopped walking. She knew he'd seen her. He was as frozen as she was. She couldn't move. She wanted to talk to him. No. She wanted to throw her arms around him and feel his arms around her, and hear him say—what? That he loved her? She already knew that. *Or did she?* He was clearly getting help to deal with his loss, but he hadn't contacted her. Maybe she was too much of a reminder. Or maybe she was wrong and he didn't love her the way she thought he did.

Her father seemed to have noticed that Daniel was no longer beside him, so he turned. Daniel nodded to him, then the two men shook hands, and her father walked toward her.

Her heart dropped into her stomach as she watched Daniel standing there, not approaching. He hadn't moved from his spot, his gaze still as intent on her as ever. As soon as her father was in the car and had shut the door, she got in as well, her eyes never leaving Daniel's. Once in, she quickly started the engine and pulled out of the spot. She couldn't just watch him not come to her. And she couldn't bring herself to go to him. Not if he didn't want her.

Her father chattered on about this thing and that, his voice becoming background noise. She pulled into their driveway with no idea how she had gotten there.

"He's in your group?" It was almost an accusation.

"You know I can't answer that, Annika."

"Yeah, okay. Fine." She needed answers. Damn her father's integrity. She glanced at her father. "How is he? I saw you talking to him, so you can at least tell me how he is."

"He's fine." He turned to face her, making eye contact. "Better."

"So, he's—he's moving on, then." Without her. Her heart sank. "That's great. I'm happy for him." She truly was, but she had thought… It didn't matter what she had thought. Maybe she had thought he would come back for her when he was in a better place. But those were her hopes. He had promised no such thing.

"Oh, I don't know about moving on, but he's better because he's getting help." Her father's smile said everything that he could not. His face held all the answers Annika was looking for.

Annika's apprehension vanished as she smiled and hugged her father. "Thanks."

They got out of the car and went into the house together.

Annika felt lighter than she had in weeks. Daniel was getting help. And from her own father, of all places. Good for him. She put her hand on her heart and let happiness flood her. Good for him.

CHAPTER THIRTY-THREE

DANIEL

DANIEL STOOD, FROZEN to the spot, as Annika jumped out of the car. For a moment he thought she was going to approach him, and he had willed her to come to him, since his own feet seemed to be glued to the spot. But she did not, though her gaze never wavered. He hadn't contacted her to tell her he was getting help. He hadn't known what to say—and the truth was, after the way he'd left her when she had needed him, he didn't think he had a right to talk to her, anyway.

What would he possibly say to her? *Sorry I broke up with you? It was the biggest mistake of my life? I want you back? I will always love you?*

Absolutely not. Especially not today. Today, she was hurting.

So he had remained frozen to his spot until she'd driven away.

She had looked amazing. Had her eyes been red from crying? He couldn't tell from where he stood. How was she coping with today? The anniversary date was never easy. She must be staying at her parents', or else why would she have been in Columbia today? He smiled to himself. She was with her family, surrounded by people she loved, who loved her, too. She would be fine.

He got onto his bike and headed for Sheila's. Aaron was all of three months old and one of the happiest babies he'd ever seen. He'd promised Jim and Sheila a night out while he babysat his godson. Annika didn't need him. He suppressed the ache in his heart as he realized this and focused on thoughts of Aaron. He'd been looking forward to this all day.

DANIEL WORKED AN overnight after watching Aaron for the evening. *Note to self—don't do that again.* He'd forgotten how much work an infant could be. In any case, by the time he arrived at the soccer field that night for his nephew's game, the match had started and Charlie was on the field. Charlie was quite intense on the ball for a ten-year-old boy, and his footwork was impressive. Daniel's heart filled with pride. The sensation wasn't new, just a bit rusty.

Ten minutes in, the coach made a substitution, and a tired and sweaty Charlie grinned and waved at Daniel from the sidelines. Daniel waved back and turned to find a place to open his lawn chair and sit down. His stomach clenched when he caught sight of his father standing just a few feet away, watching him as intently as he had been watching Charlie.

He walked over to his father. It wasn't that they didn't talk; it was that Daniel never knew what to say to him. It was easier if his sister or mother were around, though it hadn't always been that way. They'd had their share of father-son disagreements, but those were mostly growing pains. Things had really changed after Sara died. His father had supported him by telling him that it was his responsibility to take care of his wife. Men didn't need time to grieve. They simply moved on.

Except that Daniel had just shut down. And because

he still felt the pain of Sara's death as keenly as if it had just happened yesterday, he knew he had failed, not only Sheila, but his father, too.

"Hey, Dad."

"Daniel." His father nodded. "See the footwork on our boy?"

Daniel smiled. "Yeah, kid's a natural. Where's Em?"

"She got held up at work. Michael, too. That's why I'm here."

Daniel nodded, trying not to be obvious in his discomfort of having to be alone with his father. He considered standing elsewhere, but that seemed extreme.

"Nice that you made it to the game. He's talked about nothing else all day." *His father was starting a conversation. Weird.*

"He's a good kid." Daniel tried not to be too obvious as he looked around. Maybe Ba was here? "Sorry I was late. Got held up at the hospital."

"Happens." His father shrugged and looked Daniel square in the eye. "He's really happy you've been coming around."

A long-forgotten gentleness in the older man's voice jerked Daniel's attention properly to his father. He was met with that familiar green gaze but there was something softer about the older man, something—hesitant.

"He, uh, really missed you. Probably could have benefited from you teaching him some foot skills."

"He's got Michael."

"Michael's a baseball player. He doesn't know soccer." His dad's grin belied the mischief in his eyes. Soccer was clearly the better sport.

Daniel chuckled at what his father wasn't saying and shook his head to dismiss it. "I've missed him, too. Maybe

I'll come around a bit more, give him some tips on those ball-handling skills."

The older man's shoulders relaxed, and a familiar twinkle entered his father's eye. "I think he'd like that."

"Yeah." A sense of calm fell upon Daniel, one that he hadn't experienced around his father in years. "Me, too."

Coach put Charlie back on the field, so Daniel watched his nephew in companionable silence, side by side with his father. His father commented on Charlie's strengths and pointed out areas for improvement. It reminded Daniel of when he and his father would analyze his own games, and whatever tension remained in him started to melt away into the ease that fathers and sons could share.

"So, whatever happened to that girl?" his father asked with the air of someone who already knew the answer. "I was hoping that going to group would have you running back to get her."

"You know about group?" Daniel was incredulous.

His father shrugged, looking out at the field. "I hear things."

Daniel just stared at him, aghast.

"You seem more—relaxed or something." A quick glance in Daniel's direction, then back to the field.

"I am."

"So where is Annika, then?" This time his father turned to face him.

Daniel's heart clenched at the mere mention of her name. "It wasn't going to work, Dad." His turn to stare at the field.

"You don't know that."

"Yeah, Dad. I do." It seemed that whatever peace he'd come to with his father wasn't going to last.

"I'm just saying that you're not the same person you were a few months ago."

"It doesn't matter, Dad. I left her while her brother was in surgery. While her parents were terrified. When she needed me, I wasn't there. She deserves better."

"Why did you leave her?"

Daniel waved his father off. "Never mind."

"Look at me, son, when I'm talking to you."

You're never too old to have to listen to your parents. Daniel turned and faced his father.

"Danny, you're going to have to face it sooner or later. Why did you leave her?"

"Because... I was terrified, okay?" Daniel's heart sank as the truth hit him. "Terrified that I'd have to be a father again—that I'd have to give my whole heart to someone— that as much as I wanted to, I hadn't given my whole heart to her. And she deserves better than that." An admission to the man who wasn't afraid of anything.

His father remained silent for so long that Daniel was convinced he hadn't even heard. Just when Daniel was disgusted enough to walk away, his father spoke.

"I almost left your mother once."

Daniel must have heard wrong. His parents were deeply in love. "What did you say?"

"It was ages ago. While we were still dating. I was crazy in love with her, and I knew I wanted to marry her. So, I asked your grandfather's permission." Daniel's father raised an eyebrow and looked his son in the eye. "And he said no."

Daniel was speechless. No one said no to his father. Except, apparently, his grandfather. "Why?"

"He thought I was too immature and wouldn't amount to anything. We were still in college, and I was pretty aimless." He let out a small chuckle. "Looking back, I probably would have said no to me, too. Anyway, I became convinced for a time that there was no way I was good enough for your mother, that her father was right. She was better off without me. I was getting ready to break up with her when Ba contacted me. She said that if I loved her daughter, I should prove her husband wrong. I should fight for what I wanted. So, I did. Got my act together, focused on school and on how much I loved your mother. A year later, when I asked your grandfather again, he shook my hand and gave me his blessing."

"Why are you telling me this?"

"Because, son. We're all terrified of something at some point. It's what you do about it that makes all the difference."

Daniel was still unable to speak. But his normally silent father seemed to have plenty to say today. "I'm sorry."

"For what?" Daniel managed to refocus.

"I'm sorry I said those things to you when you lost Sara. I thought—well, I thought if you just went through the paces, you could get your life back. But hell, I miss my granddaughter every day—I can't even imagine what you go through. Because I know that, even now, if something were to happen to you or your sister, I'd never be the same." He hung his head, suddenly interested in the ground. He snapped his head up to look at Daniel. "I am damn proud to see you getting control of your life right now."

Daniel just stared at his father. Who was this man and where was his real father?

"Don't look at me like that. Never too old to admit you're wrong. You remember that." His eyes softened. "That girl is amazing. Lean on her. Let her lean on you. That's how that works."

"What are you saying? I should just call her up and tell her I made a mistake?"

"Why not? People who love each other make mistakes all the time. I certainly did. Your mother always forgave me."

Daniel pressed his lips together.

"You're afraid she won't take you back."

Daniel nodded, not wanting to even acknowledge that fear.

His father shrugged. "Yeah, so maybe she won't take you back. But maybe she will. How will you know if you don't try? I mean, if you don't act, I'm sure some other young man will."

Acid filled Daniel's stomach.

"She's a good and kind person, Danny. You deserve a shot at happiness. Don't let it slip away."

Daniel lowered his voice. "I love her. But if I were her, I'd want nothing to do with me. Ever. And rightly so."

His father grinned. "Well, then, I guess it's a good thing she isn't you."

NAUSEA AND DREAD filled Daniel's gut as the day drew near. He had no desire for food; trying to sleep was a joke. He avoided TV, radio and all social media so he didn't have to hear the recap on the news. It was the same every year. In the past, he had filled the approaching days with extra shifts, trying to distract himself from the impending doom of the actual day his daughter had died.

It never mattered how many shifts he worked; his body knew what his mind tried to ignore. He always woke on that day with a hole in his gut, his heart weighed down. He never actually took a shift on the actual day, preferring instead to be alone in his anger and grief and curse the world yet again for continuing on without his daughter. The first couple of years, when he and Sheila were still married, she would cry and he would drink while he held her.

After the divorce, he never contacted Sheila on this day, and she never contacted him. Not that they were ever in constant contact, but on that day, he could *feel* the connection of their non-contact.

This year was no different. Except that it was.

The familiar hollowness filled his belly as he approached the house Sara used to live in. Interesting. He'd been here a dozen times in the past two months to see Aaron, and that dread had been slowly fading away.

It was back today. Daniel had no idea what he was doing, except that, for the first time, he hadn't wanted to be alone on this day.

He knocked.

Sheila answered, her eyes red rimmed and swollen. "I thought you might come by this year."

"I'm sorry, Sheila. I can go if—"

"Don't be ridiculous. Come in." She stepped back to allow him in. "Jim's just getting dinner started. You're welcome to stay."

He stepped in. "No. Maybe. I don't know." His stomach rumbled in response to the aroma of onion and garlic sautéing. He shuffled his feet, unsure of why he was here.

Tears fell from Sheila's eyes. She wiped them away. "Sorry, but this is what I do every year."

Daniel nodded. Sheila took his hand and led him into the house. Her grip was firm. She wanted him here. "Jim, honey. Daniel's staying for dinner."

"No, that's okay. I'll just go."

"It's fine, Daniel." Jim's soothing voice reached him as they approached the kitchen. "It's a tough day—"

Jim was interrupted by a small squealing from the baby monitor that quickly turned into an outright cry.

Sheila sighed. "I just put him down."

"I'll go." Daniel spoke before he thought, and he was moving up the stairs as if he was being pulled up them.

He approached Aaron's room, which used to be Sara's room, and went straight to the crib without turning on the light. He picked up the baby and held him close, resting Aaron's head in that crevice between his neck and shoulder. The baby instantly curled up and calmed down. Daniel paced the small room until he felt Aaron fall asleep. He walked over to the crib to lay Aaron back down, but instead, he held on to the baby, finding comfort in his weight as he rocked in the chair. He shifted the baby into his arms and took in the sheer perfection that was a newborn child.

Aaron's baby scent engulfed him and sent Daniel tumbling into the past. This time, the burn of tears that built up behind his eyes was welcome, and he let them fall, allowed them to give way to sobs as he grieved for this little baby's big sister, as he grieved for his Sara.

After some time, it could have been five minutes, it could have been an hour, he felt Sheila's hand on his shoulder.

"Hey."

"Hey." Sheila moved around so she could face him, kneeling down. In the light from the hallway, he could see fresh tears in her eyes.

"I've never seen you cry before." She shook her head, her eyes filled with tenderness. "Must be Annika. She's good for you."

"That's over," Daniel croaked out.

To her credit, Sheila pressed her lips together and said nothing.

Daniel cleared his throat. "Did we keep her ER band?"

"Yes." Sheila nodded. If she was surprised at the request, she did not show it. "I have it with a bunch of her things." She stood and turned to the closet and pulled down a small box. She took off the lid so Daniel could see. A paper heart, a few awards, things she had done in school, and the ER band.

With great deliberation, he lifted his hand and reached in to pick it up, as if doing so might break him. He clasped the small band in his hand.

"Do you want it, Daniel?" Sheila's voice was soft and kind.

He nodded and clutched the small band tightly, as if now that he had it, he needed it. Maybe he did. "How are you doing it?" Daniel whispered as he held Aaron close.

"Doing what?"

"This." He nodded at the baby in his arms. "Moving on with your life."

Sheila laid a hand on his face. "Oh, Daniel. We don't move on. There's no moving on. We just live. We'll never not miss her. We'll never be okay with the fact that she was ripped from us—but maybe we don't have to be. Maybe we just live and love and honor her memory." She looked at her son and smiled through her tears. "How can you not fall in love with this little guy? Even while you miss Sara."

Daniel turned his gaze back to Aaron. The little boy slept peacefully, as if there wasn't a care in the world. He was chubby cheeks and a small pink mouth topped with a sprinkling of blond hair. He was so small and vulnerable... Daniel was filled simultaneously with a need to protect him as well as with anticipation of watching him grow. He kissed Aaron's chubby cheek.

"You can't. You have to love him. It's not even a choice,"

Daniel choked out, and he felt himself give in to that warm feeling.

"You do need to heal, Daniel. But you don't need to do it alone." She sniffled as she stood. "Want me to take him?"

Daniel shook his head. "Nah, I'm good, if that's all right with you. I might just sit with him for a bit."

Sheila nodded and squeezed his shoulder as she left. "She loves you, Daniel. She loves you no matter what."

"Sara?"

"And Annika."

Daniel melted into the sound of her name and looked back at Aaron. He put Sara's ER band into his pocket next to the one Annika had given him. Then he carefully pulled his phone from his pocket and brought up an old number. He held Aaron with one hand as he brought the phone to his ear and listened to the ring.

A familiar voice answered.

"Hey, Gus? Daniel here. It's been a long time."

CHAPTER THIRTY-FOUR

ANNIKA

THE WARM SUN beckoned her class from the window. They were particularly restless today, and Annika was sure the last few weeks of school would be challenging.

"All right. Let's put everything away and get ready to go home."

The children did not need to be told twice. It may have appeared to be a ruckus to an outsider, but Annika saw organized chaos. Every child had a responsibility in the classroom, and they took it very seriously, sunshine or no. In minutes, the classroom was in order, and the children had gathered their belongings and were seated in the afternoon dismissal circle. Annika addressed the class, recapping the lessons for the day and wishing them a happy weekend. Parents started showing up and the children left, anticipating their time outside.

"Mitch!" Annika called out as she saw his mother enter the room. Mitch popped up and came to the front of the room. He stopped in front of Annika and hugged her.

Annika hugged him back. "Thank you, Mitch."

"You're welcome, Ms. Mehta. Have a great weekend." He flicked his eyes to his mother, and she beamed at him, mouthing, *Good job*.

The sound of his voice melted Annika's heart. Mitch

was far from a conversationalist, but she'd helped his mother find the appropriate therapist, and he was making great strides. This was the most Annika had heard him say in the classroom.

Tears blurred her vision, but she smiled. "You have a good weekend, too. I'll see you on Monday."

Mitch took his mother's hand, and she smiled her gratitude to Annika as she left with her son.

Wait until Daniel hears this! It was still a reflex, her wanting to share exciting news with him. She shook her head at the thought, but the heaviness settled in her heart. There was nothing to be done for that. At least, nothing that she had found. In the meantime, she decided she'd call her dad and share Mitch's progress with him.

There had been a clip in the local news last week commemorating the anniversary of the shooting that had taken Sara. Annika had watched, her heart breaking for Daniel and Sheila, and all the other loved ones who had lost someone that day. She knew he always spent the day alone, though she'd picked up her phone to call or text him an infinite number of times. In the end she left him alone in his grief. He wasn't hers anymore.

In a flurry of excitement and activity, all of the children were reunited with their parents, and in no time her classroom echoed with silence. Annika straightened up the desks and chairs and tucked everything away for the weekend. A proud smile fell across her face as she thought of all her class had accomplished this year.

You're a damn good teacher, Annika Mehta. She could almost hear Daniel's voice beside her. Ugh. It was like she was a boy-crazy teenager who couldn't get over a crush. She needed to get a grip. And anyway, she *was* a damn good teacher. The thought made her a bit giddy. With a satisfied sigh, she turned off the light and walked out into the hallway.

Her heart nearly stopped as she recognized the muscular form of the man who was studying her class's hallway display. It was as if he'd been conjured from her thoughts.

"Daniel?" It came out as a whisper that caught in her throat.

He turned to face her, green eyes alight with amusement. "Tulip cutouts." He nodded, smiling. "I don't think there's a happier flower. The kids must love it. I was hoping you would add one more to the display." He handed her a yellow construction paper tulip as if months hadn't passed since they'd last spoken. As if he could walk into this building like anyone else. She automatically reached out and took it without looking at it, not knowing what shocked her more: seeing him, or seeing him inside this school.

"What are you doing here?" She searched his face for signs of pain. Most people would see the handsome smiling face with the twinkle in his eye. But she saw the slight twitch of his lip and the minuscule movement of his eye, the fidgeting of his right foot. His pain was hidden in those movements. But here he stood, inside this school building, waiting to talk to her. She couldn't help her smile or the feeling of pride she had in him.

"I'm adding to your display—I mean, it's five years too early, but I wanted to make sure he had a spot in your class."

Annika had never been more confused, and Daniel was standing there talking to her like nothing had happened, like he hadn't been away for months.

Like he still loved her.

It must have shown on her face, because he stopped rambling and put his hands into his pockets as he quietly jutted his chin at the flower cutout he had just handed her. His demeanor changed as if he had read her mind and decided that pretending nothing had happened between them was ridiculous.

She indulged him and looked at the tulip cutout in her hand. *Aaron.* This offered her no clarity. She looked up at him, and he met her eyes and nodded in the direction of the door, indicating she follow him. She sighed and started walking. He walked beside her, and she felt more than saw him glance at her.

"You look amazing." His voice was low and intimate, and though she knew on some level that she should fight it, she melted into the soft rumble of the voice he used only for her.

Daniel reached to open the door for her and stepped back as a man entered from the other side, the school police officer at his side. "Excuse me."

Annika froze, her pulse quickened and her back stiffened. It was Mitch's father. She hadn't seen him since the first day of school when he had insulted her. All of her interactions since then had been with Mitch's mother, whose only interest had been getting help for her son; *who* helped him seemed irrelevant to her.

He nodded at Annika, his lips pressed together.

Daniel drew himself to his full height, stepping closer to Annika, even as he made room for Mitch's father and the officer to enter.

"Ms. Mehta." Mitch's father finally addressed her.

"Mr. Evans." Annika kept her voice firm yet calm.

Mitch's father flicked his gaze to Daniel and back to Annika. "I was hoping to have a word with you, about Mitch."

"Go right ahead." Annika did not move. Daniel tensed next to her.

"Well…" Mr. Evans glanced at Daniel and the officer, then turned his gaze to Annika. "I just wanted to…thank you. For everything you did for my Mitch."

Annika couldn't speak. Daniel and the officer were looking at each other, baffled, and the man simply stood there, looking abashed. Silence echoed in the hallway.

Annika finally managed to find her voice. "Well, Mr. Evans, it was my pleasure. Mitch is a wonderful child."

"He has truly enjoyed being in your class."

"Despite your best efforts, I assume." Annika raised her chin.

Mr. Evans cleared his throat. "Well, now. That's not necessary—"

Annika narrowed her eyes, her stomach jumping. She felt emboldened. This man was thanking her for doing her job, because his son had benefited. Not because he realized that her abilities had nothing to do with the color of her skin. He certainly had not been an active participant. "Actually, it *is* necessary." She seethed, but kept her voice measured. "It's *very* necessary, since you saw fit to insult me on my first day on the job, simply based on the color of my skin. And that is anything but okay."

Daniel leaned even closer to her, tension vibrating from him.

"Well, now, what do you expect?"

Annika threw her shoulders back and took a step closer to Mr. Evans. "I *expect* to be treated with the respect and consideration afforded to any person who teaches your child. Regardless of whether I exceeded your personal expectations of what I should or should not be doing."

Mr. Evans narrowed his eyes. "Now, listen here. I came here to thank you for helping out my son—"

"And I appreciate that. You are more than welcome. I

was simply doing my job. It's a pleasure having him in my classroom." With that, Annika dismissed him with a nod. "You have a nice weekend, now."

Annika walked past Mr. Evans with a smile to Officer Keely, Daniel right behind her. She walked out into the sun, stopping to breathe.

She looked up to find Daniel staring down at her, in awe. "That was Mitch's dad?"

Annika let out a nervous laugh. "Yes! Mitch spoke to me today!" She was giddy as adrenaline flowed through her body and made her laugh. All reasons to maintain calm and remain distant not only failed her now but seemed to disappear altogether.

Daniel glanced at her, his face beaming with pride. "You did it. Just by being you."

"Well, I just pointed his mother in the right direction. They did the work." She couldn't stop smiling. Annika let out a nervous laugh. "But, yeah, I guess I did."

Daniel sighed. "I thought for sure I was going to have to punch him."

"Fists, while useful, are not always necessary." Annika grinned at him. "Daniel. Why are you here? *How* are you here? In this building."

He rested that green gaze on her, and her insides melted. She inhaled to steady herself. Seeing him again was not helping her attempts to get over him.

"Can I take you somewhere? There's someone I want you to meet." His voice was soft, intimate.

She should tell him she didn't want to play games. She should refuse to fall for that intimate tone. She should tell him to go home. Instead, she glanced down at her skirt and ballet flats. "I'm not exactly dressed for the bike."

"I sold the bike." Daniel's gaze never left her face. "Bought a car."

There was no hiding her surprise.

He grinned at her. "I know, shocking, right? What do you say?"

He looked so hopeful, so eager for her to agree, there was no way Annika could have turned him down. Not to mention she didn't want to. Being near him again felt like life was being breathed into her, and she didn't want to leave him if she didn't have to. She probably would have even straddled the bike in her skirt if it meant being close to him.

"Let's go."

He beamed at her and led the way to his car, settling his hand in the small of her back. She probably should have protested on the basis that the gesture was too comfortable, but his touch was warm and secure, so against her better judgment, she simply enjoyed it.

He opened the door to his car—a simple four-door sedan—and she sat down and relaxed into her time with him as if it were a cozy blanket on a cold day. This visit would definitely set her back in her effort to get over him. Right now, though, she didn't care. She still loved him, and it didn't seem like that fact was ever going to change.

"How was the rest of the school year?"

"Great. In fact, all the children did really well."

Silence fell between them.

"How about you? Group must be helping you out—you walked into the school." No point in pretending she didn't know.

He nodded. "Not just group. I have a therapist, too."

She couldn't hide her surprise. "A therapist and group? You'll be a new man, Daniel Bliant."

"Not that new," he spoke softly.

"Well, I'm really happy for you."

He side-eyed her as they pulled up to a small house. "Thanks."

The yard was tidy, and there was a small porch with a swing. On the swing sat a beautiful blonde woman with a bundle in her arms. Annika immediately knew who the woman was and where they were, but she couldn't imagine why Daniel had brought her here.

Daniel got out of the car and came around to open Annika's door. He offered his hand, and Annika took it as she got out, but she could not read his face. He waved to the woman, keeping hold of Annika's hand.

"That's Sheila." Daniel's voice was soft in her ear as he nodded in the direction of the swing.

Annika nodded as she walked with him, though she tried to ignore how good it felt to hold his hand. They approached the porch, and Daniel dropped her hand as he approached Sheila. Sheila stood and held her bundle out to him. Annika's heart nearly stopped when she realized what was happening.

"Is that a baby?" There was no hiding her smile or her astonishment as she looked from Daniel to Sheila. "Oh—hi, I'm Annika." She held out her hand to Sheila.

Sheila nodded, a warm smile filling her face. "I know. Nice to finally meet you." She side-eyed Daniel. "You got him?"

Daniel nodded. Sheila stepped back. "I'll just be inside." She squeezed Daniel's shoulder and went into the house.

Daniel beamed at Annika. "This is Aaron. My godson." He stepped closer to her so she could see. "This is who I wanted you to meet."

She covered her mouth with her hands even as joyful

tears blurred her vision. "You're holding *Sheila's baby*." She shook her head. "And you voluntarily walked into that school building."

"I am. And I did." He looked at her with a mixture of pride and apprehension as he rocked slightly, keeping the baby calm.

"Wait—did you say *godson*? As in you agreed to be his godfather?" Her heart rate quickened. He was looking at her with those eyes and that smile and *he was bouncing a baby*. Was there really anything sexier than that?

"Yes."

"Oh, Daniel." She started to throw her arms around him, but stopped, awkwardly freezing mid-almost-hug. "I'm so proud of you—for getting help." She dropped her arms.

"It was your dad. Came to see me." His eyes never left her, as if he were afraid she'd run off the first chance she got. "You never said anything. About your other brother."

"It never seemed like the right moment."

Daniel nodded in understanding. He held Aaron out toward Annika. "Want to hold him?"

"Thought you'd hog him the whole time." She held out her arms.

Daniel handed Aaron to her, and Annika tried desperately to ignore how much she was enjoying Daniel's proximity. Not to mention that she craved him even more when his hand brushed against hers. He did not step back after handing Aaron to her. If anything, he leaned in closer, as if he was trying to look at Aaron. Maybe he was. "Babies look good on you." His voice was soft, husky, as if he were telling her a secret.

Aaron cooed and wiggled, and she had to admit he felt good in her arms. She felt Daniel's gaze but could not look up at him. "What's all this about, Daniel?"

His finger touched the bottom of her chin, tilting her head up, so she had to look at him. "I'm sorry for hurting you. Leaving you in the hospital that day…when Nilay was hurt." He shook his head, clearly disgusted with himself. "It was selfish. Inexcusable. I'm surprised you're even here with me now."

He swallowed hard, studying her face. She was mesmerized by his every movement, his words.

Aaron wiggled, and Annika shifted to get a better hold of him. He let out an adorable gurgle, and Annika looked at the baby, giggling as he made spit bubbles. She turned back to Daniel, only to find him watching her, a vulnerability in his face she'd never seen before. "You decided all on your own that you weren't enough for me."

"You know, it was Aaron's birth that made me realize I *could* be helped. But it was you—you're the reason I wanted to be part of life again."

Annika's breath caught, but she didn't really have time to think as Daniel leaned in toward her, his gaze on her lips, and against everything she knew was wise, she tilted her head up to him, her lips finally meeting his, as if they'd been searching for each other forever. His kiss was soft and gentle, a question rather than a statement, and somehow infused with hope. Her whole body relaxed and gave in to him, asking the same question. Aaron gurgled again, startling her away from Daniel, but he stayed put, his laugh still on her lips. He turned his gaze to Aaron but then met her eyes with something like a promise.

"I have never stopped loving you. I know it's not fair after all this time, after what I did, but I had to tell you—I had to see if you still loved me, too."

Annika could not speak. There was so much to process, so much to feel all at the same time. She needed to think.

Sadness or disappointment flickered in Daniel's eyes at her silence, but he quickly replaced it with hope and amusement. "That's a lot for me to lay on you." He treated her to a smile. "Let me get Aaron back to his mother, and I'll take you to your car."

"Yeah, sure." She handed the baby to Daniel and stepped back. "He's beautiful."

The conversation in the car on the way home was easy and comfortable. Almost as if months hadn't passed. It was as though they decided to pretend that Daniel hadn't just proclaimed his love for her and she had said nothing.

He pulled up next to her car at the school. She waited a moment, stalling, but couldn't think of one thing to say to prolong her time with him. She quickly thanked him and got out.

Daniel leaned toward the open window. "See you soon?"

"Yeah, sure." Wow! Wasn't she full of words today? One kiss from Daniel and her brain became mush. "I have the wedding—Naya's getting married. Did you hear?"

"Yes, I heard."

"So, I have that next week." She smiled at him, memorizing his face for a moment before turning and getting into her car.

WEDDING PREPARATIONS TOOK up every single moment she had that she wasn't teaching. Forget sleeping and eating— Naya was getting married. One would think Annika would be too busy to think about Daniel, but thoughts of him managed to wriggle their way into her mind. Not that she was trying in any real way not to think about him. She hadn't heard from him, but he was probably doing round-the-clock shifts at the ER and the chopper.

Everyone was up early on the big day—hair and makeup

had to be done, after all. Naya had insisted that Annika have hers done as well, even though she wasn't the bride. Annika finally relented, if for no other reason than to stop the nagging. The hair and makeup artist was incredible, and sure enough, she had Annika feeling like a bride herself.

"You look beautiful!" Naya gushed. "Aren't you glad I nagged you?"

It did feel nice to be made-up, so she smiled at her cousin and gave the smallest little eye roll. "Fine—yes." She gave her cousin a once-over. "But you—you make a gorgeous bride." Naya was decked out in the traditional white sari with the red border. It was decorated with beads and sequins, but Naya had forgone all the traditional gold jewelry and opted for the basics. A simple gold set and bangles and she just glowed.

Annika's sari was a stunning shade of cobalt blue that complemented her skin. Naya wrapped an arm around Annika's shoulders and pulled her close. "You're not so bad yourself. Heard from Daniel yet?"

"No."

"You could call him."

"I might, but I've been busy getting you ready to be married this week."

Naya grinned. "I'm getting married!"

"You are! I, for one, never thought it would happen," Annika teased.

Naya nodded. "You and me both." She sighed, a slightly dreamy expression in her eyes.

"Well, if I didn't know better, I'd say we had two brides here today." Naya's father burst in without knocking.

Annika and Naya rolled their eyes at each other.

Naya's father turned to Annika. "The jaan is almost at the door. We need you."

Annika and Naya squealed like schoolgirls at a middle school dance. Naya's father covered his ears and gestured to Annika with his head. Annika squeezed her cousin's hand before following her uncle down to the crowd that had formed in front of the double doors. Annika and her kaka joined the rest of their family and went out together to welcome Ravi.

Ravi was resplendent in his cream sherwani and turban, with a red scarf that matched exactly the shade of red that Naya wore. He was glowing just as much as Naya, and Annika teared up at the happiness that exuded from him. Naya's mother approached him with the tray of sweets and performed the ceremony of welcome, in the end offering him the chance to leave or stay forever. When he stomped on the small clay pot, shattering it, Ravi chose Naya forever.

Kaka and Kaki escorted Ravi into the building, accompanied by Nilay and Annika's parents. They walked Ravi to the wedding hall and up to the mandap, where Ravi stopped to remove his shoes.

Annika caught sight of two little girls, distant nieces of hers, hovering around Ravi. Just as his feet slipped off his shoes, two little girls lunged forward, each grabbing a shoe. One of the groomsmen reached for them, but he was too late; the little girls ran off, giggling and taunting the groomsman with their prize. Annika watched the little girls, smiling to herself. She turned, then froze in place as she was met with the most familiar set of green eyes.

Daniel was the groomsman. He was stunning in a cream sherwani similar to Ravi's, though his scarf was the exact shade of blue as Annika's sari. He locked eyes with her and smiled as if he attended weddings like this all the time.

He walked toward her in that unassuming, powerful way he had, which she had loved since she'd first seen him that night outside of Phil's. Annika held back while the families took their seats on either side of the mandap. Daniel stopped in front of her.

"It's always more fun when they get the shoes," he whispered before continuing along behind the other groomsmen.

Annika's heart skipped a beat. If she had fallen in love with him the first time he'd said that, she'd fallen again, and deeper this time. She forced her feet to move. "Nice scarf," she whispered to him as she made her way back up to Naya. His rumbling chuckle was a welcome, happy sound, and she couldn't help turning back to watch him.

She took the steps up to her cousin as fast as her sari would allow and entered the bridal suite to a knowing look from Naya.

"He called me," she blurted out before Annika could speak. "Wanted to know what color you were wearing."

"Hmm." Annika could not stop the grin. "Let's get you married." In short order, Nilay arrived, informing them that they were ready for the bride, and the wedding was underway.

Annika sat under the mandap next to Naya, while Daniel sat just outside the mandap with the other groomsmen. She couldn't take her eyes off him. He spoke quietly to the other groomsmen around him, acknowledging their input, sending them to tend to things. Every so often, he would chuckle softly, occasionally catching her eye. The jolt of electricity from his eye contact was so wonderful that she didn't care he'd caught her staring. This was a more relaxed, more jovial version of the man she loved. And yes. It was definitive: she completely loved him.

Naya and Ravi took their four turns around the sacred fire and were now officially husband and wife. Naya glowed, as did Ravi. It was as if they couldn't believe their luck in having found each other. As part of the wedding party, Annika and Daniel joined them for pictures. The photographer kept putting them together—not that Annika minded having Daniel's body pressed up against hers. There wasn't much time for conversation, but Daniel took her hand every chance he could, and Annika willingly laced her fingers with his.

The photographer dismissed them when she had all the shots she needed, and Annika escorted Naya back to the bridal suite to change for the reception. Naya changed into a midriff-baring *choli* of the deepest burgundy with gold filigree design. Annika's choli, also midriff baring, was a bit simpler, in a cobalt blue and gold. She touched up Naya's makeup before taking a look at her own.

"What are you going to do?" Naya asked from behind her.

Annika took down her hair and brushed it out with her fingers, allowing the curls to do as they pleased.

"About Daniel…?" Naya prompted.

She caught her cousin's eye in the mirror. "I don't exactly know—whatever feels right, I guess."

Naya hugged her.

"Come on, let's get this party started." Annika grabbed Naya's hand and they went to rejoin the wedding.

CHAPTER THIRTY-FIVE

DANIEL

DANIEL LOOSENED THE bow tie of his tux just a bit. Tuxedos were just not his style. He followed Ravi down to just outside the reception hall. He did an automatic scan for Annika, but she was not standing with Naya.

The bride looked at him. "Caught you looking for her," Naya smirked.

Daniel inhaled. "Yeah. Well. She's been busy." He leaned in to give Naya a hug. "Congratulations. Ravi's a lucky man."

Naya smiled, and Daniel could have sworn he saw stars in her eyes. "Thanks."

Daniel nodded and turned to continue his search for Annika. He really needed to talk to her. Naya grabbed his hand and tugged.

A tuxedoed waiter approached them just then, a tray of champagne in his hands. He paused as Naya took a glass. Daniel shook his head, and the waiter left.

"What? No celebratory drink?" Naya seemed surprised.

"Not anymore." Daniel looked her in the eye. "It's for the best."

Naya nodded.

"What's up?" He glanced at her hand still on his arm, keeping him there. Apprehension made him a bit cautious.

She leaned close to him and reached up to whisper in his ear. "You know, I'm really glad it was you who was with her that night in the hospital." She sighed and turned to look him in the eyes. "Don't let anyone, me included, tell you that you don't deserve her. You do. She's a lucky girl."

Daniel pulled back to see Naya's eyes glisten with tears, a small smirk on her face.

"What?" She sniffled. "Occasionally, I'm wrong. It happens. However rarely." She released his hand and gave him a nudge. "Better find her before someone else does."

Daniel leaned down and kissed her cheek. "Thanks."

She pushed him away with a smile. "Go now. I want a minute with my new husband."

"I'll see you inside," he murmured to Ravi, and left the newlyweds to await their big introduction.

Once inside the dimly lit reception hall, he scanned the room for Annika. Naya's words sat lightly on his heart. If all went well, she'd be family soon. He felt for the ring in his pocket and relaxed at the solidity of it.

He and Annika really hadn't had any time together today, and maybe someone else's wedding wasn't the best place to propose, but he'd waited long enough. Tonight, after all the wedding hoopla, he'd ask her to marry him.

He scanned the crowd again but saw no sign of her.

"Hey, there." A gentle slap on his shoulder, and Daniel turned to face Nilay and Anil-uncle.

Warmth flooded over Daniel as he caught Nilay in a hug. "Hey, yourself. Do you really still need those crutches?"

Nilay grinned. "There are some advantages." Daniel followed his gaze to a group of teenage girls clustered together on the dance floor.

Daniel chuckled and turned to extend his hand to Anil-uncle. "Sir. Good to see you."

Anil-uncle took his hand in a firm handshake, a smile playing at the edge of his mouth. He pulled Daniel in and clapped him on the shoulder. "You can drop the *sir* bit. You asked for and got my blessing—*sir* may be too formal for us, don't you think?"

Nilay rolled his eyes. "He didn't ask her yet."

"How do you know?" Daniel raised an eyebrow at the young man. He hadn't, but how could Nilay know?

"Because if you'd asked her, Mummy would be taking notes and already have your wedding half planned."

Anil-uncle and Nilay chuckled, but Daniel had no idea what was so funny, because right then he caught sight of her. She had changed outfits but kept the color the same. The sari she'd had on earlier was conservative for the ceremony. But now her skirt was slung low on her gorgeous hips and trailed lightly on the floor. She had donned a dupatta across a very short beaded blouse, allowing it to hang loosely by her hip, but it was so sheer it hardly did anything to hide the delicious curve of her waist. His fingers tingled in anticipation of running them along that soft skin. She'd let her hair down from the complicated style she'd piled on her head earlier, allowing her curls to flow down her back and frame her face. Either way, she was easily the most beautiful woman in the room. His heart thudded in his chest, and everything else faded away.

She was chatting with some aunties, but almost as if she could feel the force of his gaze upon her, she turned toward him and smiled. It was the smile she reserved only for him, and it warmed him to his core. All her love for him was apparent and right there for everyone to see. He let himself become wrapped up in her smile, her gaze and her love. She was everything.

When finally he started toward her, he was waylaid by

a couple of the other groomsmen, who had already had a few drinks. By the time he shook them off, he'd lost track of her. He spotted her talking to the wedding planner, a slightly grim expression on her face. He caught her eye, and she tipped her chin at him.

Daniel was frozen to his spot as he watched Annika brush aside her hair. Her henna-covered hands were gently clasped together, and she was fidgeting with one of her rings. He watched more closely as she bit her bottom lip and nodded her head just a tad too fast. She started to take a step in his direction, and the planner stepped with her. She was trying to get to him. He grinned, satisfaction taking over his nerves for a moment. A final nod to the planner, and she started toward him. Just then the DJ announced that everyone should take their seats for the arrival of the bride and groom.

He caught her eye and tilted his head toward the long table reserved for the wedding party, and they made their way separately through the crowd to the table. Daniel and Annika were seated at opposite ends. Hmm. It was quite possible Naya had done that just to mess with him.

Daniel attempted to make his way to her end of the table, but the lights dimmed, and the DJ prepared to announce the new couple, so he found his seat and sat down. He tried to make eye contact with Annika, but she was deep in conversation with an auntie.

Naya and Ravi were announced to great applause and cheering, but Daniel only half heard what was going on. He kept trying to catch Annika's eye. It was taking all his self-control to stay seated and not run to her. There were lovely speeches about Naya and Ravi, their courtship and their future lives together.

They were the longest speeches in the world.

A beautifully decorated five-tier cake was rolled out. Naya and Ravi cut the cake to the tune of "Pour Some Sugar on Me," laughing as they fed each other. By the time Naya and Ravi took to the dance floor for their first dance together, and the DJ finally invited couples to join them, Daniel was about to jump out of his skin.

He fought the crowd and finally made his way to Annika. She was even more beautiful up close. He inhaled her floral scent and lost the ability to speak. She was talking to another auntie, but Daniel did not care. Not trusting his voice in any case, he simply held his hand out to Annika in silent question.

She immediately answered him with a smile and a blaze in her eyes as she took his hand and stood. Her gaze heated him as she unabashedly looked him up and down. "You should wear tuxedos all the time."

If it meant she'd look at him like that, tuxedos were now his new favorite attire.

She led them to the dance floor, where Daniel was finally able to take her into his arms. His thumb grazed the soft, warm skin of her back that was left exposed. He stifled a groan but definitely heard her breath catch.

"Hi." He kept his voice low, just loud enough for her to hear.

"Hi." She tilted her chin up at him, her brown eyes dancing. He'd never seen her this happy.

Silence stretched between them, ripe with all things unsaid.

"You are more beautiful every day." The words simply tumbled out of him.

She flushed.

He glanced over her head, then met her eyes. "I never once stopped loving you all this time. I have no right to expect anything from you, but I need you to know. My heart is yours. Always. To do with what you will. I—"

She silenced him with a finger to his lips. Just that touch was enough to melt him. "Daniel. I'm a big girl. I know your leaving was about what you had to do." A tear escaped her eye. She allowed him to wipe it away. "I'm just so happy that you did it."

"But?"

"But…I tried to move on. I had to because I…I couldn't wait around to see if you still wanted me." Her voice shook, but her gaze never left his eyes.

His heart fell. He was too late. What had he expected anyway, that she would just melt right back into his arms because he apologized? "I still want you. I will always—"

"Marry me, Daniel."

He stopped dancing. They stood still on the dance floor in each other's arms, as his mind tried to process what his heart had wanted to hear. "What?"

"Marry me." She said it with confidence, but her body betrayed her as her hands shook slightly. She gripped his arms tighter to steady them. "I don't know how not to love you. I can't remember a time since we met that I didn't love you, and I can't imagine ever not loving you in the future. I want to be there for you to lean on, on this journey of healing. I want to lean on you. I want to laugh with you, I want to grow old with you, I—"

"I want to go to bed with you every night and wake up with you every morning." Daniel paused. He cradled her face in one hand as he reached into his pocket with the other. He held the diamond ring up to her. "I want to have children with you."

She gave a small gasp as tears filled her eyes. "Is that a yes?"

"No." He shook his head and leaned down to her. He pressed his lips to hers in a kiss that could leave no doubt as to his answer. He pulled her in to his body as she melted into him. He'd never be done kissing this woman. "*That's* a yes."

* * * * *

ACKNOWLEDGMENTS

THIS BOOK WAS born from the idea that, broken though we may be, we all deserve and can find happiness. I'd like to thank my agent, Rachel Brooks, for believing in this idea—and in me—and encouraging me to investigate it. My editor at HQN, Brittany Lavery, loved just about everything about this book, and it's a fabulous feeling to have these two women wholeheartedly supporting me.

Every story, every book needs new knowledge. I met Crista Lenk when she spoke at a Maryland Romance Writer's chapter meeting, and it was listening to her talk about being a flight helicopter medic that gave me the idea to make Daniel's second job be just that. Crista has answered all of my questions for years as I crafted this book and Daniel's character. Thank you to Crista for your help and patience!

Sarah Storin answered many questions about nurses, nurse practitioners and emergency rooms. Nilay Patel, my favorite firefighter, walked me through what the fire department and EMT would do in these situations. Dr. Dahna Goldberg answered my questions on miscarriage and loss. And last but never least, Dr. Swati Jain for helping figure out when/if/how a baby could be born in a moving car!

To understand a father's loss of a child, I referred to the book *Grieving Dads: To the Brink and Back* by Kelly Farley with David DiCola. There is great insight in this small book and, quite frankly, it's almost the only thing I found that dealt specifically with a father's loss of a child.

My readers, Carrie Lomax, Delancey Stewart, Emily Duvall and Shalia Patel—thanks for amazing feedback and helping me to craft Daniel and Annika's story.

A shout-out to my amazing writing chapters, Maryland Romance Writers and Washington Romance Writers—could not have gotten here without you.

Shout-out to friends Dr. Jyothi Rao-Mahadevia for answers to medical questions and Kosha Dalal for listening to me go on and on about Daniel and Annika when I was just getting to know them.

As always, a special thank-you to my wonderful family: my sisters-in-law, Tina, Hetal, Monica; my brother, Satyan; and my brothers-in-law who like to annoy me like brothers, Prakash and Prashant. To my parents and parents-in-law, whose support is constant and solid and true.

A special thank-you to my daughter, Anjali, my favorite teacher-to-be, for making sure I got all the teacher parts correct. Shout-out to my son, Anand, who really is a light in my life.

And last but certainly not least, my personal romantic hero, Deven. Your support is without measure.